To Al

Thank you
laughing at
ook!.

Love Bob.

xxx

Small Town People

Bob Rogers

cathdubooks

Published in 2010 by **cathdu**books

www.cathdu.com

ISBN 978 0 9565840 0 7

Printed and bound in the United Kingdom

Typeset in Garamond 12pt

cathdubooks

Small Town People

Bob Rogers was born in Griffithstown, South Wales but spent several of his formative years in Stratford-Upon-Avon where he attended the same school as William Shakespeare, leaned how to say 'I'm sorry I'm late' in Latin and fell in the river.

A former local newspaper editor, radio and television writer, Bob left full time journalism to concentrate on scriptwriting and has created comedy and drama shows for the BBC, ITV and many independent companies both in the UK and further afield. Bob has written well-received sitcom series including 'Looks Like Rain' and 'Kerr in the Community' for the BBC as well as many one-off specials for BBC Radio.

Bob is the great great grandson of the famous nineteenth century herbalist, Granny Marsh. He lives in a small town and shares his home with a wife, various offspring and an assortment of surreal quadrupeds.

'They say the best of men are moulded out of faults and, for the most, become much more the better for being a little bad'
Measure for Measure
William Shakespeare

For my amazing family.
And for Malcolm Dimmick - an irreplaceable friend.

Small Town People

Small Town People

Bob Rogers

CHAPTER ONE

BIG NEWS!

AS dawn breaks there is little to mark this new day as being notably different from its immediate predecessor. The small town of Newvale yawns, throws its legs from under the duvet and sits absently scratching itself for five minutes while it waits for the last remnants of a half-remembered dream to melt away and the world of consciousness to swim into focus. Eventually it peers around the curtain to see what the weather is doing before shuffling to the bathroom where it relieves itself with a *joi de vivre* and copiousness quite remarkable considering its two-hundredth birthday is imminent.

Newvale has grown over two centuries from humble beginnings to a humble maturity. From the time entrepreneur, Thomas Fuller built his sawmill on the outskirts of the village of Meadowvale to the present day the local population has grown from fifteen hundred to almost sixty thousand and in all that time historians would be hard pressed to point to one occasion or one person and say, 'There - that's what Newvale is famous for!'

It sits in a wide valley with a temperate climate that tends to lean slightly towards 'wet'. In terms of prosperity it has seen both better and worse days and currently occupies a place about half way up the league table of success. It is too small to have a local accent of its own and so has borrowed one from the nearest big city and slightly adapted it. It is also too small to have its own radio station, university, ice rink or airport; but it has got a small hospital, a 'sport and leisure' centre, the third-cleanest railway station in the region - and a newspaper.

It is a newspaper that has, over the years, cried wolf so many times that it now has to cry Tyrannosaurus Rex in order to generate even a flicker of reaction and like many local publications it considers the pinnacle of grass roots journalism to be a front-page picture of a disgusted man brandishing a headless stuffed dog and pointing to a broken window underneath a headline such as, 'HOW COULD THEY?' or, if space is at a premium, 'BASTARDS!' A subsequent teaser of a first sentence followed by 'FULL STORY - PAGE FIVE' is usually enough to give the circulation a boost.

The desperate cries for attention are not really necessary however; regular readers of the Newvale Chronicle already know they are in for a weekly cornucopia of news, comment, speculation, rumour and fabrication woven together with a guile and subtlety rare outside the remaining bastions of totalitarianism.

The newspaper's office sits on a corner plot where Meadowvale Road and Fuller's Mill Road meet about ten minutes walk from the current centre of town. When the office first opened its doors the town centre was all around it but over the past century the commercial heart of Newvale has discreetly gravitated away from the paper like guests from an exuberant drunk at a wedding.

But it has refused to go away and every Thursday morning the Chronicle cries out its messages of titillation, outrage and exasperation to Newvalians from A-Boards and newspaper stands while for the rest of the week those whose lot it is to feed the insatiable appetite for information toil within.

'What's a shorter word for Committee?'

Chronicle sub-editor, Ian Lloyd was trying to fit a head on a single column story.

'Gang?' Editor, Monty Fox was engrossed in his own screen and only half listening to his assistant.

'Hmm, *Housing Gang Calls For More Cash*,' Ian sounded unconvinced.

'More Cash Plea from Homes Body?' suggested Monty.

'I've already used 'body' in another head on the same page – *Body Found in Nursing Home*, then a sub head, *Not One of Ours Claims Manager*.'

'How about, *Cash Boost Bid for Homes?*' Monty proposed.

'Yeah, that fits.'

The Newvale Chronicle had been - as it proudly proclaimed on the masthead - 'Serving Newvale for 112 Years' and for the last twenty-one of them Monty Fox had been at the helm.

Until he had taken over as editor it had never occurred to him to wear a dickey bow or a striped shirt but he had adopted them, along with half-moon spectacles and braces as being a uniform befitting a captain of the fourth estate.

Monty had grown round from long hours sitting at his desk and from being married to a pretty good gourmet cook. His weekly column, 'Down to Earth' featured a cartoon by-line of a fox in a Macintosh with the collar turned up and holding a magnifying glass in the manner of a sleuth on the trail of scoundrels and mountebanks.

His father, a 'Desert Rat,' had named him Montgomery out of admiration for his wartime Commander in Chief, and perhaps as a retort to those among his former comrades who had implied that the family name somehow gave him an unwarranted affinity with Rommel. Now, close to retirement himself, Monty had real concerns about who to pass the editorial baton on to.

He looked across at his sub editor, Ian; a nice enough lad and keen to do well but, like most young journalists in his position, he had one eye on the nationals and the other on the broadcasters and was unlikely to stay on a small weekly any longer than he had to. His reporter, Virginia, was certainly going to stay. She loved being a big fish in a small pond and revelled in the fear her presence in the Council Chamber's public gallery generated. But she wasn't a people person - and that was something you really needed to be in order to be a good local newspaper editor.

The only other editorial employee was photographer, Colin Gardiner, whose extra-curricular activities made him wholly unsuitable to edit anything - other than perhaps a few of the more 'specialist' periodicals aimed at couples to whom the phrase, 'The more, the merrier' was held to be a fundamental rule of pleasure-seeking.

It was deadline day, twelve hectic hours of filling the holes between advertisements and praying that nothing newsworthy happens after going to press. Ian's phone rang, he answered. 'Newsroom…. Oh, hi Virginia….. really? Good God, is that all?…. OK, we'll probably use it as page three lead, give us about three hundred words…. bye.'

Ian hung up and turned to Monty, 'The Bus Stop Flasher got off with community service!'

Monty raised his eyebrows, 'Maybe worth moving to the front - 'Court Leniency Threatens Public Safety' sort of thing. Use it as a hamper above the front-page lead.

'What is the front page lead?' Ian asked.

'TV Vet Shoots Escaped OAP in Park Drama.'

Ian frowned, 'I'm not sure about that headline, he's not really off the television is he?'

'Never said he was,' replied Monty, 'He dresses as a lady, that's what TVs do - transvestite you see.'

'Ah,' Ian forehead creased again, 'Hang on, has he actually publicly stated his penchant for… for…?'

'Wearing girls' clothes? Not as such but a few people have seen him at it, he never draws the curtains, and I was told by a reliable source that he even walked his dog in feminine attire once so he can't deny it.'

'I thought he was married? Remember the Animal Sanctuary dinner? Rather attractive woman as I recall. Do you think she knows he…?'

'Good God no, shouldn't think so,' Monty shuddered, 'would you tell your wife?'

'So,' Ian scratched his head, 'why are we outing him now?'

'Because if I took the 'TV' out, the headline would lose its balance completely, look we've got three decks…' he swivelled his monitor so Ian could see from where he was sitting …

TV VET SHOOTS
ESCAPED OAP
IN PARK DRAMA

'A really nice balance, good rhythm, not too much white space.'

'Are you saying,' Ian was rarely surprised by Monty anymore but occasionally he could still catch him unawares, '...are you saying we're going to destroy a man's marriage, possibly his career and his social life just because it will make a headline fit better?'

'Never underestimate the power and aesthetic attraction of a good headline - especially on the front page, it can put a thousand copies on your circulation.'

Ian stared at Monty in wonder, making the older man feel as if a little more explanation was in order, 'Besides, that will be the last time the bastard charges me half a grand to circumcise a borzoi!'

Monty's legendary vindictiveness made it all clear now and Ian was tempted to ask why a dog would need circumcision .... but no, if he did, Monty would only tell him, in graphic detail, and it was almost lunchtime.

The new state-of-the-art Hydrotherapy Pool at Newvale Leisure and Activity Centre had just been declared 'Open' by the mayor, councillor Gordon McIver. Virginia Wells, covering the event for the Chronicle, had anticipated a boring hour of speeches and posturing but it was proving more and more interesting by the minute.

The Newvale Neptunes Junior Swimming Club, who were supposed to have been giving a demonstration of synchronised swimming, were standing in a huddle of dripping, crying young bodies staring as if hypnotised at the middle of the pool where a dead Labrador bobbed, mostly submerged, its fluorescent yellow jacket periodically breaking the surface. The dog's owner, Jack Patterson of Newvale Association for the Blind - who had generously contributed to the cost of the facility - lay in his saturated clothing on the far side of the pool being given the kiss of life by one of the Centre's first-aiders.

He had missed his footing on the Grecian-effect non-slip tiles surrounding the pool and fallen in. Brock, his faithful companion, had dived in to try and save his non-swimming master and had been gratefully hugged by Mr Patterson who had employed the dog as one would a lifebelt. The Newvale Neptunes, who earlier in the week had watched a cautionary film in school about paedophiles, had lunged as one for the ladders screaming in their haste to get out, blocking the attempts of a lifeguard to get in. By now, a panicking Mr Patterson had held Brock underwater far longer than recommended for a Labrador and the creature's spirit had risen to that special corner of heaven reserved for the brave and self-sacrificial.

'Any comment Mr Mayor?'

'I think perhaps the non-slip tiles are not as non-slip as originally assumed,' the mayor replied with defeat dripping from every syllable.

It was rare for Virginia to allow anything approaching pity into her emotional mix but at that moment she felt a little bit sorry for Gordon McIver, he was a decent man and none of this was his fault. Even so it was his knackers on the chopping board and she had a story to write up.

It was in fact turning out to be a dog day in every sense of the word for the Chronicle. A lady had just phoned the news desk to report a missing pet. Ian had suggested she take out an advertisement and offered to put her through to the appropriate department but she had pointed out that as it was such a rare dog it might be worthy of a news story.

'A what?.... Can you spell that?.... B..U.. H..... Buhund, a Norwegian Buhund - and they're rare are they?... Only one in Newvale, I see.' Ian scribbled some details, 'Listen, it may be a help if you could pop alone to our office and drop in a picture of the dog... OK splendid, we'll see what we can do.' He hung up.

'What was all that about?' Monty had almost finished the front page and was reading Virginia's drowned dog story with interest and a trace of annoyance, this meant he was going to have to reshuffle pages one, three and five to fit everything in.

'Might be a filler for that three column hole on eight where the cancelled advert is. Woman has lost her dog, but it's a rare one apparently – it's a Norwegian Bu.. Buhund and it's called Gilbert.'

'It's going to be all bloody dogs this week, one's just been drowned in the leisure centre so I'll use that as the front hamper, keep the darted pensioner as the front lead and we'll use the bus stop flasher on three, we'll have to hold the Charity Firemen Car Wash pic until next week and drop the greenhouse wanker.'

'Shame.'

'It is a shame,' Monty agreed, 'but these buggers always do it again so we'll have him next time.'

The newsroom door opened and Virginia's perfectly groomed head appeared around it, 'There's a lady out here says you asked her to bring a picture of her dog in.'

Uninvited, the lady in question pushed past Virginia and strolled beaming into the newsroom, 'Ahhh here we are, ohh this is nice.'

Monty rose, 'Can I help you Mrs errr...'

'Camberley, Dawn Camberley – and it's Miss - Ohh I know you don't I? You're Monty Fox.'

'Yes, that's...'

'Yes, you gave a talk a few months ago to Newvale Womens Institute, a hundred years of local news wasn't it?'

'That's right... I...'

Dawn put a hand on his arm; she filled the office with her perfume, stature and her voice, 'It's awfully kind of you to help me find Gilbert, it's not like him at all to run off.'

'Well, quite so', Monty was a little intimidated although he tried hard not to show it. The lady was around the forty mark but also around the very tall and substantial mark too. She was not unattractive and gave off a predatory air as she gazed around Monty's domain.

'Perhaps you could give my assistant here...' Monty indicated Ian who also looked a little cowed by her presence, but Dawn ploughed on...

'..It's not as if he's not well fed, he had braising steak yesterday, but he's been off his food since we came back off holiday. I think the foreign food upset him, he was trumpeting like a brass band on the ferry and then yesterday he chewed a broom handle in half and he was a real foamy face.'

'A... foamy face?' a distant alarm bell went off in Monty's mind.

'Yes, a real foamy face, not like when I clean his teeth, this was much more. It looked like he had a beard; it was so funny; of course, dogs don't like you laughing at them do they? He shot out into the garden and savaged Mr Benjamin so badly his head came off, then he was over the gate and away.'

Virginia looked horror stricken, 'Whose head came off?'

'Mr Benjamin - oh it's alright Mr Benjamin is a gnome. I've had him for years; I call him Mr Benjamin because he reminds me of the man who used to live on Poplar Street years and years ago. Retired ambulance man he was, very handy if you couldn't get hold of the doctor - he's the man who pushed all my mother's bits back in with a wooden spoon after she blew her rectum inside out at Boris Perry's christening. 'That's what holding it in does for you' he told her; well she couldn't let it out in the Church could she? Anyway..'

'Hold on, hold on..' Monty could have done without this on deadline day, 'you said he was foaming at the mouth?'

'Yes, it all started with that blasted fox when we were on holiday, jumped right out in front of us it did and gave poor Gilbert a bit of a nip, he was really quiet after that.'

'And this happened ... abroad?' Ian's alarm bells were going off now as well.

'Yes.'

Monty hastily took the picture from Dawn and hustled her towards the door. 'Yes, well we won't detain you Miss err, in the meantime, leave it to us, it would probably be best if you told no one else, security you see, wouldn't want Gilbert to be dog-napped would we?'

A few seconds later a Monty that Virginia and Ian had rarely seen re-entered the office. He was animated, virtually dancing on the spot. The excitement was infectious, almost telepathic, a situation that was confirmed when they all spoke together...

'RABIES!'

'Right!' The newshound in Monty slipped its collar and ran barking around the room, 'Drop the double page quilters picture spread on nine and ten and move pages five and seven to nine and ten, then move pages one and three on to pages five and seven. Drop the inside back sports page - it's only fucking bowls anyway - and move page two on to there. Now we've got pages one, two and three for this. Virginia, let's have a panel on two - Rabies facts – just how scared should everyone be? Ian, we want that pic of Gilbert scanned in for the front; we'll use it along with a pic of a savage foaming dog under a two hundred point head – RABIES!

'I'll get on to the vet for some facts and advice,' Virginia states.

'Good idea - do it today, he won't want to speak to us after tomorrow, 'Monty was already stripping the front page ready for the new story, he picked up his phone and dialled... 'Oh hello, Park Street Junior School? Ah, it's Monty Fox here, editor of the Chronicle... is that so? Well we'll have to arrange for our photographer to pop along and..... yes but he's the only photographer we've got I'm afraid ..... no, well I agree, it's not somewhere you expect to see a glove puppet is it? Anyway, I'm calling because there's a dog on the loose near you that might be dangerous ... a Buhund... a Norwegian Buhund.... .. a bit like a husky... you're welcome.'

Monty and Virginia put their phones down at the same time. Virginia was shaking her head in wonder, 'Do you know what the vet just told me? If your dog shows any signs of rabies - hit it with a shovel!'

'Good God,' Monty was studying a picture of a snarling dog, he had decided to doctor it to try and make it a bit more 'foamy.' - 'Did he say what to do if you didn't have a shovel?'

'Yes, he said a golf club would do the job.'

'Fair enough, Ian - here's your headline for the advice column on page two,

'BASH YOUR PET'S BRAINS IN WITH A SHOVEL ADVISES CROSS-DRESSING VET'

'You really don't like him, do you?' Ian offered.

'There's a picture of him on file,' announced Virginia, '.. and get this - he's holding a shovel! It's from last winter when he organised path clearance for the OAP houses on Coldridge Estate.'

'Excellent.' Monty was delighted that everyone was getting into the spirit of things. 'The nationals will be all over this by tomorrow, thank God we're out first thing in the morning.' He stood back from his desk to admire his handiwork, the savage dog had acquired a quite convincing beard of foam and he'd put a bit of a red tint on the eyes for good measure.

'I can't fit 'cross-dressing' into this panel head,' called Ian.

'OK... hang on...' Monty's legendary headline-generating brain began to whirr, 'Here we go - FROCKED DOG DOC IN SHOVEL SHOCK!'

Ian shuddered as he typed it in, it fitted perfectly. Legend had it that Monty had once written up a story of a man who had taken a prostitute out in a boat on a lake for illicit sex and she, out of her mind on drink and drugs, had bitten his penis off. Monty had headed it up with 'OAR LEAVES ROWER WITH COXLESS PAIR'

Publication day was generally the quietest day of the week. The paper was on the street and Monty would strip the templates ready for the next issue, replace the crossword and sift through some readers' letters. There would be a few phone calls from disgruntled wrongdoers appalled at seeing their misdemeanours aired for all to see and the inevitable comments on the activities of the council.

This week was disturbingly different. Monty, Virginia and Ian sat in the office in a state of shock. They had taken the phones off the hook and locked the front door but the sounds of a Newvale under siege still reached them. Sirens wailed, some close by and some distant, screams and shouts of fear blended with running feet and vehicle horns. Virginia swore that at one point she had heard a 'woof' followed by a gunshot.

'Everyone's gone completely barking,' Ian shook his head.

'Not the most appropriate phrase given the circumstances, but accurate nonetheless.' Monty had the look of a man who had rubbed two sticks together out of curiosity and was now surrounded by a forest fire. 'On the way here this morning I saw at least three people carrying shotguns, it's like the Wild West out there.'

Ian's mobile rang. He studied the screen before answering, 'It's Colin – Hello? Colin? Eh? ..Bloody Hell, it's not his week is it?...The poor swine, is he alright?.......OK, you carry on then.' Ian hung up and turned to Monty, 'Jack Patterson, drive-by shooting outside the Town Hall.'

'Who the hell would want to shoot Jack Patterson?'

'Not Jack - his guide dog, now he can't find his way home, Colin is giving him a lift.'

Monty shook his head, 'Two dogs in a week, they're going to ask him to leave a deposit before they give him a third one - do you know how much it costs to train the buggers?'

A furious banging on the front door brought all three to their feet.

'Go and have a look who it is,' Monty whispered to Virginia.

'You go and have a look who it is, you're the leader.' Virginia hissed in reply.

The banging repeated, Ian tiptoed to the door, 'Who's there?'

'It's me, Dawn Camberley - quick let me in!'

Ian unlocked and slipped off the security chain, opening the door fraction, Dawn Camberley pushed it open the rest of the way and pachydermed into the office closely followed by a large dog on a lead.

'What?.... Is that....? Virginia and Monty quickly put as much space and furniture as possible between themselves and the dog.

'Get that rabid fucking thing out of here - stick it in... in that cupboard and shut the door. Ian, call the police!'

Dawn look horrified, 'Mister Fox, I'm... I really don't know what to say. You - a man of letters - using such....'

The dog sniffed the corner of Monty's desk, raised its leg and peed nonchalantly.

'The bastard! There's rabid piss on my desk now!'

The dog sat, seemingly at peace with the world.

'He got very frightened on the way here; someone pointed a gun at the car and there are ever so many police about - has there been a bank robbery?'

Monty looked at Dawn in wonder, had she not seen the Chronicle this morning?. Virginia gingerly picked up a copy of the paper and handed it to her at arm's length. Dawn took it and studied the cover, her mouth worked as she took in the words and her eyes got larger with each pregnant second. She looked from the page to the dog and back again. When she spoke her usual foghorn was replaced with a tiny voice, 'He had a plastic ring-pull from the top of a milk carton stuck in the back of his mouth - I managed to get it out and he was right as rain, he stopped foaming. It must have been ever so uncomfortable for him, no wonder he was grumpy - isn't that right Gilbert?' The dog looked up at her as if to agree.

Monty paced slowly from where he had been cowering until he was facing a wall with his back to the others. He placed his hands behind his back. He appeared to be reading a little notice that had been on the wall for years as if he had never seen it before. *Six Months Ago I Couldn't Even Spell Journalist - Now I Are One!* it read. Everyone waited expectantly until, after what seemed like an age, he turned around.

'Have you told anyone else about this milk carton ... thingy?' He asked Dawn.

'Well, no, I came straight here.'

Monty smiled. 'Excellent.' He studied Dawn and the dog while a wave of horrible realisation swept through Ian. 'You … you can't kill them.'

Monty looked at him as if he had suddenly grown horns, 'What the bloody hell are you talking about?'

'Ian pulled himself together; suddenly realising he had demonised his boss far beyond what the man was actually capable of. 'I… I thought…'

'Yes, well too much thought is a bad thing; it gets in the way of action. Right, Miss Camberley… Dawn.. are you, as I am, a lover of the seaside?'

'So what are we going to say?' Virginia was puzzled and for once wasn't afraid to admit it. She, Monty and Ian had retreated to the bar of the Royal Oak just across the road from the Chronicle's offices. It was a pub where the landlord had long since learned that if he didn't want to cross Monty - with all that that meant for his retirement fund - his best bet was to keep a good pint, a clean kitchen and his mouth shut.

'What we are going to say is this,' Monty leaned forward, Ian and Virginia did likewise, 'Dawn Camberley and Gilbert are now heading for my seaside home in Colin's van where they are going to spend a long weekend far from Newvale and way out of the public eye. Tomorrow we are going to announce that our photographer enticed Gilbert into his van with a string of sausages - he'll have a picture of the dog in his van to prove it - then, when he had him in there, he brained him with a shovel - as advised by the vet…'

'Hang on…' Ian was finding it difficult to find his way through Monty's maze of thought, 'Why would our photographer happen to have a shovel and a string of sausages about his person?'

'Anyone who knows Colin wouldn't be the slightest bit surprised by anything they found in the back of his van,' Virginia shuddered.

'True,' Monty continued, 'Then, fearing contamination, Colin took the dog's body to Mr Truman - the vet just out of town who does the farm animals for miles around - he's got his own incinerator - and that's where Gilbert ended up.'

'Hang on...' Ian attempted to interrupt but Monty raised a hand and continued.

'Meanwhile, Dawn Camberley, distraught at losing Gilbert, visits a breeder who lives... oh... about two hundred miles away, and returns with a new dog who bears an uncanny resemblance to her old one. Luckily, it turns out that Gilbert didn't manage to bite anything and pass the infection on, the Ministry will announce an 'All Clear' and all will be well that ends well - thanks to the quick thinking and alacrity of the Newvale Chronicle! Wouldn't surprise me if some sort of civic accolade wasn't forthcoming - another round over here when you're free Brian!'

'I can see how Dawn Camberley is going to play along, but why is this other vet, this Mr Truman, going to lie about incinerating Gilbert?' Ian asked.

'Because we've just nobbled his only competitor by outing him as a tranny and an elephant murderer,' Monty finished his glass and look impatiently across to the bar where the landlord was placing their drinks on a tray.

'A what?' Virginia's drink paused on its way to her lips.

'Haven't you read the story?' Monty raised a sarcastic eyebrow in a passable imitation of Virginia's favourite outward sign of scepticism, 'I did a bit of digging, before he came to Newvale he was sent to a zoo to put down a sick old elephant - and he bumped off the wrong one, the zoo went apeshit apparently. And once, when he was doing a wildlife job, he trod on an owl - no wonder he likes to dress up, I wouldn't want to be bloody recognised if I was him.'

'Here we are,' Brian the landlord arrived with a tray of drinks, 'Terrible business this rabies eh?'

'Yes, shocking', agreed Monty.

Brian hovered for a few seconds but it was apparent nothing more was forthcoming so he retreated behind the comforting barricade of his bar.

When outside forces stop acting on Newvale it rapidly reverts to its state of near inertia. The following week's Chronicle carried the exciting story of Gilbert's capture, which resulted in Colin receiving a proposal of marriage and an invitation from a motorcycle gang to be their patron. He was, however, in no condition to accept any outside offers having spent the previous weekend with Dawn Camberley in whom he had found someone whose appetite for sex shocked and frankly scared him. She had left him hardly able to walk and with barely the strength to drive home and now he looked around the curtains before leaving his house, fearful she would track him down.

Monty had accepted a civic accolade from the mayor, Gordon McIver and in return was going to gloss over a story involving an OAP adoption scheme. The whole rabies business had served to remind him of just why he was editor of a small newspaper and not working on the nationals. He liked small news, it was easy to manage, easy to contain and he could steer it in any direction he liked. Big news was another matter entirely; it took on a life of its own and, like a cute tiger cub, grew into something with the potential to bite off not only the hand that fed it but all the other extremities as well and Monty liked his extremities - and his Newvale - just the way they were.

*   *   *   *   *   *

CHAPTER TWO

POLICE CONSTABLE BONIFACE 'SLIM' LILLYWHITE

THE most immediately noticeable thing about Police Constable Boniface 'Slim' Lillywhite is that he is not really slim at all. In fact he is not slim to such a degree that it tends to escape one's attention until much later that he isn't lily-white either. Standing a shade under two metres tall and weighing as much as a small car, he left his native Nigeria twelve years ago dreaming of a career in law enforcement similar to those enjoyed by his detective heroes on TV. He has been on town patrol and traffic duty in Newvale ever since due to his predilection for interpreting justice in his own unique way.

He has no time - and he is sure the majority of Newvale's citizens agree - for the ponderous processes of law. To him, the wheels of justice move with the speed of glaciers and sometimes circumstances demanded a more immediate response to wrongdoing. Like the occasion he caught a man stealing a bottle of wine in a supermarket. He forced the man to drink it and then arrested him for being drunk in a public place. On another occasion he broke up a fight in a fish and chip shop and refused to let the instigator go until he had named twenty-five different species of fish. The man had only been able to name seven but Slim had tempered justice with mercy and allowed him to phone friends and relatives for help - although they probably didn't remain friends for very long after being called at a quarter to one in the morning and entreated to add to the list of aquatic ectotherms that Slim was painstakingly listing in his notebook. The process was lengthened because Slim refused to accept fish he had not personally heard of and the hooligan's exhausted exhortation that, 'My mate's brother works in a supermarket so he ought to know if there's such a thing as a fucking John Dory,' only earned him another five fish to name, this time for 'Uttering a profanity in a building where fish were stored.' The man didn't believe there was any such edict currently in force and said so, which earned him another five fish for 'Calling into question the acquaintanceship of a uniformed constable with the laws of the land.'

The keystone of Constable Lillywhite's creed was 'justice' - and if there wasn't an existing law appropriate to the situation he found himself in, then he felt himself justified in creating one. Indeed, many of Newvale's citizens had, over the past dozen years, been enlightened to the fact that it was possible to be arrested or at least cautioned for 'Leaning against a wall in a gangsterish manner', 'Growling at a shopping bag', 'Pretending to know kung-fu' and 'Blowing out your cheeks to make yourself look fatter than you actually are.' Much depended on his mood, once, during a painful attack of sciatica, he had cautioned a man for 'Lying to a police constable' after the luckless passer-by had said 'Good morning' while it was raining.

He had worked as a policeman in Lagos for four years before heading to Newvale. At thirty-eight it would have been highly unlikely he would have still been a bachelor back in Africa but over here he had never found the time for romance. He lived in the same lodgings he had taken when he first arrived and long and difficult working hours had offered little chance of spreading his social wings.

But as much as Slim was dedicated to justice and to making Newvale a peaceful place to live, his true passion - his overwhelming passion - was country and western music. It was the reason he got up in the mornings, the reason he 'moseyed' as he walked and the reason he was called 'Slim.' He had loved westerns as a child and to him the music was evocative of the chivalrous 'Code of the Cowboy' and of an age untarnished by the excesses and complications of the modern world.

His first visit to Newvale Country and Western Club had been a real eye-opener. It had been full of men and women in authentic looking western clothes, complete in some cases with gun belts and replica six-shooters. They moseyed around between acts calling 'Howdy' to each other, and they had names like 'Cade' or 'Lafe' or 'Hank.' It was clear that 'Boniface Lillywhite' wasn't going to fit right in.

Having read somewhere that the majority of cowboys were Mexican or Scottish, Slim toyed for a while with the idea of calling himself 'Pancho McPherson' but his final choice was made while passing a tobacconist on his beat a few days later. He had noticed a cigar display in the window and ever since, on Thursday evenings, Boniface Lillywhite had become 'Slim Panatella.'

Getting western clothes had proved as tricky as his initial fittings for a police uniform, which had involved lots of measuring and head scratching. Even the check shirts marked XXXL in the camping and caravanning centre were too small so he searched for a supplier online, finally coming up with one in Denver, Colorado who was happy to do mail order for 'The More Generously Proportioned.' Now he had the full uniform, the blue jeans, the size fourteen pointy-toed cowboy boots in the extra wide fitting, the check shirt and cravat and a real Stetson which he would dearly love to wear on the beat but he knew what his sergeant's reaction would be if he were to ask.

Slim didn't understand Sergeant Randall and the situation was mutual. He had suggested that he be allowed to do every other beat in plain clothes so he could blend in. Sergeant Randall had just fixed him with a blank stare before pointing out that the likelihood of Constable Lillywhite blending in anywhere at all was remote.

The shortsightedness of his superiors did not, however, deter PC Lillywhite from his dream that one day he would be a detective - and he was particular about the kind of detective he wanted to be. He had no time for the tyre-squealing, chain-smoking whisky-in-the-filing-cabinet sleuths who seemed to shout and shoot their way to success. He saw himself more in the Holmes/Poirot camp, deducing and discerning and dallying with ladies of quality along the way until, in a dazzling display of detectidigitation, he would unmask the ne'er-do-well to the gasps of the assembled suspects and victims. He had tried smoking a pipe once but it had made him feel sick so he gave it to some boys who had said they wanted it for a snowman.

Sergeant Eric Randall studied the man on the other side of his counter in the reception area of Newvale Police Station. The man was holding a sweeping brush and was dripping water into a small but expanding puddle in which he formed an island.

'I'd like to go home now and was wondering where to stick this brush?'

Sergeant Randall quickly dismissed the first answer to spring to mind; the man had begun steaming like a racehorse in the warm foyer and, tempted though the officer was to ask what the hell he was doing there, he decided against it as the double doors opened and PC Lillywhite appeared like a great thundercloud, rain dripping off his coat and helmet.

'Ah, so you've finished have you?' He addressed the dripping man.

'Yes I …ahhh, AHHHHH, SHOO!'

'I should go home and get out of those wet things,' Slim took the brush from him, 'And be careful where you throw cigarette ends in future – it's very bad for you, you know?'

The man nodded and made a rapid exit. Slim noticed his sergeant looking puzzled, 'I saw him throwing a cigarette out of his car window so I pulled him over and got him to sweep the pavement from the Hardware Emporium down to the corner of Smiths Lane, oh… and we owe Mr Donaldson in the Hardware Emporium for the brush.'

'It's pissing down out there!' The sergeant stated the obvious, 'I just hope the bugger doesn't catch pneumonia and sue us.'

'Ah, one goat cannot carry another goat's tail!'

'Eh?'

'What I mean is, he has learned a valuable lesson.'

Sergeant Randall took a slow deep breath and stared at the ceiling for inspiration and, amazingly, it came to him.

'I've got an assignment for you.'

Slim's heart leapt, 'assignments' were things detectives got while mere mortals just had 'jobs'.

Small Town People

'I want you to represent Newvale Police on the Newvale 200 Steering Committee.' Sergeant Randall silently congratulated himself; it was a brilliant idea. The Newvale 200 Steering Committee had been asking for a police representative for some time now and Inspector Snow had been pestering him to choose someone. This way he got an irritating inspector and a confusing constable off his back in one fell swoop. It would give Lillywhite something harmless to expend his energies on and something to vent the creative pressure that otherwise had a habit of manifesting itself in some of the most surreal and bewildering interpretations of police protocol that anyone had ever seen. And besides, nobody gave a toss about 'Newvale 200' so it would be pretty low profile stuff.

Slim studied himself in the mirror, turning this way and that to make sure everything was as it should be. It was Thursday and at eight he would be in the Country and Western Club. He touched the brim of his Stetson and gave a practise 'Howdy Ma'am' and was satisfied with the result. He had his eye on a lady; he had smiled at her for the last few weeks and last Thursday she had allowed him to buy her a drink. This week he was planning on asking her out for a meal. He didn't know what her real name was but on Thursday evenings she was Miss Ellie-May Quinn, a 'schoolmarm' from Meadowvale County. He gently polished the sheriff's badge on his waistcoat with the cuff of his shirtsleeve and adjusted his holster. The gun was an authentic Colt 45 copy and when Slim had first buckled it on he had practised a quick draw, which had resulted in the weapon slipping from his hand and smashing the full-length mirror on his wardrobe. His landlady had told him it meant seven years bad luck, beginning with a bill for the replacement.

He wasn't going straight to the Country and Western Club this week; first of all he had to attend a meeting of the Newvale 200 Steering Committee in the Town Hall. He had read the information pack that Sergeant Randall had passed on to him but was still unclear about what there was the celebrate. Perhaps it was nostalgia for what they perceived as 'better times. If so, from what he recalled of history lessons as a child, the past of this land was significantly different to that of his own.

The fact that PC Lillywhite was dressed as a sheriff did nothing to make his appearance through the door of Committee Room Three in Newvale Town Hall any less disturbing. Everyone in the room knew him, at least by reputation, and his garb only added to the air of ominous unpredictability that orbited him like the atmosphere of an uncharted planet. And the smile just made it worse!

He sat on one of the vacant chairs surrounding a large oblong table, joining eight others already in their places. The Newvale 200 Steering Committee had sixteen members but it was rare for more than ten to be present at any given meeting.

No one was going to ask Slim why he was dressed as a sheriff, although all were understandably curious. Had someone told him to come in fancy dress - perhaps in retaliation for some bizarre punishment inflicted in the past? Was he doing it for charity? Or had he simply crossed the invisible line between eccentric and nut case that most of Newvale assumed he had always walked. The only one in the room who knew why Slim was so attired was Mr Alan Norris, chair of Newvale Chamber of Trade who was holding up his minutes in a desperate attempt not to be spotted.

'Howdy Bat!'

It hadn't worked, resignedly he lowered his papers and acknowledged Slim's greeting.

'Howdy Slim'

He had been 'outed'. Not that Mr Norris was ashamed of his Country Music tendencies but, as his wife had pointed out, 'You're a man of position in the town, you should have grown out of playing cowboys when you were little.' At a shade under five feet three, Mr

Norris was still comparatively little but when he strapped on his six-gun and became Bat McSanchez he was one mighty tall hombre.

'Well I think everyone who is going to be here has arrived so shall we make a start?' Councillor Brenda Worrall was chairing the meeting and had brought enough enthusiasm for everyone, 'Introductions... This is umm... Constable Boney Face Lillywhite of Newvale Police,'

'It's pronounced Bonnyfass...' explained Boniface, '..But you can all call me 'Slim' tonight if you like.' He smiled, drew his gun, spun it deftly and used the barrel to nudge back the brim of his Stetson and the discomfort around the table ratcheted up another notch. 'It's OK, it's only a replica' he laughed and the others joined him in a mixture of fear and relief.

'Right.. well, welcome.. Slim, I'm Councillor Brenda Worrall, and going around the table we have, Jim Edgemont of Newvale OAP Society, Ian Lloyd of the Chronicle, Portia Mills from Newvale Garden Centre, Alan Norris - who it appears you know...'

'Sure do, Howdy Bat!'

This time Mr Norris gave a sickly smile in return as Councillor Worrall continued, '... and Simon Eddowes of Newvale Voluntary Alliance...'

'Eddowes... Eddowes.... Let me think...' Slim delved deep for a half-remembered case while Simon Eddowes visibly blanched and tried to recall any transgression he may have forgotten.

'Ah yes, Eddowes...I knew a fellow in Nigeria called Eddowes, I arrested him for buggering a doctor, he also confessed to eating a leopard - he got a damn good flogging!'

There were a few seconds of mental gear changing around the table as everyone wrestled to maintain a poker face. Slim's statement, if taken literally, could have meant that buggery in his homeland was legal unless the recipient was a medical man although the present Mr Eddowes, himself an active and enthusiastic homosexual, could see no reason why taking the Hippocratic oath should exclude one from all the fun. Perhaps the African Eddowes had got a taste of the cat for...

well, having a taste of the cat - he wasn't about to ask Slim to elaborate and was relieved when the introductions went on.

'... and this is Dick Fuller of Newvale Conservatories...'

Dick nodded coldly at Slim; their paths had crossed before, several years ago when the policeman had arrested him for 'Blasphemous use of a sweeping brush.' The charge was subsequently dropped and Mr Fuller had received an official apology but he had spent an uncomfortable hour in the company of the Constable and a further four in a cell. Slim showed no signs of recognising him.

'... and finally Robin Merrick of Newvale Historical Society...' Mr Merrick, an earnest and worthy middle-aged man with a goatee beard smiled at Slim who nodded in return.

Councillor Worrall continued, 'OK, for the World War Two parade we've managed to secure the generous services of Shortcock and Mee Tailors who are going to recreate some uniforms for those marching. I'm sure PC Lillywhite... errr... Slim won't have any objections to replica arms being carried in light of his current umm... get up?'

Slim nodded, 'As long as they are examined by the police beforehand I don't anticipate any problems.'

'Splendid,' Councillor Worrall beamed, 'Oh, just for the record, Slim, there are many in the town whose fathers and grandfathers fought in the war so I'm sure you'll understand it will mean a lot to them.'

Slim smiled politely; his own grandfather held the Burma Star; he had been mentioned in dispatches for conspicuous bravery in action but Slim had been brought up not to boast and saw no reason to educate this patronising idiot. He had already made a mental note to file the Newvale 200 Steering Committee as a typical local authority initiative, 'Well-meaning-but-wildly-out -of-touch-with-the-people-and-ultimately-pointless.'

'Howdy pardners, y'all mighty welcome.' Hank Fogarty, chairman of Newvale Country and Western Club was on stage and about to announce the commencement of the evening's entertainment. Hank - whose real name, Pete McQueen, sounded arguably more 'cowboy' than his *nom de l'ouest* was seventy-one and on the advice of his wife had abandoned his initial plan to call himself the Cold Ridge Kid. She, in turn, had been persuaded, but not without considerable pressure, to drop her planned persona of Busty Fontayne, a saloon girl and man-eater, when she had developed an allergic reaction to the fake breasts she had bought online from a company specialising in the 'Feminisation of Discreet Gentlemen.' She was now Trixie Starr - a retired sharp shooter.

'We're sure a-cookin' up a hootenanny!' Hank continued and a couple of cowboys pointed their guns at the ceiling and shouted 'Bang!' The firing of blanks had been banned after complaints from people living close to the building whose pets - and in one case grandparents - tended to spontaneously evacuate on hearing gunshots.

Slim edged closer to the bar, and the inviting presence of Ellie May Quinn who, with her Stetson tilted back and a new buckskin waistcoat, looked particularly attractive tonight.

'Howdy Miss Ellie May.' Slim touched the brim of his Stetson respectfully.

'Whah hawdy there Slim..' Ellie May tended to vary her western-speak according to her alcohol intake. The more vodka and tonics she consumed the deeper south her accent migrated. Slim estimated she was currently on the border between Virginia and Tennessee; on a good night she would be through the Carolinas and deep into Georgia by closing time and on one memorable occasion she went right through Alabama and Mississippi and was as saturated as a Louisiana bayou when they carried her to the minibus. But Slim liked a woman with spirit in her and there was no getting away from the fact she loved country music as much as he did.

'Why Miss Ellie May, you're looking as plumb pretty as a... as a prairie oyster tonight.' Slim wasn't a hundred percent sure what a prairie oyster was but it sounded 'western' and oysters were where pearls came from. Ellie May, whose Friday mornings frequently started with a prairie oyster, smiled anyway at Slim's genuine good manners and attempt at flattery.

'Why that's mighty sweet of you Sheriff, and might I say you're looking as dandy as a cottontail who's just outwitted a coonhound….'

Oh shit! Ellie May mentally kicked herself and cringed inwardly. Slim's smile remained fixed but her embarrassment must have been written all over her face. The silence became ever more pregnant until the waters broke with Slim's laugh. It was a huge and hearty laugh that filled the room and was as infectious as a yawn. Even those watching the opening act joined in, much to the disgust of the performer who had been half way through a song about coming home from the range to find his wife had been shot by bandits. Being a trouper he persevered but when the line 'I found her a-lying in the horse trough,' brought a fresh gale of laughter he admitted defeat and slunk off the stage. Ellie May, relieved at Slim's reaction allowed herself a smile too.

'I hope you didn't think I… that is, I mean….'

'I know what a coonhound is,' Slim grinned widely, '..but I'm not sure that you do - what are you doing on Sunday?'

The junior section of Newvale Town Band often played in the bandstand in the park on Sunday afternoons. Lydia Gurney sat listening to them. She was enjoying an ice cream and some pleasant sunshine. She recognised a few of the young musicians from Meadowvale Comprehensive School where she worked as a teacher.

'How's the ice cream Ellie… sorry, Lydia?'

'It's fine thanks Bony… Boniface.'

'Maybe you should stick to Slim.' They laughed together.

It had been a great day. They had enjoyed a pub lunch then visited a car boot sale where Slim had bought two Johnny Cash albums, a Latin-Dutch dictionary and a flood-damaged copy of the Complete Works of William Shakespeare with Titus Andronicus missing and a dedication on the inside cover which read, 'To George for good attendance.' Lydia had bought a china chicken with a chipped beak, a woolly hat and a set of place mats with shire horses on them.

As she ate her ice cream she realised it had been a long time since she had enjoyed a day out so much. Slim had been charming company, there was no question of off-duty anonymity for him, on a clear day he was visible from a considerable distance and there had been dozens of 'afternoon constables' on their way through the park. At thirty-three Lydia had put career before family but was aware of the ticking of the biological clock and, while she enjoyed in the main being surrounded by young people at work, had been thinking increasingly of children of her own.

Slim had told her he loved children and was one of eight, but he may have second or even third thoughts about considering her as a future wife. He was a police officer, a pillar of the community, and he had seen her being carried into a minibus singing, 'If You Ain't Lovin, Then You Ain't Livin!'

He showed no signs of being judgemental, however, and seemed to enjoy her company.

If there was one thing guaranteed to annoy Sergeant Randall it was people who were cheerful early in the morning. If he had his way the cells would be full of them. The other thing that annoyed Randall was Police Constable Boniface Lillywhite. The sergeant was therefore of the opinion that his own private hell had come into existence with the appearance of an unbearably cheerful PC Lillywhite turning up for a morning shift.

At precisely two minutes to six the main doors of the station burst open, admitting a drenched but indisputably buoyant PC Lillywhite who spread his arms wide and boomed out a dawn chorus.

'There's a bright golden haze on the meadow!'

'No there fucking isn't,' growled the Sergeant; 'what there is, is a postman who has had his bike pinched, two more garden sheds broken in to on Cold Ridge Estate - oh, and a naked bald woman is in Room Two with WPC Greenwood.... says she's been abducted by aliens.'

'Wouldn't surprise me, you remember those lights above Cedar Hill? There's no smoke without fire Sarge.'

'Yes, well anyway, I'm going home to bed!' Sergeant Randall was too tired to enter into a discussion about extra terrestrial life, especially with someone as alien as Lillywhite. He reached for his coat. Being in the same building as the constable was like mixing matter and anti matter, the longer they were together the greater the likelihood of a cataclysmic explosion.

'Pleasant dreams Sarge.' Slim moseyed down the corridor to the drinks machine singing as he went, 'Guess who I bumped into on the road to McAdoo?'

As if in answer to his question a voice from Room Two screamed, 'Fucking Aliens!'

Sergeant Randall shuddered, turned up his collar and headed out into the dawn rain.

Slim took his coffee behind the desk and tried to read the log but his mind was not on the job this morning. Lydia had agreed to see him again on Wednesday; they were going to the cinema. Then it would be Thursday, and this week he would have someone to doh-se-doh!

Funny how the world all seemed different this morning, Slim decided that if he managed to find out who pinched the postman's bike he would make the miscreant write out a list of all the addresses on the postman's round - or maybe he'd just let him of with a warning, after all, everyone deserves a second chance.

*   *   *   *   *   *

CHAPTER THREE

'ANIMAL MAGNETISM'

IT took over an hour of Internet research in order to discover that the creature languishing in the new arrivals building was a Slender Loris. With nothing to go on, phrases such as 'Big-eyed thing' and 'Monkey cat cross' had yielded little of use from the search engines.

Tony Fletcher, owner and manager of Newvale Animal Sanctuary peered through the mesh of the cage to where two huge, close-set eyes met his gaze.

'Weird looking bugger isn't it?'

'Where the hell would anyone get one of these?' his assistant, Dawn was equally baffled. 'And more to the point, why would they put it in cardboard box and leave it at our gate?'

'What else would you do with it? I can't see anyone wanting to buy one, can you? Scary-looking bugger. Still, he'll probably attract a bit of attention on our Newvale 200 Open Day.'

The only other resident of the building was a huge Brahma Light Cockerel, without a doubt the biggest cockerel Tony had ever seen. He had bought it from a breeder to see if it would cross with his Rhode Island Red hens to make extra-large birds for the table.

Melanie, the volunteer feeder wandered in, 'Ohhh, what on earth is that? It looks like an alien.'

A light bulb flared into life above Tony's head, 'Brilliant! That's it - have we still got that old milk churn behind the stables? Polish it up then bash some dents into it, cut a few bits out and hey presto, a landing module – we'll make out this little bugger was in it, charge people for a glimpse of him - keep it nice and dark in here, no torches or flash photography, no journalists or anyone who looks as if they know what a slippery…. slim….'

'Slender,' offered Dawn with a sigh.

'Slender yeah, nobody who looks as if they know what a Slender Doris is, we'll clean up! And if we're rumbled we just plead ignorance.'

'Shouldn't be a problem for you,' muttered Dawn.

'What do they eat?' Melanie asked, 'Will I have to get special supplies in or will cat food do?'

'Trial and error,' suggested Tony, 'offer it a bit of cheese or some crisps – hey, remember that ferret who would only eat curry?'

'Yes, we all do,' Dawn's tone of sarcasm was wasted on Tony, 'It exploded when a little girl picked it up to cuddle it.'

'Ah well she probably squeezed it, you should never squeeze a ferret - or any long thin creature come to that, I remember this chap I knew when I worked for the Animal Ambulance charity, terrible for squeezing ferrets he was, we all told him but he wouldn't listen - anyway, one day, pouring with rain...'

Tony's phone rang and spared his staff the rest of the story.

Five arms were raised and on three of them the hands were waving frantically, the small fists clenching and unclenching in their eagerness to be noticed.

'Simon?' Miss Gurney selected one of the raised hands to answer the question.

'Rhinos Miss?'

'No Simon, there won't be any rhinos there, it's not very likely that someone in Newvale would abandon a rhino is it?' Miss Gurney pointed to another upraised hand, 'Conor?'

'Puffins, Miss?'

'Possible, but very unlikely Conor - we're going to Newvale Animal Sanctuary, so come on everyone, think, what sort of animals are likely to find their way to a sanctuary in Newvale?'

'Pigeons?'

'Pigeons are... a possibility, any others?'

'Worms?'

'Yes Michael, I think we can safely say there will be worms there - in some shape or form - but probably not rescued worms.'

'They call puffins the Clowns-of-the-Sea Miss.'

'So I understand Conor, right, you all know who your partners are so stick together and we'll do a head count on the minibus!'

Twelve of Miss Gurney's class were making the educational field trip to Newvale Animal Sanctuary - twelve out a class of twenty-six, the rest being either considered too emotionally unstable or criminally inclined to be included. Miss Gurney's class consisted of Meadowvale Comprehensive School's most challenging young people and those who defied pigeon-holing and who had therefore been shoehorned into the catch-all category of 'Domestic and/or social issues' or 'Additional learning needs'.

Normally, on a Friday morning, she wouldn't have trusted herself to drive the school minibus but last night's Country and Western Club had been cancelled at the last minute due to a burst pipe and the subsequent disconnection of the electricity and so Lydia Gurney had given her alter-ego, Ellie May Quinn, a night off and enjoyed the rare experience of waking up on a Friday morning feeling strangely fresh and alert, and alone. Boniface had spent the night but had left at four in the morning to go back to his place in order to get ready for an early morning shift on the beat. Mrs Carter, the teaching assistant who had drawn the short straw, was busy ensuring everyone had seatbelts on when Lydia mounted the minibus and prepared to set off.

Tony Fletcher was changing his shirt. There was a school visit this morning and so a good impression was important - good impressions led to donations. He was putting on his second best shirt, his best one having been spat on by Sanchez the llama a few minutes before. He hated Sanchez and suspected the creature knew this and that the feeling was mutual. He conceded he had probably provoked it by blowing cigarette smoke into its face and calling it an 'Evil-smelling long-necked bastard' but it was an enmity that stretched back over a year to an incident the previous summer when, shortly after arriving at the Sanctuary, the llama had bitten Tony on the shoulder after he had tried to tie a bowler hat on it for the Open Day.

It would be eminently fair to say that Tony Fletcher was not the ideal person to be running an animal sanctuary. All the animals were well fed and quartered but he lacked the essential empathy that both his assistant and staff possessed. He had been a sales representative for a brewery for many years until over enthusiastic self-endorsement of his products earned him a driving ban and a conviction for damaging a police cell. On the return of his driving licence he landed a job with an animal ambulance charity after lying about his qualifications and his attitude to animality. He was fired after seven weeks following an incident involving a rabbit, which was being taken to the veterinary surgery for a few stitches in a cut ear; he had instead taken it home and eaten it - subsequently claiming it had escaped. And that succinctly summed up his feelings toward the animal kingdom; it was either edible or irrelevant.

When Tony's father died and left him the family smallholding just outside of town on the north skirt of Cedar Hill, he discovered there was also a profitable side to animals and he now made a spurious but adequate living from appeals and donations to his enterprise. Many still thought him a philanthropist despite sporadic adverse publicity backed by a degree of tangible evidence. Farming was in his blood and animals, when it all boiled down to it, were essentially a crop. Rumours persisted around Newvale that any creature taken to the Sanctuary that could conceivably feature in a recipe would very quickly be 'adopted-by-a-lovely-couple-from-out-of-town.' The rumours reached fever pitch after Huy, the Vietnamese pot bellied pig, disappeared on the very eve of the fundraising hog-roast.

The minibus slowed at the lights where the main road formed a junction with Fullers Mill Shopping Centre. Mrs Carter had to leave her seat to quell a mini-riot in the back of the vehicle.

'Now sit! All of you - put your seatbelts back on or we're going straight back to the school!

'Mrs Carter... Michael was doing sex movements at me.' Jade Overton pointed an accusing finger across the narrow aisle.'

'I wasn't - I was pulling my trousers up! The boy retorted.

'No he wasn't, he was going like this - 'Unnh! Unnh! Unnh!' - Jade recreated the offending movements for the benefit of the teaching assistant.

'Yes well I suggest you all sit down and...'

'Yeah? Well she... can I say a rude word Miss?'

'Only if it's absolutely necessary Michael.'

'Yeah - well she can talk, she master-bited Joel Gardiner in French!'

Mrs Carter blotted out the girl's rising indignation by wondering just how you masturbated someone in French? With a sort of Gallic nonchalance presumably, culminating in a flamboyant 'Et Voila!' at the *'moment de paradis'*.

'A dead goat? Where the bloody hell did that come from?' Tony got up from his desk and put on his jacket.

'Well, at a guess, I'd say it used to be a live one,' Dawn noticed the office calendar had still not been turned over from the previous month despite being two weeks into the present one; this was typical of Tony's attitude to organisation, she had given up trying to run this place as an efficient business and now just did the bare minimum in order to collect her derisory salary at the end of every month.

'Which goat?' Tony asked as the pair trudged across the concrete yard toward the goat enclosure.

'One of the Nubians, the brown one.'

'Awww, shame, I liked him.'

Dawn doubted very much that Tony had liked the creature any more than the rest of the Sanctuary's inhabitants.

'He was sponsored by Woodland Road Junior School, they called him Joe, I'll have to tell them....'

'Yes, you will,' Dawn agreed prematurely.

'No.. I'll have to tell them he's... that's it, I'll tell them he's gone to another sanctuary for a few months as part of a breeding programme. That way they'll keep shelling out for the bastard, and every few weeks I'll send them a newsletter saying he's having a great time mating with lady goats and costing money then, eventually we'll just say he had a heart attack from all the breeding but - guess what? His son has come to live at the Sanctuary and Joe hopes you will love him and look after him just like always.'

'You're unbelievable.' Dawn shook her head.

'Hang on, it gets better, listen – Joe's son has got a faulty valve in his heart and so needs regular - and expensive - visits from the vet. This is great, all we need is a small brown Nubian Goat and every time we get a visit from Woodlands School we'll get him drunk so he staggers a bit - brilliant!'

They reached the goat enclosure to discover the large Nubian Goat had chosen the most inconvenient place to expire. It had died in the small opening that led from the shelter to the grazing area and now several goats were backed up behind it clamouring to get past and out into the fresh air.

'Bugger... well it can't stay there, can it?' Tony stated the obvious.

'You'll have to call Mr Truman to come and collect it.'

Yeah, but he's not going to get here before the bloody school visit is he? Where are we going to stick it in the meantime?'

Dawn bit her tongue and then prepared to offer a suggestion when Tony cut in.

'I know, get Melanie to help you drag it over to the hay loft and winch it up there out of the way, nobody's going to stumble across it then. I'd give you a hand but this is my last clean shirt and I don't want to meet the school party stinking of goat.'

The stink in the school minibus as it pulled into the car park of the Animal Rescue Centre was significantly worse than that of a dead goat.

It emanated from a boy called Toby Rudd who had just unleashed his trademark 'classroom-emptier' precisely on cue at 10:30am. It had become a source of wonder to pupils and teachers alike that the boy erupted with all the spectacular predictability of a Yellowstone geyser every morning.

'It's two hours after my breakfast and it just happens,' the boy had shrugged when questioned. Apparently what was consumed at breakfast bore little relevance to what it later became as Toby's digestive system converted innocuous ingredients into a devastating weapon with all the misguided zeal of a terrorist. Tom Ferris was physically sick and Amber Wellbeloved was crying as Mrs Carter hurried them off the minibus into the relatively fresh air of the Sanctuary's environs. It took several minutes for the group's composure to be re-established in which time Toby stood accused of everything from witchcraft to attempted genocide.

'OK, in your pairs then, let's go!' The party headed down the narrow lane that led from the car park to the Sanctuary.

'I needn't remind you all you are representing the school so only the very highest standards of behaviour will do,' Lydia called over the marching heads. As the party approached the main gate Tony Fletcher was on hand the welcome them. He approached Mrs Carter flashing his sincerest smile, 'Mrs Gurney?'

Mrs Carter pointed to Lydia who corrected her title to 'Miss.'

'Miss… right, Miss Gurney – welcome to the rescue centre.'

Lydia had, of course, heard the rumours along with everyone else in Newvale, but the man seemed perfectly normal. He wore a disarming smile and a clean shirt, far from the overall-wearing, unshaven, brown-toothed figure she had envisaged. He certainly didn't look the type to bump off a healthy pot bellied pig, and now she had met him she was quite prepared to believe that when old Jethro the donkey's sponsor had passed away the animal had simply 'Died-of-a-broken-heart.'

'Come on in, we've got lots to show you… excuse me a second,' Tony took out his phone and dialled quickly; '… Ah Dawn? Our guests are here, is everything OK at the hay loft?'

As it happened, everything was far from OK at the hayloft. The winch - which in times past had been used to hoist sacks of animal feed - was stuck, and a large dead Nubian goat was hanging three metres above the ground swinging gently on a chain. Dawn and Melanie had found it impossible to attach the chain to the animal's feet and had fastened it around the neck, now it looked for all the world like some horrible public execution. The pair were in the open door of the hayloft trying to lasso the creature's feet so it could be dragged in out of sight when Dawn's phone rang.

'What?…. No everything is not OK, the winch has jammed, Melanie thinks she's broken a finger and there's a goat hanging in mid air…. What do you mean 'splendid?' - ah, you're with the school party is that it?… Of course, what do you think we're bloody doing?'

'Marvellous, well we'll be along shortly.' Tony hung up and turned to Lydia, 'Just having a quick word with my assistant, one of the goats has a touch of… goat fever, so we're isolating it… him.'

'Oh dear, not serious, is it? Mrs Carter looked concerned.

'Oh no no, he'll soon be up and about. Actually we're thinking of sending him to another sanctuary for a while as part of a breeding programme, so we have to make sure he's fit and well.'

'Aww, well let's hope he recovers soon,' Mrs Carter sympathised, 'A lot of our pupils still remember Huy the pig, he was lovely.'

'Yes, he was del… ightful,' Tony was suddenly distant.

'He was really sweet,' added Mrs Carter.

'…and sour,' thought Tony as he nodded solemnly.

Having failed to lasso the hanging goat Dawn and Melanie were poking it with a long-handled pitchfork in an attempt to get a 'swing' going which could bring it close enough to grab hold of.

'Go with the rhythm – poke it as it begins its swing out,' Dawn advised.

'I'm trying, it's easier said than done, I've never had a sense of rhythm,' Melanie groaned as she struggled with the pitchfork. That at least was true. Melanie Collins had nine children despite reading two books and countless leaflets on 'Fertility Awareness.' There would probably have been more but her husband, who, surprisingly, still had enough wind to play the tuba in Newvale Brass Band, ran off with a trumpeter. He had returned after six weeks begging for a second chance but Melanie had become used to uninterrupted nights of sleep and had slammed the door on him. Her absolute lack of rhythm demonstrated itself with terrible effect as she thrust forward with the pitchfork just as the goat was in the middle of its in-swing. Panicking, Melanie let go of the pitchfork and the animal swung out again, spinning as it did with the implement impaled in its side before coming to rest far out of reach and with the pitchfork pointing away from the hayloft door.

'Let's go and see some puppies, shall we?' Tony smiled at the youngsters who looked at him as if he were a paedophile. He strode off in the direction of the kennels and the troupe followed. The dozen or so current residents of the kennel block set up a cacophony of barking, whining and yapping as Tony opened the door and ushered the party in.

The noise level and the sharp smell of urine hit the visitors simultaneously, forcing some of the youngsters to attempt to cover both their ears and noses at the same time. The party walked crab-like, their backs against the tiled wall as they skirted the first of the cages, which contained a dog whose snarling and vicious demeanour labelled it as probably being too psychotic even to guard a junkyard. It actually lifted itself off the floor with every bark, showing long yellow teeth and no desire whatsoever to be adopted.

The next cage contained a huge white creature with the saddest eyes Lydia had ever seen. 'That's Snowy, sad tale there, his owner died and nobody knew; of course, he couldn't get out of the house and he had to eat something so...'

'Yes – well, sad indeed,' Lydia felt justified in cutting off Tony's tale to protect the pupils.

'In Iceland, they eat raw puffin's hearts Miss!'

The children groaned.

Yes, thank you Conor.'

'Here's a nice dog, rescued by the authorities and brought to us.' Tony indicated a pleasant-faced 'Mostly-German-Shepherd' who sat wagging his tail and studying the party with manifest intelligence.'

'He's beautiful,' stated Mrs Carter, why would anyone...?

'Ah, well he used to belong to a film maker - he was actually in a lot of the films the man made but...' Tony suddenly realised the average age of his audience, 'The man.. umm, had to go away for a couple of years and so we got Sven here to re-home,' Tony's voice dropped to a confidential whisper for the benefit of Mrs Carter, 'He would probably be better in a house with no women as he's been trained... for the films... if you see what I mean.' Mrs Carter didn't see at all but there was something about Tony's demeanour that suggested she wouldn't enjoy any elaboration.

The smell and the noise became too much for Amber Wellbeloved who took the chance to sneak outside for some fresh air. She wasn't much of a dog person but she was keen on horses and was pretty sure there must be a stable around here somewhere. She headed off to see if she could find it.

'Oh yes, I've always been a dog lover,' Mrs Carter was telling Tony, who immediately thought of Sven the German Shepherd, who was also a sort of dog lover; he suppressed a smirk as he led the party back out into the open air and away toward the C.P.S. - which stood for 'Caged

Pets Shed' but which Tony referred to as 'Completely Pointless Shitmachines.'

Amber Wellbeloved had found a llama but no horses. She didn't know what llamas ate but she had brought a few carrots from home for the horses and so offered it one of those. Carrots weren't Sanchez's favourite snack but he understood the girl was trying to be nice and so took it out of politeness. She smiled at him and walked off, allowing him to spit the carrot out and return to his natural state of nervous vigilance.

Amber had once got a part in a school play purely on the strength of her ability to scream. It was, in fact, the thing everyone remembered about an otherwise forgettable production. It managed to hit a note somewhere above Treble C that was painful to both humans and quadrupeds and was destined to ensure that over-amorous boyfriends would quickly learn that no meant no. And it carried a long way. It certainly carried over the whole of Newvale Animal Rescue Centre when Amber rounded a corner and saw what appeared to be some hellish re-enactment of a medieval witch trial.

With an order for them to stay in the Caged Pets Shed, Tony left the party and headed off at high speed in the direction of the source of the scream. It had set off the dogs again and the goats, which had already experienced a traumatic start to their day, were galloping around their enclosure like headless chickens while the chickens were leaping around in a flurry of shit and feathers bitterly regretting their decision to follow an evolutionary path that led to flightlessness.

Amber was rooted to the spot, unable to take her eyes off the hanging goat. Dawn and Michelle looked down from their eyrie in the hayloft and were about to call out reassuringly to the girl when Tony skidded around the corner and took in the scene.

'What the fucking hell's going on?' he yelled unhelpfully.

Seemingly noticing the girl for the first time his mind raced.

'Hello? What's you name love?' He waved a hand in front of the girl's eyes, 'Your name? What's your name?'

'Amber' a tiny voice replied.

'Hello Amber, listen love, it's not a real goat, it's a dummy, we use it for training... err... training staff to recognise different types of goat and... Hey, I'll bet you've never seen a real alien have you?

By the time Lydia, Mrs Carter and the children found the source of the scream there was little to see. The goat had finally been pulled into the hayloft and Tony had taken Amber Wellbeloved into the darkness of the New Arrivals building to show her a real live alien. She had thankfully calmed down a lot and there seemed to be little chance of a repetition of the scream as he led her into the dark. The only sound was the restful clucking of the giant Brahma.

'Before we look at the alien, there's something else I want to show you - and I'll bet it's the biggest cock you've ever seen!

The second scream was no less intense than the first and this time Tony was experiencing it at close quarters. The slender loris emitted a loud and angry hiss followed by rapid chattering in reaction to the pain in its ears. It's pain was nothing, however, in comparison to Tony's as Amber kicked him in the testicles and ran, still screaming, from the building.

'Fox in the henhouse' thought Tony bitterly as the editor of the Newvale Chronicle pointed out a plump chicken thus selecting it for slaughter and plucking. It was a small price to pay, however, to keep a lid on 'uncomfortable' news. Next week's paper would be telling the story of Joe the Goat who was going to a sanctuary far, far away as part of an exciting, and strenuous, breeding programme.

The sight of the slender loris and giant cockerel had added the necessary credence to Tony's explanation of his presence in the new arrivals building with a fourteen-year-old schoolgirl and he had actually received an apology from the school but not from Amber Wellbeloved who was still not completely convinced of his honourable intentions.

The slender loris had been moved to more appropriate quarters and had been 'adopted' by the Star of Bengal Restaurant who had named it Ravi.

Tony smiled, he could almost walk without a limp again and that very afternoon he was taking delivery of a small brown Nubian goat that, bless him, apparently had a heart complaint. Maybe the occasional stiff drink would help...

*   *   *   *   *   *

CHAPTER FOUR

ALL IN A GOOD CAUSE

'SAVE the Warthog!'

Katherine Walworth had been handing out leaflets, rattling her tin and loudly proclaiming her cause in Fuller Square in the centre of Newvale for three hours and ten minutes and her feet hurt. So far she had collected what sounded like three or four coins at most. Her friend Sonya was going to say, 'I told you so, ' but the few, the very few, who had stopped to learn more had at least gone on their way with a new awareness of the plight of the Southern Warthog whose tusks were being stolen by ivory poachers.

Katherine couldn't understand the mindsets of some people. 'Fuck the warthogs - ugly bastards!' One man had shouted, prompting Katherine to retort, 'It's just as well for you we don't judge people by their looks!' But realising even as she said it that, actually, we do.

Katherine's looks had never been a major worry to anyone except Katherine. Admirers regarded her as petite, shapely and pretty. She saw herself as small and plump and she didn't like her nose at all, she never had. She had once been on the receiving end of a furious row from her mother for going through the photo albums and blotting out her nose with correction fluid wherever it appeared.

Her former husband had insisted on kissing her nose and telling her it was beautiful, which had made her come to think of it as a hideous scar to be either brazened out or covered up. As a student she had worked for one summer in a food-processing factory where it had been compulsory to wear a facemask and she had revelled in the joy of what she called anonoseonymity.

Sadly, all the while her husband had been telling her she had a beautiful nose he had been telling Brenda Lovejoy she had a beautiful everything else and Ms Lovejoy, whose nocturnal activities fully endorsed the family name, wasted no time in emptying both his balls and his bank account before casting him aside to make room for her next victim. He had come crawling back to Katherine who poured a large jar of cook-in sauce over him from an upstairs window before selling his beloved vinyl record collection online and donating the money to a donkey sanctuary - a cause she knew he would hate after being kicked by one of the creatures at the seaside when he was nine leaving him with testicles that hung one behind the other and a scar the same shape as a seahorse.

She had tried a few blind dates but, after three boring malodorous gargoyles in a row, had decided the dice was loaded heavily against success. Now, at forty-two, Katherine had given up on men. She shared a flat with her friend Sonia and a tabby cat called Mister Minge and devoted her time to her job - charity fundraising for a variety of good causes.

It began to drizzle around 2:30pm so Katherine decided to call it a day and retreated to the comparative comfort of the 'American Diner' nearby for a cup of coffee and something described as a 'Frisco Feast' that failed to invoke either the spirit of California or any suggestion of calorific value. She picked up something with her fork that was probably related to lettuce somewhere along its evolutionary path and studied the now steady rain through the window.

'Everything alright with the Frisco Feast?'

She hadn't noticed him approaching her table. He wore a badge on his shirt that said 'Craig' and underneath 'It's a Pleasure!'

'Fine thanks,' she smiled tiredly. Unexpectedly, he didn't move away.

'If it wasn't for the destruction of their habitat, they wouldn't be forced into such close contact with humans.'

Katherine looked up at him, puzzled.

'Warthogs' he said and smiled shyly.

'Oh, yes… I suppose so.'

'I think you're amazing, caring about creatures no one else would give a second thought for.' This time his smile was dazzling. He was twentyish, tall with dark curly hair and deep brown eyes. Katherine found herself wishing she was twenty years younger - and with someone else's nose. She returned the smile and was about to reply when a call from the counter snatched him away.

'I told you so.' Sonya was predictably post-prophetic but not without sympathy as she handed Katherine a glass of wine. 'Nobody's going to support warthogs.'

'It's not bloody fair - they've as much right to support as anything else.' Katherine sipped at her wine and tried to bury herself even deeper into her dressing gown as she curled up on the sofa.

'What you should do,' Sonya suggested, 'Is make out you're collecting for something photogenic, like tigers or elephants, then just divert the cash to the warthogs, nobody would know.'

'I'd know, and if we weren't destroying their habitats they wouldn't have to live in such close proximity to humans!'

'Eh?'

'Something someone said to me today.'

'Stop the ivory trade!'

Same spot, same tin, next day, different tack. Katherine hoped that by linking the warthogs with elephants she might have a better response and so far things were looking decidedly up. Her tin was satisfyingly heavy after only two hours and Craig had given her a friendly wave from the diner window a while ago.

'What about narwhals?'

Someone had pulled the communication cord on Katherine's train of thought and she refocused on a little man standing in front of her peering intently through glasses that magnified his eyes so much he resembled a Japanese manga character.

'I'm sorry?'

'Narwhals - I see you've got a photo of an elephant there and one of those ugly pig things..'

'Warthogs'

'…Aye, well what about the narwhal? Only they've got ivory tusks as well you see.'

'Yes, well I suppose they have, and I certainly support….'

'.. If you cut their tusks off they don't mate - and they enjoy mating, narwhals do, every spring they go at it like nobody's business, breeding as if there's no tomorrow - they can ejaculate fifteen feet into the air!'

Katherine didn't see how this helped in procreating the species, in fact it sounded like a retrograde step and she was about to say so when she realised the man had not taken his hands out of his pockets the whole time and appeared to be attempting to give the narwhal a run for its money.' She turned and walked rapidly away.

She hadn't been planning to return to the American Diner today, the 'Frisco Feast' had been nothing of the sort but she told herself a coffee would be welcome and maybe there would be something on the menu a bit more palatable. Taking a seat she looked around hoping for a glimpse of Craig but it was a girl who approached her table. 'Laura - It's a pleasure' said the badge. Laura didn't look as if it was a pleasure as she hovered with a tiny notepad and pen and a stare like that of a circling peregrine. Katherine studied the menu uncertainly.

'What's the 'Big Apple' like?'

'It's a big apple!'

Laura was probably a nice girl when off duty Katherine told herself, but she still resented being sighed at in a bored way.

'Really, well in that case I'll have a cappuccino and a Cincinnati Sizzler please.'

Laura scribbled, spun one hundred and eighty degrees and strode off. Katherine looked out through the window, the narwhal man was leaning against a litterbin as if he was trying to shag it and across the square a row of pigeons sat on the scaffolding that surrounded the Town Hall.

'One Sizzler and a cappuccino.' The food and coffee arrived at the table and she looked up into Craig's warm smile. 'Better day today?'

'Yes, much better,' she smiled back.

'I was going to pop out and say hello and pop a coin in your tin but we've been rushed off our feet in here all morning, so how about I pay for the coffee and you can put that in instead?'

Katherine felt a blush start at her neck and begin spreading and cursed herself for having so little self-control.

'Well thanks, I'll do that!'

The dazzling smile appeared again as he turned to leave and Katherine felt the blush reach her nose which she instantly buried in a copy of the Chronicle.

'PC is first to nervously twitch a sect', something 'O' something something 'I' something?'

'Eh?' Katherine was in the office but her mind was in Cincinnati, or Frisco or somewhere and so she heard little of Sonya's plea for help.

'... at least I think it's an 'O', if 'baboon' is right ' *'Arts degree is a blessing for large monkey'* – that's B.A. - Boon, yes?'

'Hmm, probably.'

Sonya got up, walked across to Katherine's desk and waved a hand in front of her eyes, finally getting her attention.

'Eh? What?'

'Ah, so you are awake?'

'Sorry, miles away.'

Sonya studied her friend; she'd only ever known her to be 'miles away' twice before and both occasions had ended in tears. The first was in university, his name was Turgut and he had turned out to be married twice already and the other was her ex-husband.

Katherine and Sonya both worked for Newvale Voluntary Alliance, an umbrella organisation funded by Newvale Council offering support for charities and volunteer organisations in and around the Town. The pair had known each other since schooldays and had drifted together and apart many times on the sea of life. Sonya had married a man called Troy with nice pectorals and as much charisma as a wooden horse. When the sex became boring she realised everything else was too and so she left one Sunday afternoon while he was at the gym. He had called her a day later to ask how to spell metatarsus and she just hung up without even asking him why he wanted to know.

'OK, what's his name... car... job... willy size...?' Sonya prompted.

Katherine smiled, 'It's nothing, just me being silly, honestly. Come on, it's lunchtime, let's pop into town.'

'Town? We normally go over the Black Lion.'

Craig Fuller was twenty-one and currently managing a band called 'The Bloody Red Viscounts'. He was also taking evening classes in business studies. His father had his own home improvement company and, as the eldest of the three children, he would probably have taken over one day but, to Dad's disappointment, he had never been the slightest bit interested in conservatories, windows or doors.

Craig was going to strike out on his own as a music promoter and impresario and the American Diner job was just the place he felt he needed to be at present to keep his finger on the local contemporary pulse. The Diner's clientele were mostly young people, students from nearby Newvale College and the like.

Currently between girlfriends, he had been contemplating asking out Laura from the Diner but had been deterred when a Cro-Magnon driving a sound system on wheels had collected her the other evening, and this morning she had an ugly hickey on her neck and looked as if she hadn't slept. Craig had smiled at her in the staff room but had received no response.

He looked out on to the square; someone was having their photograph taken on the steps of the Town Hall, a car was about to get a ticket for parking at the bus stop while its driver queued for the cash point and.. yes, there she was, Mrs Warthog rattling her tin. She would probably be in later, thought Craig; he'd recommend the Miami Slice.

'The Miami Slice is nice - do you like pineapple?'

'Yes I do,' replied Katherine who didn't.

Craig smiled, 'Good day so far?'

'Getting better by the minute,' Katherine beamed and was rewarded with another smile in return.

'It'll be just two minutes,' he turned and walked off. 'Just as nice from the back', thought Katherine watching him go, '…what IS wrong with me?'

She hadn't felt like this for a very, very long time and was both angry and delighted about feeling like it now. 'For God's sake, you could write everything he has ever said to you on the back of a beer mat. You've spoken three times, you're old enough to be his mother, he's probably got a girlfriend, or he's engaged, or gay?' Katherine taped an imaginary gag over her inner voice of caution; she didn't want to hear, she just wanted to see him smile at her again.

She had been forced to compete with a busker for the public's money all morning. He had only known two songs and he'd had a really irritating whiney voice. She had been glad when the persistent attentions of 'Narwhal Man' had driven him to the other side of the square.

When her meal arrived she noticed Craig was no longer wearing the Stars and Stripes waistcoat that constituted the staff uniform. 'I'm off to lunch myself,' he explained.

The reply escaped from her mouth before her brain could stop it…

'Why don't you join me?'

For an instant she saw surprise and indecision flicker across his face, but then came the smile.

And he sat.

'Let me put it this way…' Sonya was pacing and when she did that there was no stopping her, '… you know when we were on holiday in Tenerife and you and that… what was his name? He looked like a vampire..?'

'Paco – and he didn't look like a bloody vampire, you were just jealous!'

'He had big pointy teeth – anyway, you know when you and... Paco spent the night on his boat and you had to rest for two days afterwards?'

'What about it?'

'Well, do you know what this Craig was doing then?'

Katherine just shrugged and allowed Sonya to continue.

'He was in infants school drawing pictures of... of gee-gees or something and taking them home so Mummy could stick them on the fucking fridge!'

'Not that you're jealous or anything?'

'Oh Katherine - look, if you want to shag him, then shag him - but don't tell me it's true love, you've got nothing at all in common.'

'Yeah? Well that's where you're wrong, he's promoting a band and I think I can help him.'

Mister Minge sat on the corner of the bath watching Katherine wallow, his indecipherable yellow eyes were half open and the tip of his tail twitched lazily, but Katherine knew he was like a coiled spring. The minute the wrapper came off her chocolate bar he would snap into life, tightrope precariously along the edge of the bath and take a small piece of chocolate gently from her hand.

Katherine was wondering how she could lay her hands on two grand. That apparently was how much it would cost to get The Bloody Red Viscounts into the studio to make their demo. She couldn't believe she was actually contemplating this. She knew nothing about music promoting - or music for that matter - despite what she'd told Craig.

He hadn't asked for money, or any help at all, he had merely told her, with a degree of infectious enthusiasm she rarely saw in her own professional life, just how dedicated the Band were, how good, how original and how deserving of a shot at the big time. He had asked his father to back them but was turned down because, One: things were pretty grim in the world of conservatories at the moment and Two: it was, he had said, a crazy idea guaranteed to lose money.

Katherine hadn't considered the commercial viability of the project too deeply, she was sure that if Craig thought they were good then surely so would countless others of his generation. All they needed was that little leg up to get them and their sound out there. She liked the idea of being an 'Angel' and she liked the idea of being Craig's angel even more. The only teensy problemette was the fact that she didn't have two grand lying about at the.... hang on, actually she did... no, NO! NOT an option! Don't even think about... hang on though... she snapped off another two squares of chocolate and broke the corner off one of them for the ever-hovering Mister Minge, hang on... if she were to just ... temporarily... then she could cover it by...surely no one would .... and it was all in a good cause, wasn't it? A thrill ran through her in anticipation of Craig's likely reaction to her generosity.

It weighed less than a make up purse or a small bottle of water but even so the envelope in Katherine's bag felt uncomfortably heavy as she walked into the American Diner. She ordered a coffee with a tremble in her voice and when it duly arrived she asked Craig if he 'had a minute..'

'Yeah! Next Wednesday, Thursday and Friday so let's have you note-perfect!' Craig was on the phone to his band's lead guitarist/singer/van driver.
'We've got a backer.... don't know mate... she's a real music lover though and we've got three days in the studio so let's go for it!'
Craig hung up, this was it! The break he had been dreaming of. He was sure that when the A&R men heard The Bloody Red Viscounts with a polished studio veneer they would be fighting for their signatures. Bless you Mrs Warthog! He pulled up; suddenly realising he didn't even know her name. What a woman! What faith! She'd turned up with two grand in cash in an envelope and just handed it over. He hoped he hadn't scared her when he had thrown himself over the table to hug her and shower her with kisses; he'd just been so excited. He

would take next week off work and drill the Band until they were flawless.

On her way home, Katherine had walked on air. She had smiled at Narwhal Man, waved at her nosey next-door neighbour and quoted part of a Shakespeare sonnet to Mr Gupta in the newsagent prompting him to ask her if she wanted a sit down and a drink of water. She could still feel the closeness, the smell, the brush of his cheek; the kisses… had there been five or six? It couldn't just have been the money, he must have liked her anyway, must have, surely? She would find out soon enough, now they had a common cause, they were… sort of… partners.

'You are joking? Tell me you're joking!'

Katherine just smiled. It was the smile drunks radiate when someone tells them it's dangerous to be walking in the middle of the road and Sonya could see there was no getting through. 'That two grand should have been banked today! It's NVA money; you and I and half a dozen others have spent the last month collecting it!'

'It's OK, I've got a loan coming from the bank to replace it, it'll be banked tomorrow and all will be well.'

Sonya just shook her head, 'You've really lost the plot this time girl. You know what I reckon?'

'If you even THINK the words mid-life crisis our friendship is over!' snapped Katherine, only half joking. She was in love! Love love love, love is all you need, love changes everything, love is all around, love is the drug, you call it madness - I call it love!

Katherine felt the colour drain from her cheeks, it was the opposite of a blush, it was as if something very heavy and very hungry had woken in her stomach and was demanding all her blood to keep it alive. She found herself trembling and looked again at the clerk behind the counter whose face, at first bank-blank and pitiless, now showed a glimmer of concern.

'What do you mean, declined?' she asked him.

He shrugged. 'As part of your application we have to run it past a credit reference agency and I'm afraid you've been declined.'

'But... I've never had any...'

'Look, here's their address, you have a right to see what information they are holding about you.'

'But I have to have that money today!'

Now that it was clear she wasn't about to drop dead in his bank, the clerk's emotional shutter came down and he simply shrugged again.

Outside the bank the reality of the situation hit home. She would have to speak to her boss, the humourless and rigid Mr Eddowes, and he was NOT going to understand.

Sonya had hugged Katherine on the morning of the court appearance and told her that their friendship was as strong as ever. Katherine had cried and apologised for the whole bloody mess and then headed here, to this soulless waiting room with the filthy floor and graffiti covered walls and people who sat with their elbows on their knees staring at their shoes.

'The fact that you have no previous convictions means that we may, hopefully, avoid a custodial sentence today,' her solicitor was telling her and her stomach lurched at the sound of the words. He had already warned her in a previous meeting that courts tend to take a very dim view of theft from charities and so she was expecting the worst. He smiled at her and moved on to another of his clients.

She had avoided the centre of town since her arrest. Craig was the last person she wanted to see. She hoped he wouldn't be too hurt by her disappearance but it was best that nothing linked him with any of this. She had told her solicitor that she had needed the money for some private medical treatment. Craig had never even known her name, was he looking for her? This was the first time in over a month she had left her own street. She wondered for the thousandth time how he was, how did the band get on in the studio, have they been signed yet? She had never even heard them play.

'Katie?'

Katherine looked up to see a middle aged woman hovering over her.

'It is Katie isn't it? Katie Porritt?'

Katherine raised her eyebrows at the sound of the maiden name she hadn't used in years. She had contemplated returning to it on her divorce but she had rather liked Walworth.

'Do I know you?'

'Of course you do, it's Miss Abbot from Beech Road Junior School.'

'Miss Abbot? So it is, I'm sorry, I didn't recognise…'

'Oh that's alright, long time, long time.'

Katherine wanted her to go away but she didn't seem inclined to. 'So, how are you nowadays Miss …. Err?'

'It's not Miss anymore, she forced a chuckle, it's Mrs now, Mrs Friendy, so.. what brings you…?' Mrs Friendy tailed off, perhaps, thought Katherine, she had suddenly realised where they were. She sighed, it was going to be public knowledge soon anyway, 'I sort of borrowed some money, but couldn't pay it back in time.'

'Ah.. I see,' said Mrs Friendy, who clearly did.

Katherine did recall Miss Abbot now; she had made her do gym in her knickers once because she had forgotten her kit. So, what was she doing here?'

'Ah, well actually I'm here with my husband; he umm… got a bit lost one night.'

That didn't sound like a crime to Katherine and she adopted a quizzical expression. Mrs Friendy, however, must have sensed a more detailed interrogation was imminent and quickly left with a, 'Got to go, Edward is waiting.'

Katherine watched her swerve between the scattered chairs towards a bench near the door occupied by a balding man in an anorak who looked tired, lost and out of place.

She stood outside the court building and took a deep breath before heading to her parked car. The relief of walking free from that awful place made her feel slightly drunk. She couldn't wait to get home and have a bath and soak away the remnants of the fear and dread that had sat on her shoulders every waking minute since her arrest. She didn't fully understand what 'Community Payback' was, but she was going to have two hundred and forty hours to find out.

Craig looked out of the diner window; he hadn't seen Mrs Warthog since she had handed over the money. His boss had told him she had been in the next day but of course he'd been off work with the band. Then she had simply disappeared. He looked out on to the Square once more then turned and headed for the staffroom. He was taking Laura out tonight to watch The Bloody Red Viscounts play at their biggest venue yet. He had invited several A&R men after sending them the studio demo and a few had indicated they would be attending, this was a big chance for the band and Craig wished he could have told Mrs Warthog how grateful he was for her help, but she had simply disappeared.

Perhaps that's what angels did?

*   *   *   *   *   *

CHAPTER FIVE

ANY OTHER BUSINESS?

NEWVALE Town Hall, on the corner of Fuller Square, had been covered in scaffolding for three years. The poles and planks had been erected by a firm of masonry cleaners engaged by the Council to remove a hundred and twelve years of grime from the great slabs that made up the building. However, the firm had gone into liquidation and the Council were claiming the scaffolding in compensation for a job only one third completed despite them having paid up front.

The scaffolding now had an air of permanence about it. Birds nested there, protesters had made attention-grabbing squats on the various levels and two Christmases ago a bank clerk had closed his account when an office party's conga line got a little bit out of hand.

The Mayor of Newvale, Councillor Gordon McIver, was inside the Town Hall chairing a meeting of the Newvale 200 Steering Committee.

'In case you are all wondering,' Councillor Brenda Worrall was announcing, 'The Newvale in Bloom Sub-Committee has begun drawing up plans for a garden bonanza.'

Mayor McIver was wondering nothing of the sort; in fact, he was wondering what it would feel like to stick an ice-lolly up his arse. His haemorrhoids were giving him hell. 'It would probably turn instantly to steam, like in cartoons,' he mused and mentally savoured the imagined relief as an icy slush of raspberry or orange splashed over a terrain resembling a fresh lava field generating clouds of angry steam.

As his colleagues waffled on he let his mind drift away to a place he had invented where it was always cool and haemorrhoids didn't exist. In 'Happy Arse World' there were glacial mountain streams, sunlit uplands of pine forest and wildflower meadows where flocks of buttocks fluttered by on angelic wings, their gentle farting calls carried on a fresh breeze. It was a superficial place, Mayor McIver had never delved into the logistics of how the buttock-birds ate or mated. Maybe they didn't? Maybe they didn't need to, maybe they were divine beings, 'Angelanus' - he liked that word and mentally filed it away for future use.

Gordon McIver was fifty-four and not a native of Newvale. He had moved to the town in his twenties to work in a then-flourishing car components factory. Latterly he had set out on his own with a small garage and now sold second-hand vans. His wife, Moira, was a teacher of languages and they had two grown-up children who lived far away. He had become a councillor because he had wanted to influence local affairs and make a positive difference, but eighteen years in the Town Hall had done to his idealism what inactivity and a lack of dietary fibre had done to his rectum.

Alan Savage, manager of Cedar Hill Retirement Home, studied the woman sitting opposite him in his tiny office and tried once again to digest what she had said.

'Are you suggesting', he asked her patiently, 'that we dress up our residents in costumes from various periods in Newvale's history and then parade them through the Town?'

'The Council feels that our senior citizens have a right to be involved in the celebrations.'

The woman was in her mid twenties and was called Jemima or Jocelyn or something, Alan couldn't remember and cared even less.

'Most of them can't ... parade, a lot of them can't even walk.'

'Well obviously, we'll provide wheelchairs for those who want them. They must be excited, knowing what year it is?'

Alan gestured wildly to the dayroom on the other side of his window, 'Most of them don't even know what fucking day it is!'

Her jaw dropped open but he was beyond caring. He had been up since 5:30 and had so far dealt with Mr Pointer who was convinced a column of army ants had stolen his teeth; then there was Mrs Luscombe who had lost a leg nine years ago and, having been told about phantom limbs, was now afraid to go anywhere alone in case hers came back to haunt her. Finally there had been a full-scale gang war at breakfast because Mr Richardson had kidnapped the Spanish donkey saltcellar and was demanding a ransom. Alan's ribs still ached from where he had been viciously prodded with a walking stick. The last thing he had needed this morning was some officious idiot from Newvale Council wanting to goad fancy-dressed pensioners through the streets in a travesty of a triumph that even Caligula would have found bizarre.

The young woman gathered up her brochures and flyers and rose to leave. 'Considering the help and goodwill you get from Newvale Council I would have thought you might have been a little more onside,' her voice quivered and Alan realised she was wrestling with either righteous anger or one of those other emotions that young gifted people have before real life erodes them.

'Listen love, I'm sorry but...' He realised there was no easy way to break the news to her, 'the fact is.. this bicentennial thing.. nobody really gives a toss.'

'Well, I think you'll find a lot of people really do and you... you're going to be left out and that's a shame.'

Alan was about to reply when his office door opened and a very old head appeared around it. 'I need a lift to go and see my husband.'

'No Elsie, you go and sit in the lounge and I'll get someone to come and sort you out shortly.' The old head disappeared.

'I'm heading back into town, maybe I could take her to..' the young woman volunteered but was cut off by a suddenly tired sounding Alan.

'Only if you've got a time machine love, her husband's been dead for thirty years.'

Mayor McIver was in his third meeting of the day; he remembered nothing of the first one and his recollection of the second was limited to a councillor using the phrase, 'Fire down below,' accurately mirroring his own discomfort. This meeting was for grant allocation and the group were considering a plea from a retirement home for financial help towards a new wing to combat what the application had described as 'Gross overcrowding.'

'He's threatening to go to the Chronicle if something isn't done,' stated Councillor Clint Moran. He brandished a letter and then read from it, 'If you don't pull your collective fingers out, I'll be speaking to the Chronicle, they can come up here and take a picture of Mr Tom Flowers who won a Distinguished Service Medal on D-Day and now lives in a shower cubicle because we haven't got a room for him. He had three umbrellas for Christmas. He was wrinkly enough when he came in here but you should see him now!'

Mayor McIver was glad he had insisted on driving himself. Granted, the battered blue van he used for work cut less of a dash than the mayoral limo but at least he didn't have to look at his chauffeur's neck, which always depressed him. His mayoral chauffeur was a nice enough man and his driving exemplary but he was entirely the wrong shape for the job. His arms were long enough for him to drive from the back seat if he so wished but his legs were hardly long enough to reach the pedals; the overall effect was decidedly simian and the tailor engaged to make his uniform had called him back three times, unwilling to believe the measurements he had taken.

Also, in his own vehicle, he could sit on his gel cushion and get a little relief. He had agreed to pay a visit to the manager of the overcrowded old folks' home to try and pacify the bugger and as he drove he allowed his mind to drift back to 'Happy Arse World'. It occurred to him that he had only ever envisaged the Buttock Birds - or Angelanuses - from the rear, so to speak. If one were to observe them from the front would they have sex organs? Watching a big hairy cock flying towards you would be a most unappealing prospect. He decided therefore to make them asexual, also, they must have at least a rudimentary brain in order to fly and sit on branches? The more he thought about it the more complex it all became - a bit like running a local authority really.

He started singing *'Campbeltown Loch, I Wish You Were Whisky'* but he stopped when it began to remind him of his late father, whose own arse had been a terrifying thing to behold. He could recall it with startling clarity, huge, red, spotty and streaked with black dust as he stood up in the tin bath in front of the fire while Mother poured in another kettle-full. He remembered praying fervently for examination success so he wouldn't have to follow his parent into the Fife coalfields.

When Mayor McIver pulled into the car park of Cedar Hill Residential Home the problems facing the establishment became immediately apparent. The number of faces at every window gave the building the appearance of the 'Last Boat out of Saigon.'

'Is Mr Savage about?' Mayor McIver asked an old man who had appeared at the small reception window and was answered with what would probably have been a prize-winning gurn.

'Onions for dinner, ohhhh, onions!' the old man replied and laughed a toothless laugh.

The Mayor backed away and decided to sit for a while and wait. The notice board caught his eye,...

'YOUR DUTY MANAGER TODAY IS A SAVAGE'

The ambiguity brought a brief smile to the mayor, unaware that the name had brought a lifetime of ridicule to the Savage in question.

'Father Frank Kavanagh will hear confessions in the TV Room on Tuesdays at 10.00am.' stated another notice and Mayor McIver wondered what any of the Cedar Hill residents would get up to that required absolution. At their age, he mused, transgressing most of the Commandments would be a cause for congratulation rather than admonishment. The thought led him to try and recall the Ten Commandments and he found himself struggling. There was killing, of course; coveting an oxen; coveting your neighbour's wife - he thought of the immense, moustachioed and evil-tempered Mrs Piedmont who lived next door to him and shuddered - and wasn't there something about graven images? His train of though was interrupted by the arrival of Alan Savage along with an elderly lady tugging at his shirt.

'There's a strange person in my room every time I go in there and she's stealing my clothes!'

'No there isn't Mrs Everett, it's a full length mirror, you asked us for one, remember?' Alan broke off when he caught sight of the Mayor, 'You're... what's-his-name aren't you?'

Mayor McIver rose and extended a hand, 'Councillor Gordon McIver, mayor of Newvale, I've come in response to your letter.'

Mayor McIver had tried to make a head count on his tour of the Home but had failed somewhere in the melee that was the common room. He had been intrigued by one gentleman who had told him he was making a model of the Holy Ghost out of curtain fabric and old coat hangers and another had tried to regale him with a story of how soldier ants had bitten off Sergeant Jackson's foreskin but, in fairness to Alan Savage, he hadn't exaggerated the overcrowding and Mayor McIver found in him a kindred spirit doing his best with his back to the wall.

'Have you gone completely mad?'

Moira McIver paused on her way to the dining table, a gravy boat in one hand and Gordon's dinner in the other. She put them down before staring around her home as if stocktaking,

'We can't have an... an old age pensioner coming here, it's completely inappropriate!'

Mayor McIver and Alan Savage had come up with what they thought of as a groundbreaking plan that could ease Cedar Hill's problem and potentially put Newvale on the map when it came to care of the elderly. They had decided to launch an 'Adopt an Older Person

For the Day' scheme and, as Mayor, Gordon McIver planned to lead the way. But his wife was clearly going to take some convincing.

'For goodness sake Gordon, we have… people around, what would they think?'

'Pensioners are people, aren't they?'

'Well… yes,' she answered grudgingly, but then qualified it with a muttered, 'only just.'

Mayor McIver had envisaged a quiet, dickey-bow wearing old chap who he could occasionally play chess with and engage in philosophical discussions, a retired doctor or lecturer perhaps, and he felt that by getting in first he could have the pick of the crop, but Moira had painted an entirely different mental picture.'

'You remember my father, Gordon, the swearing and urinating, the smell….'

'Yes' said Mayor McIver and was tempted to add, 'He'd been like that since his twenties.'

Moira's father had spent most of his adult life in prison where, on one occasion, he had set up a still producing a drink of such high quality and alcohol by volume that he earned enough from various guards during his incarceration to go straight for almost two years on release. Age, however, turned him from a loveable and inventive rogue into a violent drunk; incoherent, incontinent, indecorous and indistinguishable from the ranting spewing rabble that Moira had come to hate and fear. There was no alcohol in the McIver house. She knew Gordon had the occasional drink after work but she inevitably made her disapproval known by not kissing him and telling him he smelled like a tramp.

'It can't hurt to just see a few.' Mayor McIver persisted, but Moira only huffed and strode dramatically out of the room.

'Well I think it should be launched with a two-page spread in the Chronicle,' stated Councillor Clint Moran.

'Yes, highlighting all the chronologically enhanced persons currently available for senior companionship,' added Councillor Brenda Worrall.

'You mean,' Mayor McIver rubbed his ear, 'the same sort of thing the Animal Sanctuary does when they have their adoption drive? Something like "Can you give a senior citizen a loving happy home?"'

'Exactly!'

Mayor McIver shook his head in wonder at the enthusiasm his sarcasm had triggered. The silly sods were going to turn the whole thing into some hideous meat market. He could see it now, pages of photographs with accompanying captions...'

Fred is 86 and still has some of his own teeth; his hobbies include betting on horses and saying 'Aye Aye.' Mary is 93 and likes to talk about being bombed. She would be better in an environment where no one has a beard due to an unpleasant incident in her younger days involving a Maltese sailor and his monkey.'

'We'll use a headline like 'Homing Pensioners' or something, suggested Councillor Moran.

Mayor McIver interceded, 'Homing Pensioners? Makes it sound like we're going to drive the buggers five hundred miles away, drop them off and wait to see who makes it back!'

'That would be one solution,' quipped Councillor Moran and was surprised at the icy silence that followed and by the look of pure hatred from Councillor Worrall. He thought briefly about pouring oil on troubled waters but twenty years of marriage had taught him that any kind of oil was highly inflammable.

Alan Savage studied the two-page spread in the Chronicle with misgivings. He had already fielded several calls that morning, including one from a kissogram agency and another, probably a hoax, from someone professing to be a chimney sweep asking for a very thin pensioner with a good head of hair. But he was heartened by the fact that Mayor McIver and a few other councillors had been as good as their word and there were already four residents less in the home.

One family had turned up at the Home with a tape measure, explaining they had a garden shed with a very narrow door while another couple had introduced themselves as Beelzebub and Astaroth, all had left empty handed.

'I want a poup!'

It wasn't the finest conversation opener Moira McIver had ever heard. The little man with huge ears out of all proportion to the size of his head stood in her drawing room and turned his inquisitive blue eyes on the chandelier as if it were a hovering UFO. 'Err, this is Jim...' Gordon had said as if that explained everything. Moira had extended a hand and an insincere smile and Jim had responded by relaying the message from his bowels.

'Yes, well, how about a cup of tea, eh Jim?' Suggested the Mayor.

'OK, but what I really want is a good clear-out, only if my eleven o clock poup is late then my noon poup will be late as well and I'll end up doing two of my afternoon poups together like I did when I was on holiday the year before last. Two poups together I did, I had to be helped off the toilet.'

Moira gave Gordon the sort of look men in foxholes wear when they realise the next enemy charge is going to wipe them out. 'I'll go and put the kettle on and you can show ...Jim, around.'

He looked like a little pink monkey, thought Mayor McIver. He was wearing a suit that must have fitted in some bygone year but now hung loosely on his sparse frame, the sleeves of his jacket completely hid his hands and there was room in the collar of his shirt for another neck.

'Come on Jim, I'll show you the err.... facilities.'

'Well ours was a lovely old soul to start with.' Councillor Brenda Worrall told the meeting, 'She helped around the house, made jam and the kids started calling her Granny. Then I tried to take her balaclava off to get her to go in the bath and she screamed the house down. Dominic is a social worker specialising in the elderly and even he couldn't get through to her. He asked her to breathe slowly and she called him a… well… he's not one of them and it was a very rude thing to shout.'

'Mine only stayed for about five minutes,' offered Councillor Moran, 'We left the patio doors open and he was off like a rocket. Apparently he's living wild in Newvale Park, people who overlook it say they've caught glimpses of him darting from one bush to another - he's only wearing a vest now - and you can hear his howls at night.'

'Bloody Hell.' Mayor McIver put his head in his hands.

'So?' Councillor Moran challenged him, 'How's yours?'

'Dead.'

A gasp went around the table. They were all looking at him expectantly so he thought some elaboration might be in order.

'Found him dead on the toilet. We thought at first he'd hung himself because he was naked except for his tie but I've spoken to Alan Savage and apparently he always did that.'

'Bit of a mess Mr Mayor.' Councillor Moran offered.

'It's a fucking disaster Clint and no mistake, the Chronicle will have a field day.'

'Looking at the bigger picture,' Councillor Worrall offered, 'it's not really that bad. The adoption drive got fifteen people out of Cedar Hill and of those…' she studied her clipboard, 'Five went straight back to the home, one is living wild in the Park, one is in custody, one is completely unaccounted for and one is.. err, dead - so that leaves six successfully homed.'

'Would they be the six who are living in a squat on Coldridge Estate? Because if they are we've had umpteen complaints from residents about them!' sighed Mayor McIver. He had the look of a bunkered dictator as he paced the committee room, 'All night parties, swing music booming out, booze, prescription drugs - it's taken years off them apparently; one of them has even bought a fucking motor bike!'

With ten less residents in Cedar Hill Retirement Home, Alan Savage had a little breathing space. He also had a few uncomfortable encounters with concerned relatives but most had been at least supportive of his intentions and the son of the man currently living wild in the Park had suggested trying to coax his almost naked parent into a trap baited with a pair of long johns and a jar of rubbing liniment. Mr Savage had informed the son, however, that in the light of his father's increasingly unpredictable behaviour time might not be on their side. Only that morning the old man had leapt out in front of a woman on a bicycle causing her to swerve into the pond and the previous night a small group of local vigilantes had gone hunting for him but had scattered in terror after he had suddenly appeared in the light of their torches, his vest ragged, brandishing a wooden club. As a result, Alan Savage had discreetly called the local vet and asked him about the viability of using a tranquiliser dart.

'We could compulsorily purchase the squat on Cold Ridge Estate, rename it 'Sunshine House' or something and put a warden in it,' Councillor Clint Moran suggested. He and Gordon McIver were in the Mayor's parlour doing some serious damage to a bottle of scotch.

It wasn't a bad idea and Mayor McIver agreed to set the wheels in motion, in the meantime he would see to it that the residents of the squat got a visit from Constable Lillywhite, 'That should calm the buggers down a bit,' he thought. He would also have to raid the expenses budget and take Chronicle editor, Monty Fox out to dinner and see if he could persuade him to keep a lid on things. He closed his eyes and drifted off to Happy Arse World.

'No Mr Pointer, they've gone to live in another place, they're quite safe.' Alan Savage reassured one of his residents that the missing former members of the Nursing Home were, mostly, OK and that none of them had been carried off by army ants.

The man who had been living in the shower block now had a room of his own and was drying out nicely and the Spanish Donkey saltcellar was being locked away between meals to ensure it was not taken hostage again.

Alan Savage closed his eyes and pondered the eccentricity that different ages invoked. As a child some older kids had held him down and painted his face in an attempt to make the image fit the name. He thought of the wild man in the Park and speculated that maybe we were all just a few meals or a few misfiring synapses away from the Stone Age.

*   *   *   *   *   *

CHAPTER SIX

THE WOMAN FROM ZETA RETICULI

BY the eve of one's thirtieth birthday it's likely that a person will have experienced many things. Deborah Waghorn had not seen or done much out of the ordinary but was nevertheless destined to enter her fourth decade having had the possibly unique experience of witnessing a super-intelligent extra-terrestrial creature sticking a shining silver tube up a sheep's arse.

Deborah had been in the habit of taking nocturnal walks over the hills above Newvale for some years, dreaming in vain of bumping into her very own Heathcliff and, although her heart had not yet been stolen, it had been strengthened considerably, as indeed had her legs which were now so finely tuned that, should she indeed spot a potential paramour, he would have little chance of escape.

It had been 10:40pm, one hour and twenty minutes before the dawn of her thirtieth birthday, and she had been tramping her usual route across the hills. At a point where the path entered a small copse of trees, obscuring the view of the lights of the town below, something occurred.

Everyone subsequently involved agreed that a happening had certainly happened.

There had been an event.

The Deborah Waghorn who was standing in Fuller Square in the centre of Newvale at 4:45am the following morning, in pouring rain, with one side of her head completely hairless, naked, and staring mutely upwards into the falling rain, was not the same woman who had left her house some seven hours before.

The milkman who came across her as dawn broke was not in the mood, at that hour and in that weather, for the duty desk policeman's offer of 'Congratulations' in response to his statement that he had a naked woman in the cab of his milk float. Besides, even if he had been in that mood - and thirty years younger - his propensity had never been for semi-bald, wet, shivering women with wild staring eyes.

The police were kinder, offering her towels, warm drinks, a baggy white one-piece overall and a specially schooled WPC who became more confused by the minute as her training proved utterly unequal to the task.

'Have you been assaulted?'

'Yes.'

'Did you know the person or persons who assaulted you?'

'No, they weren't.'

'I'm sorry?'

'They weren't.'

'Weren't?'

'They weren't.... persons.'

'I'm not sure I follow, did any of them have a name that you heard?'

'Yes... and no.'

'Eh?'

'It had a name, but it's not a sound, I didn't... hear it. It was... it was more of a taste, or the memory of a taste, cold, like ice cream, but not sweet — acidic, acidic and cold.'

'Are you on any medication?' In the circumstances, the question had been very reasonable, but in her first moment of apparent lucidity since being brought to the station, Deborah seemed to suddenly realise exactly what had happened to her.

'FUCKING ALIENS!' She screamed.

'Are you saying,' the WPC continued calmly, 'that they were foreign?'

'Just about as foreign as you can get!'

Deborah's description left the police with little hope of an early arrest and a subsequent examination - which seemed to scare Deborah far more than the circumstances merited - ruled out a sexual motive for the event but highlighted some inexplicable puncture marks behind her right ear, and it was only the absence of any injury to the scalp that discounted burning as the cause of her hair loss. Not only was the right side of her scalp completely smooth but also her right eyebrow was missing and even any facial down was gone.

'You're going to have to cut what's left of your hair really short and wear a hat for a while; we'll tell people you had an accident with a chip-pan or something.' Elizabeth Waghorn studied her daughter's semi bald head in wonder for about the hundredth time.

'Why can't we just tell the truth?' Deborah retorted.

'Because we don't know what the truth is at the moment, do we?' Elizabeth put on her most patronising voice and swept out of the room.

Deborah's father's last words had been, 'I'll be down in a minute!' He had called this out from the top of a long ladder while painting the gable end of the house. His statement - inaccurate by 55 seconds - had been in response to his wife's notification that dinner was about to be dished up. At the funeral, Deborah, then twelve, had wished more than anything that she could have told him she believed him - even though she still didn't. He had gone to his maker knowing that his little girl had pooh-poohed his story that he had once seen a ghost.

He told her that he had encountered a woman in a long grey dress sitting on the river bridge where the road passed through Meadowvale Woods. On checking with people who lived locally he had been informed that the woman he described had been drowned in the river below the bridge a hundred and fifty years before. He swore he had seen her, the pale sad face gazing down at the waters and the ankle-length grey dress billowing in a long-dead breeze.

'You shouldn't scoff at these things Debbie, there are more mysteries out there that we will ever get to the bottom of.'

Her mother had scoffed, she scoffed at everything that challenged her hardwired view of the world and Deborah had fallen into the same agnostic mindset. It wasn't until her late teens, long after her father had passed over, that she regained her receptiveness to the inexplicable.

She had gone, against her better judgement, to a clairvoyant with a couple of her friends, just for a laugh. The woman told her several things vague enough to have applied to almost anyone before dropping her bombshell.

'Someone you love went away before you could tell them something important.'

It could have been a wild stab in the dark, of course. Deborah decided to say nothing and see where the woman went next but her attempt at a poker face clearly failed.

'I'm right, aren't I?'

'Yes,' Deborah had answered.

'He wants you to know that he understands; you were very young and he loves you.'

Deborah had fought against welling tears as her emotions overrode the constraints of logic. If she accepted the woman's statement as true - and she so desperately wanted to - then not only did her beloved father forgive her hurtful scepticism, but death was a great impostor with no power over consciousness and personality.

From then on, Deborah Waghorn's mind was an open house; nothing, however outlandish, would be dismissed without reasonable consideration. Her room at home became a shrine to alternative knowledge. Deborah lived at home because it was financially expedient and because, in the main, she was too accustomed to her mother doing all the cooking, washing and cleaning; tasks she would otherwise have to find time to do herself.

She had worked for some years in the office of a DIY Superstore on the edge of Newvale and knew more about larch lap fencing and grouting powder than a lady of quality should. Not that she believed any longer that she was a lady of quality. Her mother was a Bolling and insisted the name had evolved from Boleyn - which made her royal-by-marriage, but Deborah, despite the middle name of Anne, had kept her head, and her feet on the ground, thwarting her mother's social ambitions.

She was not unattractive, shunning make-up for that healthy natural look that some women can get away with as long as they smile a lot and their feet are not too big. She had attracted her share of admirers but found them all too eager to know her biblically before attempting to understand her spiritual needs, and while she enjoyed sex as much as the next woman (whoever she was) she found it only a transient pleasure.

Not being the slightest bit materialistic she never saw sex as the as the passport to accumulating possessions in the way many of her contemporaries did. She would lie there while some man rattled away, calling her 'Babe' and grunting in her ear like an adenoidal Gloucester Spot and she'd pass the time looking up at her bedroom ceiling where she had painstakingly stuck luminous stars of the constellations in their correct relative positions - using a ruler where necessary.

She had made a little game of it over the years, trying to pick out a star or constellation that began with the same letter that her lover cried out as he reached his climax. 'Arrr Arrr Arrr' would be Rigel; 'Ohh Ohh Ohh' would be Orion and so on. Occasionally she would have a challenge, like the sales representative for Barraclough Adhesives who had made a noise like an owl. She reconciled it by allowing that anywhere in the night sky would probably be appropriate for such a sound.

Deborah had never been to a psychiatrist before and was a little disappointed. He was not much older than her. He was also clean-shaven and insisted she call him Lance. She had expected a father-figure in a jacket with leather elbow patches, a goatee beard, half moon spectacles and a name beginning with Doctor and ending with something reassuringly Germanic. She had begun noisily reliving the alien encounter in her sleep and was here at her mother's insistence.

'Now then Deborah...' He hadn't asked permission to call her by her first name and she was surprised by just how much this annoyed her.

'Would you say you were religious?'

'No.'

'Tell me what you think happened to your father when he died?'

'We cremated him.'

'Do you think he might have gone to... heaven?'

'Well I don't think he turned into a fucking alien!'

She was instantly sorry when the look of hurt appeared on his face. He was probably genuinely trying to help her. He looked down and wrote something on his notepad and when he looked up again he smiled.

'Nice Hat.'

She found herself involuntarily returning the smile. It wasn't a nice hat, it was a loud and ignorant hat, if there were a cabaret circuit for hats, this hat would be the one that told cringingly inappropriate and unfunny jokes and stank of 1970's aftershave. It was a hat that invited comment in the hope of starting an argument it had neither the wit nor the charm to win. It made Deborah itch but she was reassured by a covering of bristle on her head's right hemisphere that indicated the hat might only need to be a temporary affectation.

'You told your mother the aliens made you cry?'

'Yes, but not in the way you're thinking. They were... are lachrymatory, I think it's something to do with their breathing.'

'Their world must be very different to Earth?'

'I suppose it must be, yes.'

'And yet they seemed at home here? Comfortable, no indications that the atmosphere was in any way toxic, our gravity allowed them to move with ease and the temperature didn't bother them... how likely do you think that would be given all the variables that must exist from one world to another?'

Deborah just stared at him; this could have been her mother talking.

'Are you a fan of science fiction?' He asked.

Small Town People

'In 1429,' replied Deborah, 'the then Emperor of China, Zhu Zhanji had one of his most trusted advisers boiled alive because he described to him a giraffe he'd seen on a trip to the coast.'

'No one's going to boil you alive Deborah.'

'No - just slowly grill me. And by the way, it's Ms Waghorn, I'm probably a descendant of Anne Boleyn, my father used to see ghosts and now he is one and he's spoken to me. And the aliens, all three of them, were as real, no… MORE real, than you!'

She stood up and left without a backward glance. Lance scribbled on his notebook, his office door open and his mind closed.

'I believe you!'

The three little words she should have said to her father, now someone was saying them to her. She read the email again.

'Dear Deborah;
I believe you!
We've never met; my name is Julian Skelton-Fry and I am, for want of a better description, a Ufologist.' I read of your encounter in the Newvale Chronicle and was not surprised by the frivolous way they wrote it up. You might be surprised to discover you are not alone and that others have had similar experiences. Would you like to meet for a chat?
Kindest Regards
JSF

As long as it was in a public place it could do no harm thought Deborah; besides he had two surnames which made him at worst an eccentric as opposed to a dangerous crank. She was instantly ashamed of the snobbery that her mother had ingrained somewhere on her hard-drive and as she began typing her reply she found she was looking forward to the meeting. Strange, he had called her Deborah without her permission too, but this time she didn't seem to mind.

He had dark brown eyes; stylish glasses, black curly hair and he wore a football shirt under a beige duffle coat and a striped scarf. He was drinking coffee and reading a book in the cafe where Deborah had suggested they meet. He was around her age, maybe a little younger. Slim and studious, he occasionally looked up from his book to the cafe door in expectation. She hovered outside for a moment, savouring her anonymity before realising it was probably redundant following the Chronicle's picture of her holding a drawing of the alien who had... who had... not now, she wasn't going to think about that now. She entered the cafe and he looked up, clearly recognising her instantly, he gave a shy wave and she approached his table and sat.

'I'm Julian'
'Deborah.' They shook hands.
'Thanks for meeting me'
'Not at all, thanks for getting in touch.'
'So... you've met the Reticulans then?'
'The who?'
'The aliens, they're from a planet orbiting a star called Zeta Reticuli. It's umm.. forty light years away.'
'How do you know?' It was the obvious question but Julian seemed totally unprepared for it.
'Well, it's common... that is... look, do you want a coffee or something?'
Coming here had been a mistake. Deborah had often visited the café with her father; he had always had tea and a toasted currant bun while she had a strawberry milkshake. She thought the memory would have been a warm one but it had surprisingly hard edges and was evocative of a lost innocence.
'... they're called "Greys" and several different abductees have told the same story. I really envy you Deborah, I've never had an encounter myself.'

Deborah studied him in wonder, 'So you're saying you'd like to be paralysed in some way and then intimately and intrusively examined by a creature that probably regards you as some sort of earthworm and then dumped bollock naked in the middle of town at five o clock in the morning?'

A couple of people sitting nearby turned in Deborah's direction but quickly looked away; nobody who wore a hat like that would have the restraint necessary to settle a dispute in a civilised manner. Julian looked abashed.

'It's unusual to recall so much of the encounter at first.'

'Believe me, I wish I didn't recall any of it!'

She looked around her, the cafe had filled considerably, people were eating and drinking, oblivious to the world-changing story in their midst. Julian seemed unsure of how to continue so she prompted him, 'So.. how come all of this isn't common knowledge?'

'Well,' Julian took off his glasses and polished them with the end of his scarf, 'in a way, it is. There are a few people I know of who have encountered the Reticulans, but many, many times more go to church every Sunday and they will tell you with absolute unshakeable conviction that their God is a real and tangible entity who created the Universe and who can utterly change your life - but the non religious simply don't believe it.'

Yes, but the Reticulans - sorry, I can't say that word without thinking of bloody pythons - the Aliens... are real.

'OK, now try and convince anyone in this cafe of that. You have no photographic evidence - nor has anyone else, our visitors apparently have ways of ensuring that never happens. In short, there is no physical proof at all.'

Deborah shook her head 'Why should they care? Why would it matter to them whether their existence was common knowledge on Earth or not? Why don't they just appear in the skies above the world's biggest cities for all to see and be done with it?'

Julian shrugged, 'Don't know, probably for the same reason God doesn't appear surrounded by a host of angels and proclaim his all-powerfulness; maybe it just doesn't matter to them. From their point of view, they're not visiting friends or equals, they're stocktaking.'

Deborah shuddered and saw off her gin and tonic in a gulp. 'I'll give the bastards stock the next time we meet!'

Julian was both surprised and impressed by her vehemence. A middle-aged man leaned across from the table opposite where he and his partner sat,

'I say, do you mind?'

Deborah pulled off her hat, 'See this?'

She pointed superfluously to her half-bald head. The man frowned and pulled back out of arm's reach.

'Now see that bacon sandwich you're eating? Think you're top of the food chain do you? You're probably on the menu yourself, Buster!'

Deborah lay on her bed in the dark. She had always drawn comfort from her bedroom ceiling with its familiar star patterns and during her nocturnal walks she often paused and looked up at the countless pin-pricks of light, imagining as she did the myriad civilisations that in all probability were out there; always assuming they would be benevolent - for no reason other than the illogical assumption that intelligence and benevolence go hand in hand. But now she saw only a dark, endless forest full of the glittering eyes of wolves.

It was a terrifying thought, what if the default position of intelligent life was dog-eat-dog? What if the whole meaning of creation - everywhere - was a blind and merciless game of 'King of the Castle?' She drew comfort from the fact that if she found such a concept abhorrent then so would many others, whatever their shape and home planet.

She hadn't intended to invite Julian back to her place but on leaving the café he had looked.. well, frankly, lost. He had clearly always dreamed of meeting an alien and here he was just one handshake away.

She had invited him to take a look at her bedroom ceiling and he had responded with a quizzical expression. She had been pleasantly surprised not to see the usual split-second of salaciousness flare and die in his eyes before the unconvincing facade of innocence came down. In fact, when they got into bed he had still seemed unsure of precisely what was on the menu.

He had lain on his back looking at the constellations and Deborah had lain on her side looking at him. She was beginning to think he was either a virgin or perhaps gay but too polite to have said so.

'What do you think?' She had asked ambiguously.

'I can see the square of Pegasus; I'm looking for the Andromeda Galaxy.'

She had lost patience and grabbed his balls.

When he came he made a noise like a dove, which made it impossible for Deborah to pigeonhole him, and now he was asleep.

Julian Skelton Fry had been interested in the search for extra-terrestrial intelligence since his tenth birthday when his father, a physics lecturer, had taken him to an observatory where he had been allowed to look through the big telescope at the Milky Way. Seeing the patch of naked eye luminescence resolved into millions of suns had, to his young mind, converted the possibility of life elsewhere into a virtual certainty.

Ignoring the sceptics and his peers he had, for the most part, shunned traditional adolescent pursuits in favour of furthering his knowledge of the cosmos. His sexual experiences had been sporadic and unmemorable. It wasn't that he was unschooled in such matters, he knew the theory in disconcerting detail but the practical left him lukewarm; the jousts of Venus being nothing compared to the rings of Saturn.

'Come on, it's not far now!' Deborah held out a hand to pull Julian up the hill. He was gasping for breath and, not for the first time, Deborah wondered at the fitness of the average person in the street. It seemed that the majority of the human race, at least in Newvale, were complete strangers to exercise. Deborah was not in the least breathless; she had trod this path up Cedar Hill on countless occasions and was going to show Julian the site of her encounter.

'Here we are,' she waved a hand around her at the isolated clearing in the wood. Julian didn't respond for several seconds while he waited for his heart - which was currently giving the wings of a hummingbird a run for their money - and his breathing to return to somewhere near normal.

'It's…. It's a nice… spot,' he eventually managed.

'Yes, they probably picked it out of a brochure,' Deborah replied. 'I dare say there was an advert in, 'What Species?' magazine along the lines of, 'Why go half way across the galaxy to find your abductees when there's delightful little spots like this just a forty light year hop away!'

He smiled, he had a nice smile, she thought. He was probably full of questions but the one he chose to lead with took her completely by surprise.'

'Will you be my girlfriend?'

Naturally, with his background, name and education, Deborah's mother found him 'Splendid' especially as he told her he could see similarities in her face and the known portraits of Anne Boleyn. The reciprocal visit to Julian's home had also gone surprisingly well considering Deborah's still unorthodox hairstyle. The Skelton-Frys were an irreverent lot and encouraged free thought and expression in a way Deborah's father would have delighted in. They had taken the tale of her encounter at face value and Julian's father had even gone so far as to attempt a scientific explanation for the single-hemispherical hair loss and the watering eyes.

Everything had changed and even though most of the time the new knowledge ticked away like a metronomic backing track behind the symphony of her everyday thoughts, occasionally she would become aware of it and the starkness of the message would threaten to overwhelm her, 'I have seen creatures from another world!' It was a truth that she could only share with Julian - she could only ever share with Julian, unless she should ever meet a fellow encounteree, but then she would never know whether they were making it up - and they would never know whether she was.

Zeta Boleyn Waghorn-Skelton-Fry was born during a thunderstorm. The nurse passed the small bundle to Deborah, and Julian smiled his biggest ever smile. Back in her bed the rain lashed against the window of the maternity ward. She looked at her tiny daughter and silently promised her that in the years ahead, when she came running breathlessly in with some news that none of her friends took seriously, Mummy would always believe her.

When darkness fell Deborah took Zeta from the bedside cot and lay with her cradled in her arms. The storm had cleared and mother and daughter looked back through time at the glittering lights in the endless night sky and wondered just how many varieties of bloom there were in the great galactic bouquet....

*   *   *   *   *   *

CHAPTER SEVEN

BLOODY KARAOKE

THE 4th Newvale Scouts and Guides boast - if that is the appropriate word - one of the highest rates of bronchitis of any youth organisation in the county. At jamborees, their participation in the singing of 'I'm Riding Along on the Crest of a Wave' usually produces a tsunami of phlegm that, in times past, could have only been accumulated after several years of toiling in the bowels of the earth. This condition is due in no small measure to the state of Meadowvale Community Hall where they hold their meetings.

Meadowvale is the oldest part of Newvale and the Community Hall is one of the oldest buildings there. It is damp, and heating the place up to almost infernal levels only seems to encourage the proliferation of mould spores.

As Godfrey Prendergast opened the door and switched on the lights the dank cold attacked his lungs like a zealous watchdog. He coughed as he wandered around the small hall switching on electric heaters while above him fluorescent tubes pinged reluctantly into life. The rain and wind lashed and howled against tired, ill-fitting windows. He was sixty-one and on nights like this he felt it. But, as chairman of Newvale and District Poetry Society he had responsibilities. He switched on the kettle and sat at the head of a pair of long plastic topped tables. Shaking the excess water off his satchel he opened it and took out a file.

Within fifteen minutes, and against all of Godfrey's expectations, the entire compliment of Newvale Poets had made their way into the hall in various stages of saturation and joined him at the table. Six in all now sat, sipping tea, coffee, beef extract and, in one case, a can of the sort of cider that makes men with bloodshot eyes shout 'Ayafuka' on bus stops and subsequently wonder why the bus they hailed didn't even slow down.

'Right, may as well declare the meeting open then.' Godfrey tapped the table with his pen and the other five shuffled their files and notepads accordingly. 'Matters arising - following last Thursday's Performance Night in Meadowvale Social Club there were a couple of queries; Virginia, your poem about prolapsed wombs made Mrs Geeson cry so please could you not do it again?'

Virginia Wells was a journalist and made damn sure that everyone she met knew it. She was chief reporter on the Newvale Chronicle, forty-two years old, a full-time divorcee and part time poet.

'You've got to tell it like it is Godfrey, if you had a womb, you'd understand.'

'Yes, well apparently Mrs Geeson hasn't got a womb and she understands only too well.' Godfrey prepared to move on.

'Stifling art that is.' Nudger Jones attempted to focus on the label of the can in his hand as if expecting it to tell him why it was now empty. Nudger was unemployed, probably unemployable and in his early twenties. In his more lucid moments he fancied himself as a performance poet, unaware of its designation at the last refuge of the unmusical. He could no more recite sitting down than a cowboy could walk into town. Godfrey tried to head him off at the pass..

'Yes, well…'

'My mother didn't have a womb, she had it out after I was born.'

Stable doors and bolting horse flashed across Godfrey's mind as Nudger continued

'I remember, I was eight at the time, she had a… a history-tum and we had fish and chips for a week because she couldn't stand up to peel potatoes.'

'Why didn't someone peel them for her?' the question was from Mary Benitals who, according to her mother, had been born with her eyes too near to her bladder. Fifty-nine year old Mary was a sentimental soul and measured the quality of a verse by the cubic millilitres of tears it invoked.

'I couldn't peel 'em because I wasn't allowed to handle knives.'

'Well that was very responsible of your mother,' Mary smiled.

'Wasn't her idea, it was part of my probation conditions,' Nudger produced another can of cider from his rucksack.

'Saw a camel tread on a landmine once, all that was left was its womb.' George sipped his tea and shook his head. Three months away from being an octogenarian, George was a retired Army Captain and administrator. He had been a 'Newvale Poet' since his partner, Christian, had passed over three years ago and had reached the pinnacle of poetic success the previous spring when his verse, 'Aldershot Camp' had gained a distinction in the Three Counties Poetry Slam and earned him a lifetime ban from Newvale Ex Servicemens' Club.

'How did you know it was a womb?' Charles Barr, thirty-seven year old bank manager and songwriter was curious. Charles was running to fat from a sedentary existence but still dreamed of the hobo life of railroad cars and the great outdoors - but only in summer and as long as there was a restaurant nearby.

'Well... the M.O. was with us and he said it looked like a womb, hard to tell really I suppose, not the sort of thing you see more than once or twice in a lifetime, a camel's womb...'

'How about someone actually reading some poetry tonight?' Godfrey attempted to get proceedings back on course.

'Well I've written two, one's a haiku and the other was inspired by a trip to the butchers.' Virginia stood, naturally assuming precedence here as she did in the office. She cleared her throat.

'The butchers?' Mary enquired.

'Yes, the butchers, it's called 'Pig's Brain.''

'OK, the floor's yours,' Godfrey stated superfluously, as far as Virginia was concerned, the floor was always hers.

'Right then...

"What did you think pig?

Think pig

Think pig

Where did you go pig?

Go pig
Go pig
Were you a pink pig?
Pink pig
Pink pig
What did you know pig?
Know pig
Know pig
I saw…"

'Hang on - you're supposed to tell us what it's about first!' Nudger, his survival instincts dulled by alcohol, was the only one foolhardy enough to interrupt Virginia in full flow.

Virginia huffed noisily, 'Well it's obvious isn't it? It's about a pig's brain that I saw in the butcher's window and I'm speculating on what that brain experienced when it was alive.'

A semi-stifled sob escaped from around the edge of Mary's handkerchief, 'What did you think pig? - that's so moving.'

'Godfrey shook his head, once Mary's floodgates opened there was little that could close them again apart from gin - and that made her sing!

'When… when I die…' Mary sobbed…

Oh God, here we go thought Godfrey.

'When I die,' Mary continued, struggling for composure, 'I'd like Charles to sing that song he sang the other week.'

Charles immediately hoisted his guitar, 'You mean..
Here's Fat Billy, comin' round the mountain,
A huffin' and a puffin' and …

'No' interrupted Mary, 'Not that one.'

Charles pondered briefly, 'Ah, you mean…'
In a cold and lonely boxcar,
A dying hobo lay…'

'No Charles, I'm not a hobo, I mean the one about the old engine heading for the heavenly railroad.'

'Ah, got you, you mean *Puffing Through the Pearly Gates';* I did that one at Frank Bright's funeral.

'Yes', offered Godfrey, 'And considering he died of a smoking related disease it might not have been the most tactful choice.'

'Can I read mine now?' Nudger stood. Virginia glared at him, he swayed a little and she decided not to use words like manners or chivalry, they would only confuse him. She sat, shaking her head and affecting boredom as she leafed through her folder.

Godfrey stilled Nudger with a raised hand, 'Let's have a mission statement first, shall we? We have one public outlet for our work. Every Thursday evening for years this Society has performed at the Social Club, bringing creativity and live entertainment to the masses, so let's remember that in our writing and presentation.

'Masses - huh!' Nudger sneered, 'One person was there at the end the week before last - and why did he stay?'

'Actually, there were four,' Virginia corrected him.

'Only if you count the ambulance men and the doctor - nobody stays, I can't understand why we bother.' Nudger's mood threatened to become contagious. Godfrey intervened, 'Because we're lights in a dark world, it says so on our letterhead, now, let's hear this literary offering you've got for us.'

Nudger left the table and began pacing up and down the hall.

'Do you have to do this every time you read?' Charles asked.

'I'm psyching myself up,' Nudger paced and growled before suddenly turning to face his audience, stabbing a finger at them and clutching his sheaf of papers until they crumpled in his hand. His rage bounced off the damp and tired walls...

If they can give cigarettes to a beagle,
Then I don't think cannabis should be illegal!
It's a waste of police time and I don't see the point,
In arresting young men just for smoking a joint,

In Holland they let you....

'Hang on, hang on,' Godfrey brought Nudger to a stuttering halt; it's the same as last week's isn't it?'

Nudger shook his head, his blonde dreadlocks spraying rainwater over the table. 'No it isn't.'

'I think he means old chap,' George offered, 'That the words are different but the rhythm is the same.'

Godfrey nodded as Nudger leafed through his damp and crumpled notes.

'Here are last weeks!' Nudger shuddered and growled himself up to reading pressure before exploding.

Why should I be hounded beyond all endurance?
For driving a car with no tax and insurance,
They tested the brakes, they tested the lights,
The exhaust was too noisy for that time of night,
They can't catch...'

'Yes, yes, we heard it last week - and on Thursday in the social club.' Godfrey once again pulled up Nudger in mid-rant. It's the same thing every week with just the words changing. Why don't you diversify a bit? Rap is a youthful medium so I'm told.'

'Can I do my song now?' Charles was clearly champing at the bit and Godfrey seized the opportunity to nudge Nudger from centre stage.

'It'll only be about fucking trains man,' Nudger mumbled as he sat, taking from one of his countless pockets a battered tin with a marijuana leaf on the lid.

'Well? Is it about trains?' Godfrey enquired of the tuning up bank manager.

'Not just any train,' Charles responded excitedly, 'It's about a 525 Swindon class bullied steam loco that ran for Great Western Railways from 1925 to....'

''Yes, yes, just get on with it,' Godfrey hurried him along, 'The Allotment Society have got this hall from eight, although Christ alive knows what they're going to talk about; growing bloody rice if this weather keeps up.'

'I saw Captain Barker-Mead shoot a monkey in a paddy field once,' George reminisced, 'Right off a boy's shoulder, must have been all of three hundred yards, bloody good shot fair play to him.'

'That's terrible,' Mary wiped her nose on yet another tissue, 'Didn't he like children?'

'Oh, he liked 'em alright, boys in particular, made no secret of it; of course, he was well connected so the buggers closed ranks so to speak.'

'Yes, well, in your own time Charles,' Godfrey pulled again on the reins of the meeting to keep in on course. Charles began a chewing motion and he slouched in his chair.

'OK, I want y'all to take a ride with me now on the Iron Bull, this is called 'Iron Bull Blues.''

Why Charles had to pretend to chew tobacco when he affected a cowboy accent nobody knew. He vamped a few chords.

'Ohhh, I can recall when I was a boy,
My one an' only pride and joy
Was standing by the railroad,
Waitin' fer the Iron Bull..

'If it's about a Swindon Class train,' interrupted Virginia, 'surely you should sing it in a Wiltshire accent instead of a cod American one?'

Charles huffed loudly at the interruption, 'Train songs demand a western accent, it's a simple as that; it's a fact of music.' He took a deep breath ready to set off again.

'Ohhhh...'

'Right, that'll do,' announced Godfrey.

Charles deflated with a sound similar to that of a Swindon Class 525 pulling into the station.

'It's a bloody awful night; let's go home and dry out. Don't be late Thursday everyone.' Godfrey stood and collected his papers together. Coats, still damp from the rush between the car park and the hall, were put back on. Godfrey, last to leave, shut off the heaters and the lights -

just in case the Allotment Society decided not to bother - and closed the door behind him. The dark hall echoed to the wind and the rain and the rattle of cooling heaters.

Meadowvale Social Club was neither social nor a club, and it was only just in Meadowvale, lying as it did on the very edge of the woods that separated the suburb from Cold Ridge Estate. Accepting the fact that no one would ever actually apply to become a member, the Committee had long abandoned all pretence at exclusivity and just let anyone in. The President had been President for twenty-one years because nobody else wanted the job, he didn't want it himself but all attempts to resign had been rebuffed by a committee who needed a figurehead to hide behind while they fiddled the books.

It was a friendly place, but only to its friends. Strangers were generally met with a tangible drop in the noise of conversation and became a centre of interest in a way that the 'acts' booked there could only dream of. It would, however, be wrong to think of the patrons of the Club as anti-social, they loved to socialise, but they had never graduated from the beginners' class and so regarded line dancing as a worthwhile expenditure of calories.

The committee had allowed the Poetry Society to perform there as it qualified the Club for an 'Art in the Community' grant, which they had so far used to buy a karaoke machine, some sweatshirts with the club logo on them and a box of dildoes which the entertainment secretary had spotted on an internet auction site and had snapped up in the hope of using them as raffle prizes. When it had subsequently been explained to him just how 'personal' a 'personal massager' could get he decided to offload them on his market stall and was currently bailed awaiting a court appearance after selling them to two nine-year-olds who took them home assuming they were toy space weapons.

Godfrey had long since ceased to experience any disappointment on driving into a virtually empty car park at the Club on Thursday evenings. They let the poets perform on the one night of the week when, apparently, no one wanted to go out, so they were accustomed to taking the stage in the concert room while maybe three or four club regulars played dominoes in a dimly lit far corner and one or two others wandered in and out to shout disparaging remarks or simply jeer.

Behind the main stage was a cheerless 'dressing room' for visiting artistes. It contained a wall mirror going brown around the edges, a few broken chairs, one 'easy chair' that looked as if a dog had been sick on it and a small plastic table. Piled along the wall were boxes of beer mats, broken pool cues and various other items of detritus necessary for the running of the club.

Inside, Virginia, Mary, Nudger, Charles and George prepared for their weekly performance. The room was illuminated, if one could call it that, by a single forty-watt bulb covered in dead flies. As if it wasn't gloomy enough, Nudger was wearing sunglasses. He was also wearing a hood and sneering and mumbled to himself; so far no one had plucked up the courage to asked him why.

Charles tuned his guitar, pausing to adjust the angle of his Stetson while Mary sat herself next to Virginia who was scribbling intently.

'I'm going to bring your pig back to life!' Mary announced, fishing into an oversized carrier bag. Virginia raised a painstakingly topiaried eyebrow but, in the finest tradition of journalism, remained silent, giving the speaker the opportunity to talk themselves into an abyss. Mary, mistaking the silence for tacit approval, produced a large pink blob of papier-mache from the carrier bag and only after some significant mental gymnastics from Virginia was she able to make out it was supposed to be a model of a pig's head - and it was hollow. Surely the stupid woman wasn't thinking of wearing it or something? Mary confirmed Virginia's concerns by placing the hideous creation over her own head.

'When you recite "Pig's Brain" I'm going to mime the actions of that poor creature in a celebration of its life.'

Mary, misinterpreting Virginia's look of horror for one of impressed admiration, begin miming what she imagined to be the actions of a 'thinking pig'. Virginia's mind raced as she mentally re-filed Mary, taking her from the drawer marked 'Harmless eccentric' and placing her in 'Unpredictable nutcase.' When she spoke she strived to strike a balance between pacification and firmness.

'No Mary, that wouldn't work, not a good idea at all.'

'But...'

'No - really Mary, thanks, but no thanks.'

'But I worked for three evenings on...

Virginia had already had a difficult day and her patience, never in abundance, was wearing thin.

'Mary, it's hideous. It's the sort of thing you would see if you looked at a pig after taking LSD and I don't want you tripping about like a bloody idiot while I'm performing - OK?'

Virginia was unable to make out any facial reaction behind the monstrous mask but a rhythmic shaking of the shoulders and a barely audible whimpering confirmed that Mary had reset in default mode.

When Godfrey entered the dressing room Mary was crying, Virginia was studying herself in the mirror, Charles was chewing imaginary gum and drawling to himself, George was gazing into space and Nudger was making ludicrous hand gestures and speaking gibberish, Godfrey shook his head, all this was about to end.

'Can I have your attention?'

He got it.

'Thank you; I've just been speaking to the Chairman and he's informed me that, as of next week, Thursday night here will be karaoke night.'

Responding to Charles's statement that he 'didn't do karaoke' Godfrey made it even clearer.

'We, Charles, will not be required. From next week there will be no room in the Club's busy schedule for our merry little band. Monday nights will be bingo, Tuesday, old tyme dancing, Wednesday will be big screen sports, Thursday will be bloody karaoke, Friday bingo, Saturday dancing and fighting and Sunday... wait for it... bingo again.

'Can't we have one of the bingo nights?' asked George.

'Are you kidding? I've heard of eighty-year-olds forcing walking frames through snowdrifts to get here.' Nudger enlightened him.

'So what are we going to do?' Charles, who had taken eight courses in leadership and man management, looked genuinely lost.

'We go out with a bang, that's what we do,' Godfrey punched a palm and began pacing the small room, Nudger fell into step behind him, 'Show the Philistines what they're missing. I want you all to perform as you've never performed before.'

'Yo!' added Nudger, 'Let's get out there and waste their arseholes.'

'Well, quite so,' offered Godfrey, 'and why the glasses and hood Nudger, don't you want to be recognised for some reason?'

'You said to do some rap and so tonight - I'm Bad Nudger J!'

Godfrey just shook his head. 'Right, get ready George, I'm putting you on first!'

Pausing only to straighten his tie Godfrey marched purposefully out on to the stage.

'Good Evening Ladies and Gentlemen and welcome to Meadowvale Social Club's weekly cultural event. We are the Newvale Poets - Lights in a Dark World,...'

His voice echoed across empty tables, 'So without further ado, please put your hands together for a veteran wordsmith, Captain George Webster!'

In silence Godfrey left the stage, passing George on his way to the microphone. George studied his 'public.' The audience consisted of three men at the back of the room engrossed in a game of cards, an elderly couple who appeared to be asleep and the club's steward who was taking advantage of a quiet spell to do his books.

Small Town People

George cleared his throat, 'Err, jolly good, I'd like to read for you a verse I wrote as a young officer when I was in Malaya, it's called, 'A Sudden Thought of Home.'

Who would have dreamed,
In that steaming green world
That a shock of rude pink would pierce my shallow heart?
Glittering in the prism-split light
of transient raindrops,
The young lieutenant capered like a faun in a time of magic,
His joyous buttocks reminiscent of an autumn dawn
Sin-red and siren like
They called to me
Like a sudden thought of home..'

'Yes!' the call erupted from one of the card players and for a brief moment George thought his words had touched another soul but as the others laughed and applauded it became apparent that the shouter had simply won a hand.

'I thank you...' George walked off as Godfrey once again appeared

'Thank you George, and now please welcome your very own, Mary Benitals.'

With a pained look at Godfrey as they passed Mary approached the microphone.

'I would like to perform a poem entitled, Sound.'

All the sounds of my spring have gone,
And summer's sounds too are fading into a golden past,
Only the sounds of my autumn remain,
Soon it will be as silent as winter,
And the only sound left will be
The sound of the wind.'

One of the card players chose that moment to unleash a kraken of a fart conjured from some malevolent gastro-intestinal deep where it had boiled and brooded in its wait for maturity. And now, free at last, it rattled its terrible war cry between arse and plastic chair leaving its perpetrator flushed with both effort and pride and convulsing his companions with laughter. With a huge shuddering sob Mary rushed off the stage and a furious Godfrey took her place.

'Thank you, thank you very much; yes indeed, a valuable contribution to an evening of culture, you must be very proud!'

The card-playing trio rose to leave, still laughing and wafting the air around them. The farter grinned towards Godfrey and raised a single-finger salute.

'Come on Chunk,' his friend called to him and they headed for the door. As they left, 'Chunk' pushed his arse back through the door and released a genuinely impressive series of rapid-fire farts that, unbeknown to him, spelt out 'Fish' in Morse code. The elderly couple, roused from their slumber by the methane melody, applauded politely as Godfrey left the stage.

'It's Be-knight-alls, how many times Godfrey... it's pronounced Be-knight-alls!' Mary, still tearful from her appearance was seeking a scapegoat for her misery as she sat in the corner of the dressing room clutching the soggy remains of her last tissue.

'Well it's spelt Benitals, I just say it as I see it.' Godfrey shrugged, no longer concerned with the excruciatingly thin glass that constituted Mary's emotional skin.'

Mary shuddered, 'Benitals - it makes me sound like... well, you know.'

Gordon studied Nudger, Virginia and Charles; 'There's actually nobody out there at all now so I don't see the point in any of you going on - unless you really want to?'

'Well I've got a Chamber of Trade dinner to attend with Monty Fox so I'm off!' Virginia picked up her folder and left without a backward glance.

Nudger produced a piece of paper; 'I got this off the notice board if anybody's interested.' Charles took it and read aloud, 'As part of the Newvale 200 celebrations entries are invited for a competition depicting Newvale's past and present in the written word... blah blah blah.'

'That's it!' Godfrey became animated, 'This will be our new challenge - we'll produce a book of work to commemorate two hundred years of Newvale and, in a hundred years they'll look back on this as the golden age of literature - young poets will wonder what it was like to have been there - Lights in a Dark World, what do you all think?'

Charles shrugged; Mary seemed enraptured by the prospect of literary immortality, George nodded and made a little note in his leather-covered book and Nudger... was not there.

Alone on the stage, looking out into the dark and empty room, Bad Nudger J dreamed his own dreams, his mind populating the tables in front of him with admiring fans nodding and whooping their approval at his insight and sagacity. His fervour and imagination filled in the scene ever more elaborately as brightly coloured dreams, amplified by cannabinoids and white cider, showed him what could be.

'Yo,
I didn't come hear to waste no yap,
I'm bad Nudger J an' I'm here to rap,
I come from where the streets are mean,
Been hustlin' since I was just thirteen,
Cop sees me he crosses the street,
Because he knows I'm packin' heat,
Come on my patch you gonna get hit.
I'll sneer at you an' I'll swear an' spit
Nobody messes with Bad Nudger J
I said Nobody messes with Bad Nudger J.'

Godfrey was calling to him from the dressing room door, but he couldn't hear for the cheers.

*   *   *   *   *   *

CHAPTER EIGHT

'...IF YOU GO DOWN TO THE WOODS TODAY...'

A PAIR of eights, a pair of sixes and a king! Chunk was pretty sure he was holding a better hand than either Wes or Izzy. He knew that one of Izzy's cards was the nine of spades because it had a corner missing and he also knew Wes had a rubbish hand because he was sticking his bottom lip out and scowling.

The trio met, drank and played a few hands of cards every Thursday in the lounge of the Red Lion but this week, with the Red Lion closed for a refit, they found themselves in the unfamiliar and not particularly hospitable concert room of Meadowvale Social Club. They were the only ones in the large room apart from an elderly couple who were listening to some people on stage reading lines from a play or doing poetry or something.

Izzy triumphantly spread his hand out on the table, a pair of sevens and a pair of threes with a queen. Wes folded.

'Yes!' Chunk shouted, he showed his hand and picked up the few coins in the middle of the table. The other two laughed at his exaggerated delight at winning a pretty meagre pot.

Benny 'Chunk' Scanlon was thirty-one and married with three young children. He had red unruly hair, pale piggy eyes and a markedly porcine attitude to food inasmuch as what was not toxic was probably edible. Larger than average, his somewhat forbidding appearance was offset by an almost ever present smile. He had a jovial wife who shared his passion for eating and an air of gregariousness that meant he had never been short of friends. He worked as a conservatory installer and his hobbies included holding barbecues and writing books for young children. He had achieved considerable success with the first of these pastimes but still awaited recognition for his literary endeavours, his only audience to date being Harry, Bridget and Dawn, aged eight, six and four respectively.

In his courageous attempt to take the magical world of faerie and elf and place it in a setting that contemporary youngsters would recognise he had brought into being Gabby the Goblin who got up to all sorts of adventures - frequently involving double glazing or al fresco eating. In his latest adventure, Gabby had become trapped in a conservatory and was fast approaching the end of the 'hour of invisibility' that he was allowed each day. If the householders discovered him he would, in all probability, turn into a newt. Chunk hadn't decided how to end the tale yet, he was mindful of the domestic furore his last book had caused after the children, disturbed by the graphic image his words painted in their impressionable minds, had woken up crying at three in the morning because Gabby the Goblin had inflated a greyhound with a foot pump to such a degree that it spent the rest of its life farting.

Chunk's great, great, great, great, great grandfather had reputedly been thrown overboard by Captain Bligh himself for incessant farting and in full keeping with family tradition, farting to Chunk was as natural as breathing - and almost as frequent. As he studied his new hand of cards he felt the foreshocks of an imminent detonation. Having been taught at his grandfather's knee that discreet flatulence implied dissatisfaction with the design of the digestive system and was therefore an insult to God he had spent his life mastering the release of his gaseous emissions for maximum impact with all the zeal of a dedicated virtuoso. Like a seasoned bombardier he waited for the optimum moment to fire and when he pulled the trigger the effect was devastating.

The furious genie, having been released from the bottle, roared with anger at being trapped between Chunk and a plastic chair and rattled violently until true freedom was achieved. Even by Chunk's standards the sheer volume was impressive and his friends convulsed with laughter. Chunk, red faced, stood and took a small bow.

On the stage, a woman burst into tears and strode off, clearly rehearsing a moving scene from some drama, and a man strode on to replace her.

'Thank you, thank you very much; yes indeed, a valuable contribution to an evening of culture, you must be very proud,' the man was angry and clearly didn't share Chunk and his friends' appreciation of creative flatulence. The three rose, they were leaving anyway. Laughing and wafting the air around them they headed for the door. Chunk offered a gesture of derision to the man on the stage and, as he departed he produced a staccato of rapid-fire fartlets as a farewell.

'Miserable bloody place, that.' Wes took out his woolly hat and put it on.

'Red Lion will be open again by next week,' Chunk offered.

'Good job too,' Izzy voiced his opinion, 'we won't have to walk through these creepy bloody woods to get a drink.' Iskender Aziz had never visited the Turkey of his ancestors. A promising young footballer, he had played for Newvale Youth until training nights began to clash with his pursuit of girls. He had long since given up on dreams of football stardom and worked as a lifeguard at Newvale Leisure and Activity Centre. Although only in his early thirties he was already suffering from premature baldness and premature ejaculation and once, while the worse for drink, he had covered his scalp with 'Maximus Big Man Delay Cream' before compounding the problem by applying 'Crowning Glory' hair restorer to his penis. Ironically, both preparations seemed to work far better in their new jobs than their old ones. Izzy and his partner enjoyed the best sex they had had for months and he was sure a layer of down was covering his erstwhile bald cranium. Nevertheless, he surreptitiously examined his penis carefully over the following weeks for any evidence that it was turning into something resembling a sentient meercat.

'Aww scared of the dark are we sunshine?' Wes mocked.

''And with good cause,' Chunk shuddered and turned up the collar of his coat, 'these woods are haunted you know.'

Wes laughed but Izzy looked around nervously as they approached the path that entered Meadowvale Woods and offered a short cut to Cold Ridge Estate.

'We could always walk around, or wait for the bus,' suggested Izzy hopefully.

'Nah, it'll rain again before long and the bus isn't due for almost an hour, if we put our best feet forward we'll be out the other side in half an hour,' Wes pulled his hat down over his ears and headed into the darkness and the trees, Chunk and Izzy followed.

Wesley Knutford was thirty and had already served six years in the army and eight months in jail, the latter for causing grievous bodily harm, 'Even though,' as he was still keen to point out, 'I never bloody touched him!' He had come home unexpectedly on leave and found a man in bed with his wife. He had lobbed a hand grenade onto the bed and the man had jumped naked out of the bedroom window, landing on his own car causing significant lacerations, bruising and a ruined sunroof. The fact that the hand grenade had been a dummy was held by the judge to be only a minor mitigation and he had sentenced Wes to a year's imprisonment. Wes had finished his education in jail and was now a self-employed locksmith.

'A woman jumped off the bridge into the brook and people have said they've seen her sitting on the edge of the bridge staring down into the waters...' Chunk peered ahead into the gloom where the path was barely visible through the trees.

'Well that's alright, we're not going near the bridge... are we?' Izzy hated the woods even in the daylight. As a boy he had been chased through the trees by an angry dog and had escaped a good chewing by scaling a convenient elm and sitting on a branch planning on waiting for the creature to become bored. The dog, however, seemingly had nothing else to do that day and had sat down to wait at the base of the tree panting and looking up in the hope that the young Izzy would surrender to his fate. Izzy had not found the prospect appealing and had hit on the idea of urinating over the dog to drive it away. The animal clearly saw this as provocative and a mark of the deepest disrespect and became so furious that it actually managed to get halfway up the tree towards Izzy before falling back down in a snapping snarling heap. Izzy had then decided to try and placate the creature by offering it an item of clothing to chew on. He took off his tee shirt and dropped it, the dog saw this shedding of skin as an opportunity to save face and he immediately pissed on the garment and trotted off with honour intact.

Howard Raft liked trees. He liked them better than he liked people; which is probably why he had never married - or spoken to his neighbours. He had scrapbooks and scrapbooks full of pictures of trees, pressed leaves, articles about trees and self-penned poems extolling the virtues of just about every species of arboreal life he had heard of.

Howard had lived the whole of his forty years in Cold Ridge with his mother in a small bungalow that was in serious need of modernisation. It still had a coal fire and a deep slow ticking grandfather clock that marked the passing of a time that the furniture and décor refused to acknowledge. When his mother died he had, very briefly, toyed with the idea of decorating and upgrading the property but had dismissed the plan when he realised that, in the absence of any of the requisite skills, he would have to engage trades people and the thought of strangers under his roof was just too much to bear. And so, for 'Oaklea', 12, Evergreen Lane, Cold Ridge, Newvale, each new day dawned a perfect clone of its predecessor and only the subtle deterioration of the surroundings hinted that, outside the walls, pages were falling off the calendar and the world was spinning into the future.

When it came to his personal appearance, Howard paid no more than lip service to changing trends and whether it was nature or nurture that had influenced his evolutionary path, he had become markedly tree-like. He was tall, very tall, and correspondingly thin, and swayed gracefully as he walked. If you met his gaze he looked at you through eyes that appeared to measure time in quite a different way to everyone else. He tended to dress in a long flowing overcoat and a wide-brimmed hat that had belonged to his father. His long strides carried him at quite a pace and a permanent air of deep preoccupation forbade any form of greeting from those he passed.

While Howard was content to let his home stagnate he was not about to let Meadowvale Woods do likewise. The deep ravine that ran through the woods with Meadowvale Brook at its bottom had always ensured predatory builders and property developers would need to look elsewhere for profit but that didn't mean the woods were immune from the influence of their human neighbours. Newvale surrounded them on three sides. To the north was Cold Ridge and Coldridge Trading Estate, to the south, Meadowvale and to the east the centre of Town. Howard had been saddened over the years by the appearance of all manner of human detritus left in what once must have been a pristine environment.

And so he had taken it upon himself to redress the balance. He planted trees; he talked to them and named them. He had thought long and hard about their names, he didn't want to give them human names that would be meaningless to them, instead he had tried to get inside their barks/skins and see the world from their perspective. What would they call themselves?

The great oak in the clearing next to the abandoned and crumbling stone building he had named 'N'Grumm'; it spoke to him of great age and sagacity and epitomised power and patience, a stern and paternal tree, stoic and unyielding. Just off the path where it curved around an outcrop called Smithy Rock was a sycamore called 'Frrssh' which had suffered a great trauma back in the mists of time; a scar showed where a limb had been torn off in some long forgotten storm. Close by was an infant silver birch called 'Twishck' which Howard had grown from seed and planted out just a few weeks ago.

As he looked out of his window he could see the black tops of the trees of Meadowvale Woods against the last of the day's light and a frown crossed his face as he realised a storm was approaching. He should have gone out earlier and tied Twishck to a stake as he had been planning. She was quite frail, there was no thickness to her young trunk and Howard feared for her safety. There was nothing for it, he was going to have to go out and do it now, dark or no dark; storm or no storm; he wouldn't sleep otherwise, listening to the howl of the wind and the lashing of rain against the window and knowing that young Twishck was out there all alone.

'You ever heard of Malvolio?' Chunk could barely make out the faces of his two companions in the darkness of the woods; their brisk pace had slowed considerably with the difficulty of making out the path ahead.

'I've heard the name - who does he play for? Izzy enquired.

'He don't play for nobody you dull bugger,' Wes snorted, 'He was a bloke out of Shakespeare.'

'Not this one,' Chunk elaborated, 'This one was a blacksmith, only he was like.. super-human.'

'Could he fly?' Izzy asked.

Chunk snorted, 'Course he couldn't fucking fly, blacksmiths can't fly…. what would be the point of blacksmiths evolving the power of flight?'

'So they could shoe flying horses?' suggested Wes.

'If a horse can fly he don't need horseshoes does he?' Chunk had found half a chocolate bar in his coat pocked and munched as he walked. 'In fact, if a horse can fly, metal shoes on his feet would be the last things he needs - think of the extra weight.'

'So what super powers did this bloke have then?' Asked Izzy

'Well,' Chunk searched his memory for the stories that had been passed down to him, 'He was super strong for a start - apparently he could hold a horse up in the air with one hand and shoe it with the other.'

Wes shook his head invisibly in the dark, 'Don't matter how strong you are, you'd need more that two hands to do that, think about it, if one hand was holding up the horse he's have a hammer in the other and he'd...'

'Look, I don't know, maybe he knocked the nails in with his dick, the thing I'm coming to is that people say they've seen him in these woods,' Chunk shivered as he remembered the tales of a terrifying figure still stalking the places he knew in life.

'Apparently he was only about five feet tall and he couldn't speak...'

'Not much of a fucking Superman then, was he?' Wes interrupted.

'Ah, but he was five feet wide as well and he had huge arms and hands and... and two rows of teeth - and he could bend horseshoes, and he used to make a noise like this... 'UGGUHHNNH!'

Chunk recalled his grandfather telling the tales that he'd heard from *his* grandfather — whose grandfather in turn had reputedly seen this creature in the flesh.

From somewhere in the darkness came an answer...

'BAAAARRRSTT!'

Howard had tripped over a root in the dark and fallen into a muddy puddle. He had never learned to swear but had compensated by inventing his own vocabulary of expletives that did pretty much the same job. 'Brown fladding splat!' he growled, 'Big fat brown splatting barsting plop!' He had entered the woods from the Cold Ridge side and was about two minutes brisk walking from the trio when he picked up Chunk's impersonation of Malvolio on the wind.

It sounded like... like a big cat or something. Howard had heard tell of feral big cats on the loose. There had been a story in the Chronicle about two years ago in which a schoolboy clamed to have been clawed by what he described as a cat the size of a big dog. Howard realised his cry on falling would have given away his presence and position to any predator.

Rain began to fall and the wind picked up and far above Howard's head the branches of his beloved trees groaned and bent before the strengthening breeze. The growling sound had come from up ahead, at the point where the path began it's curve to run south of Smithy Rock, close to where Twishck was planted.

Howard turned, behind him he could still just make out the streetlights of Wood Lane on the very edge of Cold Ridge, he could go back now and wait... maybe come out here in the morning when it was light and the storm had, perhaps, blown over. But what would happen to Twishck? What if she were blown over in the night? He would never forgive himself. He painted a mental picture of her thin little trunk snapped and her bark stripped and shredded. He shuddered, pulled his hat tighter over his head, and walked on carrying his hammer and wooden stake. If the 'big cat' or whatever it were made another noise he would bellow out his own challenge in return...

'Do it again,' Wes suggested to Chunk, 'Go on, do the noise again and see if the same thing happens.'

'Bugger off, I'm saying nothing until we're out of these bloody woods.'

'UNGGGH!' Wes attempted.

'Shut up you dildo,' hissed Izzy.

The three strained their ears over the sound of the wind but this time there was no reply.

'You didn't do it right anyway,' Chunk offered.

'Well go on then – it's only a bloody noise man.' Wes goaded him

'Oh alright... ready?.... 'UGGUHHNNH!'

From somewhere in the darkness ahead of them came an almost instant and unmistakeably aggressive reply.

'ROAAAAAAGH!'

'Fuck this!' Izzy turned off the path and ran into the trees instantly disappearing from sight.

'Izzy!' Chunk called after him, 'The silly sod, he's heading into the depths of the bloody woods that way.'

Wes picked up a vaguely club-shaped fallen lump of timber and strained to see anything in the deep gloom. The hairs on the back of Chunk's neck bristled and he felt that he was being watched.

'There's something out there and no mistake,' Wes hissed nervously.

A sound resembling a deep and exhausted moan came from the trees ahead.

'Shit!' Wes dropped his lump of wood and turned tail, running back in the direction of Meadowvale.

'It's only the wind you daft bugger!' Chunk called after him but, to be truthful, he wasn't that sure. Chunk's instinct was to run after his friend but Wes could cover the ground a lot faster than Chunk and if there was someone or something out there and it decided on pursuit, he would end up the sacrificial offering.

She was safe, windswept but safe. Howard knelt at her side, his knee sinking into the wet ground. Taking his stake he carefully placed it near to Twishck and began to knock it in. Eventually satisfied that the stake was firmly in place he took out some ties and began attaching the tiny tree to its new support.

Izzy fell for a second time and this time he got up much slower. There were no sounds of pursuit and he appeared to be unhurt from his fall, however, on the minus side he didn't have a clue where he was. He felt in his pocket for his phone and was relieved that it hadn't fallen out along with his coins and key ring the last time he had fallen. With cold, wet fingers he dialled Chunk's number.

Chunk was standing with his back to a large tree keeping as still and quiet as he could. Someone or something was lurking just behind some bushes about ten metres away. Chunk stared at the spot where he could make out a swaying and rustling of the foliage and a low groaning of exertion. Above him the moon broke through the clouds and a baleful yellow light brought into relief his immediate surroundings.

Chunk could now make out a figure stooping over some unspeakable task, drinking the blood of a victim, burying a body or feeding off a fresh kill perhaps? If ever there had been a time for Chunk to maintain a state of absolute silence then this was it. Unfortunately his phone rang and the shock of the sudden noise brought forth a huge fart. He cringed but the stooping creature gave no indication that it had heard anything. Not taking his eyes off the beast he slowly reached his phone from his jacket pocket and answered in a hoarse whisper.

'Yes?.... Oh, hello Izzy'

Now that the initial shock was over Chunk was surprised at just how calm he was feeling under the circumstances. The creature must surely have heard him and yet had made no attempt to attack; indeed, it had not acknowledged his presence in any way.

'Lost? Yeah, I suppose you must be... listen mate, I'll call you back, I'm a bit busy at the moment... Eh? No, no it's not Wes... actually it's...I'm not really sure'; Chunk hung up.

Wes reached the edge of the woods and ran gasping and grateful into the lights of Meadowvale. In the car park of the community centre the Route 112 bus stood ticking over waiting to make its return journey to Cold Ridge via Newvale's Fuller Square. Wheezing with the recent exertion Wes headed for the bus and got on.

Izzy could only dream of being in a position to catch a bus as he stumbled blindly through the ever thickening woods seeking some recognisable landmark. What had Chunk meant? He wasn't with Wes but he was with....? This was stupid, he was a grown man and he had ran from what was probably some idiot playing a trick on them, and now he was... God knows where he was. He stood and peered into the gloom for the hundredth time. A light passed across his field of vision, appearing and disappearing through the trees, but it was unmistakeably the headlights of a vehicle. Breathing a huge sigh of relief Izzy staggered forward toward the source of the light.

'Ahhh Twishck, Twishck,' Howard knelt and trained his torch on the little tree now firmly anchored against the mercurial excesses of Mother Nature. 'I promise to come and loosen the ties as you grow - and in about fifteen years when you are as tall as me we'll have a party to celebrate your coming of height.' Six years ago Howard had held a party to celebrate N'Grumm's five hundredth 'sprouting-day'. Of course, Howard had no way of determining whether the great oak was in fact exactly five hundred years old but he had felt that, having named it, some sort of ceremony was forthcoming and so he had made a ribbon to wrap around the tree with '500 years' written on it. He had also composed a poem for the occasion highlighting some of the events of world history that N'Grumm had lived through and finally he had invited all the other trees of Meadowvale Wood to join in the celebrations by sending out a telepathic message asking them to 'vibrate at a frequency customary for congratulation and respect'.

He had marched into the woods on a balmy summer Sunday morning ready to wrap his ribbon around the tree and recite his poem, but when he reached N'Grumm he discovered a naked man tied to it and a woman in jodhpurs whipping him with a riding crop. He had turned tail and stormed back home, furious with N'Grumm for allowing itself to be part of such a tawdry spectacle. He didn't visit the oak tree for weeks but finally relented after a nearby elm had visited him in a dream and explained that N'Grumm was truly sorry and had been singing a deep and sorrowful song at the loss of his friend.

Chunk listened to the creature talking with bemusement and a little relief. It was human, not a monster, not the ghost of Malvolio or some primeval forest beast. However, being human was a double-edged sword under these circumstances. Anyone likely to be kneeling in the woods on a night like this would have to be a certifiable nutcase. He had two choices, run or overpower the loony and render him harmless - there might even be a reward! With a roar he charged the kneeling figure.

Startled, Howard Raft quickly stood and as he rose to his full height and yelled out in alarm the figure skidded and fell backwards with a shout of pain and a loud fart. It lay on its back as Howard burst through the bushes to lean over it, hammer in hand...

Crawling up a muddy bank and through the last of the bushes Izzy found himself on the road that led to Newvale. He paused, hands on knees and panting. He was at least out of the trees if not out of the woods. The storm was receding and the moonlight showed the road as a grey ribbon twisting away to where the lights of the town made the horizon glow orange. He headed off at a brisk pace, looking around at the hoot of an owl and then ahead again to where the bridge over Meadowvale Brook made a hump in the road. As he crossed over the bridge he could hear the gurgling of the swollen brook far below and a chill of fear ran through him on recalling the stories of the ghost of the grey woman. But he was over and the bridge was crossed.

The feeling that there was someone behind him was palpable but he forced himself not to look around, ahead the lights were growing and he would soon be home, the first signs of civilisation would be Cold Ridge estate and a shower and warm bed - not to mention a stiff drink - would be waiting. The bridge was many many paces behind him now; surely he could afford a quick glance? He turned almost casually and looked behind..

Chunk pulled himself into a sitting position and winced with pain. Howard looked shocked; he stared at the place where Chunk had fallen. Kneeling, he picked up the stake that had been flattened over by Chunk's impact and as he stood he became wrapped in a cloak of towering rage.

'Twishck…. You killed Twishck!' He brandished the stake and the hammer

'I'm not a vampire!' screamed Chunk scurrying backwards.

'What?' Howard was baffled.

'You can't kill me by driving a wooden stake through my heart… well, you can… but you don't have to because I'm not a vampire, I don't drink blood or turn into a fucking bat or…. Hang on, you're that tree bloke who was in the Chronicle!'

It was 'Dentists-Waiting-Room-Syndrome' - anticipation rather than the actual event, which scared Izzy. Now that he was actually looking at a ghost he felt very little fear - in fact he was tempted to retrace his steps back to the bridge to get a closer look at the woman sitting on the ledge gazing down into the black waters far below. Even in the moonlight he could see she was young and, despite the all-encompassing dress, she was very pretty too. On an impulse he called out.

'Hello!'

She ignored the call. Getting up she climbed on to the lip of the bridge and spread her arms wide. Leaning forward she fell gracefully out of sight.

How many times… thought Izzy as he passed the first streetlight of Cold Ridge, how many times has that terrible event been re-enacted? And does it play over and over again even if no one from this side of the veil is there to watch it?

'There - it was only bent - young wood d'you see? Lots of spring in it.'

Chunk finished re-tying Twishck to her newly embedded stake and stood next to Howard who nodded approvingly.

The pair walked off together in the direction of Cold Ridge chatting amicably about trees and their habits, mahogany window frames and the possibility of creating a charcoal burner out here in the woods to 'lovingly cremate' the fallen limbs of Howard's friends and generate a bit of barbecue fuel into the bargain.

'You don't by any chance play cards do you?' Chunk asked him as they reached the road.

*   *   *   *   *   *

CHAPTER NINE

MR EDWARD FRIENDY

HE had watched a flying ant for what seemed like ages. As countless other ants milled around the freshly disturbed nest, Mr Edward Friendy, of 16, Rhododendron Crescent, Newvale knelt by his flower bed, trowel in hand, and attempted to follow a particular ant to try and determine its *raison d'etre*. Mr Friendy was no etymologist but he knew enough about ants to realise that any attempt at superimposing an individual personality on the little bugger would lead him up a blind alley. Nevertheless, he had already named it Angus.

It was difficult in the extreme to keep track of Angus as he wheeled this way and that through the teeming metropolis he called home. His left wing wasn't folded all the way in and stuck out a bit, and Mr Friendy was using this to try and make Angus stand out among his contemporaries.

He thought sadly about an incident, far away in the mists of time, when he had performed a similar exercise with a woodlouse. On that occasion he had had the bright idea of staining the creature with a drop of his mother's red nail varnish to make it easier to follow. Sadly, this had not only killed it but also caused an otherwise healthy greenfly to stick to it and suffer a death probably unique in the kingdom Aphidoidea if not the whole insect world.

Mr Friendy loved his little garden and spent a lot of his spare time in it. Given that ALL of his time was now spare this amounted to a significant fraction of his waking hours. He and Felicity had lived in Rhododendron Crescent for twenty-two years. Before moving there he had thought the name quite beautiful but now, after filling it in on a million forms and letters he sometimes wished they had chosen the house in Oak View instead. He had once tried to get and address stamp made but after they had spelt Rhododendron wrong three times he had given up. On the last occasion he had lost patience and muttered

'Illiterate twats' as he walked away. The stamp maker heard this and Mr Friendy had returned home with a bruised cheekbone, the pocket ripped off his shirt and the word 'Overdue' stamped in red on the top of his balding head.

That had been far in the past. It has been many years since Mr Friendy called anyone anything disparaging, or swore. A decade ago he found God whilst on holiday. Mr Friendy had been in a souvenir shop in a French monastery and had been agonising over whether to purchase a leather wallet or a bottle of *après-rasage* with a picture of a bearded monk on it, which, he felt, completely undermined the integrity of the product. While deep in deliberation he had suddenly experienced an overwhelming sense of peace and he knew with absolute certainty where his life was leading and what God's purpose for him was.

It was unlike anything Mr Friendy had ever felt before; almost as if whatever it was inside him that created fear and worry had suddenly been switched off and he felt a deep contentment and an overwhelming sense that The Creator was within him and that he had been 'Saved'.

He looked at the objects in his hands through new eyes, seeing now not desirable things but anathemas in this hallowed place and he understood how Jesus of Nazareth must have felt when confronted with the tables of the money changers. He dropped them in disgust and went searching for Felicity.

He found her trying on sunglasses in a far corner of the shop and breathlessly told her of his spontaneous rebirth. Felicity, still preoccupied with the sunglasses, was only half listening and punctuated his testimony with the occasional well placed 'Yes', 'That's nice Darling' or a completely inappropriate 'Do these make me look like a loose woman?' She and Edward had been married for twenty years at that point in their lives and she was well used to what she insisted on calling his 'little pecker-dildoes' - which was a story in itself and one that Mr Friendy would give his right arm to erase from her memory and his history. But as Felicity sometimes pointed out when they had an argument, 'It's one thing to try on a tea cosy as a hat but an entirely different matter to do what you did Edward.'

On return from their holiday Felicity had expected Edward's latest obsession to die a natural death as they usually did but to her surprise he began going to church, religiously. Not only that but she told him she had seen old Mr Bright sneeze his dentures out and then tread on them outside the supermarket and far from the guffaw she had expected Edward had actually said 'Poor fellow' and his face had registered genuine concern.

Felicity became so worried about Edward's change of character that she confided in her friend Meryl, a psychiatric nurse, who worried her even more by asking if Edward had mentioned hearing voices or developed an antipathy toward light sockets and power points. Meryl had looked disappointed when Felicity told her that, if anything, Edward's behaviour had improved considerably. He no longer belched or scratched at the dinner table, or swore at newsreaders, and while he had not altogether stopped masturbating in his sleep he had at least notably cut down and when he ejaculated he now did so relatively quietly instead of announcing the approaching orgasm with a loud yodel that had always finished the job of waking Felicity up; a task started by the rhythmic shaking of the bed and a low growling that in the early years of their marriage had caused Felicity to question the fantastic status of werewolves. It was a huge relief to say goodbye to the noises, it was something that had always made Felicity subconsciously fearful of anything Swiss and had led to her insisting on twin beds, which to her vague annoyance Edward had agreed readily to.

Edward, unaware that his nocturnal habits were being openly discussed, had entered into his new life with verve and righteousness. He became known in the neighbourhood as someone who was always ready to do a good deed. One day he'd be carrying someone's shopping and the next would find him putting the chain back on a child's bike. His manners became impeccable and those who had in the past avoided him for fear of his irritability and sarcasm now went out of their way to stop for a chat. Those who would have silently gloated at any misfortune befalling him now commiserated with him, particularly on the morning after one Halloween when he had woken to discover someone had painted a big red cock and balls on his front door. Mr Friendy attributed the artwork to the same scoundrels he had lectured on the evils of pagan festivals the evening before and as he had prepared to scrub the infernal thing away he had reflected sadly on a genuine talent that was being wasted.

As cocks go, and as far as Mr Friendy's experience went, this was a particularly good one, for a start it was in proportion; the shaft had been shaded in expertly to give a convincing three-dimensional effect and the glans penis had clearly been drawn by either a biology graduate or someone with an obsession for detail who had found a particularly intimate outlet. The appendage had been captured in paint at the moment of ejaculation and was doing so in a shower of red emulsion, quite decoratively, over the floral terracotta Number 16 that Mr Friendy had, in his previous life, stolen from a DIY superstore by hiding it inside a plastic flowerpot along with a tin of lawnmower oil, three packets of broad bean seeds and a book appropriately entitled 'Cut-Price Gardening'.

'Edward!'

'EDWARD!'

Felicity's voice macheted through the undergrowth of Mr Friendy's concentration forcing him to automatically look up, which instantly caused him to lose Angus in the throng of downtown Ant City. Irritation rose but was capped by the spirit of the Lord and he waved in acknowledgement before rising and heading into the house.

Sitting in the passenger seat of the car as it wove through the parked vehicles of Rhododendron Crescent, Mr Friendy watched Felicity, her face etched with concentration as she leaned forward for a better view. She had never enjoyed driving and try as she might she could not completely disguise the fact that she resented now having to do it all the time. Mr Friendy had only been advised not to drive; he had not specifically been told that he couldn't. He had a heart murmur and he observed, not for the first time, that being Felicity's passenger was significantly more stressful than driving himself - but she wouldn't hear of it. And so he sat, in his best suit, in the passenger seat as Felicity took the road for Newvale Town Centre and the Magistrates Court.

The court case had not been far from Mr Friendy's thoughts for weeks and he had played the forthcoming scene over and over in his mind a hundred times. He wondered if he was going to be going home afterwards or would he be 'Taken down' into some grim cell from where he would be transferred to a prison miles away. He had pictured the look on Felicity's face as he was being led away; it would show, he speculated, anger, pity, self-pity and resignation. His would undoubtedly show the same, but without the anger.

His solicitor had predicted a period of probation but Mr Friendy felt that the shock and disgust of the Magistrates would determine only a custodial sentence would be appropriate. And then there was the added humiliation of the Newvale Chronicle. This was going to be a front-pager for sure and soon, not only the residents of Rhododendron Crescent, but also everyone in Newvale would know what he did. Every time he went to the supermarket or even out for a walk he would be the target of their venom. Felicity had already elaborated on the scale of the shame to follow. They would almost certainly be excluded from the Rhododendron Crescent Bicentennial Celebrations Committee, which would bitterly disappoint Felicity as she had so many good ideas to put forward. Mr Friendy would probably be excommunicated from his church and the model railway society would demand the cutting up of his membership card and the return of his discount voucher for the annual World of Steam Festival - the model railway world's equivalent of the stripping of the epaulettes. And of course he had a previous conviction.

His prior brush with the law had been at juvenile court at the age of eleven when he had been charged with setting a barn on fire. He had not meant to and the Beak had agreed, dismissing the case with a warning not to play with matches in future.

He wondered if any of his former schoolmates would remember him when they read of his latest misdeed. A few probably would, in particular Geoffrey 'Plastic Ear' Moore who lost his right ear during a game of 'Spies' when Mr Friendy and a young psychopath called 'Husky' Hillier had wired him up to the mains to get the location of the plans for the new 'Deadly Death Missile'. In fairness, all Mr Friendy had done was wire him up; it was Husky who had actually switched him on, with quite dramatic results. There had been an almost simultaneous bang, flash and scream, Geoffrey's hair had caught fire and Mr Friendy had come within a singed follicle of prosecution. As it was, Husky took the rap, admitting it was his idea and that he had thrown the switch. It had earned Husky the first of his many convictions, which had culminated fifteen years later in the double shooting of his common law wife and her lover and the burning down of their house.

'When it comes down to it, I've led a very small life.'

The statement surprised Felicity enough to make her momentarily take her eyes off the road.

'You haven't led a small life Edward, you've led a relatively quiet life and that's something you should be grateful for.'

Mr Friendy sniffed; 'Too quiet' he muttered.

He began to drift away, his mind fluttering out of the car, high over the rooftops of the terraced streets and out to sea. He was captain of a huge cargo vessel called 'Bowsprite' which carried all manner of goods across turbulent oceans. Today he was carrying timber - and a mysterious man with a goatee beard who had paid in Russian gold to be taken out of Vladivostok in a hurry.

'Would you rather have had my father's life?'

Felicity cut into his musings and dragged his consciousness reluctantly back into the car.

'Wounded, captured by the Japanese, eighteen months on the Burma-Thailand Railway…'

Mr Friendy knew better than to interrupt.

'Seven stone twelve ounces! Six foot one he was and when he came home he was seven stone twelve ounces!'

Mr Friendy's father had been a Bevin Boy and he had pointed out, quite reasonably to Felicity over the years, that their sacrifice in terms of deaths and injuries made them comparable to front line troops.

'My father could do a ten-hour shift at the coal face and still go out and entertain people in the evenings,' he had told her on numerous occasions. Charles Friendy had been a singer of some note in his youth and Edward vaguely remembered being carried on his shoulders as he strolled across the hills singing 'Pretty Little Polly Perkins of Paddington Green'.

'He won prizes for yodelling.' Mr Friendy had added and had been bemused by the horrified look on Felicity's face and the coughing attack that had followed.

'I suppose by "Too quiet" you mean "No children", is that it?'

Mr Friendy sighed. It wasn't what he had meant but, come to think of it, that was probably a significant contributing factor. However, to even hint that his life had been any less fulfilling because of a lack of offspring would be to blame Felicity's Fallopian Tubes, and in turn Felicity herself, for their spick and span bungalow with its glass-topped coffee table, ornaments at waist height and complete lack of fridge drawings or pull-along toys in primary colours.

'Not at all Dear, I was merely saying…'

'I can't help my tubes!' Felicity chose to cut off any elaboration and get her defence in first.

'Of course you can't Dear, and I wasn't suggesting for a moment…'

'Anyway, the specialist didn't say I couldn't conceive, just that it was highly unlikely.'

Mr Friendy didn't like the direction in which Felicity's tirade was heading and he attempted to steer the discussion away from the potential minefield of conceptual responsibility.

'There's a chip in this windscreen, I think that's covered by the insurance.'

But Felicity was running on rails and could not be diverted.

'Highly unlikely, but not impossible. We could have... YOU could have tried harder!'

'Me? I... I don't see how...'

'Oh come on Edward, God alone knows, hang on, God and *I* alone know how many potential offspring you've fired into the duvet over the years.'

Mr Friendy chose to ignore Felicity's ignorance. If she had been in the mood to listen he would have tried to explain how half of a double helix is no more a child than a potato is fish and chips, but he was too tired and too preoccupied to argue.

'If we'd had a son I would have called him William, William Taylor, William Taylor Friendy.' He hadn't realised he'd been thinking aloud.

'William Tell would have been more appropriate given that he would have been yodelled into the world,' snapped Felicity whose blood was now clearly up. Mr Friendy allowed that her mind was probably on the court appearance too and she therefore had her own cross to bear. He closed his eyes and forced his mind back aboard the Bowsprite. He thought the man with the goatee beard was probably carrying valuable military or industrial secrets; he had asked to be dropped off in Anchorage and...

'I'll park around the side in case anyone sees the car.' Once again Felicity interrupted his train of thought as she pulled into the Magistrates Court car park. Mr Friendy thought that, given the impending front-page splash, where the car was parked was going to make little difference.

Mr Friendy and Felicity sat and tried to look inconspicuous if such a thing were possible in a place designed specifically for public chastisement. 'Justice must be seen to be done' thought Mr Friendy who suddenly found sympathy for countries where such things were dealt with behind closed doors. The majority of the people in the waiting room were young and Mr Friendy hoped he would be mistaken for a long-suffering parent here to support a wayward child who was bringing shame on to the family. The thought brought his own parents to mind, what would they have made of this?

His solicitor arrived in a flurry of cardboard folders, chatted to him briefly and told him nothing he didn't already know before moving along to speak slowly and in monosyllables to a skeletal youth with dead pale eyes that peered out balefully from under a hooded jacket.

'That's Katie Porritt over there.' Felicity whispered in Edward's ear.

'Who?'

'Over there in the blue top, Katie Porritt, I taught her in junior school - and she's spotted me, I'd better go across and have a word, in case she jumps to the wrong conclusion.'

As Felicity flitted and weaved across the now crowded waiting room, Mr Friendy thought that jumping to the right conclusion was going to be the problem. Felicity probably wanted to make sure that her former pupil was clear that it wasn't she who was about to face the righteous fury of the magistrates. She returned a few minutes later to sit at Edward's side, grim-faced but satisfied that at least one acquaintance was in no position to cast the first stone.

'Are you Mr Edward Charles Friendly of 16, Rhododendron Crescent, Newvale?

'Friendy', said Mr Friendy apologetically, this was no place for assertiveness unless you could prove your innocence. The clerk raised his eyebrows.

'Friendy' repeated Mr Friendy, there's no 'L' in it.

'Edward Charles Frrriendy' the clerk studied the charge sheet.

'And only one 'R" Mr Friendy was tempted to add; surprised at the inner calm he was feeling. He noticed a woman in his peripheral vision taking notes; 'Probably from the Chronicle' he mused.

'Edward Charles Friendy, you are charged with an offence of public order contrary to Section 4A, Subsection 1A of the Public Order Act 1986 in that at approximately 2:00am on Sunday, May 21st of this year you were seen naked in a greenhouse in the garden of 16, Rhododendron Crescent where you were performing an act of sexual intimacy on yourself, with the lights on whilst at the same time growling and yodelling - loudly.'

Despite prior knowledge of the charges it was still a shock to hear them read out in public; his shame laid as bare as he had indeed been.

'Mr Friendy, how do you plead?'

Mr Friendy's attention snapped back

'Asleep.'

'I beg your pardon?'

'I was asleep.'

'.... adjourned for medical reports with a view to a period of probation - do you understand Mr Friendy?'

'Yes Sir.'

Mr Friendy responded to the Chief Magistrate's not unkind conclusions. He had been observing the copious note taking of the woman he had assumed was the Newvale Chronicle reporter and had been trying to guess the headline they were going to put above the story.

'Newvale Man's Greenhouse Sex Shame.'

'Night Time Shock For Neighbours'

A worst-case scenario would be something along the lines of 'Residents Horrified by Growling, Yodelling, Naked Greenhouse Wanker' above a picture of Mr Friendy, with a sub head below along the lines of, 'He Buggered Himself with a Cucumber Claims Stunned Neighbour!' The Editorial, always on page eight, would likely comment on the case under the heading, 'Hanging's Too Good For Some People.'

Two days after the court hearing, and in a stroke of unbelievable good fortune for the Friendys, a case of suspected rabies was announced in Newvale and on the very same day a guide dog was drowned in the Leisure and Activity Centre's new Hydrotherapy pool. These stories served to keep Mr Friendy off the front page, or indeed any page and the rule of contemporaneousness would ensure they couldn't print it in the future.

Felicity was delighted. Mr Friendy, on Felicity's instructions, had fitted loud alarms to both doors of their bungalow designed to wake anyone who opened them at night and the psychologist appointed by the probation service was said to be hopeful of improvement in Mr Friendy after their first session. Mr Friendy too felt much better after his visit to the psychologist. He was learning to release pent-up emotions. It was like the uncapping of a volcano, he actually felt physically lighter and there was a spring in his step as he strolled home from the newsagent. He thought maybe he should get a dog? A little companion he could walk and talk with? He could call it William.

He passed the supermarket; in the window was a sign that said '2kg Potatoe's Buy One Get One Free.'

The illiterate twats!

*   *   *   *   *   *

CHAPTER TEN

'CH₃CH₂OH'

THE Red Lion Public House had been closed for two weeks. This was the longest period it had spent closed in its ninety-one year history. Even the Luftwaffe had only managed to close it for forty-eight hours after which the incumbent landlord had set up a bar out of the remains of the piano and served drinks amid the rubble. This time it was a long overdue refit that had brought about the hiatus in service.

Byron Hughes and his wife Heather had taken over the Red Lion just nine months before, determined to change it from a run-down haunt of ne'er-do-wells on the less aesthetic end of Cold Ridge Estate into a friendly and forward-looking hostelry catering for the discerning and more cerebral drinker. Byron realised it was going to be a far from easy transformation when the inaugural quiz night had ended in a full-scale brawl.

Five teams, among them two of Cold Ridge's most notorious families, the Sankeys and the Frogmores, had contested the quiz. In response to the badly phrased and ambiguous question, 'Where else, apart from around Saturn, will you find a ring?' the eldest of the Sankey offspring, twenty-one year old Dawn - who had broken with family tradition and attended school regularly - whispered 'Uranus' in her mother's ear; Ma Sankey had duly written 'Your Anus' on the answer sheet and when they were swapped for marking at the end of the round, Ma Frogmore had guffawed loudly and showed the answer to the rest of her brood who had dutifully joined in the ridicule.

During the night-long clearing up that followed, Byron had found a metal chair leg so firmly embedded in a wall that he had been tempted to leave it there as a conversation piece - a sort of modern-day Excalibur, but Heather had insisted that not only should all evidence of the brawl be eradicated but that the Sankeys and the Frogmores should be banned forthwith and in perpetuity unto the ninth generation!

Slowly, in the wake of Heather's hostile glare and the removal from sale of some of the more hideously flavoured alcohol-heavy beverages, the crowd who had made the Red Lion a no go area for civilised drinkers began to drift away. The couple had decided to make the break with the past complete with a refit that would hopefully encourage a whole new set of customers who were capable of entering a pub and leaving it several hours later without bruised knuckles and with the same dental map.

This was the couple's first venture into the world of pub running and many of Byron's preconceived ideas had already bitten the dust. He had envisaged being a genial host, propping up the bar with a few of the more coherent and educated regulars swapping tales of the big wide world and postulating on points of philosophy. The regulars he inherited however were not very philosophical or worldly at all. Most of them seemed to communicate in a series of grunts and gestures, their gravelly voices and life-blasted faces telling of an existence led far from the oak-panelled walls and dreaming spires of the great seats of knowledge.

And their capacity for drinking was voluminous. Byron was no slouch when it came to dispatching the juice of the hop, grain and grape but some of the people on Cold Ridge Estate could drink truly elephantine amounts. One giant of a man, who Byron had mentally nicknamed The Mandrill because of his quite uncanny resemblance to the colourful creature, once drank twenty-three pints of beer and ate sixteen packets of crisps in one sitting. Byron had asked him his name and got 'Mmffuddh' as a reply, prompting him to reconsider his original plan of asking the man if he felt the pub should start a debating society.

At forty, Heather was two years older than Byron and while this meant little in theory, in practice she had always felt a bit like a big sister and he had, subconsciously at least, become a naughty little brother with his fibs and his smoking in the cellar. Neither of them had wanted children and so they had drifted through twelve years of marriage on a more or less even keel and with no earth shattering dramas to date. She had hoped the pub would be a busy place to give Byron something to occupy him and leave less time for his fertile imagination to create worlds that would never stand up to practical analysis.

It would be fair to say, however, that business was slow. At 1:30 pm there were only three people in the lounge and none in the bar. Byron was sitting on a stool at the bar engrossed in a puzzle in the Chronicle. He was trying to help Simon the Squirrel find his way through the Deep Dark Wood to his store of nuts. It wasn't as easy as it first appeared, one had to avoid Buster the Badger and Wolfgang and his Wolf-Gang - although Byron was pretty sure badgers didn't prey on squirrels. The prize was an electronic robot that could learn phrases and repeat them and although the age limit for entrants was twelve, Byron was confident no one actually checked these things.

Two of the three lounge customers were there for lunch; Heather appeared at their table and dished up the food before joining Byron at the bar.

'Have you changed the Alpine Lager barrel over yet?'

'Doing it now,' Byron answered absently.

Heather looked over his shoulder, 'He's asking for trouble, passing Weasel Village carrying a pile of nuts.'

'Yeah, but the only alternative is to go around the far edge of Pirate's Pond and they'll have your nuts before you can blink.'

'As indeed will I if you don't change that bloody barrel in the next thirty seconds!' Heather's façade of concern for the fate of Simon the Squirrel's winter food supply evaporated and she bustled away to the kitchen. Byron sighed and wandered off in the direction of the cellar.

Byron liked the cellar, this was where he felt at home; this was what being a publican was all about, down here among the barrels and bottles and crates. This is, after all, was what the punters wanted, you can put on as many themed nights as you like and decorate the premises to resemble an ice palace or a bloody harem but at the end of the day it all came down to this stuff, good old CH_3CH_2OH - ethanol, drinking alcohol, booze! Without this the Red Lion would be a café, or worse, a shop!

He changed the lager barrel and then sat on an upturned crate, took out a cigarette, lit it and leaned back against the refreshing cold of the cellar wall. He checked in his trouser pocket and was reassured by the comforting feel of a tube of peppermints, he needed one of those after the cigarette to perpetuate the myth that he had given up nine months ago when he and Heather had taken over this place.

Byron had never envisaged running a pub; his career path had been a long and convoluted one. He had begun his working life as a clerk in the offices of an insurance company but one morning after he had been there for about three months he turned left instead of right as he got off the bus and, on a sudden impulse, joined the Navy. He had always wanted to be a pirate and this was probably as close as he would ever get.

He had actually enjoyed the Navy. He had been to the Far East and Malta and had contracted infections he would never have encountered in Newvale. He had a tattoo on his arm that he believed said, 'Hong Kong - Hot as Hell' in Cantonese but actually said 'I've Got a Small Penis.' He had proudly shown it to the staff at Wong's Palace Takeaway who had found it a true challenge to their inscrutability.

On his discharge he had worked in various short-term jobs but had found it hard to settle. He had finally lied his way into the position of assistant manager of a pony trekking centre just outside Newvale. The job was essentially office-based and all the while he was there Byron had been terrified that someone would suggest he rode a horse - or actually got close enough to one to touch it - but he managed to successfully hide his terror of the creatures.

It was there he had met Heather; she was a riding instructor and she had, he thought, a truly magnificent arse. Much the worse for drink at the Centre's Christmas Party he had told her so and, far from the slap across the face he had been expecting, he ended up in the tack room enjoying the most invigorating ride the Centre had ever provided.

'Are you still down there?' Heather's voice called from the top of the cellar steps. Byron hastily stubbed out his cigarette and wafted the air around him to disperse the smoke.

'Coming.'

Not many people knew about the 'Fairy Glen.' Hidden in the expanse of woodlands that covered much of the slopes of Cold Ridge, the 'Fairy Glen' had been so named by Todd Frogmore. Todd belonged to a brood whose name, when in print, was usually followed by the phrase, '...pleaded guilty at Newvale Magistrates Court.' Todd was the white sheep of the family, a gentle, twenty-one-year-old singer/songwriter still waiting for commercial recognition. He was the author of such numbers as 'Your Mole Touched My Soul', 'You Took My Heart In Your Hands and Trampled it Under Your Feet' and 'I Gave You My World But All You Saw Was An Old Table.'

Taken to wandering the paths of Cold Ridge seeking inspiration and respite from the warring and overcrowded Frogmore mother ship he had stumbled on the Fairy Glen some months ago and had been captivated by the silence and natural beauty. Birches and young sycamores filtered the sunlight allowing it to fall in ever-moving shafts to a carpet of bluebells amid the softest grass and ferns. All the sounds of the nearby town seemed to vanish leaving only birdsong. He had sat beneath the boughs of a sycamore and only then noticed the clumps of mushrooms that were dotted throughout the grass.

He knew enough about fungi to know that, unless you are absolutely sure of the species it's better not to eat them - so he took some home for his brother to try!

Randy Frogmore, two years Todd's senior and currently home between prison sentences, had once eaten a whole family-sized pizza and the box it came in for a bet so Todd had few qualms about using him as the guinea pig for his discovery. Randy ate several of the mushrooms, washed down with a can of white cider that could have been used as paint-stripper and then followed up with a home-made curry that nothing with a central nervous system should have been able to survive. Half an hour later he said he felt fine, an hour later and he was tearing down the street screaming that he was being chased by giant screaming red wasps with blonde pigtails that were going to drown him in a vat of hot butter. He would probably have run for miles if his mother hadn't waited in ambush around a blind corner and felled him with the famous left hook that had struck fear into bailiffs and rent collectors for years. Realising that these were no ordinary mushrooms, Todd had employed the family demijohns and his grandfather's recipe book and now a dozen bottles of self-labelled 'Fairy Glen Wine' were hidden in the bottom of his wardrobe.

'How about a barbecue? All we need is one dry weekend and…'

'Byron, we're trying to attract a more.. refined clientele, we should be looking into serving haute cuisine.'

'Well barbecues are hot cuisine!'

Heather shook her head. On their first date Byron had recited a Shakespeare sonnet to her and spoken of his love of classical music. She had become a little suspicious when, in response to her asking him his favourite composer, he had replied William Tell, but he had been charming company. He had taken her to a nice restaurant overlooking the ornamental pond on the edge of Newvale Park. The food had been splendid and he had regaled her with tales of his adventures as a sea captain, fighting pirates and smugglers and, on one occasion, rescuing a troupe of dancing bears from their cruel captors. The grateful creatures had apparently formed a chorus line and entertained their liberators with a spontaneous can-can. And that was how Byron was. If you let him away with the little lies they grew bigger and more elaborate until they defied not only belief, but also occasionally the laws of physics.

'I was thinking more of a musical evening,' Heather postulated, 'Local musicians, maybe a string quartet, what do you think?'

Byron shrugged, it didn't matter what he thought, Heather only solicited opinion after laying aside the hammer and chisel having carved the 'suggestion' in stone.

Todd Frogmore was stuck on some lyrics. He sat, guitar in lap staring at the opposite wall in his bedroom where a poster of an elf maiden prodding a unicorn with a stick covered a two-year-old stain left by an exploding ink cartridge. So far he had, 'Baby you're the sun in my sky, yeah you are the light in my eye…' He was trying to avoid ending the next two lines with 'cry' or 'die' as he was hoping to save those for the chorus.

'Wow yeah Baby you're the sun in my sky,' he sang.

'Give it a rest you noisy bastard!' his father called encouragingly up the stairs from the nest on the sofa from which he rarely stirred. The Frogmore Patriarch was not a music lover, or a devotee of any of the creative arts, although he had once sold a drawing in the Sixties to a man who had approached him in a pub. The drawing, nothing more than a doodle on the back of a beer mat, was, according to the man who bought it, a masterpiece of pop art. He had paid the young artist there and then out of a bulging wallet before inviting him back to his flat on the premise of seeing his art collection and hinting at future commissions. On arrival the man had given young Frogmore a large tumbler of sherry and some yellow pills that 'All the really cool artists are using at the moment.' After the young man inevitably passed out, the 'art collector' had buggered him at great length and with a degree of single-mindedness that pointed to someone who took his buggery very seriously indeed. On regaining consciousness the next morning the young Frogmore recalled nothing of the previous night but maintained for the rest of his life that sherry gave you a really sore arse.

It was, unbeknown to him, the only time in his life where the sex would actually be meaningful to at least one of the partners. Shortly afterwards he had met and impregnated the vitriolic and pugnacious future Mrs Frogmore with the first of six feral offspring destined to spread their seed throughout Cold Ridge like the rosaceaic veins on the nose of a drunkard.

'A Night of Musical Entertainment,' it said on the advertisements that Heather had posted not only throughout the pub but also in the Cold Ridge post office and the nearby Community Centre. As if to emphasise the kind of musical entertainment she was hoping to attract, she had illustrated the posters with a violin and a pair of conductor's hands holding a baton. Byron shook his head, he never knew whether to be heartened or disheartened by Heather's eternal refusal to take people at face value. He never saw the diamonds in the rocks that she imagined were there and no amount of disappointments shook her belief that humans were fundamentally intelligent, curious and creative. Life had taught Byron that if it grunts like a moron and swaggers like a moron - it's a moron. Still, maybe this time he would be proven wrong and a tattooed urban warrior would swagger in, shed his leather skin, sit at the piano, flex hands encased in fingerless studded gloves and play with such feeling and passion that the spirit of Mozart would descend from heaven to be close to a fellow prodigy.

But he wasn't going to get his hopes up.

Mr Batwell the Cold Ridge postmaster gazed through his glass screen at the queue snaking out to the door and beyond. He didn't like Mondays. On Mondays it was an interminable stream of benefit and pension payments; monotonous work, card in... 'Key in your P.I.N. number please'... card out, pay cash, 'Next please'...and another familiar and unwelcome face would loom into view.

He had just paid out the third Sankey in a row; he looked up to study the queue, just as long and not a parcel in sight. Mr Batwell loved parcels; different shapes and weights and wrapping and all those exotic addresses.

'Faraway places with strange sounding names... calling... calling me' he began to sing silently to himself. All those lovely parcels, free, escaping out into the big wide unknown world on planes and trains and ships, far away from Newvale. He dreamed of parcelling himself up in a big box addressed to Tahiti, far, far from Newvale and rain and sleet and Mrs Batwell.

Todd Frogmore stood in the queue, patiently inching forwards, studying the rack of greetings cards as he passed, 'How can you tell when you're over the hill?' one of them asked. Todd didn't care enough to open the card to find out, he inched forward a little more and drew level with the notice board. Someone had lost a cat, 'Lost, Beeches Road area, black and white cat with one eye called Coco reward - also does anybody want to buy a red child's jacket?' Todd was in the process of wondering whether the child was sunburnt or a communist when he noticed the poster advertising the Red Lion's night of musical entertainment. He had never played in public, his father had told him he was rubbish and his mother had always maintained that music was for homosexuals, but no Frogmore had been to the Red Lion since the night of the big quiz fight - from which Todd had been mercifully absent - so...

His heart raced, in his mind's eye he had imagined a thousand times the thrill as waves of applause washed over him, appreciative faces nodding at his lyrical perspicacity, feet tapping, smiling as they sang along to words he had created, calling out requests, some of the more dedicated fans sticking fake moles to their cheeks in tribute to 'Your Mole Touched My Soul' and wearing 'Todd is God' tee shirts - and it could all start here...

Heather had made a stage in the corner of the lounge bar and Byron had put up a set of directional lights. Chairs had been placed to accommodate the performers and the bar had become a veritable cornucopia of wines and cheeses and breadsticks and small round things that looked like mince pies but tasted like wet cardboard. All they needed now was people.

It was a quarter to eight, the evening had been billed to start at eight and so far there was only one person in the lounge bar, an elderly but well-kept man with white hair and a dickey bow who sat facing the stage, nursing a glass of house red in anticipation of some entertainment. Byron had kept his misgivings to himself but was disappointed for Heather who had worked hard for this night and deserved a good turn out. The thought made him even more contemptuous of the people of this end of Cold Ridge; could they really be happy in their dark, ignorant little worlds?

The door opened and a young man with a guitar walked nervously in. He looked as if neither daylight nor vitamin C played a big part in his life. Eyes that looked much older than the surrounding face took in the room and he fidgeted nervously as if wondering whether to turn around and head straight back out. Byron thought of pointing out to him that guitars didn't register on Heather's musical map but he was, so far, all they had.

'Is this the place for the musical evening?' Todd looked around the virtually empty room.

'Err yes - guitarist are we?' Byron clung to the slender thread of hope that the young man might be a stringsmith of the classical variety but a sticker on the instrument showing Alice's hookah-smoking caterpillar indicated otherwise.

'Er, yeah - singer/songwriter.'

At least he was a, sort of, composer thought Byron as the young man studied the spread of wine and food on the bar with a wariness that suggested he saw it as bait. He was clearly in uncharted territory and Byron tried to put him at his ease.

'So... how shall I introduce you?'

'Eh?'

'Your name?'

'Oh, Todd Frogmore,' the young man answered absently.

'Shit,' muttered Byron

'What?'

'Oh... nothing - look, you may or may not know, but my wife... after the riot here on the quiz night... well, we sort of told all the Frogmores and Sankeys they were no longer welcome.'

The young man looked genuinely crestfallen. It was not the expression normally seen on the face of a Frogmore who had just been told something they didn't want to hear and Byron found something genuinely likeable about the lad.

'Listen - how about if you have a stage name? Let's think ... yeah, how about Todd Tell?'

'Todd Tell?'

'Yeah, after William Tell the composer.'

'Hang on, William Tell wasn't...'

'... from Newvale, I know but it doesn't matter, it's got a ring to it, short and snappy.'

'I suppose so, if you like,' Todd shrugged.

Three more people entered the lounge and looked approvingly at the spread on the bar. Maybe by the time Heather had put on her fineries and come down it wouldn't be too bad, thought Byron.

'I knew it! I bloody knew it!' Ma Frogmore brandished a bottle as she stood between the prone Pa Frogmore and the television. He tried in vain to look around her but her girth and his unwillingness to move any more than necessary to sustain life made it impossible.

'Look' she held the bottle close to his face forcing him to focus, 'Read the label!'

Pa squinted, 'Fairy Glen Wine - where did you get that?' He raised himself up on an elbow at the welcome prospect of some unscheduled drinking.

'I got it...' Ma panted, forcing some faceless indignation to remain at bay, '... from the bottom of Todd's wardrobe! There's lots of it in there, fucking fairy wine! I told you, didn't I? All that music, the signs were there, ohh the signs were there - you should have taken him in hand when he was younger.'

'What are you talking about?' Pa scratched himself and rose to a sitting position, farting as he did so which made the movement appear to be wind-assisted.

'I'm taking about your son... OUR son - being a fucking sausage jockey!' roared the now force ten Ma Frogmore. 'Look, he's drinking this stuff!'

Pa took the bottle from Ma's outstretched hand and studied the label before unscrewing the cap and taking a long swig.

'Tastes OK.' He studied the label again as Ma stood, her mouth opening and closing mutely for a few seconds before normal service was resumed.

'You can't drink that stuff it's.... it's what fairies drink... you know, bum bandits!'

'Don't be so bloody stupid woman - they don't have special drinks, they drink what normal people drink, I've seen Charlie Day drinking a pint of beer in the pub and he's a shirt-lifter.'

'He can't be a proper one if he drinks beer, he probably goes with men and women.'

'Look maybe our Todd bought it off somebody - or pinched it?' The pair brightened at the thought of their youngest following in the family business.

'Well anyway,' Ma sounded calmer, 'We'll wait until he comes in and ask him who Fairy Glen is, and if it turns out he's been touching up our boy we'll go around his house and...' She paused as Pa handed her the bottle.

'Go on, have a pull, it's good stuff - and it probably won't turn you into a lesbian.'

There were upwards of twenty people in the lounge bar when Heather came downstairs. She had been undecided about what to wear, it had to be special but she had been afraid of overdressing and looking silly. She still wasn't sure an evening gown was appropriate but it was on now and it was too late to go and change again. She was pleased that she could still fit in it and Byron had been suitably complimentary.

The wine and nibbles were proving popular and Byron's earlier fears that their one performer would be playing to an empty room had proved unfounded. A young woman carrying a violin and a man who normally turned up every Saturday night and drank enough to drown a camel had now joined Todd Frogmore. The man had billed himself as a basso profundo; Byron had kept his ignorance in check and simply wrote down the man's name for the introductions.

Todd's heart was racing, his mouth was dry and he seriously regretted sharing one of his brother's killer curries a few hours ago. He had always dreamed of playing in public and now here was his big chance if only he could hold it all together. He closed his eyes and imagined he was at home in his room. Byron mounted the makeshift stage and took out a piece of paper; Todd's legs trembled violently as Byron briefly thanked everyone for coming.

'...And now ladies and gentlemen, please give a warm welcome to a young lady...'

Todd felt relief flow through him at the stay of execution; he was safe for a short while longer. He didn't notice Heather appearing at his elbow.

'Are we going to get any Villa-Lobos by any chance?'

Todd was spared the embarrassment of replying by a sound that resembled an anaesthetic-resistant tomcat passing through the hands of a student vet. The girl on stage sawed at her violin as if attempting to cut the instrument in two, a deed that would have met with the wholehearted approval of all listening. She had introduced the piece as 'The Wild Gypsy' and all who heard it would have agreed that one didn't necessarily need to be an itinerant in order to experience a sense of discord-induced rising ire. There was a palpable sense of relief at the end of the piece and the applause was that of gratitude for the performance's only virtue - brevity. It had, however, broken the ice and people now chatted warmly with a camaraderie born of mutual sufferance.

Todd was heartened, he was sure to sound better than that and was almost disappointed when Byron introduced the next performer as a huge man who was going to sing unaccompanied. The man took to the stage amid hearty applause, he had clearly brought his own support with him and Todd rued the fact that he had no one in his corner, however, considering what usually happened when his parents and siblings went to a pub that was probably a good thing.

'Here's a health to the Queen and a lasting peace,
To faction an end, to wealth increase....'

The huge man sang and Todd noticed Byron and Heather nodding approvingly. His heart sank again.

Pa Frogmore looked at the woman he had married all those years ago and, as if for the first time, he realised just how beautiful she was. In fact, everything in the room was beautiful, the television, the table, even the dog who only hours ago had bitten him on the foot after he had kicked it in the arse to move it out of his way. Ma seemed to be moving slowly and with a feline grace he had never seen in her before. In fact, she was very cat-like when you came to look at her, she had furry ears and slanting yellow eyes and.... good God! It couldn't be.... He looked, he felt... it was.... Bloody hell fire! He had an erection! Somewhere in a part of his brain still tenuously attached to reality a warning bell sounded - this was that bloody wine - GAY wine! Oh God, he had a gay erection!

He got up and walked in a crouch to the foot of the stairs almost bumping into Ma as she swept, trance like, down the hallway towards the front door. She glanced briefly in his direction as she passed.

'Bad back,' he muttered, feeling as if some sort of explanation was necessary. His mouth felt as if it was full of cotton wool, she couldn't find out he had a homo-hard-on. Ma Frogmore had preoccupations of her own, however, her long dead grandmother had just whispered in her ear, telling her to cast off all earthly possessions and offer herself up to the sky people and as she threw open the front door a shaft of sunlight seemed to illuminate the rubbish dump of a lawn that fronted Chez Frogmore and as she walked down the garden path to the road, she began to disrobe.

Todd was glad they had provided a chair for performers, he was shaking too much to stand up. He sat, guitar on lap, adjusted the microphone and looked out at a room full of expectant faces. He took a deep breath and began to strum, he was hoping they would chat among themselves but they were actually listening. Singing your own words, exposing your own thoughts to public scrutiny, it was like bleeding... the best and the worst of feelings. He sang....

Ma Frogmore's audience were even more attentive. This was something most people went through life without ever seeing - or ever wanting to! It was clear there was only going to be a window of a few minutes before the police arrived so they were making the most of the spectacle. Most of the street had come out to watch as the huge naked she-walrus raised her flabby tattooed arms to the skies and howled like a timber wolf. Pa Frogmore, crouching like a weasely Quasimodo, was trying to throw a duvet over her but she was having none of it. Neighbours usually cheered the police when they arrived at the Frogmore house but this time they were booed, as no one wanted the surreal entertainment to end.

There was no way he was going to sleep tonight; he lay on his bed looking up at the ceiling as the evening replayed itself over and over again. They had applauded, they had actually applauded, and a few of them had said, 'Great' to him as he had passed on leaving the stage. The landlady had patted him on the back and invited him to return and play there again. And then there was her.... Her name was Dawn, she had approached him as he stood at the bar and told him she loved his songs, and she had smiled - and his whole world had flipped on its axis.

Heather was pleased, and so, therefore, was Byron. The evening had been a success beyond all expectations and Heather was already planning a follow-up.

'Maybe I'll book a professional string quartet to headline next time?'

Byron smiled; she was already probably considering a 'Newvale 200 Music Festival' for later in the year, and why not? It would in all probability be better entertainment than some of the twaddle the council were coming up with. The Red Lion was going to be a hub of culture. He decided to look online for a couple of William Tell albums to play over the sound system.

'Yes, I know her name's Dawn, you told us - but do you know what her other name is? Sankey! That's what!' Ma Frogmore looked at Todd as if he had gone completely mad. She had spotted her youngest and his new girlfriend in the American Diner on Fuller Square holding hands over a pair of Knickerbocker Glories.

'For God's sake Ma - at least he's not a fairy!' Pa interjected from the sofa. It seemed to placate Ma but made him feel suddenly uncomfortable as he half-remembered the incidents of a few days ago. He had felt well enough again by the following morning and Ma had been released with a caution but, disturbingly and inexplicably, ever since the incident he had really, really fancied a glass of sherry.

*　　*　　*　　*　　*　　*

CHAPTER ELEVEN

THE HONOURABLE MEMBER

UNFORTUNATELY for headline writers, Oberon Oliphant, Member of Parliament for Newvale, was not fat. In fact he was rather more sylph-like than an MP had any right to be. He looked as if the rough and tumble of debate would shred him like a straw in a storm and his genteel mannerisms had lulled many a political adversary into the surreal sensation that attacking him in the chamber would be somehow ungallant and that they should be holding doors open for him or throwing their cloaks over puddles in his path.

Oberon had held Newvale at the last general election with a substantially reduced majority, partly due to a nationwide dissatisfaction with his party but also as a result of the fact that he had been photographed in a rabbit costume coming out of a house in Cedar Hill and hurrying into a waiting taxi. The subsequent explanation from his office that it had been a charity fundraising event had been called into question by a tabloid revelation quoting a 'reliable source' who claimed that the event was by no means a 'one-off' and that on the second Wednesday of every month - parliamentary business permitting - Oberon became 'Bunty Bunny' and joined several other like-minded 'Woodland Folk' in a world of their own making far from the responsibilities of their high-powered careers.

The truth was that Oberon sought a comfort in his rabbit suit that he had never found in his own skin. He had always known there was something fundamentally wrong. It was as if his public persona was completely at odds with the real Oberon inside. He felt like a tortoise whose shell was entirely the wrong shape for the creature trapped within, subjecting it to a lifetime of inescapable discomfort. In short, there were bits he didn't have that he dearly wanted and there were bits he DID have that he most certainly wished he hadn't!

He was, by and large, a good MP. He cared about his constituents, worked long hours and embezzled very little. He had always borne barbs about his sexuality with dignity even though they were generally inaccurate. 'Oberon never leaves his friends behind!' was a case in point; suggesting as it did that he was unwaveringly loyal while simultaneously being only an apostrophe away from implying that he spent every waking minute engaged in sodomy. Oberon had never had a homosexual experience in all his forty-five years and both his heterosexual ones had been deeply disappointing. He just didn't get sex - either actually or cognitively. He got love, he understood love perfectly and longed for it, but he had felt for some time now that if Cupid's dart were ever going to strike he would have to make himself a more appealing target.

Monty Fox, editor of the Newvale Chronicle, had just spent forty-five minutes watching Meadowvale Junior School's play with the theme of road safety and there was still no sign of it drawing to a close. His reporter Virginia Wells had been set to attend but she had phoned in sick and so he had been forced to come along with his photographer, Colin. The young performers had just joined hands and formed a sort of chorus line.

'Oh great, 'Monty sighed inwardly, 'They're going to sing another fucking song.'

A teacher struck a chord on the piano and the children launched into a ditty entitled 'Look Both Ways' complete with appropriate actions. The requisite number of 'Awws' and 'Bless thems' came from the audience of parents and relatives while Monty squirmed on a chair designed for someone much smaller and younger and prayed for a speeding truck.

Monty usually liked children, he had once been one, but watching the little buggers performing with their reedy voices and robotic dancing was becoming more irritating by the minute. He was due to have lunch with Newvale's MP and if this lot carried on much longer he was going to have to feign illness and leave.

Fortunately, the song had been the finale and as the young performers took a bow Monty applauded, more out of relief than anything else, and rose to leave. Colin would be staying behind to take some pictures. He smiled this way and that at parents and teachers as he headed for the exit.

'Oh, Mr Fox,' the headmistress caught up with him in the corridor, 'I'm sure you haven't forgotten, but you promised a few weeks ago to donate something from the Chronicle for our Activity Centre Fundraising Auction?'

'Ahh, of course, indeed I did Mrs Birch..'

'It's Beech, actually,' her smile never wavered.

'Of course it is, of course it is,' Monty smiled warmly while inwardly cursing his photographer for instigating the Freudian slip. For the last half hour of the concert Colin had been whispering in his ear, describing in graphic detail just what he's like to get up to with the headmistress, what she would be wearing at the time and where online you could buy the equipment. 'I hadn't forgotten,' reassured Monty, who had, 'I'll have something for you well before the event.'

Monty couldn't understand why children needed an 'Activity Centre', when he was their age they had used Meadowvale Woods where nature had provided everything a growing mind and body needed for optimum fitness. They had climbed trees, fought duels and built dens and their free-range imaginations had created world after world without the help of television, computer games or 'Play Leaders'.

'Full of fucking flashers now probably,' he mused still thinking of Colin.

Oberon's private secretary, Polly Barring, studied her boss across the restaurant table as if seeing him for the first time.

'Well, go on, say something.' Oberon prompted her.

Polly shook her head. She had worked for Oberon for thirteen years and genuinely liked him. One of the things she liked most about him was his honesty - rare in a politician and particularly endearing in someone for whom the truth could be as dangerous as a bomb. They had become firm friends and confidants and she thought he had always told her everything.

'What you've just told me is that you've been going through gender reassignment for some time and now you're going to have a sex change operation and, not only that, you're going to tell Monty Fox all about it - have I missed anything out?' Polly wasn't the slightest bit surprised by the gender reassignment, only that it had taken so long for Oberon to get around to it.

Oberon sighed, 'I know how it must sound but in my experience people respond to openness. They like their representatives to be frank.'

'And now you're about to tell them their representative is going to stop being Frank and become Francesca!'

'Titania, actually.' Oberon replied almost apologetically.

'The Queen of the Fairies?'

He sighed.

'Look,' Polly had begun speaking with gestures, 'Honesty's a valuable commodity in this world, particularly in our business and we shouldn't be wasting it on journalists.'

'People have a right...' Attempted Oberon.

'Indeed they do, but let's manage this; it might actually be better to present the public with a *fait accompli*. You can do a sympathetic chat show and bare your bos... that's a point, will you actually have..?'

Oberon smiled, 'I'll look like a woman, yes. I still believe it's better to prepare people for a surprise, soften the blow.'

Polly poured them both another glass of wine, 'Maybe, but Monty Fox? Have you forgotten all he's written over the years? For God's sake Oberon, just a couple of months ago he stated in his paper that the reason you joined the trade delegation to Seoul was because you wanted to see what it was like to bugger a duck!'

Oberon smiled and shook his head, 'That's just Monty all over, he was miffed because I couldn't swing a couple of tickets to a Commons garden party.'

'Yes, but your constituents read these things and some of them are stupid enough to believe it; it can cost votes. What sort of angle do you suppose he will give to the story of your gender modification?'

'That's quite a piece of equipment you've got there,' Mrs Beech was admiring Colin's camera.

'Oh yes,' his weasely eyes twinkled. That morning, as he did every morning, Colin had sprayed his underarms with a product he had bought online called 'Rutting Stag' guaranteed, claimed its makers, to induce uncontrollable urges in females when employed in confined spaces. Colin was trying to give it a hand by making chicken movements with his arms as he and Mrs Birch chatted in the corridor.

'Are you feeling OK?' she asked, concerned.

'Err, oh yeah, just.. adjusting my... my shirt - so, are you interested in photography at all?'

'I have a camera but I have to say it's not as impressive as yours.'

'Would you like to hold it?' Colin struggled to keep a tremor out of his voice as he handed his camera to Mrs Beech. He failed to stifle a slight whimper as she ran her fingers delicately over the telescopic lens, 'I've got a Long Tom at home,' he offered.

'I've always wanted to pose for a professional,' Mrs Beech sighed.

Colin closed his eyes and offered up a silent prayer of thanks, 'Well, I'd be more than happy to shoot...' he said, feeling as if he was about to.

Mrs Beech smiled at him, 'Let's arrange something then, shall we?'

'Sorry I'm late, a thousand apologies, you wouldn't believe the morning I've had, fucking kids!'

Oberon raised an eyebrow; it always took a few minutes of mental gear changing when one met up with Monty Fox. Oberon knew him well enough, however, not to fall into the trap of thinking crude meant stupid. Many adversaries had learned to their cost that the editor of the Chronicle was vulpine enough to fully justifying the family name.

'Wine?' Oberon offered the bottle, Monty held out a glass.

'No Polly today?' Monty queried.

'She had to rush off.'

'So - to what do I owe the pleasure of this invitation?' Monty took a sip of the wine and frowned. He picked up the bottle and studied the label.

Polly had made Oberon promise not to give too much away. They had reached a compromise in which Oberon would tell the journalist that he was about to undergo a change but reveal little else.

'A couple of things really - I've noticed my column hasn't been used for the last two weeks, is there a problem?'

'Only one of space,' Monty absently studied the menu looking for the most expensive dish, he was veering towards the lobster, 'There's been all this furore over sending little Chloe Davies to Disneyland prior to her bone marrow transplant; four and a half grand our generous readers raised - and then the organisers end up sending the wrong Chloe Davies!'

'Unfortunate.' Oberon commiserated.

'Too bloody right, all we can hope for now is that the one we sent actually gets leukaemia otherwise it's all going to go tits-up. I fancy the lobster.'

Monty's turn of phrase reminded Oberon of the real reason for the invitation, he beckoned a waiter over 'Yes, well I wanted to forewarn you that I intend making a big change in the very near future...'

Newvale Chronicle sub editor, Ian Lloyd was studying Page Nine on his screen and trying to avoid an unfortunate juxtaposition of picture and headline. On the left of the page he had a golden wedding picture in which Arthur and Muriel Skinner of Trinity Crescent, Cedar Hill posed with their pet West Highland Terrier and directly opposite was a story headlined 'Couple Plead Guilty to Animal Cruelty.' Ian knew if he didn't make it abundantly obvious that the two weren't connected there were plenty of self-righteous vigilantes out there who would give the old kippers a golden wedding to remember.

Ian remembered an occasion a few years back when Monty ran a serious background piece on post natal depression and, in his rush to get off stone on deadline day, had flagged the story on the front page right next to an ad for a competition. The paper had hit the streets and the shit had hit the fan almost immediately as furious readers jammed the Chronicle switchboard. Monty had used a white-on-black head for both pieces which now appeared to read, 'COULD YOU BATTER YOUR BABY? A BRAND NEW CAR MUST BE WON!'

Monty had called an hour ago, saying he was 'stuck in traffic'; meaning as Ian knew and Monty knew he knew, that he was in no hurry to return to the office as someone else was paying for lunch. Ian was finally satisfied that the page passed muster and so filed it away. He thought about having an early getaway, as it was unlikely Monty would be back before...

The office door suddenly burst open and a florid Monty barrelled in.

'What's our front lead?'

'Probably Gordon McIver's promise to boost council spending on regeneration.' Ian replied.

'Fuck that now - I've got a big one, Oliphant is crossing the floor!'

'He's doing what?'

'He's crossing the floor - changing parties!'

'Oberon? Are you sure?'

Monty sat at his desk and started burrowing into the Matterhorn of paper and folders that served as his filing system, he pulled out a dog-eared sheaf of paper and studied it

'He's just told me he's about to undergo a major change, what else could it be? I tried all ways to get more out of the bugger but he wasn't budging.'

'I just can't believe he'd join a party he's spent all his political life fighting against; he's opposed to everything they stand for!' Ian got up and paced as his boss drummed the desk with his fingers, a sure sign he was entering headline mode.

'Here we go' Monty announced writing in the air with his hands as he spoke, 'Headline - BUCK OFF! - Strap line - Grass is greener on the other side for Newvale's flop-eared Fairy King! We'll get Tom the Cartoon Man to do a drawing of a rabbit with Oliphant's face carrying a suitcase or something.'

'Did he speak to you in confidence?' Ian asked.

Monty looked at his assistant as if he had suddenly grown a second head; 'In confidence? Nobody EVER tells a journalist anything in confidence. If they tell you something it's because they want you to tell everyone else. Oliphant's no fool, he knows damn well anything he tells me is going to be all over Newvale before he can blink.'

'Yes...' Ian hesitated but felt it his duty to point out an inescapable fact that Monty seemed to have overlooked, '... but he hasn't exactly told you anything, has he?'

'Aha! Exactly!' Monty looked and sounded triumphant, 'He knows I'm no fool either. He can't actually tell me outright what he's going to do because he has to tell his party grandees first - but he obviously can't stand the buggers which is why he's given me the ammunition to have a pop at them on his behalf. He's shot himself in the foot though - he's going to get a right whipping at the next election.'

Colin was hoping he wouldn't have to wait that long. He had lengthened his camera strap until the instrument hung almost in front of his groin and, with his Long Tom lens attached it looked for all the world like some space-age dildo. Mrs Beech had raised an eyebrow at the sight on answering the door for their prearranged meeting; the symbolism wasn't lost on her but she was no professional photographer and maybe this was how they were carrying their cameras nowadays.

She offered Colin a drink and they sat. She had given some thought to how she would like to be shot; maybe a few formal poses in businesslike attire and a few in a softer focus, relaxed, smiling, approachable, ideal for newsletters aimed at parents of her younger pupils.

Colin had also given some thought to the shoot; in fact he had thought of little else all day! His preferred poses were leaning more towards the disciplinary aspects of a headmistress's professional life. He had thought about turning up for the shoot dressed as a schoolboy but had decided not to put all his cards on the table just yet - however, he had brought along several props in the event of things going according to plan.

'So, are you busy?' Mrs Beech broke the ice.

'I haven't got a lot on at the moment,' replied Colin who had optimistically left his vest and underpants off for ease of disrobement.

'OK,' Mrs Beech smiled warmly, 'I thought perhaps we could do something on the couch?'

Colin gripped his Long Tom excitedly, his mouth went dry and the butterflies in his stomach turned into seagulls.

'So, when are they actually going to...?' The investment and portfolio manager of Newvale's biggest bank was curious about Oberon's forthcoming procedure.

'Friday morning,' Oberon brushed back his huge furry ears and nibbled delicately on a carrot stick.

'Are you nervous?' The banker was too fat to be a convincing stoat. Oberon doubted he would survive long in the wild being unable to follow his prey into narrow nests and burrows but what he lacked in tubularity he more than compensated for with enthusiasm and an excellent costume that he'd had professionally run up by a friend who worked for a major theatre.

'Not really nervous, no - I'm actually rather looking forward to it - well, at least looking forward to it being behind me.'

'Come on you two, we'll be late for Bessie Badger's tea and cakes!' A breathless magistrate/squirrel chivvied Oberon and the banker into the kitchen ...

Colin was hunched over the steering wheel as he drove; Mrs Beech's knee had found its target with painful accuracy. His eyes were streaming and he had a tissue plugging up each nostril to stop him from bleeding on his shirt, 'Fuckin' lebbian - I'be a bloody good bind to sue her!' he muttered.

Colin's ratio of success with women was low. It was so low that a change of tactics to doing and saying nothing at all would likely increase it. But even though it was very low, the fact that it wasn't *zero* told Colin that his approach was basically sound but that ninety per cent of women instinctively recognised a lover of such power and magnitude that they felt unworthy and this, for some reason, manifested itself in hostility. The other ten per cent were just dykes!

He regretted the turn of events at Mrs Beech's house but he was sure that when she had calmed down she would recognise the misunderstanding and blame herself for her inability to keep her passions under proper control. As he recalled, he had been taking a few preliminary snaps of her as she had disported herself on the couch and she had said; 'You seem to be shaking, have you got a stand?' Without the restraining effect of underpants his trouser tent must have been all too apparent. He had been delighted by her playfulness and had joined in the banter, 'I think you know the answer to that,' he had said huskily, and she had replied, 'Well, I suggest you get it out then...'

But the very appendage that had brought Colin a lifetime of, mostly self-induced, pleasure had always appeared to be an extraneous waste of flesh and blood to Oberon. He lay on his back watching the white lights of the hospital corridor pass overhead as a porter trollied him to the theatre. He felt eerily calm as if all this were happening to someone else, which, in a sense, it was. He would certainly not be the same person when he woke up.

He thought, strangely enough, of his parents; of all the incidents of his childhood, the one that always came most readily to mind was the occasion of his mother and father having to be called to the school where he boarded to be told, while he sat dumb and shamed next to them, that matron had caught him in her quarters trying on her underwear. His mother's expression of disbelief and his father's look of utter contempt would stay with him forever.

They were both gone now, his father into a wholesome and manly afterlife where the angels smelled of carbolic soap and pipe tobacco and his mother into the living death of advanced dementia. There was only Oberon, and in a few hours he would be gone too.

'The thing is Mrs Beech, as he wasn't on Chronicle business I really don't see...' Monty held the phone away from his ear and Ian could clearly hear the outraged headmistress in full flow on the other end of the line. Monty tried again to placate her 'Yes... yes... I see, no, alright YOU saw, but the thing is...' Once again he was forced to hold the phone at a distance to mute the rant. Monty, not the most patient or diplomatic of men at the best of times was rapidly tiring of the one-sided conversation. Did the silly bitch have any idea who she was talking to?

'Listen... LISTEN!' The voice on the other end trailed off. 'I'm his boss not his bloody father - a man showed you his cock, you kneed him in the balls and punched him in the nose and he left. Christ almighty, it can't be the first fucking cock you've seen!'

There were a few seconds of heavily charged silence before both men heard Mrs Beech scream - 'You ought to be bloody well hung!'

Monty smiled coldly; 'I AM bloody well hung, if you like I'll come over and show you what a real cock looks like!'

Marlon Sumner knew exactly what a cock looked like. He had worked as a hospital theatre assistant for twenty years and there was little about human anatomy he didn't know, which made him a boon on quiz night in the pub and a bloody nuisance on any other occasion. With a deftness that would have earned a nod of acknowledgement from any professional pickpocket, Marlon removed the bloody organ from the clinical waste bag and slipped it into a jar and into his pocket. He left the theatre and headed for the locker room.

The first thing Titania Oliphant saw when she opened her eyes was a huge bunch of flowers from Polly; then she saw Polly. Still groggy, she managed a weak smile.

'How are you feeling?' Polly asked.

'Tired, really really tired.'

Was it Titania's imagination or did her voice sound different? Polly seemingly hadn't noticed.

'Get some rest, I'll come and see you tomorrow,' Polly smiled again and departed.

Titania closed her eyes, she wanted to check how things... felt, but everything was heavily bandaged. Ah well, it was done, it was really done and her new life started here. She had already assumed that even if she decided to stand she would lose her seat at the next election. It wasn't that Newvale was a particularly intolerant place but the herd tended to be frightened by the unknown and she was not at all convinced she wanted to go through the arduous process of introducing the Queen of the Fairies to the electorate and striving to convince them that she still had the heart and stomach of a king. No, she'd go for a consultancy somewhere out of the public eye and maybe change Bunty Bunny's costume from grey to faun.

Colin could easily have passed himself off as one of the Woodland Folk at present with his two raccoon-like eyes. He sat in the corner of a bar far from Newvale watching the door over the top of his newspaper. When a man entered wearing a red scarf, Colin rolled up his paper and waved it discreetly until he had caught the man's attention.

'Have you got it?' Colin asked

'I have - my goodness, have you been in an accident?'

'Bit of a run-in with a lesbian headmistress, but never mind that, let's have a look at it.'

The man looked around before surreptitiously taking a small glass jar from his pocket and passing it under the table to Colin. Colin peered through the liquid within.

'Euggh! That's horrible. Are you sure....'

'A hundred per cent, my brother took it out of the bag himself; he saw it actually coming off as it were. Now then, have you got something for me?'

Colin took an envelope out of his coat pocket and passed it to the man who opened it and checked inside.

'Are they all here?'

'Every last one, all the negatives and a contact sheet; now nobody will ever know about your... regular rural rendezvous.'

The man tucked the envelope into his jacket pocket. They chatted for a few moments more about the website of mutual interest on which they had first found each other before the man said his goodbyes, rose and left. Colin took a sip of his drink and smiled, 'Thank you vicar,' he called quietly after him.

Polly was struggling to hold her temper as she re-read the Chronicle's lead story in Monty's office.

'And you maintain that this is what Oberon told you?'

Monty Fox smiled slyly. 'I ask questions dear, I don't answer them - now, you tell me, is there anything in there that you want to dispute?'

'Well let's see..' Polly had sworn to herself she was going to keep calm and maintain an air of professionalism but her limits were being sorely tested, 'I'd say just about ever word, it's rubbish - all of it,' she studied the editor seeking a reaction but the sardonic grin was still in place. She continued, 'Do you seriously imagine Oberon would ever go over to the other side of the House? He's a man of conviction!'

'He's a man of two convictions actually - driving whilst disqualified, November 23rd 1986 and obstructing a police officer, May 17th 2007,' Monty offered.

'In the first instance,' retorted Polly, 'He was just out of university, a young man who made a mistake in the exuberance of youth and in the second case he simply asked that bloody annoying Constable Boniface to leave his meeting unless he was prepared to stop laughing ever time someone said Oliphant!'

Monty leaned back in his chair and regarded Polly. He quite liked her, she reminded him of his wife when she was younger. She was earnest and well meaning and genuinely cared about Oliphant. He wished he had someone of the same calibre watching his back. 'So, what would you like me to do?' he asked her.

'I'd like you to print a retraction, and if you do I might in return offer you an exclusive on the real change that your MP has made.'

Monty smiled warmly, 'I like Oberon as you know, the last thing I would want is to make his life any harder than necessary,' He appeared to be mulling something over, 'I'll tell you what, we'll run an exclusive in the next edition on these... real changes and when Oberon returns from his... urgent business, we'll all get together and this time lunch will be on me, how's that my darling?' His smile seemed genuinely warm and Polly felt her anger subsiding.

'It's a great story, you'll be impressed,' she told him.

'I'm sure I will.'

They rose and he escorted her from the office. Returning he slid open his bottom desk drawer and took out the jar that sat there. Lifting it up to the light he wrinkled his nose at the contents.

'Euggh!' He said.

Prosthetics, oestrogen, cosmetics and the ministrations of a skilled beautician had transformed Titania dramatically. She got out of the car in the car park of Newvale Town Hall and was challenged by the security guard. She laughed out loud while Polly took the confused man to one side and explained the situation. He was still scratching his head as the pair entered.

In the committee room, Gordon McIver, mayor of Newvale and the Chronicle's editor waited in anticipation. 'So, come on, Monty, what's the big deal? Why has he asked us to be here?'

Monty poured himself another scotch from the mayor's secret stash and winked knowingly.

'All will be revealed Gordon, don't you worry.'

When Polly Carringdon entered the room with another female Monty initially assumed the woman was some town hall gopher but as they approached the lady had smiled an unmistakeable smile and the prior knowledge of Oberon's big secret did nothing to blunt the shock of seeing Titania in all her glory for the first time. Monty had expected a less than convincing transvestite in an ill-fitting wig teetering on inappropriate heels but Titania actually looked far more like a woman than Oberon had ever looked like a man. The editor had intended to say something cuttingly witty but all he could manage was, 'Well bugger me!'

Gordon McIver, without the cushion of forewarning looked as if he was about to pass out. '...Oberon?'

'It's Titania now Gordon,' she held out a hand, Gordon took it and shook it automatically, noticing as he did the nail varnish. He was at a complete loss for words but decided to say some anyway. 'Err, will you be doing this now instead of the rabbit thing or will you be keeping that up....?'

Polly raised her eyes skywards while Monty stifled a giggle. The editor held out a hand, which Titania took and Monty shook it warmly.

'Fair play to you old bo… girl, fair play!'

In an event so scarce as to be almost unprecedented, Monty actually felt genuine admiration for someone's courage and fortitude. He began to understand the lifetime of emotional pain Oberon must have endured. To undertake this metamorphosis would have been a monumental upheaval even for someone living far from the glare of fame, but to go through all of this with the added burden of a career that relied totally on public acceptability took an inner strength he doubted he'd be able to find in himself! He shook Titania's hand again and, leaning forward, kissed her on the cheek.

'I admire your balls,' he said, she laughed.

It had better be a peace offering and some sort of apology thought Mrs Beech as she opened the small package with the Chronicle's address label on it.

'Hope this will stimulate some interest in your raffle!' The note read.

The parcel contained a small jar; she examined the contents.

'Euggh! She said.

*   *   *   *   *   *

CHAPTER TWELVE

SAND TO THE ARABS

'EVERYONE lives by selling something!' - Robert Louis Stevenson.
It was written below a cartoon of a sales representative trying to sell a lifebelt to a drowning man and today Dick Fuller knew how he felt. The poster adorned his office wall along with several other 'inspirational' quotes that Dick had displayed in the hope of motivating his sales force to go the extra mile.

'If there is no wind, you can always row!' said another one. It was the second time he had put that one up, the first one had to be taken down after someone had added, *'Not if you're up shit-creek without a paddle!'*

Outwardly, Dick's lifestyle belied the struggle it was becoming to maintain the façade. At 45, he had the trappings of moderate success, a nice house and car, a wife, three children on the cusp of adulthood and a wristwatch that looked really expensive from across the bar of the golf club.

The last year had not been easy for Newvale Conservatories, people were tightening their belts and Dick was finding it harder and harder to radiate the positive mental attitude that all good salesmen need. An incentive scheme offering a weekend in a health spa for the first representative to hit their monthly target had gone unclaimed and so Dick had given the voucher to his wife, Karen who had gone away on the Friday evening and returned Sunday morning with a broken ankle and food poisoning.

There was just one job on the books for the current week; a house in Cedar Hill was having a conservatory and two new windows; the crew and materials had been dispatched and the factory floor on the other side of Dick's office window was eerily quiet. In the office, Dick was putting the finishing touches to an advertisement for the Chronicle. He couldn't decide between, 'Let The Outside In With a Newvale Conservatory' or 'A Newvale Conservatory - Where Home and Garden Meet.' Karen had suggested something along the lines of, 'Our Conservatories Are Definitely For Sale' or 'Please Buy a Conservatory, Or a Window, or Even a Letterbox - We Beg You!' But that was Karen; when the going got tough, she got sarcastic.

Dick looked across the office to where his internal salesman, Larry Hodge presented a rear view as he sat talking on the phone to a prospective customer. Dick never tired of looking at the rear view of Larry and wondering how such an immense bulk could ever walk upright. Huge folds of superfluous fat hung down both sides of the chair seat like the jowls of a bloodhound. The legs of the chair bent under the burden and the vast steppe of the man's stomach forced him to sit at arm's length from his desk.

At least once a month the office got a visit from the police following up a complaint from some traumatised housewife owing to Larry's habit of beginning every call with ten seconds of heavy wheezing. He was awaiting a date for a gastric band operation in a last ditch attempt to lose weight. They had tried stapling his jaws but it had made him speak with a growl and everything he said had sounded like a threat, which inevitably impacted on his sales figures. Besides, it didn't make him eat less, it just took him longer and he began drinking huge amounts of coffee to ward off sleep so he could eat well into the night and maintain his terrifying calorie intake. Only recently, Dick had taken a surreptitious look in Larry's lunchbox and discovered it contained four pork pies, a large chocolate bar, a cold lamb chop and, bizarrely, a low-fat yoghurt. But Larry could, respiration permitting, actually sell. In the last six months the few conservatories and windows the company had sold had been down to him.

Dick's field sales team consisted of just one long-term employee and two others who never seemed to last long; tiring of the interminable evenings of tramping the streets of Newvale knocking on doors, waiting for them to open, speaking a sentence and a half and watching the same doors slam again. Dick acknowledged it was difficult to maintain a positive outlook in the face of almost constant rejection but his role in the organisation, apart from keeping steady hand on the tiller, was motivation and training. Dick had inherited Fuller Construction when his father, Tom had retired and had decided to specialise in conservatories and windows, much against the old man's advice, and he was determined to prove it was a good move.

He had also inherited a good and loyal workforce and had treated them with the same respect and fairness they had enjoyed under his father. He put up with their practical jokes and horse play as long as the work got done and, despite the hard year, he had kept all of his small team in full time employment. He had lost count of the number of times he had turned up for work and discovered that someone had changed the 'F' to a 'P' where it said 'Dick Fuller' on his office door. He thought of giving up and letting the alteration stay but that would just spoil the fun for the next apprentice to believe he was the first to think of it.

Dick stared at the phone on his desk, willing it to ring. The job up at Cedar Hill would take the rest of the week and half of next but after that there was nothing, the firm's reserves were dwindling and he really needed a good run of work to get things back on an even keel. Earlier that morning he had sent his sales reps out on to the streets of Newvale with motivation ringing in their ears. That was the key to the whole organisation, the God-given ability to sell! Sometimes Dick despaired of ever finding someone who knew the magic formula, the elusive alchemy that led people from the darkness of doubt and resistance into the epiphany that their lives had been a mere sham without the enlightening presence of a new conservatory.

Mrs Lynn Mortiboys was a regular churchgoer and, as such, had always had a pretty good idea of what Hell looked like, now she also knew what it smelled like. She had just visited her downstairs toilet five minutes after one of the conservatory fitters. Operating on early morning autopilot she opened the door and went in. She managed only one breath before staggering out, eyes streaming, into the rear garden where she leaned against a wall for support and waited for the world to swim back into focus.

No one who knew Benny 'Chunk' Scanlon would have braved the smallest room so soon after his visit. It was advisable to wait at least an hour before entering - and then only after the ministrations of a powerful cleaning agent, two cans of air freshener and, where at all possible, an exorcist. But Mrs Mortiboys had never met Chunk or his workmates before and now she was beginning to doubt her Christian capacity for forgiveness.

The gang of four workmen had turned up at eight-thirty sharp to begin installing her new conservatory. In the three hours since then she had been assailed with a radio station that broadcast a continuous stream of cacophony mostly comprising, to her refined ears, lots of drums and shouting and men making what she believed to be sex noises. But that sound was as nothing compared to half dozen or more thunderous farts that the perpetrator seemed compelled to follow with some witticism designed to not only draw attention to the flatulence but to invite praise for it.

This was all confirmation to Mrs Mortiboys that the end days were here and that soon the righteous would be lifted up into paradise, leaving behind the farting, smelly beasts of the field to repent belatedly. In the meantime, however, she would enjoy her new conservatory along with Joshua the cat and the ashes of Mr Stanley Mortiboys who had never farted and who would have died peacefully in his sleep if Mrs Mortiboys hadn't woken him up to complain about the choking noises.

'Nice view from here,' Chunk observed. He and his workmates were eating their lunch in the garden of Mrs Mortiboys house. 'You can see all the way down to St Peters Church, you'd see the town centre if it wasn't for those trees!'

Joshua the cat approached, his tail in the air and his whiskers twitching at the scent of food. Noel 'Woody' Woodward took a bit of filling out of his sandwich and offered it to the creature. The cat accepted it gingerly, chewing on it and, with an expression of extreme distaste, managing to wrestle it down.

'He didn't look as if he enjoyed that,' Chunk observed, 'What was it?'

'Chicken,' Woody replied, 'I think it was the curry sauce that put him off, but he swallowed it, fair play.'

'I had a dog once, lived entirely on shoes,' Ed Ogiazu studied a pasty with a degree of suspicion.

'Shoes?' Chunk was intrigued.

'We used to get them for him from the charity shop, mens' brogues were his favourites but he didn't mind a boot as long as we washed the polish off first. It's only like beef after all as far as they're concerned.'

'When Sian was pregnant the time before last she used to eat sausages with jam on them offered Gaz Price.'

'Where's the evolutionary benefit in that?' Chunk pondered aloud.

'I suppose when times were hard and there was famines and that, it paid to be able to eat anything,' suggested Woody.

'Yeah, but she's never known a bloody famine,' Gaz shuddered as he envisaged the reaction of his rugby-playing wife on being told there was nothing for dinner.

'I reckon it's a lack of minerals or something; if women don't get folic acid and chocolate they go mad - look at that one in the Chronicle, thought she'd been abducted by aliens!'

Woody's outburst prompted Chunk to respond, 'Maybe she really was abducted by aliens?'

Woody scoffed, Ed seemed more responsive, 'Do you believe in all that then?'

'All I'm saying...' Chunk lowered his voice as if afraid galactic ears were wagging, 'is that I've experienced things I can't explain and I'm not about to say something don't exist just because I haven't seen it.'

'There must be something in it, she had her picture in the Chronicle and all the one side of her head was bald,' said Ed.

'Yeah? That's Alpaca that is, my sister had it!' Gaz announced.

'Alpaca?' Chunk was curious.

'Yeah, makes you hair fall out.'

'That's a fucking llama!' Chunk shook his head and studied Gaz in wonder.

'Uh?' Gaz looked puzzled.

'An Alpaca is a type of llama!'

'It's caused by stress', Gaz insisted

'I can believe that, 'Woody offered, 'We took the kids up to the animal sanctuary and they've got a llama, I gave it a peppermint and it spat on me - nasty bastards they are, enough to stress anyone.'

'Yeah - but it didn't make your hair fall out, did it?' Chunk challenged, 'Gaz is thinking of Appalachian…. Alpacino.. or something, but that's not what the woman in the Chronicle had I'm telling you. It wouldn't just bald off half your head, would it? No mate, women eat weird things because it's in the genes, I've been reading about it. Genes explain a lot of things, the reason we like going to parks for instance is because the big expanses of grassland dotted with trees reminds us of Africa. It's the type of environment we evolved it.'

'My ancestors left Africa a lot later than yours and I'd rather go ice skating - explain that!' Ed offered the last of his pasty to Joshua the Cat who, with the taste of curry fresh in his memory, sniffed it thoroughly first before taking it and carrying it off under a nearby bush.

'I can't, you've probably got a bit of Viking in there somewhere mate.' Chunk rose to his feet, dusted the crumbs off his overalls and headed reluctantly back to the job. The rest followed.

The day Karen MacLennan became Karen Fuller she decided to give up singing with the family cabaret showband to concentrate on helping Dick with the business, but the way things were going she was sorely tempted to dig out the glittery dress and give her father a call.

The showband was still playing the local pubs and clubs on a more or less regular basis despite - or perhaps because of - a reputation for unpredictability thanks to Old Man MacLennan's propensity to get a bit 'emotional' as the evening wore on. He had never been able to reach the end of 'The Tartan Shawl My Dear Old Mother Wore' and on particularly fraught occasions the tears would be streaming down his cheeks as soon as son, Terence, played the opening chord. He had once tried to perform 'Old Shep' but had cried so much he needed treatment for dehydration.

The audiences, however, lapped it up. Fans would buy drinks for the Old Man prior to his performance in the hope he would 'Hit the ground crying' and the booze usually worked its maudlin magic. On one memorable night in Newvale Ex Services Club he had staggered on to the stage in a flood of tears because a duffle coat in the cloakroom had reminded him of a beige mongrel he had owned as a boy. The subsequent show had opened with the most unconvincing rendition of 'Happiness' ever and just fifteen minutes in he had given up and grandson, Sean, had taken over the vocals despite a falsetto voice and an inability to pronounce the letters 'R' or 'S'.

Karen didn't miss the late nights and she seriously doubted she could still hit the high notes, but there was no getting away from the fact that Newvale Conservatories could do with a boost in the order book department. It's a pity, thought Karen, that Craig's seemingly boundless energy couldn't be diverted from music promotion to conservatories; he would make a good salesman with his dazzling smile and easy eloquence, but her son had his own Yellow Brick Road to follow.

She picked up her handbag and checked the time. She was meeting Dick for lunch at a pub just out of town. Dick had recently let his golf club membership lapse, he rarely played and the cost had been hard to justify. She had hated the crowd there anyway; the men talked incessantly about property prices and the women about expensive clothes and accessories. She smiled as she recalled how she had once brought such a pointless and superficial conversation to a dead stop by announcing she had bought an ivory dildo with detachable pearl testicles in Thailand. One of the women - whose name she had never committed to memory but who she had always mentally referred to as 'Agent Orange' due to her fake tan - had almost choked on her marguerita. Taking pity on them, Karen had decided to expose the joke by telling them the objects were made in a village called Toikok Phuc. None of them got it and two of the group had discreetly approached her later asking if they did mail order.

Despite the current pinch, Karen had rarely regretted marrying Dick. He was a kind and unassuming man whose only crime was to have an ambition that outstripped his ability to achieve it - but those things were called dreams and Karen had always believed everyone had a right to them. No one who met him would have guessed he was the current head of Newvale's 'First Family', indeed, he had never shown a lot of interest in genealogy and it had been left to son, Craig to unearth the unbroken line back to the birth of the town when Thomas Fuller and his young wife had moved to the area and build a sawmill on the edge of the tiny village of Meadowvale. Dick tried really hard to provide for them but - and he was the only one who didn't know it - he was not a born salesman! Karen had sometimes cringed to hear him on the phone telling prospective customers about the benefits of his products.

'Have you ever considered the advantages of a Newvale Conservatory?... No? Well there's never been a better time to let the outside in and....hello?......hello?.......Fuck you then! Oh, sorry, I thought you'd hung up... I don't suppose you'd....... hello?'

She had urged him to join the Newvale 200 committee, not only because he was a Fuller, but because it presented the opportunity to ally the name of Newvale Conservatories with an image of longevity, continuity and dependability. However, the majority of the locals did not share their centuries old attachment to the Town and the name Fuller meant little to anyone outside the Local History Society.

The name Fuller, however, certainly meant something to Mrs Lynn Mortiboys and she was using it to subtly remind the team of craftsmen on her property that they should behave in a manner in keeping with the tradition they represented.

'I don't think I can tolerate any more of that frightful noise from the radio gentlemen. I'm all for music while you work, but that terrible racket is beyond the pale. I'm sure Mr Fuller would agree.'

'Sorry Missus, we'll turn it down a bit,' Chunk was conciliatory.

'Yes, well…. very well then - only I've known Tom Fuller all of his life, charming man, although of course, it's his son running things now. I used to see quite a bit of Dick when I was younger, over at the golf club.'

'So er…' Chunk knew he shouldn't but he couldn't help himself, 'You don't see a lot of Dick nowadays?' Woody and Ed struggled to keep straight faces; Gaz failed and had to turn his back.

'Not as much as I would like, not since Stanley died, he used to come at least once a month but it's been ages now.'

Woody was silently shaking and Ed was biting his lip painfully, Chunk surged on, 'Yes, well you'll probably see Dick quite soon - big erection like this, he's sure to come… to admire it.' Mrs Mortiboys paused and looked thoughtful. For a moment Chunk feared he'd gone too far but he realised he was still in the clear when she took up the thread, 'Yes, well I hope he will, it will be nice to see Dick again; they shoot up, don't they? They seem to grow before your very eyes….'

Dick was animated; he was already on his third gin and tonic in the pub when Karen arrived. He was not by nature a lunchtime drinker but he had just had a really good idea and so he was going to celebrate - and Karen could drive home! When she arrived she found him hopping from one foot to the other, eager to tell her his great plan. She managed to calm him enough to order her a drink and retire to a table with the menus but she could see he was simply bursting to let it out so she gave him the green light.

'It's great!' he began, 'Newvale 200 OK? So what we do is launch a new range of products, the '200 Range', fantastic conservatories to celebrate two hundred years of Newvale combining traditional craftsmanship handed down for generations with space-age twenty-first century technology - and the first two hundred who order get a big discount!'

Karen was impressed, it wasn't that bad an idea and Dick, used to being shot down in flames, was pleasantly surprised to see his wife nodding thoughtfully with just a ghost of a smile playing across her face. 'Let's send the canvassers out in nineteenth century dress, it will buy them a bit longer on the doorsteps to get their message across.' She offered.

'Brilliant!' Dick was already mentally phoning the Chronicle to try and convince Monty Fox that it was worth a news story. Maybe he and Karen should dress up as... who were they?.... Thomas and Jane Fuller, the founders of Newvale. He could phone Newvale Amateur Dramatic Society and ask about some suitable clothes and stick-on whiskers!

Harry Scanlon considered himself far too grown up at eight to listen to bedtime stories but sisters Bridget and Dawn aged six and four respectively looked forward to Daddy's tales. Chunk was in the habit of writing about a page and a half before he got tired of the discipline of committing things to paper and from there on he tended to ad lib. Harry sat on the edge of the bed feigning disinterest as the tale unfolded.

'Gabby really wished he hadn't eaten all the green beans from Farmer Jack's garden as he now had a sore tummy. He decided to go and visit Jenny Rabbit to get some medicine. He knocked on her door but there was no reply, going around the side of her house he saw her in the conservatory, he called out but she couldn't hear him, can any of you tell me why?'

Both of the girls raised their hands gleefully. Chunk nodded to young Dawn, 'Because of the gap between the panes of glass?'

'That's right, well done darling.'

Harry scoffed, 'Yeah, but not just any gap, it's got to be wide enough hasn't it Dad?'

'Well, yes I suppose….'

'…and there's got to be a good seal..' offered Bridget.

Chunk smiled and stood.

'That'll do for tonight,' he smiled and crossed the landing to his own room.

He picked up a stovepipe hat off the bed and tried it on, studying himself in the wardrobe mirror. It was part of the Newvale 200 costume that he'd agreed to wear to help promote Dick's new product range and it gave him a strange feeling. Chunk was a man who loved the comforts of modern living but, unlike his boss, he also felt an affinity with those long-gone pioneers who had left their mark on the town. He had been lucky enough to have a grandfather and a great-grandfather to tell him tales of his ancestors and he delighted in passing them on to his own children. He thought of all his long-gone ancestors, right back to his namesake, Benjamin who had fought at Trafalgar. It was something to be proud of and reminded him that his name was stamped indelibly on the history of this town. He listened to the sound of his children chattering from across the landing and made a mental note to incorporate a bit of family history into future Gabby the Goblin adventures.

'Four already today! Four!'

Larry Hodge's face, always florid, was like a rising sun as he passed on the news of his success. He had made four sales in one morning and the good news didn't end there.

'The canvassing team have got six leads for this afternoon and evening!' Dick was beaming. The 200 Range was succeeding beyond his wildest dreams, Karen had been on the phone to the materials suppliers all morning continually increasing the order to keep pace with sales. Dick would have to consider taking on more fitters and maybe setting up a second team.

He was taking out a double page advertisement in the Chronicle to further promote the 200 Range with photographs of Fullers down through the ages and in the same edition they were running a story about the fact that both the very first Newvale Fuller and the present one seemingly had a right-hand man called Ben Scanlon. Not only that, but his father had called to say how proud he was of the way Dick was taking the firm into its third century. He felt like celebrating and promised himself and Karen a bloody good holiday after the Newvale 200 celebrations were over.

'Where would you like to go?' he had asked her and been puzzled by the reply.

'Toikok Phuc' she had suggested.

*   *   *   *   *   *

<u>CHAPTER THIRTEEN</u>

DIZYGOTIC TWINS

ROBERT Bonnaire's surprise at being pulled over by the biggest policeman he had ever seen was almost immediately topped when the officer asked if he could take a photograph of the vintage Citroen's engine. It was only after popping the bonnet and waiting while the verbose constable explained he was trying to get it all in the viewfinder on his mobile phone that Monsieur Bonnaire realised the officer had addressed him throughout in fluent French.

'You are originally from Cameroun or Le Cote D'Ivoire perhaps?' Mr Bonnaire had politely enquired.

'Nigeria actually, but it's only next door,' The constable had boomed out a laugh that had startled Madame Bonnaire in the rear seat and caused the chauffeur to recall in disturbingly graphic detail a thoroughly unpleasant experience he'd once had in a changing room in Marseille.

'Parlez-vous Anglais?' The officer asked.

'Indeed,' responded Mr Bonnaire, eager to demonstrate that the policeman was not the only skilled linguist present although he got the feeling the officer had at least a smattering of any number of tongues.

'And may I ask,' the policeman enquired, 'what brings you to Newvale - holidays?'

'I am, Officer, the Mayor of Nouville, France and I am here at the invitation of your mayor, Monsieur Gordon Maceevere to see if our towns can become twins.'

Gordon McIver, Mayor of Newvale was beginning to regret using après soleil on his haemorrhoids. He had uncharacteristically run out of his usual stuff and had figured, on seeing the tube in the bathroom cabinet, that something designed to take the sting out of sunburn might perform a similar service in the place where the sun don't shine! Unfortunately, the application had, if anything exacerbated the problem and his mood had not been helped by an uncomfortable confrontation a few minutes earlier with wife Moira.

'Don't you dare,' she had shouted, bringing him to a halt halfway up the stairs as he had headed for the bathroom carrying a packet of frozen peas. Her father may had been a violent drunk, she reasoned, but at least it had been possible to sit down to dinner secure in the knowledge that as one ate one's greens they were entering the proximity of a human orifice for the first time.

Gordon couldn't see what the fuss was about, what did she think he was doing with them for God's sake? He never actually took them out of the packet. He had been dumbstruck on one occasion as they had sat enjoying their evening meal when Moira had paused, holding a corn on the cob, and then asked, as bold as brass, 'Are you sure you've never stuck this up your rectum?' As dinner time conversation openers go it was devastating. He couldn't imagine it ever being a line in a Hollywood love story.

Anyway, it was too late now to do any more about his affliction, he would have to endure the discomfort. His driver was due to take him to the Town Hall to receive his guests from France. He stood looking out of his front room window while Moira put the final touches to her make up in the hall mirror.

'Fucking idiot' he muttered.

'What was that?' Moira called out.

'Oh... nothing,' he replied. He had been thinking of Councillor Clint Moran whose idea this twinning thing was. With two hundred years of history under their belts, Councillor Moran had suggested it was time for the Town to be looking outward for new partners and new horizons. Gordon had spoken against it on the grounds of cost but had been outvoted. With the whiff of a junket to France it was surprising how many of the councillors had forgotten their natural xenophobia in the name of 'Trade and cultural exchange opportunities.' But with the exception of Clint none of them had been aware of the existence of Nouville a couple of months ago and Councillor Brenda

Small Town People

Worrall was still insisting they should have gone with her suggestion of twinning with an Aboriginal encampment she had come on the Nullabor Plain in Western Australia while on holiday. Councillor Doug Deveer had laughed and reminded the meeting of the time Brenda's husband had posed in their front garden wearing nothing but a penis horn to highlight the plight of some tribe in New Guinea whose river had been diverted or something.

'At least he was trying to draw attention to something important,' she had retorted in a voice quivering with emotion.

'All it drew attention to was the fact that he's got small bollocks!' Councillor Deveer had goaded, causing her to storm out of the meeting in floods of tears after which Gordon had been forced to call it a night.

'It is nothing at all like Nouville,' Josianne Bonnaire failed to keep the disdain out of her voice as she viewed the centre of town through the car window.

'Well it was never likely to be,' her husband responded, 'but people are people wherever you go, there are sure to be less superficial similarities when we meet them.'

Mme Bonnaire snorted; she was a Monteneau D'Orleans - or at least she had been until she had become a Bonnaire. She could still see her father's look of horror on hearing she intended to marry a professional footballer. He had relented on discovering what top footballers earned and had mentally begun prioritising repairs and renovations to the crumbling family chateau. The wedding had been an *evenement specataculaire* and anyone who was anyone had received an invite, the town had bloomed for the occasion and the Champagne corks had competed with the firework display to blaze a *salut* to the happy couple.

Three months later a crunching tackle by an opposition defender had ruined Robert's left leg and his career and now, twenty years on, football was a distant memory and Robert *'Le Fantome'* Bonnaire had become a successful businessman whose silky dribbling skills were remembered only by diehard fans.

Mayor McIver's heart sank as he entered the reception room of the Town Hall. 'Oh for fuck's sake, the silly bitch,' he muttered and got a dig in the ribs from Moira for his troubles. The subject of his consternation was Councillor Brenda Worrall who, for reasons only she knew, had decided to dress in nineteenth-century peasant rags. Her husband, Dominic, was dressed in shabby brown culottes and a battered tricorne and looked as if he was about to be dragged to the guillotine - a fate the Mayor would readily have authorised had he only had the power.

'I just thought it would be nice to wear our 'Les Miserables' outfits', Brenda explained in response to Gordon's one word question; 'To demonstrate our *concorde* and *esprit de revolution*. We went down ever so well in last year's production.'

Gordon tried and failed to keep the exasperation out of his voice, 'He's the mayor of Nouville, it's a 21st Century town with a manufacturing base primarily geared towards information technology and semiconductor refinement - or so I'm told - he's probably never even seen a fucking guillotine...ooof!' Moira's elbow dug home but Councillor Clint Moran took up the baton.

'I told them that, Gordon, but they wouldn't listen. I mean, how likely is it that when we go over there for the return visit they're all going to be dressed up as beefeaters or... or pirates or something?'

'The idea was to put them at their ease,' Dominic Worrall spoke as if addressing a retarded five-year-old.

'It's embarrassing and stupid - they'll think we're taking the piss,' Councillor Moran snapped.

'I have to agree,' Mayor McIver added, 'I think you should go and change, and quickly before they arrive and see you.'

As a tearful Councillor Brenda Worrall and her husband left by the rear doors, Mayor Robert Bonnaire and his wife entered at the front. The Town Hall of Nouville was a small building situated between a boulangerie and an opticians. It was a functional and unpretentious suite of offices. Newvale's town hall, however, had been built to impress at a time when the future had no limits; prosperity, both local and national, was increasing and great men were blazing empire-building trails into unknown worlds where unimaginable wealth awaited. Nowadays it was covered with scaffolding and pigeon shit and sat on the corner of Fuller Square like a tired old soldier with a story to tell of battles fought for causes that became less relevant every day.

Gordon McIver stepped forward, hand outstretched to welcome the visitors. He smiled his warmest council smile, 'Bienvenue a Newvale.' He had inadvertently pronounced it 'Noovale' and immediately hoped it didn't sound too much like Mr Bonnaire's hometown. Mayor Bonnaire took the hand and shook it warmly. 'It is a pleasure to be here, *je vous presente mon femme*, Josianne,' Mme Bonnaire smiled a cooler smile than her husband and tentatively extended a hand which Gordon shook, 'My wife, Moira.. and councillor Clint Moran...' more handshakes followed and Mayor McIver guided the party toward the refreshments prepared in his chamber.

A parking bay for VIP town hall visitors was currently occupied by a beautifully maintained gleaming white 1952 Citroen 15CV and also by a somewhat less well maintained 1968 Raoul Loupiac - professional chauffeur, amateur poet and would-be actor. A small crowd had formed to admire the lovely vehicle and Raoul was trying to lean nonchalantly on it with just the right balance of pride and disdain. At forty-two Raoul had still not given up on his dream of one day playing the leading man in a dark romance and he never passed up an opportunity to 'smoulder' in a Gallic way.

'That's a beauty mate, an absolute beauty,' a townsman peered in through the window of the car, 'What's it handle like?'

Raoul's English didn't extend beyond 'hello, goodbye, please, thank you and fuck off' and he suspected none of those would be immediately appropriate. He could tell by the man's expression and the inflection of the strange words that he was being asked a question and that it was clearly something to do with the Citroen but the detail was lost to him.

'*Parlez-vous Francais?*' the chauffeur asked more in hope than expectation.

The townsman frowned as he tried to exhume a francophonic skeletal remnant buried since schooldays, 'No... *Mon Oncle il a barbe rouge!*'

Raoul couldn't see why having an uncle with a red beard should preclude the man from speaking French, '*Oui? Well my aunt has got a black fanny!*' he responded in his native tongue and the local's puzzled look confirmed Raoul's suspicion that they shared no common linguistic ground.

'I'm sure we're going to discover we have a lot of common ground,' Mayor Bonnaire handed his Newvale counterpart another glass of red wine from the vineyards around Nouville while close by Moira McIver and Clint Moran took it in turns to confuse Mme Bonnaire, whose Latin was impeccable but who had attended a school which regarded anything '*Anglais*' as '*Americaine*' and anything '*Americaine*' as '*Grossier.*'

Moira looked across disapprovingly at her husband as he raised his glass. They were laughing and seemed to be hitting it off but she mentally set her alarm to watch for any signs of excess bonhomie. Councillor Moran was attempting to tell Mme Bonnaire that he was a professional painter; deliberately neglecting to make it clear he was more artisan than artist. Later Moira would join her husband to escort their guests on a tour of Newvale taking in prominent businesses and sights of interest followed by a full civic reception and a migraine.

'Of course,' Mayor Bonnaire explained, 'semiconductor refinement requires a whole support industry and there could be scope for Newvale companies to get involved - what do you think Gordon?'

'Sounds great.' Mayor McIver replied, he didn't know what a semiconductor was. As far as he was concerned something was either a conductor, like a copper rod, or not a conductor, like a stick. What the bloody hell was a semiconductor supposed to be? He didn't want to show his ignorance and cursed himself for his procrastination. He had gone online the previous evening with every intention of learning a little about Nouville in general and semiconductors in particular but he had become sidetracked by a website where people dressed up their dogs as historical figures and photographed the results. A dachshund, converted by its owner into a pretty impressive Julius Caesar, had particularly impressed him. Considerable effort had clearly been expended and the animal had stood, toga draped nonchalantly over one 'arm' and a laurel wreath on its head as if about to address the Senate. Gordon had laughed out loud but had stopped short of calling Moira to see it. She would not have approved. She always took a dim view of anything approaching animal exploitation. Her father had once drunkenly placed a live duckling on a record turntable to see if it enjoyed the ride. The unfortunate creature had promptly shit on 'What's New Pussycat' and Moira's father had retaliated by having its father for Sunday lunch.

Gordon admired Mayor Bonnaire's suit as they paused to study a painting of Alderman Richard Fuller who had walked in the Mayor's shoes a century before. It was a very nice suit, had a bit of sheen to it, Gordon thought, and it fitted perfectly. He supposed he looked like a sack of shit in comparison, Moira always said that no matter what he wore he managed to look as if he'd slept in it - under a hedge. Mayor Bonnaire was also trim and athletic, a fact that Moira would have filed away to be used later whenever Gordon reached for an extra roast potato or slice of cake. 'It seems as if fate deals a kinder hand to some', Gordon thought as he studied first his French counterpart and then Madame Bonnaire who was sexy, elegant and carried her years better, he thought, than Moira. He was immediately contrite on reflecting that

Mme Bonnaire's life had almost certainly not begun in the fear and poverty that had stalked his wife's childhood.

Moira McIver's childhood was a time of plenty, however, in comparison to that endured by some of the tribes of the Nullaboor Plain - a fact that the people of Newvale had been ignorant of for far too long! If you counted body paint as covering then Dominic Worrall was not actually naked. He and his wife Brenda had fled the town hall with the derision of Brenda's fellow councillors ringing in their ears and now, after spending a hour in front of the bathroom mirror and twenty minutes in the car they were pulling into a parking space in Fuller Square opposite the Town Hall. Dominic was going to do an 'Emu Dance' accompanied by Brenda on clap sticks to draw attention to the couples' own alternative 'twinning' campaign.

Earlier rain had ceased and there was enough blue in the sky to make a shirt when Dominic stepped from the car; he felt both the breeze on his skin and a moment's hesitation. Somewhere behind a dustsheet in the attic of his psyche lay the long neglected mirror of self-judgement once polished to pristine clarity by realist parents but dulled and finally covered over the years by Brenda's myriad causes and his desire for a quiet life. Her conscience was pricked more often than a rose-grower's thumbs but inevitably it was his prick that stood in the firing line - and here he was, yet again, the prick with no clothes on. Every instinct was telling him to get back in the car and stop being such a stupid bugger but Brenda nodded encouragingly to him and began tapping her clap sticks. He sighed and started his dance, crouching and scanning the busy square and growing crowd of amused onlookers for any signs of an emu. With luck he'd be in a warm cell within minutes.

Raoul Loupiac had flared his nostrils at a passing woman who had been intrigued enough to pause and smile in return and now her basic French had allowed them to strike up a rudimentary conversation.

'Camberley - Dawn Camberley, delighted to make your acquaintance…'
'Raoul Loupiac – actor, I am enchanted Madame.'
The chauffeur bowed and kissed Dawn's hand.
'Actually, it's mademoiselle,' Dawn blushed.
'Ah mademoiselle…' the nostrils flared even more furiously and the dark eyes twinkled with a predatory light….

The Emu Dance lasted a little over seven minutes. Constable Lillywhite had actually arrived after three minutes but had been intrigued by the performance and had allowed it to continue, much to the delight of the crowd and the despondency of the shivering 'Aboriginal'. It had only come to an end thanks to the arrival in the Square of the Mayoral touring party.

Madame Bonnaire had never seen a blonde Aboriginal before and, bereft of the benefit of local knowledge, was unaware of how to react to the performance. Was this a regular or acceptable thing in Newvale? She looked to her husband for guidance but he clearly shared her bemusement. Mayor McIver realised only too well what was going on and he glowered thunderously at the performing couple. His mind raced, how could he explain this? He would need to employ a degree of subtlety. Councillor Clint Moran, however, had never downloaded the subtlety or forethought add-ons to the basic programme of his personality and so tended to react unhindered by the need to contemplate repercussions.

'You fucking idiots!' He shouted, earning him a chorus of boos from the crowd and the unwelcome attention of Constable Lillywhite. Dominic paused in his dance and, disregarding the exhortations of Brenda to 'Ignore him and keep going' strode purposefully towards Councillor Moran who, recognising the look of someone who had been pushed beyond reason and was no longer capable of restraint, retreated behind the formidable wall of PC Lillywhite who pointedly drew his riot stick.

The sight of the constable in his path brought Dominic to a halt and, as if only then realising he was naked, he covered himself with his hands and walked crab-like to his car. Brenda, on seeing her husband's ignoble retreat, reacted by throwing her clap sticks in quick succession with all the force and precision of a natural martial arts warrior. The first one hit Councillor Moran on the nose bringing forth a stream of blood and swearing which neither Mayor Bonnaire or his wife had any difficulty in interpreting; a cheer from the crowd also told them this was a popular act. The second knocked off Constable Lillywhite's helmet and the reaction was quite different. A pregnant silence fell on the square; Gordon McIver looked on in fascinated horror as Dominic Worrall carefully picked up the helmet and handed it without comment to the officer.

Brenda's anger dissipated as the full realisation hit her. She had knocked off Constable Slim Lillywhite's helmet - in public! The officer's face spoke of internal turmoil at this unprecedented show of disrespect, he began to quiver and the crowd backed off to give breathing room for the inevitable eruption. Brenda Worrall raised her hands above her head as she had seen 'perps' do in American cop shows which prompted someone in the crowd to shout 'Assume the position Motherfucker!' There was a collective nervous giggle. A deep rumble emanated from somewhere inside Constable Lillywhite just before his roar broke over the onlookers.

'EVERYONE IS UNDER ARREST!'

In the silence that followed people looked at each other for clarification. A few tentative hands were raised to attract the attention of the still rumbling policeman.

'Errr,' a nervous man on the edge of the small crowd had got Lillywhite's attention and was eager to get rid of it again as soon as he could, 'When you say everyone - does that mean... like... everyone? Only my mother is in a nursing home in Cedar Hill - should I go and tell her she is under arrest?'

'Of course your mother isn't under arrest you fool - when I say everyone, I mean everyone here!' The Constable barked.

'Yes, but how far away can you be and still be here?' A man wearing a dickey bow joined in, 'I was on the other side of the square when all the activity was going on and I only came over here a few seconds ago to see what all the fuss was about - so does 'here' extend to 'over there' or not?'

The policeman studied him carefully. He recalled advice he had been given when still a fresh recruit out on his first patrol with a seasoned officer, 'Never arrest a man who is wearing a dickey bow' he had been warned, 'They know their rights inside out and they're probably friends with the chief constable.' Lillywhite took a deep breath, 'You see that litter bin on that side of the square... and the bus stop on the other side? Well draw an imaginary circle with those at the edge - now anything inside that circle is 'here' and anything outside is 'not here' OK?'

A few people on the edge of the crowd had begun to surreptitiously creep away while others, not initially involved had joined the gathering, making Lillywhite's arrest list a fluid and increasingly uncontainable entity. Gordon McIver decided it was time for a bit of leadership.

'Well done Constable, for dealing with everything so efficiently, now why don't you tell these people that the show's over and to be on their way!'

The officer, realising his initial edict was going to be embarrassingly unenforceable grasped at the offer of a dignified way out. 'Yes, well perhaps on this occasion - and in light of the fact that we have special guests present..' he gave a perfunctory nod in the direction of the now totally confused French couple, '...very well - THAT'S YOUR LOT - THERE IS NOTHING TO SEE HERE NOW, SO OFF YOU GO... GO ON!'

The majority of the crowd gratefully vacated the Square leaving only the Mayoral party and Dickey Bow Man who was still uncertain of whether he should go as, he argued, he was technically under arrest.

An off-duty nurse had stemmed Councillor Moran's nosebleed and Brenda Worrall had driven off in a squeal of tyres while Dominic hastily got dressed in the rear seat.

On Level Five of the multi-storey car park adjoining Fullers Mill Shopping Centre there was only one car - but it was a beauty. The Citroen 15CV's renowned suspension was being tested to its limits. Raoul Loupiac was offering up promises to a God he had not acknowledged since his schooldays that, if he was allowed to live through this, he would never flare his nostrils at a woman again. He was sure he had at least one cracked rib. His screams of *'Cela suffit! Mon Dieu! Suffit!'* had only served to spur the demoness on to ever more violent exertions. The chauffeur had prided himself on his encyclopaedic knowledge of *'Les Arts de Boudoir'* but was going to have to write several new chapters following the current liaison. The mad creature had dug her nails so far into his arse he was going to have to drive standing up on the return journey to Nouville.

Dawn Camberley had waited for quite a while to encounter a lover of such urgency and eagerness. His entreaties in French, groaned through clenched teeth, were all the confirmation needed that she had met a soul mate. Not since that long yearned for summer in Lanzarote when she had completely worn out a lounge trio had she encountered such dedication to pleasure seeking. She had written to the musicians for weeks without reply and had finally phoned, only to be told they had left the resort and gone their separate ways. Apparently the piano player was now in a monastery, the drummer had gone to work on a sheep ranch in Australia and the double bass player was in prison at his own insistence. But Dawn was determined Raoul was not going to slip from her grasp.

Raoul, for his part, would have found it easier to slip from the grasp of an Olympic wrestler. The woman's powerful leg muscles were making any kind of withdrawal impossible. He was attempting to operate the rear door handle with his foot, figuring if he could open it he could cry for help but his contortions only seemed to goad her on to ever more furious exertion.

'Of course, we have street theatre in Nouville but perhaps not so… radical as that which we have seen here.' Robert Bonnaire paused as his wife delivered a rapid stream of French and then continued, 'Oui… my wife asks if it would be possible to get out of the rain?' The request snapped Gordon McIver back to reality, he hadn't realised it had started to rain and he hastily waved over the mayoral limousine to escort the party back to the relatively sane surroundings of the Town Hall.

'You should have waited until we got home and washed the paint off before getting dressed.' Brenda Worrall admonished her husband who was still shivering from his prolonged exposure to the elements.

'Yeah?' Well fuck waiting, fuck riding around in the rick - and while we're at it fuck the aboriginals and their fucking emus, they can all fuck off!'

Brenda pulled over and stopped the car; she turned and looked back at her husband as if seeing him for the first time. 'Are… are you feeling all right?'

'Never fucking better,' he was using his shirt to wipe the last remnants of face-paint away.

'Have… have you any idea what you just said?' Brenda couldn't escape the feeling that Dominic had suddenly become inexplicably possessed; 'You care deeply about the plight of the Western Aboriginals, we agreed over dinner at the Merricks, remember?'

'Yeah? Well that was then - fuck 'em now, fuck 'em all - and those other bastards, who were they? The ones who cover themselves in mud, the Moleskin Titwanks or something…'

'You mean the Molay Tetwanga?'

'Yeah, them - fuck them as well, dirty cunts, if I ever meet one I'll kick him in the balls and tell him to have a bath!'

Brenda's bottom lip began to quiver, 'There are less than a hundred Molay Tetwanga left you know.'

'I can well believe it, would you want to shag one of them?'

'Look,' she grasped at straws to come up with the reason for Dominic's seemingly total failure of social conscience, '... the Queensland Shell People believe that if a man catches a chill in his private parts it can cause temporary insanity, perhaps you have...'

'Private parts? PRIVATE parts? I wouldn't call them fucking private, would you? Everyone in Newvale has seen them except for the frail and bedridden in the Retirement Home - and why should they be left out? Maybe I should go up and wave my cock at them as well?' Brenda turned and resumed the journey. It was clear Dominic was not himself, or anyone else she knew; she would have to make a detour past the surgery and hope their doctor could bring him to his senses.

Raoul would have given anything to be receiving the ministrations of a sympathetic doctor. He lay across the back seat of the Citroen gasping for what little oxygen remained in the vehicle. He recalled as a boy seeing a picture in a war book of a man who had been run over by a tank and now knew with a grim certainty how the unfortunate combatant's last minutes must had felt.

Dawn Camberley lay beside him panting and perspiring like a well-ridden thoroughbred, wet golden hair hung across her florid face and her breasts heaved like twin hillocks over a tectonic fault.

'Ohhhh Raoul *Mon Cherie*, such... such fire!'

'*You can say that again,*' he gasped. '*For the next week I will be able to use my prick as a fucking torch!*'

Fortunately her French did not extend to translating Raoul's summary of their joint experience and she levered herself up onto an elbow, wiped the condensation from a window and peered out.

Colin Gardiner, Newvale Chronicle photographer, had missed the Emu Dance while on his lunch break in the Red Lion and he knew his boss would have his guts for garters if he went back to the office without at least one circulation-boosting picture from the twinning visit. He had just missed the mayoral party in the Square as they had climbed into the limousine to return to the Town Hall where a boring dinner would follow with very little in the way of photo opportunities - and now it was pissing down with rain!

But sometimes, just ever so rarely, the gods smile on journalists; Colin had returned to his car meaning to lurk around outside the Town Hall and hope for the best when the several beers that constituted his lunch had made their presence felt on his bladder. The normally deserted upper deck of the car park was a closer option than the public conveniences back in the Square and so he had strolled up the ramp to relieve himself - and there it was.

Why was the Citroen up here? Had the chauffeur decided to take an unscheduled tour of Newvale on his own - or had it been stolen? It began to rock - and it rocked for a very long time indeed. Colin had spent enough time in rocking vehicles with steamed up windows to draw the inevitable conclusion. Here was his scoop, and Monty Fox was going to be over the moon.

Colin crept from concrete pillar to concrete pillar approaching the car ever closer, he could hear grunts now and he gleefully began concocting headlines to accompany his exposé. 'Le Wanc' - perhaps in red white and blue lettering.. or something along the lines of 'Chauffeur pulls off into on-coming traffic' or 'Un vite one off le wrist!' He reached the car shortly after the rocking stopped and raised his camera ready to strike. Then a hand wiped the window clear and a flushed face peered out.

Colin's face, in complete contrast, immediately turned a terrified white!

'But Raoul would not have moved without letting us know where he was going? Josianne Bonnaire could see that her husband shared her concern. The Citroen had been a wedding gift from her father.

'He has probably gone to get fuel,' the mayor of Nouville responded, immediately translating for Gordon McIver's benefit. Newvale's mayor did not share his confidence. There had been a spate of car thefts from the centre of town over the last few weeks and the embarrassment of having the French Mayoral limousine stolen would probably deal a fatal blow to Newvale's reputation on the continent. He was about to excuse himself and make a surreptitious call to the police when the gleaming vehicle rounded the corner into Fuller Square.

Mayor Bonnaire's initial conclusion that his chauffeur was drunk proved unfounded. The man's difficulty in standing unaided, dishevelled appearance, wild staring eyes, furiously flaring nostrils and torn trousers surely pointed to some sort of violent trauma, possibly an animal attack. Raoul had managed to get out of the car and now leaned on it for support. Gordon McIver feared he had been mugged and prayed that the culprit would be caught quickly so that justice could be seen to be done.

'Let's get him in the Town Hall and get a drink down him' Mayor McIver suggested, keen to get him off the street before the Chronicle's photographer made an appearance. Supporting him on both sides, the Mayors helped the staggering and gasping figure out of public view.

They needn't have worried, there was no way Chronicle photographer, Colin Gardiner was going to show his face in town again that day. He had never been a Francophile but at that moment he felt nothing but compassion for the poor chauffeur. His own back still gave a twinge on cold mornings and he still recalled in chilling clarity the relief that came from lowering overheated genitals into a champagne bucket of crushed ice.

Jésus, Mary et Josef' Raoul gasped, *'Mère Sainte de Dieu.'*
'What has happened Raoul? Tell us who did this to you?' Josianne Bonnaire took the chauffeur's hand in her own and patted it. The

silence of the Newvale Mayoral Parlour and the effects of a stiff whisky had begun to bring a little colour back to Raoul's cheeks and the panting had slowed enough to allow short bursts of speech but he had resisted all attempts to get him to sit down.

'*Un animal sauvage…. sauvage.*'

'He says he has been attacked by a wild animal - what could it have been in this vicinity?' Mayor Bonnaire quizzed his Newvale counterpart. Gordon McIver couldn't imagine what could have left the chauffeur in such condition. He was about to suggest the semi-mythical and highly disputed 'Goblin of Meadowvale Woods' when Raoul enlightened them further. Robert Bonnaire translated his chauffeur's account of his liaison with a 'Demoness of Sex' and all became clear.

Gordon McIver was nonplussed by his counterpart's reaction to the dalliance. If his own chauffeur had confessed to using the council limo for such an event the bugger would have received an official kick up the arse but the French dignitaries seemed to understand and even sympathise with their driver's agonies. Robert Bonnaire turned to his counterpart and shrugged, '*Un blessé dans la guerre d'amour* - a… casualty in the war of love.'

Even with decades of experience as a general practitioner, Dr Douglas McKinnon-Law at Cedar Hill Surgery could find nothing physically wrong with Dominic Worrall and, despite Brenda Worrall's pleas, was reluctant to refer him to a psychiatrist, explaining, 'Lots of people couldn't care less about primitive tribes, I'm not particularly excited by them myself.'

'Perhaps,' Brenda persisted, 'But to say you'd kick a Molay Tetwanga in the testicles is a bit …. well, isn't it?'

'Oh I don't know,' the doctor scratched his head, I once kicked a pygmy in the balls when I was with a medical mission, little bugger was trying to pinch the cotton wool, they probably make nests out of it or something. And this other chappie was stealing medicine from us and selling it so we held him down and rubbed Fiery Jack Horse Liniment all over his gentleman - the wee scunner did the best war dance any of us had ever seen.'

Brenda walked numbly to the car leaving Dominic and the doctor happily chatting about indigenous people they had abused. 'You think you know someone...' she said to herself.

Gordon and Moira McIver and Councillor Clint Moran were waving away the French limousine as it set off on the journey back to Nouville. In a change to the order of things from the outward journey, Robert Bonnaire was driving with his wife in the front passenger seat and with Raoul the chauffeur lying on his stomach across the back seat.

'Do you think it will do any good for the Town?' Gordon McIver asked Councillor Moran.

'Yeah, reckon so. We'll make sure local firms are on message, get them to pitch to the Nouville *Chambre de Commerce* and in six months we can all go over there for a fact finding visit and a good piss-up eh?'

Moira McIver's icy stare told him he would be fighting an uphill battle to get a party atmosphere going on the ferry.

Fortunately for Colin Gardener, a reader had submitted a few pretty good pictures of Dominic Worrall's Emu Dance and Monty Fox was going to use one of them as a front-page panel under the headline *'Quelle Surprise'* and a sub head, 'Coq-up Shock for Crocked Soccer Frog!' There would be little mention of any commercial ramifications, people didn't give a damn about twinning, but a good flashing story... that's what got them talking. Monty also made a mental note to follow up on an intriguing advertisement in the personal columns.

'Such fire. I will find you and we will set Nouville aflame! Call me. Dawn'

*   *   *   *   *   *

CHAPTER FOURTEEN

MR EDWARD FRIENDY'S JAGUAR RELOCATION CENTRE AND PENGUIN-SHIT-POWERED ANTARCTIC GREENHOUSE!

MR EDWARD Friendy sat in the reception area of the opticians waiting for his new glasses. The walls were adorned with advertisements depicting young handsome men and women posing in spectacles that as far as he could see - which admittedly wasn't very far at present - were probably unnecessary and didn't suit them at all.

If they wanted to paint a realistic picture of spectacle usage they should, he felt, show something along the lines of an old man in glasses with the accompanying caption, 'Ahh that's better - I can read the paper now.' Or maybe a tear-stained and wrinkled old lady peering through new varifocals into the angelic face of a much-loved great-grandchild with, 'So that's what my Timmy looks like!'

Mr Friendy sniffed derisively at the ridiculous portrayal; a square chinned, designer-stubbled young man was smiling at an attractive young woman and they both wore cheesily obvious glasses. 'Bloody Idiots' Mr Friendy muttered; the receptionist on the telephone momentarily raised her eyes but quickly returned to her conversation. Mr Friendy silently speculated on the odds of two such beautiful young things:

1. Needing glasses,
2. Choosing ridiculous frames like those,
3. Subsequently meeting up; and …
4. Forming a relationship!

Was mutual astigmatism the attraction? Or maybe they were brother and sister but, if so, why was his hand on her arse?' Maybe fate, on realising they had been endowed with perfect bodies and symmetrical features had attempted to redress the balance by giving them poor eyesight? If that was the case then Mr Friendy felt that his less than perfect frame and unremarkable features should have entitled him to the eyes of a hawk.

He wondered if he should ask about contact lenses that change the eye colour. He could have coal-black penetrating eyes capable of a thousand-yard stare and then he would dress all in black and be.... mysterious and erotically sinister. 'Is he a vampire?' people would ask and sensitive young ladies of breeding would be drawn like moths to a candle by his aura of dangerous unpredictability and otherworldness. After all, if 'handsome' is out of the question then 'intriguing' is a damn good substitute.

But then, vampires are never plump - and they never wear anoraks or paisley socks. And he couldn't imagine Felicity going along with the idea of him becoming mad, bad and dangerous to know. She wouldn't get into the spirit of it at all. He sighed; maybe he'd be interesting in his next incarnation.

September Plenty was interesting. Not only did she have a name that made her sound like a cross between a Harvest Festival hymn and a James Bond girl, but she was also six feet tall, spoke five languages and played the flute. Her parents had named her September after a song that topped the charts on the day she was born. She had often speculated that, had she been a week premature, she might have gone through life as 'Sixteen Tons'.

She had been raised in Switzerland where her father had been a physicist and now, with grown up children of her own, she had moved to Newvale, her mother's hometown and bought a share in an opticians business with the insurance money that came when Frederick had died in a wanking accident.

Of course the death certificate had cited a gas explosion at their holiday home as the cause of his demise but the build up of gas from a faulty boiler in the en-suite bathroom may well have dissipated harmlessly had it not been for the frenetic rubbing together of Frederick's metal watchstrap and belt buckle. The cataclysmic spark had caused an explosion that left little to identify him by. September often wondered whether Frederick had come before he went; she hoped so, it would have been a frightful waste otherwise.

'Could you just try and read the last but one line for me?' September made a small adjustment to the lens combination perched on her patient's nose and waited while the elderly lady leaned forward and squinted mole-like at the mirror image of the letter chart.

'A...X....N... M - no, not M, another N.... P.... umm, I don't know how to pronounce the next one..'

'What do you mean?'

'Well it's one of those Indian squiggly ones isn't it? I don't know how to say them.'

'Actually, it's a V.'

'Avee - ah there you are you see, I'd never have know that. You should have an all English chart for English speakers and an all Indian one for Indian speakers, there wouldn't be any confusion then.'

'Yes,' September pinched the bridge of her nose, 'A great idea Mrs Stansfield, I'll see what I can do.'

'Won't be long now Mr Friendly.' The receptionist called across and smiled.

'There's no L in it,' he responded with a sigh. But she had resumed her telephone conversation and had tuned him out. He picked up a magazine and idly flicked through the pages. It was full of pictures of thin women eating Knickerbocker Glories and even thinner women sitting on bales of hay and pouting petulantly in ridiculously overpriced clothes. He replaced it on the pile and was about to rummage through for something more interesting when the door to the test room opened and two women emerged. The one was short, elderly and squinted in the light and the other was probably the most striking woman Mr Friendy had ever seen. She crossed to the receptionist's desk, picked up a file and studied it.

She was no longer young but her poise and presence would have been the envy of many thirty years her junior. She was tall, very tall, slim and with a figure her white coat failed to conceal. Her eyes were so blue they seemed ultra-violet and she wore her almost waist-length hair - strawberry blonde with just a hint of grey - tied back in a ponytail. She had a face that suggested a smile was its default setting, the passing of years had, if anything, made it even more appealing adding wisdom and laughter lines and when she spoke it was like warm honey being poured over ice cream, a delightful combination of hot and cold that left the senses struggling to maintain a balance. Mr Friendy felt himself wishing he had worn his leather jacket instead of his anorak, he could have turned up the collar and slouched indolently.

The woman spoke briefly to the receptionist who nodded and walked off, she then turned her formidable attention on Mr Friendy and smiled. He instinctively smiled back and immediately hoped it wasn't his Monkey Smile. He hated his Monkey Smile and it inevitably reared its simian head at the most embarrassing moments. He no longer smiled on photographs in case the Monkey Smile ruined them as it had so many in the past. He remembered the huge row he had been given as a child for scribbling out his face from the class photograph his parents had bought. He had inadvertently done the Monkey Smile and was determined no one else was going to see it.

If he had done the Monkey Smile on this occasion the lady in the white coat showed no indication of it. She studied the file again before returning the ultra violet gaze to him.

'Mr Friendy?'

She had got it right; people rarely did at the first attempt. 'Yes', he found himself smiling again and his hands instinctively went to his ears to hold them back.

'This way please,' she headed back to the test room door and he followed.

The only reason James McKenzie knew he was James McKenzie was because a doctor was showing him a driving licence with his name and photograph on it.

'Can you remember anything at all Mr McKenzie?'

Mr McKenzie couldn't. He remembered driving a car then nothing until he woke up here with these bright lights and white walls and bleeping things and a man in a white coat asking him questions.

'Where am I?'

'You're in hospital, you were involved in a road accident, it's quite normal to suffer a bit of amnesia, try not to worry, you're in safe hands now.'

A road accident? He tried to lift his head to do a stock take of his bodily parts but it hurt too much and so he rested on the pillow and sent his mind on a journey of discovery to his fingers and toes and all points in between.

The name James McKenzie meant nothing to him, it wouldn't have meant much even if he hadn't lost his memory. No one had called him James for years. To the few fans he had left he was Mickey McKenzie, stand-up comedian; three television appearances a few decades ago and a handful of pantomimes since.

These days he made a precarious living doing after dinner speeches and the occasional guest appearance. A fledgling second career as a childrens entertainer had to be abandoned after he was fined and put on probation for throwing an eight-year-old boy into a duck pond. He had been halfway through his balloon animal act when he asked his young audience, 'Anyone know what it is yet?' The little boy had called out, 'It looks like a big prick - and so do you!' Coming as it did hot on the heels of an extortionate tax bill and a divorce Mickey had been in no mood for the little bastard's quip and so had dragged him out of the marquee and across to a nearby duck pond. The other children had followed happily and had cheered when the lad was thrown in. That would probably have been the end of it if had the brat's mother not been a magistrate.

Mickey tried to remember something.. anything. There was some vague recollection of heading to Newvale. What the hell would he have been going there for?

It would be a month before Mickey fully recovered his memory and by that time there would be no need to go to Newvale.

'A….D…X….R…W….N…J….U….S'

'Splendid, well that's the left eye done, now we'll just swap these over…'

Mr Friendy could have listened to that voice all day. She smelt nice too, a cross between lavender and Bakewell tarts.

'Are you not from around these parts?' he enquired.

'I grew up in Switzerland, but I've been a Newvalian for almost a year now.'

'Ah, I see,' Mr Friendy smiled, safe in the knowledge that the dark room would hide any chimp-like expressions, 'Thought I detected an accent there.'

'OK, now you see the two circles, which would you say was the dominant colour, the red or the green?'

Mr Friendy was about to answer when the optician's mobile phone rang. She 'tutted' and answered it.

'Hello?….. Yes…..Yes….. What?….Oh gosh, is he OK?…..Yes…. bit of a nuisance….. not at this short notice, I'm afraid I don't know anyone who could….hmmm, I'll call you lunchtime…OK bye.'

She sighed to herself and muttered, 'Never rains but it pours…'

'Oh dear', Mr Friendy offered, 'Bad news?'

'There's a dinner for Newvale Chamber of Trade tomorrow night and I've just been told the after dinner speaker we had booked has been in a car accident and won't be attending. I've now got the task of replacing him in twenty four hours.'

Fifty years earlier, an eight-year-old Edward Friendy had listened attentively with the rest of the class while the teacher had told them a tale about a little boy growing up in the jungles of Brazil. At the end of the story the teacher had said that, if they were lucky, one day they might travel to where the little native boy lived and see all the amazing creatures that shared the jungle with him.

An hour or so before hearing the story Edward had seen Pamela Freeman kissing Michael Boyd in the playground and his jealousy had burned fiercely. Edward was ordinary and being ordinary meant being ignored and overlooked.

He didn't remember his hand going up but now he had the teacher's attention.

'I've already been to Brazil, Miss.'

The teacher had raised an eyebrow, 'Are you sure Edward?'

'Oh yes, I had a parrot and a … a piranha and a baby jaguar - two baby jaguars actually.' The class had looked at him in disbelief - but at least they had looked and for a brief moment he experienced the sweet and dangerously addictive taste of fame. When it was snatched cruelly away hours later by his forced admission that he had never actually been abroad at all reality seemed colder and blander than ever and it was a long, long time before Edward tried to make himself interesting again.

So why had he just told this woman he was an experienced after-dinner speaker who would be happy to step into the breech and regale the Chamber of Trade with tales of his worldwide adventures?

'I just bumped into Albie Ferle and he says you phoned him to tell him you won't be going to Model Railway club tomorrow night?' Felicity was doing things to a cabbage that reinforced Edward's oft held suspicion that she watched too many forensic shows. The question had been asked off-handedly but Edward knew from past experience that his response had to be watertight.

'That's right, I promised I'd pop around to Dick Blackwell and show him where he was going wrong with his curly kale.'

'He brews his own sherry doesn't he?'

'Hmm, I'm not sure you actually brew sherry dear, I think you just make it.'

Yes, well I was talking to Mrs DiStefano who lives next door to him and apparently he's got a bath full of amontillado so I'd be careful if I were you.'

Edward shook his head, what did she think the man would do? Lure him up to the bathroom on some pretext or other and then push him in? He needed to be alone, to think, to panic quietly, he had little enough time as it was and could afford no distractions.

'I think I'll go and write a letter,' he announced.

'Who to?'

He sighed, would it be possible, just once, to do something without cross-examination?

'To the Chronicle.'

'What about?'

He sighed again and failed to keep a hint of terseness out of his reply, 'The amount of dog shit in Newvale Park.'

'There's no need to swear Edward, honestly, I don't know what's got into you these last few months. Besides, nobody cares about that.'

'I do.' He replied, too quietly for Felicity to hear.

'You should write to them about the statue.'

'What statue?'

'You know what statue - the one in the entrance to the cemetery, the soldier. That was a disgusting thing to put on a soldier!'

Edward saw no harm in a bit of high spirits but he didn't have time to debate the point with Felicity today. The statue, that of Captain Stewart Bennett - Newvale's only VC - had been adorned with a strap-on penis by a passing hen party and the Chronicle's photographer had been fortuitously on hand to record the addition before the police arrived and removed it. The picture had made the front page under a headline of 'ATTEN-SHUN! CAPTAIN'S PRIVATE IS A MAJOR COCK-UP'

'OK, Edward headed for the door, 'I'll write about that instead.' He disappeared before Felicity could reply.

'Who?' Alan Norris, chair of Newvale Chamber of Trade was puzzled.

'Ed Friendy.'

Alan Norris at just short of five foot three couldn't help but feel a little overshadowed by the six foot of September Plenty currently standing next to him in the lounge bar of the Happy Wanderer.

'Can't say I've heard of him,' Mr Norris had heard of just about everyone who was anyone in Newvale, 'what's his M.O.?'

'He's travelled a lot. He built a railway through parts of the Matto Grosso and while he was there he set up a relocation centre for displaced jaguars. And while in Antarctica he supervised the building of giant greenhouses to grow vegetables in the six months of perpetual daylight they get there.'

'Good God, what did he use as a growing medium?'

'I asked him that, apparently they propagated their crops in a mixture of penguin droppings and powdered fish bones, it's all been very hush-hush, he's patented the stuff and is preparing to launch it worldwide very soon.'

'Sounds quite a man,' Alan Norris muttered, hating him already.

'Indeed, and he's still had time to write a book about his adventures.'

'I'll have to see if I can get a copy,' stated Mr Norris, failing to keep all of the bitterness out of his voice.

'No point, it's in Portuguese apparently ...'

They say the eyes are the mirrors of the soul, but they're not. Eyes, in isolation, can tell little about what's going on behind them; it's the surrounding face that gives the game away! September had looked deeper into his eyes than any woman ever had - and that was probably why she hadn't spotted the fantasies that had gatecrashed the get-together reality was holding to commemorate fifty eight years without any form of real excitement.

Edward, for his part, was trying to remember all the things he had told a strange lady in a dark room. If it hadn't been for the absence of light he wouldn't have dreamed of letting his imagination run riot. But there, in almost opaque velvet anonymity, his eyes shielded by selections of lens and his Monkey Smile safely caged, he had allowed free rein to his dreams. There, where no one could see him, he became the Edward Friendy who should have been. The dashing Ed Friendy, jodhpurs and white teeth, black curly hair and bass-baritone manliness; interesting, confident and …. Oh God, what was he going to say? He couldn't get out of it; she had his address on her records. He could picture the worst-case scenario… He would simply not turn up and Ms Plenty would knock on his door, Felicity would answer and Ms Plenty would ask her where the jaguar-breeding, penguin-shit-vegetable-growing Portuguese-speaking author was? Felicity would call him to the door and he would try and smile his way out of it and the Monkey Smile would appear and September Plenty would shake her head, mutter, 'Wanker' and turn on her well-shaped heels and walk off leaving Felicity to do her famous resigned sigh and say, 'I despair of you Edward, I really do.' And then she would tell all her friends.

Edward looked at what he had written; it was about three pages and concentrated mainly on trying to get a baby jaguar to drink from a bottle. He hoped there would be no Portuguese speakers present.

The Function Room in the Town Hall had undergone a metamorphosis in readiness for the Chamber of Trade's Annual Dinner. Mindful of the fact that this was Bicentennial Year a large Newvale 200 logo backed the small stage where a string quartet had been engaged to play throughout the courses. Crisp white tablecloths bedecked the chandeliered tables along with serviettes in the livery of Newvale County Borough Council. September had popped across Town in her lunch hour to personally ensure everything was as it should be. As the Chamber's newest member it had fallen to her this year to organise the dinner. Fortunately, she didn't have a hard act to follow after last year's debacle. It had been arranged by the now incarcerated William Steed, renamed the 'Mad Chemist of Meadowvale' by the Chronicle after he had become over-fond of his own stock. The meal had been a terrifying game of culinary Russian roulette with many not even daring to sip the bottled water. A few brave souls who, through sheer hunger, had a bash at the starter - pepper stuffed mussels - were later found naked on the bus stop in Fuller Square trying to form a human pyramid in a bid to touch Jupiter to see if it was hot.

September took in the room and felt satisfied; at least it was going to look OK. She hoped the Borough's caterers would be up to the job. She had chosen the menu carefully, ensuring those with specific dietary needs were all catered for. As far as she could see she had left nothing to chance. The string quartet had come highly recommended by Newvale Amateur Operatic Society. The only wild card was Ed Friendy; she hadn't been able to find out anything about him online. Searches linking his name with keywords such as 'Jaguar' 'Antarctica' and 'Guano' had all proved fruitless. She discovered he had been a customer of the opticians for more than twenty years and had lived for all of that time in Rhododendron Crescent so his exploits abroad must have been in his youth. She hoped he had a good memory.

Edward also hoped he had a good memory, He had taken copious notes and had spent hours in Newvale Library and online boning up on the habits of jaguars and penguins and the climates and fauna of both the Matto Grosso and the Ross Ice Shelf. He now knew lots of things he hadn't known, or wanted to know, twenty-four hours earlier but he still had no idea how to deliver this information in an entertaining manner. He had another worry too. Somehow he had to get out of the house tonight in evening dress and a dickey bow ostensibly to go and potter about in Dick Blackwell's garden. He'd never get past Felicity, his only option would be to go out in his gardening clothes with his posh suit hidden in a bag under some tools or something and get a taxi from the end of the Crescent.

He wished he'd had the forethought to tell Ms Plenty he was a model railway expert or something. Not as interesting perhaps but at least he knew a bit about it. He doubted the ups and downs of office administration in a printing company would have held an audience for long but it was what he had done, who he had been… boring, boring Edward Friendy. The most unorthodox thing he had ever achieved was to have a wank in the greenhouse - and he'd missed it because he had been sleepwalking! He could imagine the reaction of the great and good of Newvale if he told them that tale.

The only other time in his adult life he'd made a public announcement had been at his wedding when he'd got to his feet and thanked everyone for attending and for the gifts and had then attempted to tell a joke. It had been about a wedding reception for nursery rhyme characters and only when he was three quarters of the way through did he remember the punch line was going to be utterly inappropriate for the several children present, not to mention his mother and Felicity's uncle - a verger. He had petered out pathetically with an uncomfortable, 'Errr, I'd better not finish that one…' and sat down to a very sparse and embarrassed applause. Much later, in the hotel, Felicity had insisted he finished the joke and, being young and slightly drunk, he had, *"…..and so Little Jack Horner said to Bo Peep. "What did you expect, fucking mint sauce?"* Felicity had looked stunned, her face drained of colour and she had run into the bathroom, locking the door behind her. Edward had sat on the end of the bed for fifteen minutes listening to her crying through the thin walls and when she returned to the bedroom she had looked washed out. She had got into bed, switched off the light and said, 'We'll talk about this in the morning.'

Edward couldn't think of any jokes about penguins or jaguars, or any jokes at all if it came to that; but he was going to have to think of a way to make himself sound interesting.

'It's "Spring" from Vivaldi's Four Seasons,' Karen Fuller was trying to educate her husband who had asked what the string quartet were playing.

'Fair enough, I thought it was the music from that farming programme,' Dick Fuller hated wearing evening dress and had already managed to loosen his bow tie and undo his top shirt button without Karen noticing.

'Yes, well they probably use it for that, although I'll never understand why you watch it, you're scared of animals.'

'I'm not scared to eat them,' he retorted picking up a menu from a nearby table as they headed for the bar.

'Put that back - we'll read it when we sit down,' Karen hissed.

He ignored her, 'What's App… Apfelclothesline?'

Karen snatched the menu from him and put it back on the table. The room was filling up with Newvale's movers and shakers. She had insisted they attend tonight, reminding Dick of the importance of networking. She smiled at the wife of the manager of the Newvale Building Society and got a cheerless 'business-smile' in return. The string quartet, having given Vivaldi an unseasonal airing turned their attention to Mozart as many of the assembly began milling around the tables looking for the places with their names on them.

Karen and Dick found themselves on a table with Portia Mills of Newvale Garden Centre and her son Adam who vied with the long gone stegosaurus for the title of living thing with the widest disparity in brain and body size. Dick's attention was immediately torn between studying Portia's cleavage and her son's hands, which resembled the buckets on a hydraulic digger. The huge fingers made the condiment set and cutlery appear like miniatures. 'God knows where they find clothes to fit him,' Dick thought.

'All very nice,' Karen attempted to break the ice. Portia smiled in return and was about to respond when her son dragged her attention away.

'Music's good isn't it Mum?' His loud bass drew attention from nearby tables but they quickly looked away.

'Yes Adam,' she took the saltcellar from him to prevent him from unscrewing the top and eating the contents.

'So, how's business?' Dick attempted.

'Oh, it would be alright if I hadn't spent the last week doing the books - are you with Frobishers the Accountants?'

'Err.. no, we're with Hollands,' Karen volunteered.

'You're lucky, Portia continued, I've had old man Frobisher in and out of the office and on the phone all week.'

'Mr Frobisher's a fucking nuisance isn't he Mum?' Adam's voice rumbled across the sea of expectant diners, mercifully breaking on a beach of serving trolleys before reaching the table island occupied by the pedantic Mr Gawain Frobisher who prided himself on his professional thoroughness. Those near enough to have heard the second-hand opinion grinned and looked away. Portia fired her giant offspring a withering glance, which bounced unnoticed off the clumsy shield of his innocence.

'Yes, well I've heard he's very thorough,' Karen tried to gloss things over.

'Who's the turn tonight?' Dick queried.

'Chap by the name of Ed Friendly, can't say he rings a bell,' Portia offered.

'Sounds like a comedian,' Karen suggested.

'Hope so, I could do with a laugh,' Portia sighed and took the pepper pot off Adam.

Mr Edward Friendy was much closer to panic than to laughter. He was in a public toilet cubicle just across Fuller Square from the Town Hall and he had just discovered his evening suit trousers were several inches smaller than his waist. Granted, it had been many years since he had cause to put them on but surely they wouldn't have shrunk that much? The legs were still the same length but there was no way that button was going to reach that buttonhole!

Further experimentation with the rest of his attire confirmed his fear that years in the dark cause shrinkage when his dress shirt only just stretched over his paunch and his jacket gave up the unequal task without trying. In fact, of all his clothes, only the dickey bow was still going to fit. He began to consider doing the speech in the gardening clothes he had sneaked out in when that option was snatched away, quite literally. He had hung the old trousers, shirt and jacket over the adjoining partition and now a grubby hand had briefly appeared and whipped them. All he could hear was a receding smokers cough and running feet. He thought about shouting out but wasn't sure he wanted to get on the wrong side of anyone desperate enough to steal clothes that Felicity had been trying to get him to throw away for years.

He shrugged in his tight jacket and shirt and resigned himself to what lay ahead. At least he still had his wallet so he would call a taxi and go home. He would explain all to Felicity and hopefully she would see the funny side of it, realising even as he considered it that Felicity didn't actually have a funny side. He had always pitied her for that.

Taking off his dickey bow he used it as a makeshift belt to hold up his trousers; he removed his jacket and held it discreetly in front of him as he left the cubicle. He had deliberately 'forgotten' to take his phone with him to stop Felicity from catching him out and so he had to make the walk across the Square to the phone booth outside the Town Hall. In a carrier bag were his gardening shoes, the only remnants of the horticultural uniform now adorning some tramp. As he approached the phone booth he noticed a few people in evening dress smoking outside the Town Hall and realised he would have to call Ms Plenty to explain his absence. He would say he had been mugged - not entirely untrue - and he would find a new optician and try to forget. And in future he would embrace his uninterestingness and wear it like a warm, all-protecting cloak.

He was deep in thought and concentrating on reaching the phone booth and so didn't instantly register that the call of 'Ed!' was directed at him.

'Ahh there you are, I was beginning to think you'd stood us up' September approached Edward who cringed instinctively, one hand on the phone booth door, and held his jacket even closer to conceal his 'undoneness'.

'I'm sorry, I'm afraid I…'

'That's alright, you're here now,' She shot down his fledgling excuse and, taking his elbow, steered him toward the bright lights of the Town Hall foyer. 'There's a little room just off the main restaurant that we're using as a dressing room. You can say hello to the String Quartet and relax for a short while.

Edward was more unrelaxed than he could ever remember and his sense of impending doom deepened as September herded him through a door into a room he now saw as his very own condemned cell. From the other side of the door he could hear music and the babble of multiple conversations. There was no way out.

'It's Swiss, Apfelküchlein, it's something to do with apples, apple crumble or something probably,' Karen tried to ease Dick's fear of eating anything he couldn't pronounce. The starters and main courses had been excellent and she doubted she had room for the sweet. Portia Mills, sitting opposite had failed to finish her meal but her giant son had ensured there would be no need for doggy bag.

'The meat was nice, wasn't it Mum?'

'Yes Adam, now don't interrupt.' Portia and Karen were talking about the possibility of putting a window and conservatory display somewhere in the Garden Centre. Adam squirmed uncomfortably; making the overworked chair creak, 'I'm going to the toilet' the announcement was just about loud enough to qualify as a broadcast. He stood, towering over the table, his arms extending a long way out of the sleeves of his jacket as he looked around for the facilities.

Edward had decided to leave the shirt hanging out of his trousers to cover the shortcomings at the front and roll up the sleeves in the hope that the effect would make him look at little bit like an adventurer who just couldn't be bothered with the niceties of civilisation. He thought he'd walk to the stage with his jacket slung over his shoulder to enhance the effect. It would make the best of a bad job. He poured himself a glass of wine from the refreshment table and resumed his nervous pacing. From out in the restaurant there was a ripple of applause followed seconds later by the adjoining door opening to admit four musicians. They smiled at Edward and got a grimace in return that wouldn't have looked out of place on the face of a constipated macaque. It was a visage that prompting them to give him a wide berth and concentrate on the post-performance nibbles. The door opened again and September's head appeared briefly around it, 'I'm about to....' she paused to take in Edward's unorthodox appearance but didn't comment on it, '... I'm about to announce you, OK?' Edward, still impersonating a primate with a serious intestinal blockage, managed to nod. He felt in his pocket and was reassured by the feel of his notes. He headed for the door and peered through. The room was frighteningly full. He could still run away, or at least walk briskly, but the consequences would be even more embarrassing than staying. His heart was racing and it wasn't supposed to, the doctor had said! What if he dropped dead during his talk? The thought made his heart beat even faster.

'...and so we're really grateful to our speaker this evening for stepping into the breach with such alacrity. He's a Newvalian who has travelled the world and demonstrated what a little enterprise and a sense of adventure can achieve, so please give a warm welcome to, Ed Friendy!'

The applause was both welcoming and chastising. It was like a smile from a mother who has yet to see your school report. He didn't really deserve it and very soon everyone would know. He'd been a fool to think he could carry this off. His mind flashed back half a century to the little patch of wasteland behind the cycle sheds of the junior school. A circle of children, Edward in the middle, their mocking voices, '...*Brazil ha ha ha...baby jaguars ha ha ha...*'

He noticed September's eyebrows were raised as he approached the stage and he instinctively pulled his shirt around to ensure full frontal concealment. Her smile carried a whiff of concern as she backed away from the microphone to make room from him.

'Err, thank you..' There was a whistle of feedback and September briefly adjusted the microphone before abandoning him on the stage. A sea of faces looked his way. 'Well, here we are then,' he stated the obvious and fished his notes out of his pocket. Even before he studied them he knew there was something terribly wrong. He looked down at the pieces of paper, they had been folded a long, long time ago; Edward's heart sank. Unfolding them revealed a list of accessories for a model railway layout. The last time he had worn his evening suit, for a long forgotten function he had sat next to a fellow model railway enthusiast who had given him these notes. He had forgotten all about them and now stood wondering if one could still buy half of these accessories. The murmuring of his audience brought him back to reality and as he snapped up to study the sea of expectant faces he went beyond the border controls of fear into the wild and lawless land of 'Fuck it!'

'I had made some notes but they are in my other jacket which was stolen half an hour ago by a tramp!' The audience seemed unsure of whether to laugh. 'I'll try and continue from memory... *When I first arrived in Brazil they explained they'd never built a railway through the jungle because it was full of jaguars....*'

Outside, the rain that had been threatening all day began to fall. In the gathering dark the lights of the town gave the wide valley the look of an encampment, spreading as they did all the way out to Cedar Hill. The only patch of dark being the black semicircle of Meadowvale

Woods, which, with the exception of the road now running through it, showed little signs of being affected by the two centuries of human habitation all around.

'...there was little in the way of coal so we used mahogany which seemed to power the narrow gauge trains quite nicely and the clearings left were used to house more jaguars and....mappa mundies....'

'I was in court that day and I'm telling you, that's him - the Greenhouse Wanker,' reporter Virginia Wells hissed in her editor's ear as they sat listening to an increasingly hesitant and desperate-sounding Edward Friendy as he fidgeted onstage. Edward still sometimes couldn't believe his luck that the somnambulistic escapade that had landed him in the dock had escaped publication due to a rabies scare. Now, in the audience, the editor of the Newvale Chronicle, Monty Fox, grinned wolfishly; he hated it when prey got away and was always delighted to be offered a second bite.

'...of course once you get it lit a killer whale will burn for weeks as long as you keep the wick well trimmed, they're virtually made out of oil, whale oil.... Like a great big black and white candle and.... and that's what kept it warm enough inside the greenhouses to let the plants grow... err, and that's it really'

Edward checked his watch and was surprised to note he had spoken for fifteen minutes. He couldn't now remember a single word of what he'd just said and had probably repeated himself several times. There had been no laughter from the audience as such, just a bit of bemused murmuring and coughing. He suddenly remembered he had been told to do half an hour and so prepared to launch once again into a world so tangible it existed only for the time it took to describe it. He was pre-empted by September Plenty who ascended the small stage and held out a hand for the microphone. Edward passed it to her with a mixture of relief and foreboding.

'Well,... thank you Ed for that.... most... yes, well unless anyone has any questions we'll...'

A hand went up and was spotted by September.

'Yes? You sir?'

'Monty Fox, The Chronicle.' A hush descended on the gathering akin to ones that envelop saloons when the gunslinger walks through the batwings. 'Tell me Mr Friendy..' Edward's stomach did a double-flip. '...Scientists at the American base at McMurdo in Antarctica only manage to grow plants in an underground hydroponic propagator - and yet you managed to *pull it off* in an ordinary greenhouse?'

So intent was Edward on parrying the harpoon he failed to notice the wicked barb of the double entendre.

'Well we were lucky with the weather that year and thanks to a couple of beached whales...'

'Yes..' Monty interjected, '.. but in a greenhouse? Perhaps you could tell us exactly how you got it up in the cold?'

He let himself in through the back door. Felicity had clearly retired and so, with relief, he took off his evening suit and pushed it under the bed in the spare room. He would pretend to have flu or something and stay indoors for a while. September had sympathised when he said he'd had an 'off night' and he'd made his excuses and left before anyone else could ask him things or sting him with *'Brazil ha ha ha, baby jaguars ha ha ha'*.

He sneaked as carefully into bed as he could and closed his eyes gratefully. In the twin bed Felicity mumbled something in her sleep and turned over. She would find out of course; someone would tell someone who would pass it on to somebody who would tell her. He decided to take the bull by the horns and make a full confession in the morning. Then she could despair of him that much sooner. And tell all her friends.

*   *   *   *   *   *

CHAPTER FIFTEEN

SHORTCOCK AND MEE

THE fact that one can mention Shortcock and Mee anywhere in town without generating even a snigger indicates just how long the clothing store has been part of the fabric of Newvalian society. There have been Shortcocks in Newvale for more than a century and for most of that time there have been Mees alongside them.

Founded in 1907 by Earnest Shortcock the store, originally a 'high class gentlemens outfitter' has traded continually ever since despite increasing competition from cheap imports and the World Wide Web.

In 1945 Oswald Mee, on his release from a German prisoner of war camp, threw in his lot with Captain George Shortcock and the store underwent an expansion before entering the golden age of the 1950s on a sound and promising footing.

Captain George Shortcock R.N. D.S.C. M.B.E. had been a man whose bearing immediately marked him out as one to whom the concept of defeat or humiliation was utterly alien. Had he been captured in wartime he would have been head of the escape committee and first over the wire - eager to get back to the front to give the enemy a bloody nose. He had been a leader of men whose steely gaze was honed to eagle sharpness by the bitter winds and razor-blade fogs of the Arctic Convoys, a man who thought of ladies as highly-strung and unreliable fillies but loveable nevertheless, a man who measured a fellow by his handshake and the look in his eye; in short, a man who had had the common decency to shoot himself to protect the family name when arrested for buggery in a caravan in 1951.

His son, Nicholas Shortcock, had taken over as partner but had never hit it off with the straight-laced and pious Oswald Mee. On Oswald's retirement the Mee mantle had fallen to his Olympic shot-putting daughter Fanny and a joyous age of ribaldry and general piss-taking began. Coinciding as it did with the Swinging Sixties, Shortcock and Big Fanny gave endless hours of mirth and good value clothing to Newvalians and helped to establish the punning reputation of junior reporter, Monty Fox whose stories in the Chronicle fully entered into the spirit of the era of the double entendre.

In the early seventies Nicholas Shortcock had been struck by lightning and killed while wearing a devil costume at a fancy dress party. The event had made an instant Christian of his widow and a premature managing director of his nineteen-year-old son, Ralph. In the same year, Fanny Mee defected to East Germany to be with her lover who she had met at a hammer-throwing event and the Mee mantle had fallen to her twenty-three year old nephew, Charles.

The young Mr Shortcock and Mr Mee confounded those who had said they were too green to take the reins of the business and through hard work and fast learning had kept the store on an even keel. The pair were cut from the same cloth and thought as one when it came to the future direction of the business while agreeing the need to show due deference to tradition and the sterling efforts of Mees and Shortcocks who had gone before. Now, almost forty years on the pair were still at the helm and steering a steady course.

Charles Mee was elegant to a point stopping just short of exotic. His golden youth had coincided with the worst fashion excesses of the seventies and he was reluctant to let go of the inner peacock. He was fiercely proud of his luxuriant full mane of silver hair crowning a perfectly symmetrical face illuminated by striking blue eyes. He had the hands of a concert pianist, a trim waist and a way of walking that combined economy of effort with a poise that people have paid money to try and perfect. Many initially mistook his natural lissomness for femininity but he was in fact very heterosexual and had once paid a woman to claim he had made her pregnant and then given Monty Fox a bloody good bespoke suit to write about it. The scandal had killed off all conflicting rumours once and for all.

Ralph Shortcock, by contrast, was ruggedly masculine and as gay as a daisy. But the pair genuinely liked each other and the lifelong friendship had always made for a profitable and steady business relationship.

Shortcock and Mee employed six members of staff and had expanded from their core business of gentlemens outfitting to ladies fashions, childrens clothes, school uniforms and latterly into household linens. But Mr Shortcock and Mr Mee never forgot their roots and, being tailors of some ability, remain the first port of call for the discerning gentlemen of Newvale and its environs while Ms Francine Waite employed as a dressmaker, enjoys a similar good name in the world of local ladies fashion.

It was Monday, and a pleasantly warm morning breeze was drying the night's drizzle off the pavements of Newvale Town Centre. Just off Fuller Square on Meadowvale Road, shop assistants Reeta Chopra and Sheryl Frogmore were in the window of Shortcock and Mee changing the clothes on a pair of mannequins. Reeta and Sheryl had joined the staff of the store on the same day six years previously. Sheryl, now 29 had married noted Newvale ne'er-do-well Jack 'Header' Frogmore on her twentieth birthday in a ceremony still talked about in awed and respectful tones on the rough end of Cold Ridge Estate for the sheer scale of the violence that accompanied it. Header was currently serving three years in jail for burglary and Sheryl tells anyone who asks that she doesn't miss him, freely admitting he only ever came home to procreate and change his socks.

Sheryl's three children, Chastity, Dirk and Sergio, were given names inspired by the cheap romantic novels that provided an escape from their mother's routine grind. Sheryl however has remained a striking redhead and it is only the fearsome reputation of her husband and the knowledge that one day he would roam the streets again that keeps potential suitors at bay. Sheryl's friend and workmate Reeta is 27 and still waiting for Mr Right. Tall and skeletal, with unfashionable spectacles and long, straight hair; she is a makeover waiting to happen. She still lives with her widowed mother whose demands on her mean her social life is all but non-existent. She relies on Sheryl to fill in the gaps in her worldly education.

A man wearing glasses with lens that hugely magnified his eyes was standing with his hands in the pockets of his coat staring in through the window watching Sheryl and Reeta work. He was bobbing his head like an expectant sparrow chick in an attempt to make eye contact with the women who were studiously ignoring him.

'I wish he'd go away.' Reeta was fitting a bra on one of the models, which seemed to drive the man to new heights of bobbing excitement.

'Take no notice of him, he'll be off soon enough.' Sheryl was trying to decide which wig would go with the clothes she had been given to dress her mannequin in.

'I think he's…. you know…'

'Yes, well he does that quite often - show him a bit of leg.'

'What?' Reeta wasn't sure whether her friend was referring to human legs or mannequin ones.

'Whip the dummy's skirt off and let him see the knickers, the quicker he comes the quicker he goes.'

'Alright, but I'm not going to stay here and watch him, I'm going for a cup of tea.' Reeta whipped off the dummy's skirt and without a backward glance headed into the store. Sheryl shook her head, smiled and followed.

'You know when you've died, right?' Reeta unwrapped her biscuit with all the care of one dismantling an unexploded bomb. She rarely managed to do it without breaking the biscuit.

'What about it?' Sheryl was trying to read her book.

'Well - do you *know* that you're dead?'

'Hmm, not sure,' Sheryl was only half listening, in her book the new owner of Bleak Hall, Brent McAllister was "smouldering with passion" as he studied a serving wench.

'Well, you know when you're alive. If you got murdered would you suddenly think, Oh bother! I've been murdered and now I'm dead?'

Sheryl sighed; she'd had a late night and didn't really feel like talking today, especially to Reeta. She was fond of her friend but sometimes having a conversation with Reeta was like being pecked to death by a persistent goose. She was far more interested in where Brent McAllister's smouldering was going to get him.

'I'm only thinking, If I died I'd like to know about it' Reeta persisted, 'I mean, do ghosts know they're ghosts, do they go around going "Whoo! I'm a ghost", or do they not know and when they go to eat their dinner the food comes off the end of the fork and drops on the floor?'

Sheryl put her book down with a sigh, 'Right… well - the *Holy* Ghost probably knows he's a ghost but ordinary ghosts probably don't know they're ghosts until they go to open a door and can't get hold of the knob.'

She picked her book back up more in hope than expectation but several seconds of silence followed in which Brent McAllister smacked his riding crop against his jodhpurs making the serving wench's bosoms "heave and tremor". *He advanced on the panting wench, a fire of desire flickering in his steely eyes, she could see the corded muscles beneath his shirt, he stood over her, he smelt of the great outdoors and the wench felt herself letting go of her inhibitions, Brent reached for her and….*

'My mother won't use the downstairs toilet because she says it's haunted by my father!'

This time Sheryl's book hit the canteen table with a 'slap' and she turned to make deliberate eye contact with Reeta. 'What?'

'Well she says if you pass the door early in the morning you can hear grunting noises and the sound of a pencil scratching on a betting slip…and one morning she swears she heard the words "Beaten by a length".'

Sheryl was about to ask Reeta why she imagined any spirit, free at last from the shackles of mortal flesh, would choose to forsake the undoubted delights of paradise in order to sit on a toilet trying to win money it could no longer spend but the question remained unasked as dressmaker, Francine, joined the pair and turned the conversation over to the forthcoming Newvale 200 window display featuring costumes through the ages.

'They must have been frightfully hot in the summer,' Mr Mee was examining a swatch of thick black material from which he was going to make a gentleman's formal suit fashionable in the year 1830.

'And wet when it rained, this stuff wasn't at all waterproof,' Mr Shortcock replaced a similar swatch on the table in their tailoring room, 'Let's see if things had improved at all by the dawn of the twentieth century.' He picked up some brown material and teased it between thumb and forefinger, 'Ugh, rough rough rough, I'd be fidgeting and scratching all day if I had that next to my skin, pity the poor sod who has to wear it in the parade.... let's have a look at the list, Richard Ellwood, 42-36-39-31 .... He's going to be a prosperous townsman circa 1902.'

'I know that name, Ellwood...Ellwood, ah yes,' Mr Mee snapped his fingers, 'Richard Ellwood, Newvale Am-Dram, played Gloucester in King Lear about seven years ago, they had an Arts Council grant and we dressed them, d'you remember?'

'Ahhh,' Mr Shortcock smiled as the memory wandered out of the wings and on to centre stage, '*that* Richard Ellwood, gorgeous thighs.'

'Hmm, he'll need them, they're expecting people to walk five miles around Newvale, dressed in these clothes and goodness knows what on their feet,' Mr Mee picked up a swatch of rough khaki, ' and pity the poor bloody infantry if they have to carry a full pack; people are like clothes, they're just not made of the same material any more.'

'True,' Mr Shortcock sighed, 'did you know a Roman soldier could walk fifty miles in full armour without a rest?'

'Well thank goodness they're not asking us to go back that far - although Meadowvale's been around for about seven hundred years...'

'Hush, don't put ideas into their heads,' Mr Shortcock murmured.

Despite the business's century of existence, neither man saw much point in the bicentenary commemorations. Nobody outside Newvale would be interested and nobody inside the town would have any extra money to spend on clothes as a result of the anniversary so there seemed little point in it. However, the Newvale 200 Committee had been given a budget to spend and they had seen fit to steer some of it in the direction of Shortcock and Mee for the 'Newvale Through the Ages' parade, which meant the pair would be busy for the next few weeks creating costumes to challenge both their tailoring skills and historical knowledge.

'One suit, that's all, it's not as if they're going to miss it…' Ma Frogmore fished a teabag out of a cup and squeezed it between thumb and forefinger before throwing it out of the kitchen window '… and a nice shirt and tie, there's a good one in the window display at the moment.'

'I've told you Ma, I can't just pinch a suit, they stock-take you know.' Sheryl Frogmore took a sip of tea and tried not to grimace, it was like its maker - strong, thick and bitter.

'Some daughter-in-law you are - poor Randy is going to have to stand in that dock in rags. The Beak will take one look at him and give him five years, you know how they hate scruffy people.'

Sheryl was tempted to ask why Randy Frogmore, a hardened recidivist, hadn't bothered to steal himself a good set of clothes whilst in Newvale's largest supermarket at three in the morning instead of weighing himself down with games consoles and palmtop computers but Ma was clearly in no mood to see any fault in her second oldest son.

'Poor Randy, he's never had a fair crack of the whip,' Ma eased her amplitudinous form into a creaking chair.

Sheryl was tempted to suggest that maybe Ma had unwittingly put her finger on the reason why the young man had turned into such an antisocial light-fingered little shit. Randy was fifth in the infernal series of six Frogmore offspring. Marcia at 31 was the eldest and was currently in the process of raising a lawless brood of her own just a few streets away; next was Sheryl's husband Jack, 29, currently languishing in jail then came Lucille 28 and Sandra 26 who had moved away and were 'Doing very well for themselves', then came Randy, 24, a younger clone of his father and testimony to the fact that human and rat DNA can exist on the same double helix. Finally there was Todd, 21 who seemed to be bucking the family trend having never been in trouble and who was actually showing signs of leading a conventional and even productive life.

'A nice suit and a shirt and tie, he might even get off with probation...' offered Ma, '...although I'm hoping for Community Payback, you get a new pair of boots with Community Payback and he's the same size as Pa.'

As if reacting to the mention of his name, a fart that managed to convey in its fruitful resonance all the unpleasantness of its originator echoed from the adjoining room where Pa Frogmore was watching racing on TV.

'We've got visitors you dirty bastard!' Ma shouted, quickening the pace of a passing mother and her children.

'Bollocks!' came the affectionate reply.

'Actually..' a spark of an idea flickered into life as Sheryl pondered the problem of Randy's apparel, '...does Randy enjoy a good walk?'

'I don't even know what one of them is!' Randy's ratty eyes darted this way and that. Even in everyday conversation he managed to convey the impression he was defending himself against interrogation thus confirming there could be no such thing as an innocent chat with someone utterly bereft of innocence.

'They were well off young people in the 1980s and the point is they all wore nice suits and drove fancy German cars,' Sheryl sometimes wondered what direction her life would have taken if she had married her other suitor, Geoffrey Lovelace, a trainee chartered accountant with a nice car and impeccable manners. Unfortunately, he had lost interest in her after Header had thrown him in Newvale Park Lake chained to a washing machine. Luckily the lake is shallow and the hapless young man had stood there waist deep in murky water feeling quite miserable until the fire brigade had come along and cut him loose.

'Yappy?'

'Yuppie, you just go along and tell Mr Mee or Mr Shortcock that you're in the Newvale 200 parade and you're a Yuppie from 1985.'

'And they'll believe that, will they?'

Sheryl studied the young man in front of her and was forced to admit it would probably be easier to pass off a New Guinea mud-man or a Siberian yak herder as a Yuppie than to perform the same illusion using Randy Frogmore as the model. If he were going to be in the Newvale 200 parade at all then surely 1860s footpad or backstreet pickpocket would have been the ideal role. But Ma Frogmore had given the plan the green light and it was therefore carved in stone.

'If your father was alive he would have something to say about a young woman who abandons her own mother to fend for herself for hours on end,' Ravinda Chopra was laying it on with a trowel as her daughter prepared to go out for the evening.

'I'm going to the Amateur Drama Club Mother, I've been promising myself for ages, I really fancy having a bash at acting; they've been in and out of the shop all week getting measured for the parade and they seem a nice lot,' Reeta was wearing her least boring cardigan and had toyed briefly with the idea of earrings before deciding not to push the boat out too far.

'I'll probably scald myself trying to make a cup of tea with my wrists - and I can't reach the cream crackers where you've put them.'

'I've made a flask of tea for you and the crackers are on the tray next to it,' Reeta sighed.

'I'll never manage to lift that flask, Ohhh I can see it in the Chronicle now….."Tea-Soaked Old Lady Left to Starve!"

Reeta shook her head and bent to kiss her mother on the cheek, 'I'll be back about nine thirty.' Her mother's voice followed her down the passage to the front door, "Hero's Widow Scalded After Daughter Abandons Her" ……. "Lonely Old Lady Chokes on Cream Cracker!'

Reeta closed the door behind her and strolled to the bus stop. He had said she had beautiful eyes and a great voice. He thought she would be a 'natural'. He in turn had a voice full of richness and resonance and a lovely smile…'

Going in through the front door of a store during opening hours was a rare occurrence for Randy Frogmore and he was feeling a little disorientated. He went over the script in his head once again before slinking towards a counter.

'I'm here to see Mr Shortcock or Mr Mee to get measured up.'

The counter assistant took in the furtive demeanour and rapidly darting eyes and measured him up in seconds. 'Just wait here, I'll fetch someone,' she said and headed off. Randy felt strange and uncomfortable, not just because he'd had a bath and was wearing what passed for clean underwear in Chateau Frogmore, but because he was operating outside his *domaine de l'excellence*. His personal world of crime was a lonely and silent place and his skills lay not in the silky charms and poise of the confidence trickster but in the nocturnal skulduggery of the burglar. He was about to turn and run from the shop when the counter assistant returned accompanied by a man whose impeccable appearance immediately suggested private detective to Randy.

'Ahh, you're another for the parade are you?' Mr Mee sized up the young man with a professional eye aware that the subsequent tape measure would only confirm what he had already deduced.

'Err yeah - I'm a… I'm a yuppie from 1985.'

When executed correctly, the raising of one eyebrow can convey in two seconds a whole encyclopaedia's worth of disbelief, distaste and disparagement and Mr Mee succeeded in conveying all of that and more as he struggled to imagine who in their right mind could have envisaged this… creature as a yuppie! The only thing it appeared to share with the acquisitive generation was bipedal motion and stereoscopic vision. But who was he to question the Council's casting policy? It was clearly something to do with the same 'all-inclusiveness' that had so far seen him measure up a morbidly obese Victorian street urchin and a one-legged Chinese teddy boy.

'I see…' said Mr Mee, 'Well, we'd better get you fitted for a suit and a personal organiser then.'

'A what?'

'Never mind, just walk this way.'

Randy tried to walk that way but failed and reverted to his nervous sidle.

'…. and then he took me in his arms and stared out across the stage and said, "It's a big country Emily, I'm gonna carve us a homestead out of this wilderness!" - and then I had to say, "…and I'm gonna make it a little home to be proud of," and then a coyote howled in the distance only it wasn't a coyote it was Mr Beard the prompter and then as the lights went down we kissed and it was, ahhh, it was wonderful - then when I got home Mother had eaten a whole packet of cream crackers and I had to help her on to the toilet and…' Reeta waved a hand in front of Sheryl's face, '…are you listening to any of this?'

'Eh?' Sheryl had tuned Reeta out several minutes earlier. She had been watching Mr Mee measuring up Randy and was trying to ensure he didn't catch sight of her. She had drummed into him that, if anything went wrong, he was not - absolutely not - to mention that he knew her.

'His name's Richard, he's thirty five and divorced and he works for a law firm and he's got two children, Dick and baby Sam… are you listening?'

'Yes - you said he's a lawyer and he's got a dick like a baby's arm!'

'I said no such....' Reeta's mouth moved for a bit without doing anything useful and then tried to resume speaking '....I never mentioned his... and I've no idea how big....'

'You've snapped your biscuit again,' Sheryl helpfully pointed out.

'Right then, you remember how this is going to go,' Ma Frogmore stood over Randy as he ate his breakfast, '...you've got to be at the court by ten thirty and your fitting in Shortcock and Mee is at nine thirty so....'

'I know Ma... as soon as the suit is on make a dash for it and get to the court on time.'

'That's it - we'll all meet you there, I can't wait to see you in a suit, I've asked Todd to bring his camera it will be nice to have a picture of us all dressed up.' Ma absently straightened the pictures on the mantelpiece of various Frogmores in their best clothes; there was one of Pa (handling stolen goods), one of Lucille and Sandra together (immoral earnings), a nice one of Marcia holding baby Conan (affray) and one of Ma herself (violent conduct), she bunched them up a bit to make room for one of Randy (burglary).

They were unlike any suit trousers that Randy had seen before but he supposed the experienced Mr Mee would know what he was doing. They were purple and velvet; tight at the top and very, very baggy below the knee, and now Mr Mee was approaching him with a shirt that looked like the middle page spread of a seed catalogue - an explosion of flowery life! Mr Mee must have seen the doubt flicker across Randy's face and reassured him.

'Trust me, this is exactly the thing old boy, exactly the thing - when we get the wig on you'll begin to see the full effect...'

Randy was beginning to doubt his initial conviction that the last minute change of plan would have little overall influence on his appearance. He had arrived at the Store at nine-thirty prompt to be informed by Mr Mee that apparently there was already a 1980s yuppie in the parade and so Randy was going to be a 1960s hippy instead. Randy had shrugged, they sounded similar and free clothes were free clothes. Now, as the wig went on and the hair hung down to his elbows it occurred to him that fashion must have undergone a truly seismic shift in the twenty years between hippy and yuppie.

A pair of yellow tinted round-framed sunglasses completed Randy's ensemble. 'Take a look in the mirror,' Mr Mee gestured to the full-length glass. There was no time, the clock was ticking; Randy took a brief look in the glass then burst into 'police pursuit' mode; dodging and swerving at high speed between displays and shocked customers he flew out through the door, long hair flying behind him and tore across Fuller Square in the direction of Newvale Magistrates Court. Mr Mee raised the eyebrow again and wondered what challenge the Council would set him next.

Ma and Pa Frogmore and Todd took no more than a casual interest in the colourful creature speeding towards them and it was only when it skidded to a halt and took off the sunglasses that Ma's deeply buried maternal radar bleeped on recognising the apparition as her offspring. Randy gasped, hands on knees as Ma struggled to find her voice, eventually she located it, 'WHAT THE FUCKING HELL HAVE YOU GONE AND DONE?' Her foghorn tones, a familiar clarion over the rooftops of Cold Ridge, rang out over Fuller Square bringing Randy to the attention of those who had initially failed to register the bizarre refugee from the age of free love.

'They.... they already had a yuppie so... I'm a hippy,' Randy gasped. Ma snatched the camera from Todd who had been snapping away at his brother.

'Good God, I looked exactly like that when we met, remember Ma?' Pa Frogmore was shaking his head in wonder, 'Exactly like that - well I'll be buggered!' A chill ran through him as, deep in a mental dungeon, a suppressed memory struggled against its chains.

'Mother… this is Richard - Richard, this is my Mother' Reeta made the introductions. The foyer of the theatre was filling up for a special morning performance with free entrance for pensioners. Reeta had gone to great pains to get her mother to attend, eventually bribing her with a new handbag that currently contained several cream crackers.

Richard chose a smile from his 'dazzling' range and beamed it at Ravinda.

'Are they all your own teeth?' he got in reply.

'Your daughter is a natural actress Mrs Chopra, you must be very proud of her.' Richard prided himself on discovering 'Diamonds in the Rock.' A previous protégé of his had gone on to do very well in radio drama and had appeared on national television as a woman with indigestion who sucked a lozenge and ended up doing the samba with a man on a yacht. He had seen in Reeta a potential tigress concealing herself in an undergrowth of nondescript beige clothes and shy accessories designed to blend in rather than stand out.

'Reeta tells me you are a lawyer?'

'Well, I'm a legal clerk but I…'

'Why do you want to waste your time acting when you have a law career?'

Richard smiled, 'I suppose there are those who would ask why I would want to spend my time in law when I could act?'

He got a look in reply that reminded him of an eagle owl he had seen in a zoo as a child.

'Well,' he floundered, 'I can see where Reeta gets her looks from.'

Ravinda, who had always regarded her daughter as plain, took this as an insult and the glare sharpened to a point where Richard thought she was actually going to attack him. He backed away; 'Right… well better go and get the old greasepaint on, see you in a tick Reeta…' he beat a nervous retreat leaving Reeta to escort her mother safely to her seat.

The chief magistrate had actually laughed, and then they had retired to consider their verdict. When the bench returned they handed down to the hippy in the dock two hundred hours of Community Payback. Pa had shouted 'Hooray' at the prospect of a new pair of boots and Randy, relieved at not going to prison, had said 'Thank you' to the magistrate who had responded by saying 'Love and peace man' before giggling again.

Following his appearance, Randy hammed it up for the Chronicle photographer on the steps of the court and, in a gesture of hitherto undetectable civic pride, swore to take part in the Newvale 200 parade....

'...And ahm gonna make it a li'l home we can be proud of.' Reeta looked up into Richards eyes and they kissed. The lights dimmed and the audience applauded. In the front row Ravinda Chopra nudged the man next to her; 'That's my daughter, she's a natural you know...'

*   *   *   *   *   *

CHAPTER SIXTEEN

EDUCATION

LYDIA Gurney was a born educator. She had dreamed of being a teacher ever since she was a small girl. Of course, there had been distractions along the way, phases she went through when she wanted to be a dancer, or an actress or a woman who washed elephants with a long brush and a hosepipe or, on one short-lived occasion, a newsreader. She had set up a desk in the living room and read a prepared news bulletin to her amused parents, which had consisted mainly of family events with a special emphasis on the recidivism of her younger brother.

Lydia's parents had set great store by education and had ensured their offspring had grown up surrounded by books and in particular atlases. Her father was an armchair adventurer who loved maps and faraway places. Lydia had sat with him for hours as he had pointed out the countries of the world and encouraged her to learn them. She could now name almost any capital city on Earth and on a relief map of the planet would be able to pinpoint the location of any given country. And now even if she didn't always know what she should be doing, she always knew where she was.

Unlike her father Lydia had not been content to study the faraway places in the pages of an atlas, she wanted to go there and see them for herself - and so she did, travelling to every continent, absorbing knowledge and experience and storing it for future use.

She had qualified as a teacher and brought to bear her wealth of knowledge and experience in the task of educating some of Newvale's most challenging youngsters - those who had not sat for hours with their father and an atlas and those who had learned that parental approval, and often safety, lay in not drawing attention to oneself in the family home. Lydia now had the challenge of leading them back to the path of enlightenment, finding a way through the emotional barricades and encouraging crushed spirits to pick themselves up and have one more go with the promise that they had been lied to and that the world was really not that bad a place.

But when you have the hangover from hell and you've walked to work in the rain and the heating is broken again in your classroom and every one of the students seems to have watched the same violent TV show the night before it can be hard to recall with any clarity the original mission statement.

'QUIET!'

Lydia's shout rang in her head like a rhino colliding with a pyramid of galvanised steel buckets. Most of the class calmed down. A pair of boys were still giggling and miming something that, try as she might, Lydia could think of no innocent interpretation for.

'When you're quite ready…'

At last, the final few faced the front. A hand went up.

'Yes Amber?'

'It's cold Miss.'

'I know Amber, the heating…. JACK! You've been warned about that!

'I was scratching my head Miss'

'You were not scratching…SIT DOWN SEAN!….you were not scratching your head Jack, you were making horns; you've been told not to make horns and not to tell people you're the devil. Now then, the heating is broken but Mr Farr hopes to have it back on by lunchtime. You can all put your coats on if you want to.'

Amber Wellbeloved's hand rose again, 'Jason just swore Miss,'

'I didn't, I said dung - dung's not swearing is it Miss? You get dung on farms.'

'SIT…. DOWN! No Jason, dung is not swearing but..'

'See - I fucking told you!'

Lydia rubbed her temples and mouthed a silent platitude to the ceiling, 'Thank fuck it's Friday!' She checked herself and immediately apologised to Pamela Parish whose deafness had made her an expert lip-reader.

Police Constable Boniface Lillywhite was admiring the display in Shortcock and Mee's window. One of the mannequins was wearing a really nice suit with a herringbone pattern and a gold tie that really complimented the jacket and shirt. The material had a pleasing sheen to it and the officer considered, not for the first time, asking Mr Shortcock or Mr Mee to measure him up.

At just under two metres tall and with correspondingly larger than life vital statistics, he had never, as an adult, been able to buy clothes off the peg but he was contemplating a serious change of direction in his life and he felt the occasion merited looking the part. He entered the shop.

It wasn't long before he was approached. In the case of PC Lillywhite it was always best to be the approacher rather than the approachee, if only to get the experience over with as soon as possible.

'Can I help you Constable?'

No matter how fastidious a person was in matters of dress and personal grooming, standing next to Mr Charles Mee always made one feel like a tramp that had just rolled down a steep field of cowpats and brambles and then dried off in a wind tunnel. The word 'impeccable' was a starting point but didn't begin to describe the effortless panache and poise he radiated.

'Ah, yes well I'd like to be measured for a nice suit.'

The tailor's left eyebrow rose momentarily. Mr Mee was proud of his professional skills and relished a challenge.

'Jolly good, well lets see what we can do then shall we?'

Boniface Lillywhite had only ever owned one suit. It had been a present from his grandparents on the eve of his twelfth birthday and had been run up in an afternoon by the Blessed Man From Galilee Tailors and Outfitters store in downtown Lagos. Even as a boy he had been big for his age and the tailor had wanted to charge extra for the amount of material used but his grandfather was an expert haggler and had even got the hapless artisan to throw in a shirt and tie for the same price.

The suit had been for his confirmation and he still remembered standing in the church with his entire extended family in attendance listening to the priest shouting to be heard over the ceaseless sound of the traffic and the whirring of the ceiling fans. Later there had been a party and he'd had asun barbecued goat meat, pepper soup and coca-cola.

Mr Mee measured him twice, and then checked what he'd written down and measured him a third time.

'Special occasion?' Like everyone else in Newvale, Mr Mee was fully aware of the eccentricities of the Town's biggest single law enforcement operative but he prided himself on being able to relate to people of all backgrounds.

'Yes, I'm going to ask a lady to marry me!'

Unseen by the policeman, the tailor's eyebrow rose again; 'Well the very best of luck to you old chap.'

Lydia Gurney and her class were watching an educational film about alcohol. Friday was not the best day of the week for Lydia to be reminded of the effects of alcohol on the human body. For her, Thursday night was Country and Western night and the 'likker' generally flowed free as Newvale's latent cowboys and cowgals threw off the shackles imposed on them through being born in the wrong time and place and became the rootin' tootin' gunfightin' cowpunchin' horsebotherin' ornery critters their hearts told them they really were.

There had been an impromptu karaoke contest last night and Lydia vaguely remembered singing 'I'm a Galveston Gal in a Ten Gallon Hat' and then there was some disjointed recollection of shouting 'Giddyap you goldurned coyote!' to a cab driver and then very little until the morning alarm wrenched her from the arms of Morpheus into her own private hell where her head was full of bells and her tongue felt as if a coyote had been sleeping on it.

The film drew to a close and Lydia was now expected to chair a question and answer session based on what they had all just seen.

'Right - we've all just seen the effect alcohol has on the human body - who can tell me the safe and suggested daily limit for a man and woman?'

Several hands went up.

'Yes Jade?'

'If that man had put his arm around me and tried to drag me away I'd have kneed him in the gentiles and screamed!'

'Yes, Jade, but the question was...'

'Five units Miss - but ten on Saturdays before seven pm because they're half price!'

'The cost has very little to do with it Justin, it's a matter of...'

'My mother went to sleep on the toilet once and my dad got up in the night and peed on her Miss!'

'Really Lara, well perhaps that illustrates...'

'Our neighbour fell over his own hedge and then pooed himself...'

'You know Carmel McQuillan? Her father was sick over a police dog!'

Lydia took a deep breath and just let things go; sometimes the sheepdogs know better than the shepherd and it would be lunchtime in twenty minutes.

Sergeant Eric Randall had a problem. He had a job to fill and a very thin list of potential candidates to fill it. WPC Greenwood had announced she was going to have a baby and would therefore be seeking maternity leave. Not only did this leave the sergeant with a hole in his already stretched team but it also left Newvale without a Police School Liaison Officer. Discounting the traffic teams there were only three other constables in the station; PC Vickery had a shaved head and cauliflower ears; he spoke in a series of grunts and monosyllables.

Sergeant Randall generally used him as a sort of 'law-enforcement-scarecrow' by standing him in potential trouble spots. He would be thoroughly unsuitable to the task of building relationships between Newvale's young people and the police.

Then there was Detective Constable Rickman who looked and smelled as if he slept on a compost heap. He swore profusely and lived on a diet of vodka, coffee and cigarettes - not the image of local policing Inspector Snow wanted to project.

That left Lillywhite, Sergeant Randall shuddered - and yet... there was that time when Park Road Junior School had brought a class along for a tour of the police station and Lillywhite had locked the teacher in one of the cells before taking the excited and chattering crocodile of little people out on to Fuller Square and into the American Diner where he had suggested that considerable good will would be generated by the provision of twenty-five complimentary milkshakes - not needing to underline the implication that to refuse would be to generate the exact opposite. Afterwards the children, under Lillywhite's watchful eye, had taken it in turns to stop the traffic then wave it on again. Unorthodox maybe, but they all returned to school determined to be police officers when they grew up and for weeks afterward a wall in the station's reception area had been covered in drawings depicting the visit, invariably figuring large in most of them, the unmistakable figure of PC Lillywhite with a huge smile on his face - the smiling face of Newvale Police and that, Sergeant Randall reluctantly acknowledged, was exactly what Inspector Snow wanted.

PC Lillywhite was, at that moment, smiling very widely indeed. He had just left Shortcock and Mee having ordered a suit like the one in the window with a nice sheen on it and a new shirt and tie as well. Now he was heading back into Fuller Square and around the corner to the station where he would do his paperwork before signing off for the day. He spotted a furtive figure in a long shabby coat lurking outside the American Diner and bore down on the man while his attention was diverted by the sight of an attractive young woman getting off a bus.

'Aha!'

The man turned, his eyes, already magnified by thick glasses, grew even wider at the sight of a beaming PC Lillywhite looming over him. He began bobbing up and down like an excited pigeon.

'Not up to anything naughty are we?'

'Err n..no officer, I was just admiring the… umm…'

'Yes, well I'm well aware of what you admire - you haven't been playing the tummy trombone again have you?'

'No! No not at all…' The man raised his hands.

'Hmmm, well I should hope not, did I ever tell you about a man I knew from Shagamu?'

'Where?' The man looked perplexed.

'The place doesn't really matter, he was like you, overly fond of milking the mongoose and he was warned what would happen but he took no notice and do you know what happened?'

Any inclination the man might have been harbouring to 'milk the mongoose' had evaporated and he simply shrugged.

'Well I'll tell you shall I? One day he went down to the market and was soon up to his old tricks until a group of men grabbed him and bundled him into a molue and…'

'A what?' The man queried. If he was going to hear a cautionary tale he may as well understand it.

'A molue, they were like buses but much more dangerous; anyhow, they bundled him in and took him ten miles out of town where they found a huge anthill…'

'I'd… I'd like to go home now.' The man interrupted

'Yes, well that's probably a good idea, but before you go it might help if you were to get yourself a new coat, the one you have on looks… well it looks the sort of coat a man might wear if he were overly fond of self abuse, they've got some good offers in Shortcock and Mee at the moment.'

'Oh.. err, thank you.' The man scurried off in a bizarre sort of lurch almost colliding with a lamppost in his hurry to get out of the square. PC Lillywhite smiled to himself and passed through the double glass doors into the police station.

Sergeant Randall was putting up a crime prevention poster in the reception area when the constable entered. 'Ah Lillywhite, just the man, I've got a little assignment I'd like you to consider...'

The brass band that had been playing in Lydia Gurney's head since dawn had thinned down to a couple of trumpets and a snare drum by mid afternoon; she had a free period, which meant a coffee and the chance to do some marking. Opening the first book she was initially impressed by the neatness of the handwriting particularly when it belonged to Joel Kennard who always looked as if he had dressed in the dark in a room full of other people's clothes. The essay was, however, a triumph of style over substance. The class had been asked to write about the most memorable event of their previous weekend and Joel had taken four pages to describe a television programme he had watched in which a dinosaur had picked up another dinosaur in its jaws, shook it and then thrown it up in the air where it got caught in a tree. He then added as an afterthought the fact that his mother's boyfriend always cleaned his teeth in the nude and had a scar on his 'buttacks' the same shape as a grill from where he had got drunk and sat on the barbecue the summer before last. Lydia sighed and gave it a 'good effort' before moving on to the next one in the pile.

Amber Wellbeloved had used her essay to compare herself favourably with several of the other girls in her class, pointing out that her weekend had been spent helping her mother to decorate the spare bedroom, then she had taken her little niece to the fair but they had to go home early to avoid the Punch and Judy show; and then she had gone shopping - unlike Jade Overton who had allegedly "Done something to two boys behind Cold Ridge Youth Club that I'm not allowed to say but it begins with a W, you know what I mean Miss, only I didn't tell you right?"

Lydia looked forward to Amber's essays which always included at least one encounter with a Punch and Judy show. The regular inclusion of the traditional puppets had caused the teacher to question whether they had indeed figured in some incident in Amber's life. Gentle and persistent coaxing had revealed that, on her eighth birthday she and her friends had enjoyed a party at which a Punch and Judy show had been part of the entertainment. Later in the afternoon Amber had heard shouts of 'That's the way to do it!' coming from the garden shed and, expecting a repeat performance, had peered in only to see her mother kneeling in front of the Punch and Judy man - who it turned out was none other than her uncle Darren - doing something inexplicable. But although Amber couldn't fathom what her mother was up to it was clearly being done with a high degree of aptitude made evident by Uncle Darren's whoops and shouts of approval. Years later when it became obvious to Amber what her mother had been up to she had chosen to partially suppress the incident by conditioning herself to truly believe that Punch and Judy men have evil powers which they can use to force women to eat sausages.

'Excellent - I've got some great ideas about this already!'

This was exactly the sort of reaction Sergeant Randall had feared. 'There are set rules and regulations about how an officer conducts himself on school visits you know,' he reminded the constable as they changed into their civilian clothes at the end of their shift.

'And quite right too,' Lillywhite agreed, 'we wouldn't want the youngsters thinking it's all fun and games in the police would we Sarge?'

Randall gazed at the ceiling for a few seconds and decided against replying. He combed his thinning hair in the mirror and watched as the constable put on a pullover that he said his mother in Nigeria had knitted for him, a statement that had led Randall to speculate on the

Lillywhite matriarch's powers of endurance and the sheep population of West Africa.

'Did I tell you Sarge? I'm going to propose.'

'You're going to what?' Randall was genuinely surprised. He had given the fledgling romance a fortnight when Lillywhite had first announced he was walking out with a lady but it was still going strong - so strong apparently that wedding bells were a real possibility. He must have hidden depths or she, like so many others, had been hypnotised by the sheer size of the man.

'I'm going to ask Lydia to marry me.'

'You're not going to have a fucking cowboy wedding are you?' The Sergeant was already picturing his inspector's raised eyebrows.

'No, I've been measured up for a suit in Shortcock and Mee's!'

'That should give them something to talk about over lunch,' Randall thought to himself before forcing an uncustomary smile on to his face, 'Well congratulations.'

'She hasn't said "Yes" yet, I'm going to take her out for a special meal on Friday after I pick up my suit.'

PC Lillywhite had considered proposing at the Country and Western Club, resplendent in his cowboy gear, but he wanted the occasion to be really memorable and part of that was going to be the surprise when she saw him dressed up to the nines. As he strolled to his car he pondered once again on the role he had just accepted as Police Schools Liaison Officer. He had often thought about taking his girlfriend out on patrol to show her his professional world, now he would have the opportunity to experience hers.

Lydia's professional world was lasting longer today. It was parent's evening and along with most of the teaching staff she sat in the school hall at one of a row of desks awaiting the next parent who had made an appointment to speak with her. A chimp-like man with huge fleshy ears sat himself in the chair opposite. He wore a shirt and tie so unmatched that Lydia thought of the resistance felt when forcing together the kindred poles of magnets 'I'm Jason Quinn's father,' he announced; Lydia smiled politely and searched through the pile of reports for the one pertaining to Quinn the Younger. Unbeknown to the man she was actually playing for time as she racked her brain to try and think of something positive to say about his son.

'He's a very quiet boy in class.'

'He's always been a deep thinker, our Jason.'

'So deep that a coherent thought has yet to reach the surface,' said Lydia to herself, 'Well,' she smiled, 'He's making progress in science, we've been studying colours in nature this term and...' she was momentarily sidetracked by the shirt and tie, speculating that this was probably the first time in history outside establishments for the criminally insane that the colours in front of her had been deliberately placed in such close proximity. '...err, yes, colours, he may have mentioned it at home?'

'He don't talk much at home, he's always been a deep thinker.'

'Yes, I see... well...'

'Follows his granddad, he was a deep thinker.'

'Indeed, however we like to encourage participation in class discussions, sharing ideas and...'

'Ohh, our Jason don't have ideas, his mother had ideas and a fat lot of good it did her.' The chimp man folded his arms signifying any further debate about the merits of pooled knowledge would be futile.

After an hour and a half the faces started to blend together into a sort of 'parent identikit' and Lydia felt herself switching off and handing over the task to the autopilot. 'Yes, he tries hard..... Indeed, she's making good progress.... Well, there have been a few behavioural problems....' As always, she consoled herself with the knowledge that the parents she was seeing were the ones who cared enough to turn up.

The extendable coat hanger didn't extend enough and Mr Mee had to get one especially made for the finished suit to hang on.

'If it were anyone other than you I'd say there's been a little hiccup over the measurements.' Mr Ralph Shortcock studied the garment in wonder.

'Well, you've seen the bugger, if anything I'm hoping it's not a little too snug. He's going to propose marriage in it apparently, do you think we should offer a discount in return for him mentioning us in his reception speech?"

Ralph Shortcock shook his head, 'I think everyone will take it as read that he bought it made-to-measure, the only place you'd get a suit that size off the peg would be on a film set or something.'

What had started out as a sunny day had deteriorated throughout the morning and now, approaching lunchtime, the skies above Newvale were battleship grey and a fine drizzle ensured people walked quickly from shop to shop around Fuller Square.

A little man more accustomed to staring in through the window of Shortcock and Mee now found himself inside where he stood polishing the steam from the thick lens of his glasses. Replacing them he approached an unwary sales assistant and tugged on her sleeve.

'I want a coat that makes me look respectable.'

'One moment please Sir, I'll fetch someone to help you,' Reeta Chopra beat a hasty retreat from the furtive figure who continued to gaze myopically around the shop floor. He repeated his request as Charles Mee approached causing the tailor's eyebrow to migrate half way to a perfectly coiffured silver hairline.

'I see' said Mr Mee, 'Hmmm, respectable...' he looked the figure up and down as if struggling to find a shred of common ground between the word and the image before him. 'Perhaps something in fawn with a detachable lining? And has Sir ever considered a hat?'

Lydia entered the staffroom of Meadowvale Comprehensive School closely followed by Police Constable Boniface 'Slim' Lillywhite causing a clearly audible gasp from those assembled within. Being in the main law abiding it was the first time most of them had encountered the officer up close and the sheer scale of the man was causing a rapid re-evaluation of the parameters within which 'human' sat. Taking off his helmet went a little way toward making him less intimidating but it was a huge smile that broke the ice.

'A very good afternoon to you all!' he boomed and was rewarded with a chuckle of relief.

The gasp was much more apparent when, following a cup of tea with the staff, he entered Lydia's classroom. A few 'Wows' and at least one 'Fucking hell' greeted the Constable whose smile as he faced the class was markedly more crocodilian than the one he had used on the teachers. He was recalling his father's advice that between an officer and the public was a wall with barbed wire on the top, a wise officer will remove the barbed wire but a foolish officer will also dismantle the wall.

A hand shot up. 'We haven't started yet Conor,' Lydia explained.

'I know Miss, but I wanted to ask the copper if there's puffins in Africa?'

The class groaned.

'There are no puffins in the part of Africa I come from so… err….' It wasn't the first question Slim had anticipated and had thrown him a bit, Lydia came to the rescue, 'We'll get around to questions in a minute after I've done the introductions.'

'We know who he is Miss!' a number of the class offered. The officer bared his teeth in a humourless smile; the familiarity was mutual in the case of a few of the faces before him.

There was very little of the cockiness often displayed by miscreants in the presence of the police. In places other than Newvale they might conceivably hide behind the shield of 'We know our rights,' but they were all too aware it would be a pointless defence in the case of P.C. Lillywhite who considered only their wrongs when dishing out justice. There were few among Newvale's errant youth who did not have a tale to tell about the constable. Some of the stories were passed on so much they had grown considerably in the telling but had remained bizarrely credible. Another hand went up.

'Just a moment Amber, now then, this is Constable Lillywhite of Newvale Police, he's our new Schools Liaison Officer and...'

Amber's hand waved and clenched in increasing urgency.

'Very well Amber, what is it?'

'Miss, I'd like to ask the policeman if it's against the law to do something beginning with a W to two boys?' There were chuckles from many in the class and a look of pure venom from Jade Overton.

'That's quite enough of that Amber, PC Lillywhite has come here to...'

PC Lillywhite raised a reassuring hand and smiled a gentle smile to Lydia, prompting her to stop before turning his attention to Amber who suddenly took on the demeanour of someone who had dipped their fishing net in the canal to catch a minnow and pulled out a shark.

'...Something with a "W" eh? Let's see...' The officer put his hands behind his back and paced as if in deep thought, 'Hmmm, W...W...' a nervous giggling ran around the class, Thomas Reid put up his hand, 'The second letter's "A" Sir.

'Aha!' Lillywhite boomed making several of the children and indeed Lydia jump, 'You mean... Wash!' Well I should imagine it's perfectly OK for this girl to be giving the boys a wash. My eldest sister used to have to wash my brothers and me because my mother would often have left for work before we got up. Does that answer your question?'

Amber was intelligent enough to realise she had an opportunity to extricate herself from a very uncomfortable situation. She smiled weakly and gave a barely perceptible nod. PC Lillywhite beamed, 'Splendid, now who can tell me what a police officer's best friend is?'

Several hands shot up and Lillywhite nodded to them in turn before dismissing the answers with a shake of the head

'The stick you hit people with?'

'Handcuffs?'

'Police dog?'

'I know who your best friend is, it's Miss Gurney there,' Tom Ferris' snigger died away as PC Lillywhite strolled down the aisle between the desks. He bent and whispered something in the boy's ear, which brought a look of horror to the young face. The officer then turned and headed back to the front of the class.

'It's this!' he announced pulling his notebook from his pocket. 'I can't remember every name and face, so I write them down. It wouldn't do for someone me to end up arresting the wrong person, would it?'

Several of those listening saw nothing untoward in the wrong person being arrested as long as it meant they in turn got away with whatever it was they had been doing.

'It all goes in here,' he waved his notebook, 'For instance, so far today I've cautioned a man for parking in the disabled bay outside the Town Hall, I made him hop all around Fuller Square on one leg to see how he liked having a disability. I actually made him do it twice because he fell over the first time.' The class laughed.

'Then later this morning I had to pop out to Cedar Hills Nursing Home because an elderly man had stolen all the tea cups and locked himself in his room and was refusing to come out until they gave him his clown costume back. They were afraid he would hurt himself but I managed to get him out by singing through the letterbox' This brought a hearty laugh from the assembly.'

Lydia watched as the class, without even thinking about it, were collectively put at their ease. This wasn't a taught skill this was something that came naturally to Boniface; he just seemed to know how to engage people; the word pulled her towards an oft-visited speculation, she was sure that as far as their relationship was concerned he was in it for the long haul, he had said so and had seemed interested when they had stopped to look in the window of an estate agents and she had pointed out a modest two-bedroomed house in Old Meadowvale.

Her mind was brought back to the present by a gale of laughter from the students; Boniface was chuckling with them,

'.. and the funny thing is, when we opened the cell door in the morning to let him go he was fast asleep under the bed and he was wearing his socks on his hands!'

The youngsters laughed again and even though Lydia had heard only the punchline of the story she found herself laughing too.

He had been thoroughly impressed with the workmanship of Charles Mee and had told him so. 'You are a craftsman Sir!' he had boomed as he admired his reflection in the new suit. The tailor had smiled a fleeting smile and quietly congratulated himself on the successful completion of the biggest outfit he had ever created.

Now, at home, Boniface Lillywhite was dressed to the nines; he manoeuvred himself around so that he could study himself a bit at a time in a wardrobe mirror designed for someone of far more modest dimensions. He was pleased with the result; it was a really nice suit and the new shirt and tie set it off perfectly.

His landlady stared open mouthed as he left for the restaurant. Normally, he would have swung past Lydia's and picked her up but her wanted to meet her there to maximise the surprise. This was the night - this was it! He had told his mother on the phone just a few hours ago of his intentions and she had insisted he bring her 'home' to meet the extended Lillywhite clan.

He had booked a table in the Lakeside Restaurant adjoining Newvale Park; it was possible to watch the wildfowl and evening dog walkers as one ate. Lydia had always like it there and the chairs were generously sized. She arrived as he was in the process of checking his watch for the twentieth time and, to his delight, she actually stopped in her tracks as she caught sight of him. Gently he guided her to her seat and gave a barely noticeable nod to the barman who immediately brought champagne.

Lydia's heart raced; he was going to propose surely. He looked great in the suit and she had been about to tell him so. He was clearly nervous and... yes, he was taking a little box from his pocket. Surely he wasn't going to go down on one knee? No, he sat on the chair next to her and took a deep breath...

'Lydia, I am most profoundly fond of you and I would like you to consider becoming Mrs Lillywhite!'

That was it, that and a most engaging and appealing smile. He opened the little box and took out not a ring but a gold cross on a chain. Lydia's confusion must have been evident as he offered an explanation.

'It used to belong to my great grandmother. I was going to get a ring but I wasn't sure of your size but if you say 'Yes' We'll go and get one tomorrow and then we'll go and have a look at that house in Meadowvale - I was thinking we could have a few chickens, only for eggs of course, I wouldn't expect you to cut their heads off although my grandmother used to, not only that but she could dispatch a goat quicker than ...

'Yes.'

'....you could say... you could say... say that again?'

'I said... yes!'

If you counted the invited guests, then it wasn't a big wedding, but if you counted the actual number who turned up and multiplied by the size of the groom then it was one of the biggest matrimonial events Newvale had ever seen. The Newvale Chronicle photographer had attended along with many of Newvale's Country and Western Club, Lydia's parents and sister were there, Sergeant Randall had been privately flattered to have been asked to officiate as best man and would not be short of tales to tell at the reception. But the guest of honour had been Boniface Lillywhite's mother who had made the journey all the way from Africa unbeknown to her son as a surprise.

Small Town People

Boniface had introduced her to her new daughter-in-law and his many friends from the town he had grown to love and call home. Most of Lydia's students and just about everyone who had crossed the policeman's path throughout his career seemed to be outside the registry office. It heartened him to see so many of Newvale's criminals cleaned and polished and eager to shake his hand - a fact that did not escape Sergeant Randall's attention. There was one scary moment when a little man in bottle-bottom glasses appeared to be making and exhibition of himself but it turned out he was just showing some bridesmaids the lining in his brand new coat.

* * * * * *

CHAPTER SEVENTEEN

MOURNFUL OLD DANIEL

THERE are no specific guidelines relating to the treatment of stoats in the Hippocratic oath; even so, it was rare for any significant length of time to go by without Doctor Douglas McKinnon-Law deeply regretting having shot a stoat with an air rifle then paying to have it stuffed and mounted on a wooden plinth.

What could he have been thinking of? He knew how living things worked; he was on first name terms with all the amazing mechanisms, harmonious systems, wobbly bits and fluids that made it possible for large lumps of matter comprising calcium, protein, water and various trace elements to not only see the night sky but to ponder on their place in the vastness. So what had possessed him, on seeing a playful stoat in the woods above the loch all those years ago, to send 14 grams of lead towards it at two hundred metres per second?

Occasionally he dreamed about the stoat. It would come to him with disturbingly human characteristics vaguely reminding him of his long-deceased father, the same wistful smile - a difficult feat for a stoat - and a tone of voice that succeeded in being at once affectionate and slightly admonishing. He would wake with the same regrets, calling to mind all the things he would like to have said to his father and how he dearly wished he had slipped on the wet ferns in that long gone loch side wood and his pellet had flown wide. If that had happened then the stoat would had skipped happily back home to his family and today his descendants would be capering with carefree abandon in the pale sunshine.

He sometimes felt that keeping it all these years had been some kind of penance and that the lifelong guilt might well diminish if he were to simply throw the bloody thing away, it was looking moth-eaten now anyway; but on the one occasion he had bitten the bullet and put it in the bin his housekeeper of twenty-two years, Mrs Mary Merryman, had taken it out and cleaned it and put it back on the shelf.

'You'll never guess who I found in the bin,' she had told him as she dished up his dinner.

'The postman?'

'Eh?' she regarded him quizzically.

'The postman - or perhaps Mr Ahmed who runs the paper shop, or was it maybe a quartet of agoraphobic dwarves? You see it must have been a living entity because you referred to it as 'Who' and not 'What.'

Mary had given him the affectionately quizzical look she reserved for times when he was saying 'Educated doctory things.'

'All I'm saying is that I found Mournful Old Daniel in the dustbin; I can't imagine how he got there?'

Dr McKinnon-Law had pinched the bridge of his nose and studied the potatoes on his plate; one of them was an almost perfect sphere, bloody impressive!

'Yes, you see Mary, this is why I sometimes have cause to wonder whether I'm actually doing you a kindness in letting you near sharp objects. Now what you found in the rubbish bin was a stoat, a dead stoat, a very very dead stoat - the fact that it is comprised of organic material makes it only as alive as a wooden spoon, so why, in the name of whoever you believe created dandelions and the great spirals of the cosmos would you call it Mournful Old Daniel?'

She had explained, at laborious and convoluted length, that the unfortunate creature always looked so sad and reminded her of her old Uncle Daniel who had died of a broken heart after Aunt Minnie had gone out one day to buy lemon curd and was found five days later in a bus shelter seventy miles away with a carrier bag full of cucumbers and absolutely no idea of where, or indeed who, she was.

The Doctor had reluctantly placed the creature back on the mantelpiece in his consulting room between the photograph of him in the uniform of a naval lieutenant and the small cup for 'Second Runner-Up' in a long-ago annual Kingdom of Fife Open Shooting Championship.

The creature had long since ceased to look like a live stoat and was often mistaken for a wooden model; this was due in no small part to Mary having used brown shoe polish on it a few years previously to try and give it back a bit of sheen. It subsequently resembled a turd with teeth and more than one person, assuming it was some sort of rare medical aberration, had suffered nightmares as a result.

Dr McKinnon-Law was a busy senior general practitioner at a surgery in the relatively leafy and comfortable Newvale suburb of Cedar Hill and also did rounds in various local clinics, while off duty he enjoyed a busy and fulfilling social life as a member of Newvale Caledonian Society and the Golf Club.

He had married as a young man but his wife had left him after just nine months for a Norwegian oceanographer she had met in a shoe shop in Aberdeen. Afterwards the young Douglas became disillusioned with all womenfolk and for a short time seriously contemplated entering a monastery but instead, following a boozy garden party, he entered the daughter of a prominent church minister and then, for an encore, entered her brother as well which left him so emotionally confused he spent the next four years on the banks of the Congo at a medical mission. On his return he had found work at the practice in Newvale.

His home was adorned with various mementos of his African years including a picture he had drawn during a bout of malaria of a member of the Bambenga people that, in the height of his delirium, he had imagine talking to him and encouraging him to drink some foul-smelling medicine which had, nevertheless, broken the fever and set him on the road to recovery. The experience had left him receptive to not only conventional medicine but also folk remedies and various fringe treatments.

Tony Fletcher, owner and manager of Newvale Animal Sanctuary, was also receptive to unconventional treatments if it meant avoiding an extortionate veterinary bill and was trying with limited success to convince his deputy manager, Dawn of the need for an open mind when it came to animal health.

'I'm having nothing to do with it,' she stated firmly, 'It's a limping sheep with a cough, it could be worms or pneumonia or something notifiable, we should get Mr Truman out to have a look.'

'Yeah? We might as well shoot the fucking thing; it would cost us less to lose the bastard than to get Truman out - bloody highway robber. Look, this cough syrup works great on me and it's cheap as chips; I'll get the bugger in a headlock and you pour it in right?' He handed her the bottle and Dawn studied the label.

'It says the dose for an adult is two small spoonfuls; you want to pour the whole bottle in? It contains alcohol Tony.'

'Yeah? Better still; take its mind off the cough. I remember once, I had a bit of a cold, went out and had a bloody good piss-up and a curry - right as rain the next morning - hey, that's a thought, there's half a lamb madras in the microwave in the office, that'll sweat it out of the bugger!'

Dawn looked at him in wonder, 'You want to feed sheep to a sheep?'

Tony shrugged, 'Remember Huy the pig? Loved a pork pie - and are you telling me that if you were really hungry you wouldn't eat a person? I know I would... well, bits of one anyway as long as it was a stranger, I couldn't eat someone I knew.'

'You knew Huy the pig.'

'Yeah, but he was a pig, they like being eaten that's why all their insides are shaped like chops and stuff.'

The sheep, as if sensing it was about to be forcibly inebriated, stopped coughing and walked off.

'Mrs Dugdale of 8, Dahlia Crescent is next with her son Simon,' Mary put the case notes on Dr McKinnon-Law's desk.

'OK, show them in would you please Mary.'

The housekeeper was doubling as receptionist due to the no-show of the regular incumbent who was at home with one of her migraines.

'He's got sticky eyes; I asked her if she thought he'd been touching his gentleman because he's twelve and you know what they're like at that age; my brother Peter couldn't leave his alone for five minutes, I was glad I didn't have one, I'd never have got any knitting done...'

'Yes Mary, we've been through this before - you show them in, I'll diagnose them OK?'

'As you say Doctor – COME ON THROUGH MRS DUGDALE AND SIMON!'

A woman steered her son into the surgery, giving Mary a bleak look as she passed her in the doorway.

Morning surgery generally ran on rails in the Cedar Hill practice, a regular column of minor ailments and chronic conditions requiring a bit of fine-tuning with a healthy dose of oddities to break the diagnostic monotony. As the day wore on Doctor McKinnon-Law found himself treating a middle-aged woman whose head kept turning to the left completely of its own accord; a man who asked for inoculation against Green Monkey Disease because he'd had some shit thrown at him in a zoo and a carpet fitter attempting to obtain grounds to sue his employer because he'd started having nightmares in which he was chased through a bleak, post-apocalyptic world by huge creatures made from underlay.

'That was the last of them Doctor,' Mary finally sounded the 'All Clear' as the last patient of the morning left. 'Only one visit for this afternoon, Mr Rosetti, Bramble Cottage, Sycamore Street - sounds like 'flu but if I were you I'd check him down below, Celia Paterson saw him coming out of that place above the launderette on Cold Ridge Road and then Tony Fletcher from the animal sanctuary called, could he please have a prescription, he's got a cough and he's limping.'

Dr McKinnon-Law sniffed, 'Hmmm, I suppose that's slightly more plausible than the last time he phoned in claiming he had chapped udders.' The doctor sat at his desk and checked the contents of his case prior to leaving. He caught sight of Mournful Old Daniel in the corner of his eye and unconsciously swivelled in his chair to eliminate the object from his peripheral vision.

Tony Fletcher was driving into Newvale for a meeting in a pub with a man who had a female Golden Guernsey goat. Tony had a male of the same breed and he was hoping to negotiate a good stud price. The man had suggested coming up to the Sanctuary to see the goat for himself but Tony had fobbed him off with an excuse in order to buy a little time. In actual fact, the Sanctuary's male Golden Guernsey was not so much golden as bright green after knocking a pot of paint off a stepladder as it walked beneath it and Tony had left Dawn and Melanie, a Sanctuary volunteer, with the task of cleaning the unfortunate creature. He had downloaded a picture of a similar goat and printed it off to show the potential owner

'Bum tit tit, bum tit tit, bum titty titty, bum tit tit...' Tony sang to himself, the diesel engine of his 4x4 ticked over as he waited at the lights. Sven the German Shepherd panted in the passenger seat. The dog had originally ended up at the Sanctuary when its owner had been sentenced to three years in prison for pornography offences. He had been a filmmaker and Sven had appeared in many of his 'specialist' productions, making the animal particularly difficult to re-home. He was a friendly enough dog, however, as long as you kept an eye on him and ensured he never got between a lady and the only exit.

It was Friday and Newvale was busy with early weekend shoppers. He watched as an attractive young woman chatted on her phone while waiting at a bus stop, he noticed Sven studying her too. A honking of horns behind him told him the lights had changed while his attention was elsewhere and so he pulled off and headed for the centre of town.

The Animal Sanctuary was never going to make Tony a millionaire but thanks to donations and sponsorship it paid the bills and allowed him a reasonably comfortable life. He could have sold up - a farmhouse and several acres would fetch a tidy sum which would allow him to buy a modest semi in town and still have a tidy nest egg, but Tony was a countryman at heart, he would suffocate in a small house with a postage-stamp garden and while he couldn't, by any stretch of the imagination, be described as an animal lover, he certainly loved the potential for fiscal self advancement that animals made possible and, like many a tropical dictator before him, had come to realise that native fauna was potentially worth far more *vitae intacta*.

Pulling into the car park of the Red Lion, Tony noticed Dr McKinnon-Law getting out of his car and so he subsequently disembarked his own vehicle and crossed the car park with a pronounced limp.

'Ah *cough* Doctor, I'm glad *cough* I bumped into you, ohh, damn this limp, I was wondering if you could give me something   *cough* for this damn lameness and this *cough* cough?'

Dr McKinnon-Law frowned heavenward as if attempting to conjure a name from the clouds, 'Mr… Mr.. err..'

'Fletcher, Tony Fletcher…. *cough*' Tony offered helpfully.

'Fletcher… ah yes - how's the udders? Did the cream help?'

'The udders? Ah, the old udders,' Tony nodded vaguely downwards in a forlorn effort to endow 'udders' with a rural euphemistic quality both men immediately recognised as being pointless. 'Much on the mend doctor, much on the mend - aye, 'tis this old cough and limp that's causing the trouble…' Tony's voice was becoming more rustic by the sentence.

'You don't think it might be a zoonosis?' The doctor queried.

'Hmmm, no it's real enough I'm reckoning.'

'No, a zoonosis is a disease that has transferred from an animal to a human.'

'Oh, arr, that it be and no mistake..' Tony's voice was rapidly leaving the rural backwaters and heading for the more choppy currents the Spanish Main, '.. Yarr, transferred from a blarsted animal it has I'm a-thinking.'

'What sort of animal might it have transferred from do you suppose?' The doctor was beginning to enjoy the exchange and was intrigued to see where Tony's accent would head next.

'Well now it wouldn't surprise me if it turned out to be a sheep - we've got a sheep with these exact same symptoms at the moment.'

'I see... sounds notifiable, have you spoken to Mr Truman?'

Tony was aware of the potential for painting himself into a corner and thought carefully about his reply, 'Aye, well of course I've told him about the sheep but I thought I'd mention me to you ... as I'm human.'

Doctor McKinnon-Law studied the clouds again as if seeking some divine confirmation of Tony's claim. He looked at his watch and was disappointed to note that other pressing matters dictated this exchange would have to be drawn to a close, 'Right, well if you pop by the surgery later I'll write you out something.' He smiled bleakly at Tony who offered a sickly and somewhat relieved smile in return, remembering to offer a last *cough* at the back of the retreating doctor.

He looked more like a bank clerk than a goat breeder, small, fussy in his movements and clearly fastidious in dress. He half rose to shake Tony's hand then sat again. Taking a gentle sip from his half of bitter, he took a picture from his jacket pocket.

'This is Edith,' the man pushed the picture across the barroom table towards Tony.

'Edith?' Tony studied the picture of a Golden Guernsey goat.

'Yes, Edith - we, that is the wife and I, decided to call her Edith after hearing her do this amazing bleat one morning, it sounded for all the world like the opening line of 'Je ne regrette rien."

'Fair enough', Tony responded. The goat appeared to be well groomed and in a fine state of health.

'Have you got a picture of yours?'

'Er, yeah,' Tony took the downloaded picture from his pocket. 'This is.. Gaspard.'

'Gaspard?'

'Gaspard, yeah, we… we thought we'd give him a French name as he's such a passionate lover and that.'

'There's a coincidence, both our goats have a French connection, it must be fate.' The man smiled.

'Yes, fancy that.' Tony smiled in return.

'So - do you think it would be possible to pop up to the Sanctuary at some point and take a look at, err… Gaspard? If all is well and we come to a satisfactory agreement I can Bring Edith down next weekend.'

'Shouldn't be a problem, I'll just pop out and make a phone call,' Tony smiled.

Against all the odds Dawn and Melanie had washed, dried and groomed the Sanctuary's Golden Guernsey goat and it looked as good as it ever had, so when Tony had called they were able to give him the green light for the breeder's visit. Dawn was putting the hair dryer back in the cupboard just as Tony's vehicle entered the yard closely followed by the car of the goat breeder.

'This is my assistant, Dawn and one of our volunteers, Melanie, and this is Mr…'

'Oh, Wheeler, George Wheeler - breeder of goats,' he announced as if it were not so much a hobby as a legendary heroic title.

'So, let's go and take a look at Gaspard then,' Tony chivvied them along toward the goat pen.

'Who?' Dawn's query died on her lips as a glare and barely perceptible shake of the head from Tony alerted her to the risk of incoming bullshit.

'There he is,' Tony superfluously pointed the creature out.

'He seems a little smaller than his picture?'

'Aye, well he's standing next to that big Nubian, don't worry about size though, he's big enough where it matters,' Tony grinned salaciously and nudged the goat breeder who winced.

'I would imagine you'd give Edith and... Gaspard their own quarters if we can agree terms?'

'No problem - they'd have a virtual honeymoon suite, the very best of everything.'

The little man nodded, 'Only she's very sensitive you see.'

'Yes, well as I said, Gaspard is the smooth and sophisticated type; soft music, bottle of wine... you know.'

Dawn and Melanie exchanged a glance but the goat breeder seemed to have made up his mind.

'Very well, let's talk money.'

Tony beamed.

'Well it seems to be mending very well Mr O'Donnell...,' Dr McKinnon-Law lowered his patient's leg gently back onto the padded rest, '...but it's going to be a while before you're up and about again.'

'Ohh, I'm hoping to be out and about by the end of next week Doc, I'm one of the organisers of the Cold Ridge Earthquake Appeal and we've got posters to distribute and everything.'

'Cold Ridge Earthquake?' The doctor queried.

'Loretta Hillier - The Coldridge Earthquake, she's a lady wrestler, we're raising money to buy her a new costume and a mask and we're paying for her van to be repaired. She does a lot for charity when she's working so it's only fair to put a little back. She's the only benefactor Cold Ridge has ever produced, apart from Vibrating Des Devine.'

'Hmmm, again you have me at a disadvantage,' the doctor clipped shut his case.

'Vibrating Des Devine, lovely singer so he was, he had such a vibrato in his voice that he used to move across the stage when he sang. He was demonstrating his vocal range to a bus queue on Meadowvale Road and he vibrated out in front of a van and got knocked down. Sure it was a lovely funeral, a few of the lads rested the coffin on two washing machines with a curtain chucked over them in the church and at a signal they switched them on and the coffin vibrated, everybody laughed, even the priest, fair play to him.'

'Well I'm sure a good time was had by....'
'... and did I tell you about One-Lung Wilson? Now there was a man who could make balloon animals - and d'you know, the funny thing about him was....'
'...See you next week!' Doctor McKinnon-Law called from the hallway as he let himself out.
As the doctor drove back towards the centre of Town on his way to Cedar Hill his car slowed in a stream of traffic allowing him the time to look in through the window of a sports shop. A rack of air rifles caught his eye; his own weapon had not been fired for many years now and probably never would be again. He had often half thought of getting a new one but then his mind would turn, as it often did in the presence of firearms, to the bloody stoat.
He could recall as if it were yesterday lowering his rifle then trudging up the hill and seeing the small brown body lying next to a fallen tree branch. It pained him to bring it to mind now but all those years ago he had thought so differently. He had wrapped it in a handkerchief and put it in the boot of his car with his gun before driving back to the holiday lodge for a hearty lunch.

By the time the Goat Breeder brought Edith to the Sanctuary, Tony and his assistants had created a private enclosure for the courting couple. Tony had achieved this by kicking out seven of his eight goats, leaving only Gaspard the Golden Guernsey in the goat enclosure.

Gaspard's erstwhile housemates had been sent to join the sheep in the neighbouring pen.

When Gaspard's love interest arrived Tony had to admit she was the best-kept goat he had ever seen; a lustrous coat and clear eyes indicating a young female in the very best of health. Slightly smaller than Tony's male, Edith trotted curiously around her holiday home before spotting Gaspard standing in the entrance to the shelter. She strolled across for a sniff and a 'hello' before walking off. Gaspard did not follow.

'It's bound to take a short while for them to get to know each other,' Tony reassured Edith's owner.

'Yes, well probably best not to rush things, shall we say three weeks? She's wagging her tail and bleating to show she's well in season.' The breeder was clearly nervous about being parted from his pride and joy.

'Three weeks should be plenty then,' Tony agreed.

Forty-eight hours after the breeder's departure, however, Gaspard had still shown no interest whatsoever and Tony was perplexed. 'What's wrong with the bugger? Why isn't he giving her one?'

'Maybe she isn't giving off the right signals just yet?' Dawn suggested.

'Oh no? Look over the fence, listen to them - the billys in there are desperate to get at her so what's wrong with this one? D'you think he's gay?'

'Let's just give it a day or two more.'

'Well he'd better get some lead in his pencil, I'm being well paid for his services but only if the man gets a pregnant goat back.'

After four days of disinterest from Gaspard, Tony decided to give nature a helping hand. The website described 'Man Magnet' as the 'Most Potent Pheromone Spray Available' and apparently any female foolhardy enough to put a dab behind each ear would have men throwing themselves from aeroplanes as they passed above her. Tony bought two bottles, paid the extra for express delivery, and awaited the postman with anticipation.

The next morning Edith was wagging her tail and bleating with increased urgency causing the billy goats and rams in the next pen to answer her calls with ever more heartfelt promises of what they would do if the dividing fence wasn't there. Gaspard, however, stood with his usual nonchalance in the entrance to the shelter chewing aimlessly.

'A small dab behind each ear eh?' Tony read the label on the bottle, 'Right, Gaspard - let's see if this gives you the idea.'

He took the stoppers from both bottles and poured the entire contents over the female goat before exiting the pen wrinkling his nose at the pungency he had released. 'I wonder how long it takes to work,' he thought as he closed the gate behind him. The answer came in seconds as a black and brown shape mounted the fence and then mounted the goat with an expertise and deftness that spoke of well-practised skills and an urgency far beyond human senses.

'Sven! No!" down boy, DOWN!'

Tony dived back into the pen and grabbed the frantic dog by the collar but Sven had the goat in a furious grip and Tony almost lifted the pair of them off the ground. Panicking, he lunged for the drinking trough and threw the entire contents over Sven, which shocked the dog enough to ease his hold allowing Tony to pull him clear.

Trying to avoid multiple bites he managed to lock the panting German Shepherd in the rear of the 4x4 where the frenzied creature began shagging the spare wheel with a fury that fully endorsed the tyre manufacturer's claim that their product gave you 'The Ride of Your Life.'

Back in the pen, the little female goat looked stunned by the unexpected turn of events and was wagging and bleating ever more frantically. Sven wouldn't necessarily have been her choice of paramour but she had been running out of patience and maybe his attention would give Gaspard a clue. Gaspard, however, seemed impervious to the lure of a chemically induced romance and Edith must have been wondering if the few seconds of excitement with Sven were going to be the highlight of her stay in this strange place.

Sven's forthrightness, however, had merely been a hors d'oeuvre for the veritable feast of fucking that was to follow as, with a crash, the combined weight of four billy goats of various breeds and three rams brought down the dividing fence. The pheromone-crazed creatures charged the little female and a furious ruck developed as they fought for first go. A big powerful Nubian goat succeeded in the initial battle for supremacy and, mounting Edith, ravished her as only a mad goat can before finally falling off exhausted to make way for a Jacobs Ram whose behaviour was far from biblical.

'Oh for fucks sake!' Tony fulfilled the requirements of a cartoon enraged man by taking off his cap, wringing it, throwing it furiously to the ground and jumping on it. He then put it back on, covering his head in goat shit before calling for help.

'DAWWN!'

Dawn and Melanie came running and the orgiastic scene brought them to a shocked halt. 'How much did you put on her?' Dawn asked, already guessing the answer.

The Jacobs sheep had finished and staggered away. Edith tried to bolt for the relative safety of the shelter but was tackled in full flight by a Welsh Mountain ram that had clearly been raised on a diet of fast flowing rugby. Edith's bleats of desire had been replaced by bleats of fear; Tony, Dawn and Melanie entered the pen on a rescue mission and within seconds all three were knocked off their feet in the maelstrom of ruminant rape.

It took several frantic minutes to finally force the males back into the adjoining pen and as all three fought to shore up the broken fence a crash from behind informed them that the battle had opened on a second front. All three turned to witness the fence of the goat pen collapse under the weight of Sanchez the llama who, crazed by a combination of the pheromone scent and several years of enforced abstinence, was determined to make up for lost time.

'Oh NO!' RETREAT!' Tony ran for the opposite fence closely followed by Dawn and Melanie. The trio vaulted the barrier just as the sex-crazed Llama bore down on the shell-shocked goat.

'I'm going to get the shotgun from the office,' Tony headed off with Dawn calling after him, 'For God's sake Tony - you can't shoot Sanchez, he's the most popular animal we've got, everybody likes him.'

'I don't - I've never liked the fucker,' Tony stopped and began retracing his steps, drawn by the bizarre noises the llama was making as it struggled to overcome the significant difference in sizes between itself and the object of its desire. It was trying to spread its legs to lower itself to the optimum height for action, much like a drinking giraffe but Edith had performed far beyond the call of duty and sank to her knees leaving Sanchez furiously shagging fresh air, much to Tony's glee.

'Ha ha - Yahh! You missed! You stupid, spitting long-necked South American bastard!'

At the sound of Tony's voice hatred overruled lust somewhere deep in the llama's brain and it turned, red-eyed and sprang toward its long-term tormentor. Tony saw the danger and with reflexes he hadn't realised he could call on he turned and dived into the rear of the 4x4 and slammed the door a split second before an enraged Sanchez collided with it.

'Ha Ha..... arrgggh! Get off my leg you sex-mad mutt!' Tony struggled to dislodge Sven who had got two lungfuls of the pheromone while it was still at its most potent and who was clearly going to take a long time to wind down.

Meanwhile Sanchez, realising he was going to get no satisfaction from either Edith or Tony wandered back to his field feeling slightly embarrassed.

Edith was still on her knees and breathing heavily. Dawn approached her and felt for any obvious fractures. She could find none but the goat's heart was racing and she seemed to hanging on to consciousness by a thread.

'Tony! Get out here!' Dawn called and Tony, seeing Sanchez disappearing into the distance, opened the back door of the 4x4 and fell out into the mud, finally shaking off Sven whose attention returned to the far more compliant spare wheel.

Edith now lay on her side, only the faint and rapid rising and falling of her chest revealing signs of life.

'We're going to have to call Mr Truman.' Dawn looked up at a clearly concerned Tony who was rapidly weighing up the comparable costs of a veterinary visit and a lawsuit from Edith's owner. He came to the only sensible conclusion.

'...and you say this is as a result of her mating today?'

'Yes,' Tony's glib astonishment causing Dawn to shake her head.

'And this is the goat she mated with?' The vet nodded toward Gaspard who couldn't have cared less.

'Yeah,' it all seemed to go well and then....' Tony shrugged and indicated the comatose female Golden Guernsey.

'She seems terminally exhausted - are you sure this small male is responsible?' The vet studied Gaspard in wonder as he chewed vacantly, completely unaware of his sudden thoroughly undeserved reputation as a killer sex-machine.

The vet knelt and applied his stethoscope to the goat's chest.

'Probably just needs a bit of a rest eh?' Tony hovered expectantly.

The vet rose and put his stethoscope away. 'I'm afraid not, it's heart failure. The kindest thing I can do for her is give her a little jab and let her go.'

Dawn gave Tony a look of pure hatred and stormed off holding her handkerchief to her eyes.

Tony was already calculating the cost of replacing the goat and facing the fury of the little man who clearly loved her deeply. 'I'd like to give her a few hours just to see,' he told the vet who shrugged as he left.

Doctor McKinnon-Law was watching patterns floating by on the inside of his eyelids. He had only meant to close his eyes for a few seconds to rest them but it felt really nice and a patch of light almost exactly the same shape as Scotland had just glided silently across before dissolving and being replaced by a kaleidoscopic display of snakes heads and clothes pegs.

There was a tap on the consulting room door, which he ignored, in the sure knowledge it would be repeated in a few seconds followed by the door opening and Mary's head appearing in the gap. Another set of patterns - a series of neon bars and what resembled the front end of a sperm whale rising up out of the waters to meet them. Another tap followed by the sound of the door opening.

'Doctor?....Doctor... are you awake?'

He reluctantly opened his eyes, 'Sadly, yes - what is it Mary?'

'Well I know surgery's over but Tony Fletcher from the Animal Sanctuary is in the waiting room and he seems really agitated - says he has to see you urgently.'

The doctor sighed, 'Probably got hoof-rot or something, very well, show him in.'

There was no denying the man who entered the consulting room was in considerable distress. He was wringing his cap and pacing and brought to mind a man the doctor had encountered on the Congo who had sat on a fishhook.

'And what can I do for you today, Mr Fletcher?'

'Well, I've been.... I mean... several animals suddenly.... Look - it's not me!'

The doctor raised his eyebrows in surprise at the rare outburst of honesty, 'It's not you?'

'No - it's... Edith.'

'I see, and is Edith with you?'

'No, I think her heart is failing, she's lying down and won't get up, she's been... sort of.. attacked.'

'What?'

'She's been... well, raped.'

'Well raped?'

'Oh yes, very well raped.'

'Good God, have you called the police?'

'No... no, sorry. She's been raped by... by some goats.'

The doctor studied the man before him. He had heard the rumours of course; basically when it came to animals in the Sanctuary they had to earn their keep through sponsorship or get themselves adopted pretty damn quick. You were either a winner - or dinner!' But mass rape? By goats?

'What sort of goats?'

The question was utterly irrelevant but the doctor thought he would seek a little more elaboration prior to calling the police himself.

'Well, a Nubian, two Toggenburgs and a Black-Faced British.... and a Jacob's Ram...'

The doctor studied the man in wonder.

'... and a Welsh Mountain Ram and another one we're not a hundred per cent sure of but it might be a Norfolk Horn...'

In his decades as a medical man Doctor McKinnon-Law had heard nothing like it, he shook his head in amazement.

'....and a llama... and... and a German Shepherd.'

The doctor had heard enough and rose angrily, 'For fuck's sake man - what sort of a place are you running up there?'

'It wasn't planned, I was trying to get this other goat to give her one but he wasn't interested so I...'

The doctor struggled to controlled his fury but it seeped out between every word, 'Give me one good reason why I shouldn't call the police right now. You should swing for what you've done to this poor lady.'

'Oh no, she's no lady.'

'Aye well you would think that you misogynistic wee bastard!'

'No.. no, listen; Edith's a Golden Guernsey - a goat.'

Doctor McKinnon-Law took in the unfamiliar surroundings of the Animal Sanctuary before turning his attention to his unorthodox patient.

'It might indeed be heart failure, but there again it could be shock. I'm going to take her back to the surgery, put her on a drip and keep an eye on her - and you don't breathe a word of this to Mr Truman or anyone else at all or the shit will hit the fan for you and me both, d'you understand?'

'Absolutely doctor - and thank you again for coming out, really, really appreciate it.'

What the hell could he have been thinking of? At three-thirty in the morning the only sensible place for a sensible man was dreamland. He had done his share of hospital rounds as a young doctor at all hours of the day and night but that was then and this was now - and this was a bloody goat!

He put his stethoscope to the creature's chest for the hundredth time that night; the breathing was still shallow and too rapid but it seemed to have slowed just a little. He had rigged up a drip, got a line in for fluids, and ensured the airways were clear. All he could do now was watch and wait.

There had been one occasion at ten past midnight when, with a shudder, her heart had stopped and she had ceased to breathe. The doctor had applied cardiac massage and mouth to mouth, not an experience he was in a hurry to repeat, but it had worked as, with another shudder, the little creature's soul had turned around and trotted back down the tunnel of light to re-enter the small golden body lying on blankets in the consulting room. Above the mantelpiece, and the unblinking gaze of Mournful Old Daniel, a heavy clock gave off a heavy tick as, hidden in the shadows, an ethereal black goat in a cowl studied the tableau through timeless eyes and hovered impatiently.

Daylight was showing around the edges of the consulting room curtains when Dr McKinnon-Law was jerked out of his half sleep by the weakest of bleats. He rubbed his eyes to witness Edith raising her head.

'Well done lassie, bloody well done!' He left the room and came back in with a baby's feeding bottle full of tepid milk containing some crushed vitamins and a shot of single malt. Edith dispatched it greedily and to his delight rose shakily to her feet.

'Well she certainly seems happy, did the mating go well?' The breeder was clearly pleased to be reunited with Edith. She trotted around the pen ignoring Gaspard, her head held high, a picture of ruminant health.

'Oh yeah, went... very well.' Tony forced a smile.

'Excellent, well we'll just see what happens in about five months then shall we?'

'Err, right,' Tony scratched his nose and exchanged a fleeting glance with Dawn. 'I was wondering... you wouldn't be interested in selling her, would you?'

'Hmmm,' the goat breeder's eyes twinkled, 'She's very dear to me you know, a fine pedigree too...'

'So?' Tony prompted him.

'I couldn't let her go for less than... shall we say, two grand?'

Dawn failed to suppress a snort of derision - it was a ludicrous price and she was sure Tony was about to tell him where to get off.

'Done.' Tony extended a hand.

Dawn gasped and the Breeder, who had been limbering up for some prolonged haggling, looked stunned but the little man recovered in time to shake the offered hand.

As the breeder's car and its empty trailer disappeared around the bend and out of sight Dawn could contain herself no longer, 'She isn't worth anywhere near that - and even if he'd sued you he would never have been awarded two grand or anything close to it!'

Tony smiled, 'Ah well, she'll be company for Gaspard and to be honest I'm curious to see what the offspring will turn out like.'

Dawn studied him as he turned his attention to the two little goats. Could it be? Good God it was! He was actually fond Edith. To his shock she kissed him on the cheek before heading off to clean the cattery.

Doctor McKinnon-Law slept for twelve hours the following night but it wasn't only the repayment of a sleep debt that had allowed him to rest for so long. He felt strangely light, as if a weight had been lifted; a weight that had been with him so long he had forgotten what it was like to be without it. He tacked his breakfast with relish and greeted Mary with a smile as she bought in a second pot of tea.

'Nice to see you in such a good mood this morning Doctor.'

'Aye, well it's a fine day Mary, a fine day indeed.'

'Yes it is - and you'll never guess who I found in the bin this morning?'

*   *   *   *   *   *

<u>CHAPTER EIGHTEEN</u>

LOST IN TRANSLATION

A MORTAR shell exploded nearby and he instinctively ducked but kept up his report to camera; *The insurgency is now in its third day and shows no signs of diminishing in its ferocity...*' a burst of automatic gun fire forced him to duck again as stray rounds threw up puffs of dust on the rim of his foxhole. His face streaked with sweat and grime, he persevered, *'I'm going to try and make a dash for it across to that white building to try and get a word with the rebel leader...*'

'... not only for their size but also their texture - anyone can grow a big leek but it's the taste that counts - any questions?'

With a jolt, Ian Lloyd's attention was dragged back from his dream of reporting a breaking story on the world stage to the even grimmer surroundings of Meadowvale Community Hall and the monthly meeting of Meadowvale Village Allotment Society. They were discussing manure now and Ian, sub editor and relief reporter on the Newvale Chronicle, was half listening to the speaker and half watching a pair of youths who were gurning in through one of the grimy rain-streaked windows. An earlier storm had abated but water still dripped from the windowsills where the wind had blown it through the ill-fitting frames.

Monty Fox, editor of the Chronicle, had impressed on him the importance of showing one's face from time to time at these parochial things as it paid to occasionally touch base with the grass roots readership. Inevitably, however, it was rarely Monty's face that did the showing and Ian suspected that his presence here tonight had little to do with touching base and much to do with the large box of fresh vegetables in the boot of Monty's car.

Across town Monty Fox was also finding his mind in two places at once. He was sat superficially watching as a fourteen-year-old musical prodigy performed selections from 'Die Fledermaus' in Newvale's Senate Theatre. Monty was at the tail end of a very stressful and busy day and had lasted only around two minutes before his mind had wandered off on its own to find the comforting sanctuary of a well trodden path.

The young musician reminded him a little of a childhood friend who had once pulled the arms off every plastic mackintosh in the school cloakroom but Monty felt sure such a free spirit would nowadays have been discovered and squashed long before reaching an age where it would have been capable of such unbridled self expression. He studied the young performer and seriously doubted whether he had ever so much as ripped the pocket off a blazer or pulled a tie in half and while Monty conceded the youth was technically a very good young musician the newspaperman still came from a generation that viewed with suspicion anyone of such tender years who had attained such a height of artistic proficiency. In order for all that ability to fit in, he reasoned, lots would have had to be left out. He found himself wondering if the lad had ever got his hands dirty or spat on a shop window or swore?

'All I thought about at fourteen was motorbikes and Marcia Berry,' Monty mused to himself before sidetracking, 'Fair play to the Germans, "Fledermaus" is a fucking great word,' and what have we got? Bat! Who first looked up into the darkening sky and caught sight of the silently flying creature of the dusk and thought - "I think we should call it a bat!" It doesn't even make a noise that goes anything like "Bat!"

Monty's musings were interrupted by applause. The young man had reached the end of a particular piece and had turned to acknowledge the accolade with an insincere and well-rehearsed smile.

Monty hoped it would be the last piece, but no, the youth turned back to his keyboard and flexed his fingers indicating there was at least another section to go. 'Strauss must have watched this fucking bat flapping about for hours,' Monty sighed and adjusted his position to try and let some life flow back into his left leg. His wife gave him her 'stop fidgeting' look and he fished in his pocket for a mint.

Mr Batwell's wife rarely looked at him at all - and he only looked at her to determine her whereabouts so he could remain at a comfortable distance. They had been married for thirty-nine years and for the last twenty-six of them had run Cold Ridge Post Office. Stanley Batwell was sixty-two, his father had called him Stanley in the hope he would grow up to become a great explorer or at least a trail-blazer in some walk of life. He had started out promisingly well, hitchhiking across Europe working in vineyards and juggling in village squares for the price of a croissant and a coffee. He ended up in Corsica where he worked on a tomato farm and met a girl called Hortense Cuypers who hailed from a small town in Belgium where they made surgical supports and built-up shoes.

Hortense was ideally built for strenuous farm work; she had corn coloured plaits strong enough to tow a tractor with, muscular arms and a way of walking that the word 'purposeful' was made for, and when she turned and looked at you the stare landed with the force of a blow. But Stanley was young and relished a challenge; he pursued Hortense until she caught him and their love ripened with the tomatoes throughout a blissful summer.

He told her he was a painter and she had begged him to do her portrait; having painted himself into a corner he had to tell her he only did landscapes - and he only did those in abstract! On a boozy night in a Corsican bar he told her he was planning to walk from Cairo to Cape Town and she asked to go with him. He had been about to tell her it was too dangerous for a young lady, but at that moment a pair of drunks had put their arms around her and tried to kiss her, she had felled the one with left hook and thrown the other expertly over her shoulder. Stanley had decided at that point it might be a safer option to stick to the truth in future.

They had gone to Belgium to meet her parents and siblings and she had proposed to him over the kitchen table while her mother stood at the sink chopping cucumbers in half with what looked like a bush knife.

They had been married in her home town with a further civil ceremony in Newvale a few weeks later at which Stanley's mother had cried and his father had shook his hand with a solemnity and finality more suitable for a departing emigrant than a bridegroom. Within weeks the magical freedom of the tomato summer faded to be replaced by the world of work and responsibility. Hortense had turned into a slave driver, forever comparing Stanley to her industrious father and brothers who all had their own businesses and were 'going places'. Stanley began to wish Hortense would go places too, ideally without him, but he was trapped and little by little the explorer in him shrank away behind defensive walls to exist only in his daydreams. Now he sat in his glass prison looking out at the procession of faces and dreaming of far horizons while a few feet away Hortense, her plaits now grey, sat at her own window eating nuts and stamping forms and shouting 'Next!'

It was approaching the day when Stanley would have been married to her for forty years and he supposed he should do something to mark the occasion. He could organise a family get-together, invite the children - at least the ones who were still within travelling distance - and Hortense's innumerable tribe, but the last time there had been a gathering of the clans it had degenerated into a blazing row in which Hortense's brother Jans had called him an under-achiever and he had called Jans a pointy-headed Belgian cunt. Their eldest son, Denzil, then seventeen, had got roaring drunk and climbed on to the roof of Cold Ridge Community Centre then fallen off, breaking his collar bone while Stanley's octogenarian mother, oblivious to the fact that she was sitting next to Hortense's uncle, a Lutherian minister, went all out to break the world farting records for both volume and essence throughout dinner.

He decided therefore to commemorate their milestone in some other way.

Ian Lloyd looked at his notes from the previous evening; he was supposed to fill a double column with about five hundred words, but it all boiled down to 'Use the right type of shit for the longest and fattest leeks!' How was he supposed to stretch that out? He thought about starting with a history of the domestic leek but it would mean interminable internet research and he just couldn't be bothered. He wished he had taken an opportunity to collar the speaker before he left to try and squeeze a few anecdotes out of him but it was too late now.

All he had to go on were two pages of random notes he didn't really understand and a third page containing a doodle of a character he had named 'Throbbin' Hood' who was using an unfeasibly large penis as a longbow. He wondered what the reaction would be if he were to scan it in and put in the space provided with a caption along the lines of, 'I went to a meeting all about leeks but it was very dull so, instead, here's a drawing of a man with a huge tool.' Instant dismissal obviously but also a place in the local journalism hall of fame alongside the careless sub editor who forgot to replace the headline over a local government story which subsequently went to press as, 'Boring tossers waffle on about planning regulations.'

Ian felt like a formula one racing driver at the wheel of a family saloon or a national hunt jockey on a seaside donkey. He was capable of so much more and he wanted to be doing it - now! His boss, Monty Fox was old and didn't understand the potential of the information super highway. A piddling weekly paper in the back of beyond might be enough for him but Ian was young, the decades stretched ahead, glittering with promise, calling him on with the lure of prestige and awards and Pulitzer Prizes and gala dinners and sex - aha! Sex, that's what it was all about of course, sex sold papers, he had tried to tell Monty that on many occasions but the old man would have none of it. It wasn't that Monty was a prude, far from it in fact, but he just didn't seem to see how a bit of glamour fitted into the parochial world of the weekly rag.

'You can't put fannies in the Chronicle,' he had stated.

'I'm not suggesting we do, 'Ian had retorted, '...not fannies, but a nice pair of legs here and there and maybe the occasional tit?'

Monty had explained to him that tits worked in the nationals because the likelihood of the reader seeing the same tits in real life was distinctly remote - they were unattainable tits - but the Chronicle was a local paper and if you were to put local tits in it there was a strong possibility that you would encounter those very same tits on the bus stop or in the pub and men would assume that because they had seen them in the paper they were in the public domain and would try to get them out to have a better look at them. 'You make them sound like animals,' Ian had told him. Monty had just smiled.

Ian got up from his desk and made his way to the mens' room where he studied himself in the mirror. His father had begun to go bald when still young and Ian checked regularly for signs of following the trend. In his mid-twenties he should have been further up the career ladder and it was a source of constant frustration that his ambitions seemed no closer to fruition than they were a year ago. He was vaguely displeased with his reflection; he had a university degree and yet still looked vaguely thuggish. A broken nose from varsity rugby and a largish chin from his mother's side of the family gave him the appearance of one who would probably instigate a late night public disturbance rather than report on it. 'Maybe I should wear glasses?' he thought before turning with a sigh and heading back to his leeks.

Stanley Batwell was studying an online English / Flemish dictionary and composing a greeting for publication in the Chronicle. He felt it would show a thoughtful touch if he were to use his wife's mother tongue to announce his love and admiration for her on the occasion of four decades of togetherness. Whether he actually felt those sentiments was another matter; he was pretty sure he still cared for her on some level but it was probably more habit and familiarity than hearts and flowers.

He typed in the phrase, 'I awoke and disbelief was erased and like a storm you filled my heart with the thrill of thunder and light!' It was one of his favourite quotations and while, not by any stretch of the imagination, did it sum up his years with Hortense, he hoped she would accept it as a sentiment worthy of their matrimonial longevity. He hit the translate button and carefully copied the result.

Against all the odds Ian Lloyd had managed 237 words about Meadowvale Allotment Society's talk on leek growing and was going to use a picture of a leek to fill the rest of the space. He was pleased to have put the boring assignment behind him and was reaching for his jacket in order to accompany Monty, Virginia and photographer Colin Gardiner to lunch in the Royal Oak.

Such was Monty's reputation that the cosy corner under the bay window was always surprisingly vacant when lunchtime approached. The quartet seated themselves, Colin picked up the lunchtime menu while Monty gestured to landlord who arrived as if on roller skates.

''What's the fish like?' Monty didn't bother looking at the man who thought carefully about his reply. Anyone else would have been reassured as to the freshness and deliciousness of the offering but it was better not to promise too much to Monty as his disappointment usually came at a high price.

'To tell you the truth it's not up to much this week,' Brian the landlord replied, his shoulders dropping - the gammon's not bad and the steak's passable but if it was me I'd have the chilli con carne, she's got it almost right today.'

Monty nodded and followed the man's advice. Having ordered the four sat with their drinks awaiting the arrival of the food.

'I could eat anything as long as it didn't have leeks in it,' Ian took a sip of his beer.

Monty grinned, 'All part of the rich tapestry of life that makes up Newvale.'

Ian snorted, Virginia and Colin, by contrast, had experienced a most illuminating morning in Newvale Park where they had initially gone to cover the retirement of a park keeper with fifty years service on the clock but had ended up encountering a man hiding in some bushes who claimed he was waiting to spot a Penduline Tit although he appeared to be at a loss to explain why he was wearing pyjamas and a lady's hat. He seemed agreeable to having his picture taken, however, and even offered to pose up a tree.

The week's edition was going to press and, like most weeks, there was nothing earth shattering to report. The front-page lead was a rant against the continuing road works around Fuller Square and the letters page contained three missives concerning the Chronicle's ongoing campaign to limit the number of takeaway restaurants in the Town Centre. They all heartily supported the Chronicle's stance, unsurprising as Monty Fox wrote them all. It was a journeyman issue, eminently forgettable - apart from one small announcement in the personal columns.

Inspector Nigel Snow, head of Newvale Police, had been unaware that the Secret Service had a branch whose function was to monitor local newspapers for anything suspicious. He knew now because they had contacted him and drawn his attention to a small personal advertisement in the Newvale Chronicle, written in Flemish and translating into something that could be a coded message to a terrorist sleeper cell.

He had asked them, quite reasonably he thought, why a terrorist organisation would:

1. Choose Flemish as a medium of communication and...
2. Choose Newvale as a centre of operations

He was told that the country's enemies were sometimes very strange and unpredictable and to find out what he could and let them know. He studied a copy of the announcement in the paper and the translation he had just received from Special Branch. It read, 'Wake you sleeper, and eliminate the disbelievers in a storm of light and thunder!' It certainly sounded fanatical, a call to the Chronicle's advertising department quickly established that it had been paid for by a Mr Stanley Batwell who had given his address as Cold Ridge Post Office which Inspector Snow admitted didn't sound like the sort of person who would smite unbelievers or the sort of place a fanatic would choose to call home, but he would send someone along to check just to be on the safe side.

An announcement in Flemish followed up by a police enquiry was enough to suggest to Monty Fox that there may be a story hiding behind the unobtrusive little six centimetre by two column box half way down page thirty-three so he dispatched Ian Lloyd to find out what was what. It was newspaper policy to insist on a full translation before publishing anything in a language other than English but this one must have slipped through the net. The policy had been initiated after a Portuguese woman living locally had used her native tongue to accuse her estranged husband of a string of indiscretions with other women, boys and even a tortoise, almost landing the Chronicle with a libel case.

Ian, with the lethargic fog of leeks and manure not fully dissipated hoped there would be something worthy of his journalistic talents in the story as he set off for Cold Ridge.

Stanley Batwell had bought two copies of the Chronicle and left one near to Hortense's counter position and another by her chair in the living room but as far as he could ascertain she had not spotted the announcement yet; he might have to point her in the right direction soon if she didn't notice it. In a lull between customers he stole a glance across to her window and watched as she absently crushed two walnuts together in one hand as she stamped a passport application with the other.

'Anything interesting in the Chronicle this week?' He asked matter-of-factly.

'Haven't had a chance to look yet,' She replied, her face a picture of concentration as she picked out bits of crushed shell from the flesh of the nuts.

He was about to point out that there was something that looked a bit like Flemish on page thirty-three when he was interrupted by a customer who hoisted a parcel up for delivery and as Stanley opened up the window to receive it the twin barrels of a shotgun pushed through the gap and pressed against his midriff.

The last time Stanley had been held up at gunpoint it had been a local youth from Cold Ridge Estate with a clearly fake gun. Hortense had pretended to pass him the contents of her money drawer before felling him with a truly fearsome blow and tying him up with sticky tape so efficiently it took the police twenty minutes to unravel him to a point where he was able to stagger into the patrol car. This person however wore a balaclava and a flak jacket - and there was nothing fake about his gun. He spoke only three words.

'All of it!'

Stanley felt strangely calm as he took the notes out of the drawer and began filling a cloth bag. Hortense noticed what was going on and the gunman indicated for her to do the same. She hesitated, weighing up the raider with a flinty stare before turning her gaze to Stanley and then to her money drawer as if calculating which of the two would represent a greater loss to the business.

'Move it!' The raider barked.

Stanley speeded up his bag filling and, with an obvious reluctance, Hortense also began emptying her cash drawer.'

'Come on, come on..' The raider was clearly in a hurry to get this over and done with before another customer entered and, if he had begun his raid thirty seconds earlier he might just have made it, but as Stanley was about to hand him the bag of cash Ian Lloyd of the Chronicle entered and walked straight into a scoop.

'What would a terrorist come to Newvale for Sarge?' PC Boniface Lillywhite had squeezed his huge frame into the passenger seat of the patrol car leaving Sergeant Eric Randall little room to change gear.

'Well you came here!' the Sergeant responded.

'Aha! But I answered a job advertisement in the Police Gazette, I doubt there's a Terrorist Gazette advertising vacancies for bombers.'

'Ah, well this one is a Flem apparently.'

'A what?'

'A Flem, according to Inspector Snow.

'What's a Flem Sarge?'

'A particularly nasty sleeper terrorist, they speak Flemish.'

PC Lillywhite frowned, 'You... you mean a Belgian?'

'Belgian?'

'Belgians speak Flemish Sarge - some of them anyway, the ones who don't speak French.'

'Good God, I never knew that. I thought they just made chocolate. Still it stands to reason, I went to Brussels on a school trip when I was a boy and some bastard stole my rucksack.' The patrol car turned into Cold Ridge Estate and headed for the Post Office.

'Just lie down on the floor and nobody gets hurt!' The raider swung his gun barrels wildly between Stanley, Hortense and the now prone Ian Lloyd. 'Now hand over the bags - MOVE IT!'

'No!' Stanley sat back in his seat and smiled coldly at the raider. Hortense looked at him as if he had grown a second head.

'You tired of living old man?' The raider brandished the gun menacingly under Stanley's nose.

'Yes.' Stanley smiled and folded his arms.

The raider turned the gun in Hortense's direction.

'I'm tired of her living too,' Stanley said conversationally, '..and before you point the gun at the guy on the floor, I don't know him from Adam so I couldn't care whether you shoot him or not.'

'You're trying my fucking pat....'

The raider never finished the sentence as Ian grabbed both his ankles and pulled with all his strength. The man fell forward, his forehead crashing into the post office counter and his gun discharging with a loud 'Bang!' blowing a hole in the plaster of the ceiling and showering the area with dust and debris. The man hit the ground and in a split second Ian had him in an arm lock, Hortense flew around the counter with a roll of sticky tape and with the dexterity that comes from practice proceeded to bind the unconscious robber.

Outside the post office the sound of a gunshot stopped Sergeant Randall in his tracks.

'Shit! That was a gun that was - I'll radio for Armed Response.'

'Armed Response could take an hour to get here Sarge, the terrorists could have shot everyone - or blown up half of Cold Ridge by then.' PC Lillywhite joined his superior in ducking behind the patrol car as a small crowd gathered.

'Back - everybody back! There's a Belgian in there!' Sergeant Randall gestured to the onlookers.

'There's always a Belgian in there,' a tall skinny youth jeered.

'Eh?' The Sergeant queried.

'Mrs Batwell, the postmistress - she's Belgian!'

A wisp of dust and gun smoke began to seep through the window fan. PC Lillywhite broke cover and dashed into the building. A shout of 'Get back here you silly bugger,' from his superior going unheard in the adrenalin rush of the moment.

When Police Constable Boniface Lillywhite charges a door it generally ceases to be a door, or anything that could conceivably be made into one. In a crash of splintering panels he entered the post office much as a buffalo would to find most of his work done for him. The raider lay groaning, and expertly taped. Ian Lloyd was standing, furiously scribbling on his notepad, stopping every now and then to take a picture with his phone. Hortense was standing, hands on hips, like a Jolly Grey Giant, glowering at the still sitting Stanley Batwell who was smiling beatifically at all and sundry. Having stared death in the face he no longer felt intimidated by his wife's icy stare and it showed in his eyes. Things were going to be different in the post office from now on.

Ian Lloyd had his picture on the front of the paper he had helped to fill so anonymously in the past. He was posing, arms folded in a 'job done' sort of way under a headline in which the word 'Hero' appeared. Two girls had smiled at him in the American Diner on his way to work and even reporter Virginia had seemed impressed. He was going to ask Monty for a raise or an official designation of 'Deputy Editor' or something - but not yet; he had depleted his bravery reserves and needed time to recharge them.

Hortense Batwell had just squeezed Stanley's thigh in a way she hoped wasn't too predatory. He had responded with a smile, she realised she hadn't seen him smile for a long time; she would have to see what she could do about that. She'd had no idea that he was brave; she had always assumed his desire for a quiet life demonstrated a fear of confrontation. She suddenly realised how years behind a post office counter must have been a cheerless prospect for such a man. Maybe it was time they sold up and went travelling?

'You weren't brave, you were bloody stupid Constable - what if there had been a gang in there?'

'Yes Sarge, I just thought I'd catch them unawares before they could aim.'

'They wouldn't have to fucking aim, would they? You fill a room man! Don't do it again!'

'No Sarge.'

'Leave it to the experts.'

'Yes Sarge.'

'Just because you dress up as a fucking cowboy doesn't mean you've got to behave like one.'

'No Sarge.'

'....Pint?'

'Yes Sarge!'

*   *   *   *   *   *

<u>CHAPTER NINETEEN</u>

THAT'S THE WAY TO DO IT!

'THAT'S the way to do it!'

Mr Edward Friendy gave the dummy's head a quick turn and a nod but was displeased with the result. He regretted not painting Mr Punch's face the previous night and now he wasn't at all sure if it was going to be dry in time for the show he was planning to stage for the children of his street.

He wasn't happy with Mr Punch's expression, it was supposed to be a grinning face stopping just this side of manic but he'd unintentionally given it the look of someone coming out of a brothel; a mixture of guilt and furtiveness that really wasn't going to fit in with the tale of crocodiles and sausages.

Rhododendron Crescent was holding a Newvale 200 street party; singing, dancing and tables groaning under home made cakes, sausage rolls and those things that smelled fishy that no one ate. Bill Fredericks from number 12 had given Mr Friendy a knowing wink yesterday when the subject had turned to refreshments. He had promised some cakes that would 'break the ice' which had intrigued Edward who assured him he would try one or two.

He looked up; the clouds were clearing, promising a fine day. Felicity had been in the kitchen since first light making cakes and sandwiches. He had offered to help but to his relief she had sent him out into his shed to get him from under her feet.

The big day had finally arrived, the big day in the big year. The specific date of Newvale's birth had been determined from the day Thomas Fuller had registered his company, Fuller Timber and Construction Supplies, all those years ago.

The original site of the first sawmill was now somewhere beneath Fuller's Mill Shopping Centre and a tyre depot appropriately stood on the spot where the blacksmith had once shod the draft horses of the infant enterprise.

Newvale 200 banners festooned the centre of town, schools had been given a holiday, the council had pulled out all the stops to get everyone on message - 'Happy Birthday Newvale!'

A HAPPY
BIRTHDAY
NEWVALE

The banner headline on the front of the Newvale Chronicle boomed out. For one week only, the newspaper had amended its masthead to incorporate the Newvale 200 logo and although the organ's personal history fell significantly short of two hundred years an eight-page pull out recorded stories from the very first issue in the year the Town Hall had been completed, through wars and various triumphs and traumas right up to the present day.

'Listen to this,' Ian Lloyd read from an archived issue, '*The Defendant denied the assault but was clearly lying as his face marked him out as an obvious member of the criminal classes.* - no libel laws in those days then.'

'Hmmm,' Monty Fox, editor of the Chronicle was preoccupied, he had been asked to speak at the Newvale 200 Civic Luncheon and had left writing his speech to the last minute. The obvious topic would have to be significant achievements with a Newvalian link over the last two hundred years but he couldn't think of any offhand. There was that woman in the seventies who had made it big in the music world for about eighteen months before sinking back into obscurity. She had briefly returned to Newvale several years later to declare a shoe shop open and had been utterly and embarrassingly unrecognisable. Or he could mention the fact that for a short period between the wars Newvale had been responsible for most of the nation's clothes pegs. Neither fact had initiated a tourist boom. He was going to have to concentrate instead on the uniqueness of Newvale's people, their warmth and individuality, enterprise and industriousness. It was the type of bullshit people were used to at these events although he would attempt to weave in a few lightly veiled digs at the great and good of the Town past and present and try to inject a thread of humour.

Despite his earlier misgivings Mr Edward Friendy had to admit everyone had made a splendid effort on Rhododendron Crescent; tables with white cloths and a multitude of different plates and dishes now filled the road in the bowl of the Crescent where many of the residents had already gathered. He had pitched his Punch and Judy tent on the level square of concrete left behind when they had taken the phone box away, it was a perfect fit.

The plan was to give a show while the adults were setting up the tables in order to keep the youngsters occupied and Edward was putting the last of his characters in place in his little tent when the back flap opened and the head of close neighbour, Bill Fredericks popped through. He beamed his almost ever-present smile, 'All OK Edward?'

'Getting there,' Mr Friendy replied. He still wasn't happy about Mr Punch's expression but it was too late to worry now.

'Here, have a few of these,' Bill pushed a plate of small cakes through the gap.

'I don't want to spoil my appetite,' Edward took one out of politeness.

'Oh they won't do that old boy, far from it.' Bill grinned even wider, 'I've made loads, I'll leave these here shall I?'

They were actually very nice cakes, if a bit spicy, and Edward hadn't realised just how hungry he was. He had skipped breakfast and only had a mid-morning sandwich as he struggled to get everything ready for his performance. He had polished off five or six of the little cakes before he knew it.

Mayor of Newvale, Gordon McIver, was hungry too. He sat on the edge of the bed trying to tie his bowtie on autopilot. Doctor

McKinnon-Law had put him on a diet and told him to get more exercise. Moira had eaten bacon, sausage, eggs and toast in front of him that morning while he had a yoghurt, an orange and a cup of green tea with no sugar in it. Now he was getting ready for the Newvale 200 Civic Luncheon.

He had been looking forward to this bash. There was a six-course meal and lots of booze, it was a chance to let his mayoral hair down on a celebratory occasion that cut across party politics. The Member of Parliament for Newvale, Titania Oliphant would be there as well as the leading lights of the Chamber of Trade and most of the Council. And now he was going to have to sit there like a lemon watching everyone gorge themselves at the expense of the ratepayers while he nibbled on a lettuce leaf and drank a mineral water or something. He brightened a little at the prospect of smuggling a pork pie, some beef sandwiches and a bottle of red into the mayoral parlour, locking the door and having a private little banquet of his own.

'What am I supposed to do if I'm in the ladies and the Member of Parliament comes in? I'm so used to calling him Oberon?' Moira bustled into the bedroom spraying her hair as she went.

'Her name's Titania now and she's a lady, just treat her like any other woman you bump into in the loo.'

'Hmmm,' Moira had put one shoe on and was looking under the bed for the other one, 'Well I can't help remembering she used to have a doo-dah, it's all very uncomfortable.'

'Well she hasn't got a doo-dah now so there's no chance of catching a glimpse of one.' Gordon replied.

'You can't help wondering,' Moira had found her other shoe and was now rummaging for lipstick on the dressing table.

'I'm surprised you can remember what a fucking doo-dah looks like,' Gordon muttered.

'Eh?'

'Oh, nothing, I'll go and check if the limo has arrived.'

Small Town People

Monty Fox usually wore a bow tie to work, but it was always an unorthodox bow tie. He was currently wearing a very formal bow tie and a dinner suit and he didn't like it one bit. It was turning out to be a warm day and the last thing he needed was to be wrapped up like a penguin. Never one to turn down the chance of free food and wine, he was nevertheless, not really looking forward to the Civic Luncheon. He was unhappy with his speech. The exercise of having to compose it had surprised him, despite being editor of Newvale's newspaper for the last twenty-one years and having been born and raised in the town and having lived in it for sixty of his sixty three years he had been amazed at how little he could find to say in its favour.

It was not that there was anything particularly wrong with the place, it's just that, among the hundreds and hundreds of towns in the land, Newvale just didn't stand out as being worthy of particular praise. It had recently risen to brief national prominence due to its status as the only constituency in the country with a transsexual member of parliament and the local people had, to Monty's surprise, accepted Titania Oliphant to such a degree that she had reversed her decision to stand down at the next election. It was also home, as Monty could testify, to a fair number of eccentrics and he often wondered how other towns measured up in the madcap stakes.

He had wanted his speech to stand out from the others, which were sure to be dry, and motivated by politics and business. But try as he might, he had been unable to rise to the challenge of injecting anything like the sparkle he had hoped for. Even so, he tucked the notes into his jacket pocket and checked his watch.

In the mayoral limousine, Gordon McIver had no such worries. He had written his speech weeks ago, it concentrated on his time in office and the achievements, or otherwise, of the one hundred and eighty seven mayors of Newvale who had gone before him. It had virtually written itself and he looked forward to reeling it off before excusing himself for his surreptitious feast. He generally took seriously the advice of his doctor but it was unreasonable to ask a man to suddenly stop eating and drinking nice things, he planned cut down gradually.

The car pulled into the specially designated parking space at the front of the Town Hall and he and Moira got out, not waiting for the chauffeur to open the doors - a practice Gordon had never found himself comfortable with. His stomach rumbled in anticipation of the fare within and he nodded to a couple of councillors having a smoke on the steps before entering. He noticed Monty Fox getting out of a cab and gave a friendly wave in his direction. He felt pretty safe today as just about all of Newvale's great and good would be listening to his speech so there was little chance of him being misquoted in the Chronicle. It was a celebration after all, a happy occasion, he reminded himself and smiled as he put his hand in his trouser pocket and closed it around the half bottle of whisky therein.

It was certainly a happy occasion on Rhododendron Crescent; in fact, Mr Edward Friendy couldn't remember when he had last felt so happy. It was as if…. as if all his cares had been carried away by big pink flamingos into the candy floss clouds. The music from the sound system Mr Beverstock had set up in his front garden had seemed irritating a short while ago but now it was beautiful and for some strange reason actually seemed to be coming from inside him. A few minutes ago a child had poked his head through the flap at the back of the tent and asked how long it was likely to be before his Punch and Judy show started. Mr Friendy knew that deep inside there was another Edward Friendy, an uncool Edward Friendy, who would have told the child to bugger off but as he had looked into the expectant little face, into those bright copper-coloured eyes and angelic smile he had felt his hostility melt away. He had beamed and simply said, 'Everything's cool man.' The child had looked confused but had disappeared and Edward was now just about ready to put on a show.

He was going to break with tradition, there would be no one beaten with truncheons or made into sausages today; it was too beautiful an occasion for that, he was going to weave his magic like a travelling troubadour, a teller of timeless tales, a skimmer of flat stones on a crystal pond above which a rainbow arched, turning the warm sunlight into a liquid paint box, a multi-coloured firmament drowning the thirsty unicorns in sweet sweet.... Where was he? Oh yes, concentrate Edward, it's showtime...

The Mayor's Annual Charity Dinner was usually a glittering affair but this, the Bicentenary Lunch, was the finest event Gordon had attended in his tenure as the Town's figurehead. The Town Hall's Function Room was bedecked with Newvale 200 banners and around the walls, courtesy of the Chronicle and a few local families, were old photographs blown up and framed showing old Newvale scenes and people of years gone by.

'Gordon, come on, over here,' He turned and noticed Councillor Clint Moran beckoning him to his place. He and Moira sat at a table in the company of Clint Moran and his partner, Dick and Karen Fuller representing both Newvale Chamber of Trade and the Town's oldest family and Titania Oliphant who had brought her private secretary, Polly Barring, along as a partner. Titania rose as the McIvers approached; she shook Moira's hand then Gordon's and gave him a kiss on both cheeks causing Moira's inner Presbyterian to find itself standing on shifting sands where there had always been cold hard stone.

Clint poured Moira and Gordon a glass of wine, which Gordon raised and drank before Moira could stop him. Her look suggested he'd better not try that again but he was shielded against the gloom of cold sobriety by his secret stash.

Across the room, Monty Fox found himself on a table with Simon Eddowes deputy chairman of Newvale Chamber of Trade, Inspector Snow of Newvale police with his wife, Councillor Brenda Worrall and her husband Dominic, Charles Mee and Ralph Shortcock.

'Should have been a copper with a name like Fox' Inspector Snow addressed him.

'Should have been a heroin dealer with a name like Snow,' Monty retorted and smiled as the policeman's discomfort flashed briefly across his face. Inspector Fox felt his stomach turn over; surely the bastard couldn't know about one tiny indiscretion in a university gap year three decades ago on the other side of the world? But this was the legendary Monty Fox who allegedly had a photographic memory and a very detailed photographic library. The inspector gave the editor a glassy smile before pulling in his horns and turning to strike up a conversation with Brenda Worrall on community policing.

Monty refilled his wine glass - he had noticed it was a particularly good wine - and decided to talk fashion for a bit with Messrs Shortcock and Mee.

It looked like being a long afternoon and evening, he loosened his bow tie and decided to enjoy himself....

The young audience began to mutter, Mr Punch had not said anything now for about thirty seconds, he had stared furtively at the sky then fallen over on his side then got up and wiggled about as if in the grip of a seizure, and now he was just staring again and there was a shade to his expression that suggested he had done something he was profoundly ashamed of.

Out of sight in the little tent Mr Edward Friendy was studying the sunlight as it illuminated the blue and white stripes. Here and there flecks of dust floated past and Mr Friendy wondered if they may be tiny spaceships carrying microscopic but highly intelligent beings on voyages of discovery across what must be for them the unimaginable voids of Rhododendron Crescent. 'Be safe tiny brave travellers,' he whispered, afraid to speak aloud in case the vibration upset the agonisingly delicate mechanisms that drove their craft.

Felicity Friendy, who in common with the rest of the audience was concerned with the lack of Mr Punch monologue, discreetly sneaked around the back of the tent and popped her head through the flap. Edward failed to acknowledge her.

'Is everything alright, Edward?'

He held a cautionary finger to his lips before whispering, 'Chill man, everything's cool.'

Felicity frowned. Edward hadn't said 'Chill man' since 1967 and he'd only said it then to impress her older sister who'd had a real Afghan Coat and nice legs.

'Make Mr Punch do something for God's sake, the children are getting restless.'

Edward seemed to snap out of it a little at Felicity's commanding tone. Outside, the watchers saw Mr Punch suddenly jerk and twist around and resume his chat, 'Right, ah, OK, yeah... wow.... unreal man... a crocodile.... far out!'

Monty Fox, to his surprise, had emptied one wine bottle and was a third of the way down another. He had been engrossed in Charles Mee's account of a time the tailor had created a morning suit especially for a man to be buried in. The suit hadn't been a problem but the deceased had left specific instructions that he was to be buried in a top hat. His widow was on a budget and this would have added to the length of the coffin and also the hole to accommodate it, significantly increasing the cost of the burial. They had got around the problem by using a top hat two sizes too large and pulling it down over the man's ears all the way to his neck and then cutting a door in the front which could be opened to show his face.

Basking in the warm glow of the wine Monty was genuinely enjoying the occasion and had applauded Gordon McIver's speech heartily even though he now couldn't remember a word of it. He realised he had transgressed one of his own rules by drinking before speaking in public but it was a one off occasion; he hadn't been around for the Centenary and wouldn't be here for Newvale's Tercentenary so to hell with it, let the good times roll, he was actually looking forward to delivering his speech now anyway.

The Master of Ceremonies was on stage, Monty couldn't remember his name; the man was a councillor from Meadowvale with long arms and big ears. He was waffling on about Newvale's proud heritage of the written word - God knows why, as far as Monty could remember nobody from Newvale had ever written anything worth reading - present company excepted of course. His mind was about to wander off, lost in the comfortable fog of intoxication when the phrase, 'Newvale Chronicle' nudged his attention back to the speaker.

'.... who needs hardly any introduction, the editor of the Chronicle, Mr Monty Fox!'

There was a ripple of polite applause, Monty rose and headed through the tables to the front of the banqueting hall where he climbed the two steps on to the low stage. The applause petered out as he reached the lectern. He gripped the sides and peered into a vast nothingness. Bloody spotlights... he could see very little of his audience but they could see him OK and that's what mattered.

For the life of him, he couldn't imagine why he had never tried this before. The words, he knew, would just flow. It was as if a tsunami of wit and perspicacity was about to break over his audience. He tucked his notes into his pocket; he was going to fly by the seat of his pants.

A hush of anticipation ... the term 'Pan Troglodytes' entered his head and he put it down to the master of ceremonies in his peripheral vision. He swayed a little and gave what he hoped was a smile that implied a familiarity that stopped just short of friendliness. He boomed out a greeting.

'Never argue with someone who buys ink by the gallon!'

Silence. What a bunch of fucking idiots! Monty shook his head sadly. For the best part of his life he had been slaving over typewriters, notepads and keyboards in an attempt to enlighten and entertain these... these cretins! Homo Sapiens my arse!

'So... two hundred years eh? Two hundred years....'

He paused to look out into the void. The pause went on long enough to allow a low murmuring to begin. His shout snapped them all back to attentiveness.

'Rubbish! That was the first word ever spoken to me in the Chronicle office and it was spoken by old Jack Peterson who some of you might remember. He was an editor of the old school and I had just put my first ever story proudly on his desk. He read it and then threw it right back at me. Rubbish! - he shouted. And he was right.'

Another pause, and this time the murmuring from the audience was laced through with a nervous giggle.

'I'd worked bloody hard at that story and he pulled it to pieces - but he was right, it had been full of my own opinions and it was a harsh wake-up call to the world of journalism in particular and to the world in general. Nobody gives a flying toss what you think.'

Monty looked briefly to his left to gain some relief from the glare of the lights and noticed Pan Troglodytes scratching himself in a remarkably simian way. 'Monkey-faced fucker' he muttered and the immediate gasp from the audience told him it had been picked up by the microphone and transmitted to most of the hall. Within a second or two, however, the part of the brain that blots out trauma told the listeners they hadn't really heard it at all and so Monty continued.

'No, nobody gives a flying toss. Each week we put out the Chronicle and we tell you who is in court, or we tell you that so and so is dead and most of you didn't even know the bugger was alive in the first place, or we'll tell you what your council is spending your money on but frankly they could spend it on jelly, glove puppets and sex toys that light up in the dark and you wouldn't really care because as long as you've got four hundred TV channels and discount booze you're perfectly content.'

This time the muttering broke over the beachhead of the stage like approaching waves and opinion in the hall seemed to be torn between indignation and curiosity. A couple of 'boos' were silenced by a chorus of 'Sssshhhes' indicating that a majority, tired of the dry and scripted offerings from local dignitaries, wanted him to continue.

'Well there's nothing wrong with that. When I was young I was going to change the world; my words were going to mould public opinion and galvanise the masses into action against injustice and... and corruption. But now, quite frankly, I couldn't give a horse's fanny as long as you keep buying the bloody paper. I've only got eighteen months to go and then it will be some other bugger's worry.'

There was laughter now; Monty heard it and saw it as a sign to take off all the brakes. Why not? It's time somebody told 'em what was what.

'You see all these councillors,' he indicated the gathered dignitaries with a sweep of his arm, 'All bloody terrified about what you'd think of them if you knew everything that was going on. But they needn't worry, the law stops people like me telling people like you about people like them.' He paused to allow a hiccup to escape, 'So I'm afraid I can't reveal which of them.... I'll tell you what, let's have a bit of fun shall we? I'm going to tell you something and you've got to guess which of these worthies it applies to, right? OK here we go.... Which of them do you think seduced an Egyptian boy whilst on holiday?'

The deputy chairman of Newvale Chamber of Trade, Simon Eddowes, who had boasted extensively about his expensive 'Luxury in Luxor' vacation, began feverishly muttering to those closest to him, 'It wasn't me.' The audience, much to Monty's delight and the dignitaries' horror, joined in enthusiastically calling out the names of councillors they particularly hated. Monty encouraged them with shouts of 'warmer... warmer... hmmm, interesting suggestion.....oh I couldn't possibly confirm....'

The deputy chairman of Newvale Chamber of Trade was torn between an overwhelming desire to flee the room and the need to maintain an air of injured innocence. He was relieved when Monty called a halt to the questioning and moved on to another target.

'OK, here's a good one - which currently serving councillor bought some cream for erectile dysfunction off the internet and it dyed his old man bright yellow? Looked like a banana according to his wife - a small banana I might add.'

With the exception of a handful of people who stone facedly made their way to the exit, the audience loved it. Hands were raised to answer while at the back of the room Councillor Brian Pipe cursed his spouse's loose tongue and the generous amounts of free wine at last month's 'Meet the Press' bash organised by the Chronicle.

'Not that erectile dysfunction is anything to be ashamed of!' Monty continued.

He swayed a little and was aware of slurring his words a bit. He gave another smile meant to reassure.

'No, nothing to be ashamed of at all; are we ashamed of being bald? Of course not! We might have had lots of hair in our youth so things tend to balance out. And it's the same with your old chap. The reason you can't stand to attention now might be because you did it so often when you were younger. I know I did!'

A couple more sour-faced people rose and made their way, crab-like between tables to the exit; someone shouted 'Shame' but the majority appeared to be ready for more.

'Good God yes...' Monty warmed to his task now and thundered on, '...it must be something in the water down at the Chronicle. We had this reporter a few years back, Derek Michelson - some of you might remember seeing his by-line in the paper, he broke the story about the Meadowvale cow painter, you all remember that I'm sure....' One or two more of the assembled dignitaries discreetly left their seats and hurried to the welcoming embrace of the room's dark corners, eager to be away but held in thrall, like the rest of the audience, by the need to see how this was going to end. 'Oh yes, Derek Michelson - now there was a chap who could get a panhandle. He boasted that it would take the weight of an oven-ready chicken and it bloody well did too! He did it right there in the office!'

Monty had gained several new fans and their laughter instilled an 'Emperor's New Clothes' effect on many of the rest who suppressed their discomfort and chuckled along out of politeness in the hope there wasn't much more of it to come.

But Monty wasn't ready to end just yet ...

Mr Edward Friendy was sitting in the kitchen of his home drinking a cup of strong coffee, much against doctor's orders but in line with Felicity's orders and as she outranked the doctor he had quietly acquiesced. Felicity bustled around the kitchen piling up plates for washing and gathering nibbles together for later distribution. She gave him the occasional distasteful glance and muttered something along the lines of 'Man of your age,' as she passed by.

It had been a strange experience, 'a strange experience on a strange day,' Edward thought. He remembered it all clearly but it no longer made the perfect sense it had an hour or two ago and he wondered which of the two realities he had lived through was the one he could trust. Certainly the other one, with its vivid colours and heightened senses and profound joy was superficially attractive but there had been an air or impermanence about it. Maybe beautiful things don't live for long because the ugliness of reality corrupts them, he thought. Felicity passed and 'huffed' again and Edward got up.

'I'm going for a walk,' he announced.

Gordon McIver had sat in a stunned silence throughout Monty's speech while Titania Oliphant had laughed uproariously. Monty was still in full flow and a spot poll would have shown he still carried about sixty-five per cent of the audience who took delight in puncturing pomposity. They had a choice of whether to buy the Chronicle or not but the Council took their money without a by or leave and that counted for a lot when it was time to draw a line in the sand and choose which side of it to stand on.

Moira McIver had left the room in a state of righteous outrage a few minutes before when Monty Fox had told a lurid tale about a former Mayoress who had been a music teacher and who had also given evening classes. She had failed to see anything scandalous in what the newspaperman was saying until Councillor Clint Moran had explained to her exactly what kind of instrument a 'pink oboe' was.

Monty had paused in his speech to allow the latest outburst of chuckles die down. He raised a hand..

'Seriously….. Seriously ladies and gentlemen; I am a Newvalian and believe it or not after all I've said, I care a lot about this place.

'There are villages and there are big cities; in villages you'd think everyone would know everyone else but that's not the case any more because most villages are no more than hotels with all the rooms separated by gardens. Just knock on the doors in a village and try and find out how many of the resident's parents lived there!

'And in big cities you have the same impersonality, people coming and going, millions living there but few actually belonging any more.

'But we're not city dwellers and we're not villagers, we're small town people and there's just enough here to hold our children but not enough to attract the attention of the world.

'And I'll tell you something else….'

Mr Edward Friendy sat on a bench in Newvale Park and studied the mallards on the pond. He was curiously happy, as if his little sortie into another dimension had left an echo of joy like the aftertaste of something sweet. Try as he might he could not re-enter the happy place, the only key to unlock that particular door was a few more of Bill Frederick's cakes and.. and well, he was just too… 'Edward' to bother.

But he had decided he liked his life in general, he even liked Felicity - and, whether they all realised it or not, in common with the majority of the people in his little town, he liked Newvale.

It was the same as him, eccentric, lived in - and not particularly famous for anything.

● *'A farting horse will never tire - a farting man is the man to hire!'*

If the adage was true then Thomas Fuller had that morning surely hired a truly excellent fellow. The chap was loading newly cut lengths of timber on to a cart outside Mr Fuller's sawmill and while doing so he was farting almost continuously. Thomas could not help but speculate on the man's diet. He looked sturdy enough and had, he claimed, spent the last twelve years at sea, so perhaps it was the effect of eating fresh food on Terra Firma that caused him to produce so much gas. Thomas' wife, Jane, would be along in a few minutes with lunch for her husband and he made a mental note to send this new scoundrel off to do a job well out of ear and nose shot before she arrived.

The man passed by again with a length of wood to place on the great cart, tearing off a thunderous voluntary as he did so. Thomas could contain his curiosity no longer.

'I say... Benjamin isn't it?'

'Aye Marster?'

'You seem to be a very... flatulent fellow don't you?'

'Begging your pardon Marster?'

'Well, you tend to expel wind a lot?'

'Oh, you means the farting Marster - aye, I've allus done that, and my dear old father afore me, 'tis the curse of the Scanlons, my grandfather was thrown overboard by none other than Captain Bligh hisself an' there were bubbles still coming up for nigh on ten minutes they do say.'

'I see.. well, Mrs Fuller will be along shortly so why don't you go and find Mr Raft and help him to stack the bark for the charcoal pits.'

'Aye aye, right you are Marster.'

Thomas Fuller looked out over his little empire. He had inherited £10,000 from his late father who had made his money buying and selling and supplying tools and equipment to the East India Company. Thomas had left the family business and moved here with his bride and a dream of striking out to make his own fortune. Now five years on, with two young children and a third on the way he was quietly pleased with his progress.

Small Town People

The tiny village of Meadowvale, just two miles away from his sawmill had been his original home but he was on the verge of moving into his grand new house here in the growing community surrounding his enterprise. He employed sixty workers, business was booming and the families of his employees needed to be catered for. Already a draper, candle maker, cobbler and butcher had set up their own businesses and a doctor/dentist was on the way. Thomas was planning to build a school to cater for the needs of the burgeoning population. The place had the look of a small town already.

Malvolio had arrived one rain lashed night two years previously, coming out of the darkness of Meadowvale Woods like something elemental. A shade over five feet in height but almost as broad, a bent back, huge arms ending in hands like shovels, fiery red hair and green eyes that glinted like shards of an emerald heaven in the middle of a face that could only have come from Hell. He could not speak but indicated by sign that he followed the trade of a blacksmith. Thomas already employed a smith but there was ample work for another, particularly one who was willing to turn his hand to others tasks at quiet times and who seemingly had the strength of ten men.

Malvolio inspired awe and fear in equal proportions, when he swung his hammer it was said that the metal bent even before the blow struck home. Children would approach nervously to watch him at work but because there was little to differentiate between a smile and a snarl in his face they always kept an escape route open.

It was Thomas who had given him his name, 'Because he looks like a Malvolio,' he had explained. Jane had never personally pictured the Shakespearian character in such an otherworldly guise as this creature who spent his days hammering white-hot iron in his own private Hades of smoke and flames.

While Jane loved Thomas and did not doubt for a second his capacity for hard work or his business acumen she did not share her husband's optimism that this new community was going to be the Utopia he envisaged. For a start, a lot of these people were from the Lower Orders and if you started educating them, as Thomas planned, then surely no good could come of it. Jane's father, The Reverend Percival Pollard, never employed household staff who could read and write; goodness knows what the simple creatures would poke their noses into; they'd gain more knowledge than was good for them, that's for sure.

Jane walked along the muddy path to the sawmill carrying a basket containing a repast of eggs, cold chicken, bread and sliced fruit for her husband's midday meal. She raised the hem of her dress with her free hand to keep it from the mud and only then did she spot the man, sitting on a pathside log and staring brazenly at her exposed ankles. He noticed that she had observed his curiosity yet made no attempt to look away.

'Do you not know, it's the worst of manners to stare at a lady?'

'Begging your pardon Missus,' the man touched his forelock, 'my eyes were on you but my mind were miles away.' He grimaced, raised a leg and unleashed the most blasphemous fart Jane had ever heard. Speechless with horror she simply stared at the man as, seemingly unabashed, he took out a clay pipe and proceeded to fill it.

'I... I...' Jane simply couldn't get the words out.

'Sorry 'bout that Missus, it's the curse of the Scanlons; I'm never free of it, day or night.'

Jane recalled her father's guidance, 'You may as well ask a horse to speak as to seek refinement in these unfortunate creatures,' he had told her.

She studied the man more closely, noting in particular his hands as he worked the plug of tobacco into his pipe. They were broad, strong hands, calloused and with cracked nails. His face too reflected a life alien to gentility. It was a hard face but not unkind. Eyes, a piercing blue that carried in them a reflection of past pains, and an inner strength to offer a shield against future hurt. She had seen such faces before in the pews of her father's church.

The man calmly lit his pipe, wrapping himself in a cloud of acrid smoke, which a gentle breeze dispersed.

'I have not seen you in these parts before Sir, are you a Meadowvale man?'

'I'm a Newvale man; leastways I will be if the Marster is satisfied with my work.'

Jane sighed, 'Newvale indeed;' she had tried to persuade Thomas to call the new community 'Fullerstown' but to no avail. With the slightest of nods in the direction of the smoking man she walked on. Behind her a monstrous fart that sounded for *all the world like a canvas sail being torn in two was quickly followed by a 'Sorry Missus.'*

Jane shook her head.

Upon such foundations 'Newvale' would be built.

* * * * * *

Bob Rogers